ALFRED A. KNOPF

1915 · 100 YEARS · 2015

THE
BANGKOK
ASSET

JOHN
BURDETT

THE
BANGKOK
ASSET

ALFRED A. KNOPF

New York · 2015

THIS IS A BORZOI BOOK PUBLISHED BY
ALFRED A. KNOPF

www.aaknopf.com

Knopf, Borzoi Books, and the colophon are registered trademarks of
Penguin Random House LLC.

Burdett, John.
The Bangkok asset / John Burdett.
pages ; cm
ISBN 978-0-307-27268-3 (hardcover) ISBN 978-0-385-35320-5 (eBook)
1. Sonchai Jitpleecheep (Fictitious character)—Fiction.
2. Police—Thailand—Bangkok—Fiction.   3. Bangkok (Thailand)—
Fiction.   I. Title.
PR6052.U617A9   2015
823'.914—dc23   2015006232

Jacket photograph © Charles Walker/TopFoto/The Image Works
Jacket design by John Vorhees

Manufactured in the United States of America
First Edition

FOR NIT

*And in grateful memory of F. W. Burdett and
Patrick Harry Wilson (sometimes it takes two)*

*I thank Sandra Bacon for her unflagging support
and friendship over the years*

*and Joel McCleary
for introducing me to MKUltra*

Author's Note

This novel was all but complete before May 22, 2014; therefore, it has not been possible to address the many changes that have taken place in Thailand since the military coup of that date.

Phenomena have no signs.

—The Buddha (corroborated by Ludwig Wittgenstein)

THE
BANGKOK
ASSET

Prologue

So I'm at my desk in the open-plan area of District 8 Police Station when a rumor blows through the room similar to a gust of wind in a rice paddy. Like Big Data, Big Rumor has no obvious source or contact point and is not coherent until you join up all the different packets of information: *Behind the station; In the market square; Male or female? Not sure; Young or old? Unclear; So, what? Dead; How? Murder or natural causes? Unclear; When? Who knows? Who found the corpse? Dunno.*

One day someone will produce an award-winning thesis to show why information that arises from close in is invariably more garbled than that which comes from a distance. In a more remote case I would have expected precise detail and a named informant and clear orders to investigate. Here, though, with the scene of crime less than five minutes' stroll away, cops and staff simply turn their heads and stare at me. Pretty soon everyone including the tea lady has turned to look at the only homicide cop in the room on duty and available. I shrug and stand up, ready to do my duty: even if there was no foul play, in a case of sudden death you still need a murder cop to say so before anyone will believe it. Anyway, I'm as curious as everyone else. And, yes, it is easier to descend the emergency stairs to leave the building by the rear entrance and cross the *soi* to the market and ask the first vendor I see where the body is than to wait for some official order to investigate.

"Over in one of those shop houses in the corner behind the roti vendor."

It is true there is a small crowd just behind the roti vendor, who is doing a brisk trade. Does the proximity of death give people a sweet tooth? We know about sex and death, but what about death and other appetites? About ten people are lining up to buy pancakes, which we call *rotis* thanks to our Hindu community, wrapped around bananas smeared in a Swiss chocolate spread, a culinary form long since mastered and perhaps even invented by the stall owner—and it is to these enhanced bananas in wheat-flour wrappings that the small crowd has resorted in its grief and confusion.

Okay, not grief and confusion: there's nothing like sudden death-cum-murder to provide an excuse for a break, a chat, and a snack. There are no Thai bosses so insensitive that they would force people to work under such pressure of curiosity, for gossip is a force of nature no more deniable than gravity.

Do you detect a slightly frivolous mood on my part, Reader (I'll call you R if you don't mind)? Please do not label me and my people as callous, you see the common assumption at this moment is that the body, wherever it is, will be that of an older person, probably a male vagrant who drank too much rice whiskey and drowned in his own vomit, or a younger person not necessarily male who OD'd on *yaa baa* (crystal meth). I'm afraid it is incidents like that, rather than your great operatic homicides beloved of the media, that form the bread and butter of a murder squad's humble servant such as I. Even the unexpected presence of a forensic team at the S of C does not faze me. They would have experienced the Big Rumor earlier than the rest of the station, for their laboratory is on the ground floor at the back: they would have felt the invisible pressure to stroll over quite a few minutes before me.

Now I see they have left one of their young gofers at the bottom of the three-story shop house, who greets me and jerks his head at the stairs. "Top floor," he says, without calling me *sir*. I am sufficiently irritated by this insubordination, a more severe transgression in these parts than corruption, to give him a double take. He looks away. Once I have checked his face I think it was not insubordination; I think he forgot himself out of some kind of embarrassment or inhibition. His strangeness is sufficiently odd for me to check his face again as I set foot on the stair: he looks slightly scared and seriously embarrassed, as if I will find something personally compromising on the third floor. I put his attitude down to youth and stupidity. I am confident that if a murder were committed on the third floor it was nothing to do with me. I even have an alibi: I was at home with my wife all night.

At the top of the stairs forensics have placed another gofer, who also looks away as soon as he sees me, directing my attention to an open door where I glimpse a crime scene specialist in white coveralls squatting over something on the floor. It is A-Wut (Weapon), an old pal from way back. A glance into the room reveals more old pals: Channarong (Experienced Warrior) on the video camera and Khemkhaeng (The Strong) standing around. But I know them all too well to use their official forenames; intimacy built up over more than a decade requires and expects nicknames of cozy vulgarity (e.g., Damned Aye, Bloody Toei, and so on). I enter the room on tiptoe. When A-Wut, aka Effing Tam, catches sight of me he looks surprised, as if I am the last person he expected to come across right now; as if there is something important that he assumed someone would have told me already. He gives a quick look behind him, which seems to me somewhat furtive, then gestures for me to step farther into the apartment. At the far end Bloody Toei is standing in front of a mirror holding the video camera and panning monotonously across the crime scene with grim determination. There are also two women from forensics, who I've not met before although I've seen them around, and who are slouched against a wall, one stone-faced with a thousand-yard stare, the other softly and continuously weeping over something that lies between them

Their anguish possesses a mystic force that takes you back to the Fall: primal loss. So why is the team in two separate groups, with the women squatting against a wall and A-Wut, the leader, about ten feet away from them? A-Wut gestures for me to look first at what he is squatting over: a Thai girl laid on her back, probably about twelve or thirteen years old, still fully dressed in the blue-and-white costume of secondary school children and minus a head.

It is the head the two women are watching over on the other side of the room, the two body parts joined by a trail of what must have been spurting blood from a snapped jugular not too long ago: crimson and pink splashes, mists and sprays have penetrated everywhere, including the ceiling.

I am in shock, my professional reflexes reduced to idiot-level slowness. Only one thought emerges clear and strange: against all the rules of psychological profiling the face is undamaged. This is unnatural: terrorism aside, your deranged perp resorts to the extreme violence of decapitation because he must punish and destroy the Other who, as a projection of himself, he blames for everything that has gone wrong and will continue to go wrong in the tormented world he inhabits. Destruction of the face is basic. Here, though, the face is not only undamaged, it shows no sign of trauma at all. It is delicate, beautifully modeled, tan, big-eyed, slender-necked, innocent, like the golden head of an alabaster Buddha. A shudder convulses my body when I realize that the neck is so very slender—hardly more than an inch in diameter—because of elongation. *Someone pulled her head off with bare hands? Isn't that impossible?*

Now I am throwing A-Wut a look of anguish—and still there is a reserve about him, a certain distance, almost as if he suspects me in some way. Then I realize the two women also are staring at me. Silence. The weeping has stopped, the women's eyes shift to the far end of the room where Bloody Toei the video operator has moved to a corner and also is staring at me. When his eyes shift to the mirror I follow the cue and finally begin to understand:

Detective Sonchai Jitpleecheep, I know who [smudge] father is.

The words are written in blood in neat handwriting across the top of the mirror. What I have described as a *smudge* is an elongated spurt of blood between the words *who* and *father*.

I am being hollowed out by something even more toxic to mental health than fear. I find my features pinching in some kind of caricature of righteous rage. A-Wut is no fool, he sees what is happening to me.

"Who . . ." My mind wanders, searching for an escape. I force it to return to the scene of the crime. "Who reported it?" I demand.

A-Wut puts an arm around me and squeezes hard. "That's your job to find out, good buddy," he says in a consoling tone. "We're only forensics."

"But . . ." I lose track, try again. "But somebody must have . . ."

"We came because of the rumor. Think about it, who in Bangkok is going to own up to being the first to see a corpse like that? If superstition doesn't faze them, fear of law enforcement would have the same effect. No one wants to be associated with anything so extreme. Bad joss. Very, very bad joss. You know that."

"Right," I say, gulping and staring again at the mirror, all too aware that a great heap of very bad joss has landed on me also. "Right." I fish out my phone to call Sergeant Ruamsantiah, who says he will detail half a dozen constables to start taking statements from the people in the market. For the moment I am unable to bring myself to tell him about the writing on the mirror. For the moment I cannot face the world, either. I wait downstairs for the Sergeant to arrive.

By the way, my name is Sonchai Jitpleecheep, Homicide Detective, attached to District 8 Police Station where one Colonel Vikorn presides, at your service.

PART I

THE
RIVER

1

These are strange times on Planet Thailand. Even Colonel Vikorn is acting out of character. He called me at around four-thirty this morning to tell me to find my own transport to take me to a specific point on the east bank of the Chao Phraya River.

"The team is already there. Sergeant Ruamsantiah will explain."

"Is it related to—"

"Not clear."

He closed his phone before I could ask what it was about, and why he would need me to meet the Sergeant at such an hour at a location some ten miles from District 8. And what team, exactly, was he talking about? And why would he choose the filthiest morning I've witnessed since the last typhoon season twelve months ago? And most troubling of all: why was I being distracted from the case known as the *Market Murder*, in which the victim has been provisionally named as *Nong X*? A case, after all, with my name on it.

Like a dutiful serf I grabbed a pair of jeans, T-shirt, and waterproof jacket, kissed Chanya on the lips while she snored, took a peep out of the door at the sheets of rain that were flooding the street, which would be a river of brown mud in an hour or so—and called a cab. I had to promise to pay triple before the driver would consent to take me to the river. He showed up in ten minutes, his wheels sloshing through the mounting torrent, and he turned out to be more valiant than I expected. We were within half a mile of the location given by Vikorn when he stopped. The flooding by that time was up to the level of his exhaust pipe, forcing him to keep gunning the motor while slipping the clutch, to stop water from entering the cylinders. I gave him his full fee and wished him luck on the way home and watched him drive back through the muddy floods, his engine screaming. According to the GPS on my smart phone, all I had to do was find the river and walk a few hundred yards north along its bank.

I found the river by following its thunder. I don't think I've ever heard it so loud or been so drenched. I was shocked, too, by the way the wind roared through in gusts, temporarily tearing up the mist and revealing a churning brown monster in a rage bathed in clear end-of-the-world light. I wondered how the cargo ships were faring at the port. And where had they stored all the long-tail passenger ferries, the tourist vessels, the floating restaurants, the rice barges. No boat was built for this leviathan.

From the east bank of the Chao Phraya it was easy enough to follow the GPS on my smart phone in a northward direction. Visibility was so low that even if I reached the coordinates the Colonel had given, there was no guarantee I would be able to see the people I was supposed to meet. Unless the wind conveniently cleared the air again.

For a moment it did. A sudden gust screamed down the river valley, tearing up the mist in one long howl. I was at a bend where the river made an abrupt turn to the west. I knew that bend; so did everyone who had spent Sundays hanging out on the Chao Phraya. It was a tourist spot that jutted way out into the water where you took selfies of you and your loved ones smiling and playing at happy families. Not today, though, not in this storm. According to my phone I was no more than fifty yards from the meeting point Vikorn had given, which was about twenty yards from the riverbank. I forgot about that when I caught sight of a small flat-bottomed tourist vessel downstream in the middle of the torrent, held fast by a stout rope fastened to a stanchion on the extended promontory. I stopped, gripped the safety rail, and stared.

At first I thought the only human on the boat was a tall *farang* with startling blond hair. He stood in some kind of high-tech parka with feet apart, arms folded, compensating for the rolling of the deck without visible effort. Then I realized he was standing over a group of terrified Thais, two men and two women. The Westerner opened his mouth to speak in what seemed like slow, deliberate instructions. Then he clapped his hands and the two Thai men fell upon the two women. It took less than a minute to throw them into the raging current, where they disappeared instantly. I stared openmouthed at the *farang* on the boat, the wild river, the point where the women had been instantly engulfed. Frantic for some kind of explanation, some clue that would orientate me in a moment of confusion, I turned away to search for the people I was supposed to meet. A white van was parked a few hundred yards back from the river and I made toward it.

In the couple of minutes it took to run in that direction, the wind died and the mist returned. I had to use the GPS to locate the van when it was no more than thirty feet away. I beat on the sliding door, which opened to reveal Sergeant Ruamsantiah, Colonel Vikorn's most trusted aide, who pulled me inside. I told him in a gush what I had witnessed. He wrinkled his brow and turned his head in wonder at my report. He had not seen anything himself. He had arrived nearly an hour ago and become inured to zero visibility. Fleeting breaks in the fog had ceased to seduce him out of his torpor. He told me that Vikorn had ordered him up here some time before he had called me. The weather was so bad no willing driver could be found, so Ruamsantiah drove the police van himself. He had no better idea what it was all about than did I. All he knew was that he was supposed to meet what he called "a third party," at the same coordinates that the Colonel had given to me. Now we watched through the windshield while a figure emerged out of the mist no more than ten feet from the van and made its way toward us, crouched, soaked and monochrome in black coveralls with a hood tied under the chin.

"That's her," Ruamsantiah said, and pulled the door open.

She was average height for a Thai woman, about five three, in her late twenties or early thirties. As far as I could tell she was pretty in a sharp-featured kind of way, but her personality hit you before you had a chance to concentrate on her sex appeal. Even without the cute black-rimmed spectacles, like miniature windows smeared with rain, you would have guessed she was a smart cookie from the new generation of Thais. She did not want to climb into the van. Instead, she jerked her chin toward the river and led us toward it. Her own van was about a hundred yards away, invisible in the dense mist. When he saw us her driver opened the sliding door. The Sergeant and I held back for her to enter first, but she shook her head to make us precede her. We obeyed.

Inside a van rocked by gusts we introduced ourselves. Her name was Krom, Inspector Krom. When she pulled back the hood I saw how close-cropped was her spiky black hair. I told her what I had just seen on the river, half hoping she would have some happy explanation, although I couldn't think of one myself.

"I know," she snapped. She jerked her head at the front bench of the vehicle where her driver was sitting and called my attention to the out-size gadget clamped onto the dashboard. I'd already stored the impression that it was bigger and stranger than any GPS or satellite navigation instrument I'd seen in a police van before, but technology rules by outpacing us a little more each day. Now that I examined it more carefully I saw it had some unusual black buttons with Chinese characters stamped on them in white.

Inspector Krom ordered the driver to join us in the back. He got out and reemerged at the rear door, soaked from the ten-second exposure to the storm. Then the Inspector beckoned the Sergeant and me to move forward to the front bench with her, while she sat dripping in the driver's seat. Now she was manipulating the buttons.

"We have it on the hard disk," she said. "About five minutes ago, right? When the mist cleared. This machine automatically switches between radar and video. The video is in color, quadruple HD, with about a thousand dots per inch, that's nearly double the pixel density of the most advanced screens and cameras commercially available. They're keeping the technology secret for the moment."

"Radar, too? I didn't know satellites used it."

She jerked her chin at the gadget. "Synthetic aperture radar: SAR. It can penetrate cloud, even the earth up to about six inches. The Chinese were allowed to steal it from the U.S."

She cast me a glance, aware, I suppose, of how odd the phrase *allowed to steal* sounded. Also, how was I to react to the information that we were using the "borrowed" Chinese version of the gadget?

"Intelligence is complicated. Actually, it's a mess. The most over-governed democracy in the world privatizes government so they can pretend they're not overgoverned. The most crowded nation juggles about fifty local governments with the population of large countries. Of course it's all out of control." I thought I detected genuine irritation when she added, "And everything they say, everything they do, is said and done in a spirit of absolute denial of the truth. We're screwed. There!"

She had mastered the controls and now we were looking at a replay of what I had just witnessed on the river. Perhaps the clever machine had a way of enhancing its own video, or perhaps the weird clarity of that fleeting moment had made the scene unusually photogenic; either way, the definition, detail, and color were amazing as I watched a replay of the double murder by drowning.

"You know who these people are?" I asked.

"Yes. The two Thai men are low-grade thugs." She paused the video and turned to stare at me. "You just saw the older one throw his wife overboard, mother of his three kids. The younger one drowned his own mother."

"WHAT?" I glared at her, refusing to believe what I had heard.

Sergeant Ruamsantiah stiffened on the bench next to me. We exchanged a glance. I shivered. "Could you say that again?" the Sergeant asked.

"No. You heard it right."

"Play it one more time," he said. He didn't care that she was superior in rank to him; that was an order. She replayed the video: there was no doubt about it, a Thai man about thirty years old threw a woman his own age into the raging torrent. At the same time a young man in his twenties drowned a middle-aged woman. The Sergeant was still not satisfied and neither was I. We didn't say so, but he wanted proof that what the Inspector had said was true. In Thailand matricide is virtually unknown. It is one of those crimes so extreme, inviting a sentence of millions of years in a hell starker than stone, before the perpetrator reemerges in some primitive life form, that most of us, including me, believe it to be exclusively Western. Inspector Krom, though, seemed to take the unnatural crime in her stride.

"That's as much as you saw, right?" she asked me.

"Yes. After that the wind died and the fog returned."

"So, here's the continuation in real time. It will have to be radar, which is monochrome, because of the mist. Look."

I studied the screen, now black and white, as the tall *farang* threw off his padded parka to reveal a magnificent torso under a black T-shirt, removed his pants leaving boxer shorts, took a couple of paces to the stern, poised like a professional swimmer, and dived elegantly into the churning water. The two Thai men stared after him but made no effort to move.

"Who in hell *is* that?" I muttered.

"I don't know his real name, if he has one." The Inspector waited to see if I would react to that. I didn't. "They call him *the Asset*. Or, if you prefer, *Goldman's Asset*—that could be changing, though."

"What could be changing?"

"Goldman's ownership of his Asset."

"Who is Goldman?"

Krom played with the buttons some more to change focus. Now we were looking at a great shadowy hulk standing on the riverbank no more than a hundred yards from where the van was parked. Even in monochrome with nobody around to compare him with he appeared gigantic, in a weatherproof jacket the size of a bedsheet, hands in his pockets, thinning hair blown about by the wind.

"Meet Joseph George Goldman," Krom said. "Former CIA officer, retired." She cast us a glance. "He still works for them, though. On contract." I looked at her, waiting for more. "He's too old, really, but they can't do without him."

"Why?"

"Wait and see."

"This is the weirdest day," I muttered. "Really, the weirdest day of my entire career."

"How so?"

"I'm investigating a murder by beheading that happened last week in the market behind the police station. Suddenly I'm told to come here in this filthy storm. When I asked if it was related, the Colonel said he wasn't sure. Now two women are murdered—drowned—with no clear motive and no reason for supposing there's a link with the case I'm working on."

"Get used to it," she said.

"Why?"

She shrugged, as if to say that if I didn't understand yet, I soon would.

Now she manipulated the radar to return to the river. She used the boat as a point of reference—the two men were huddled in the stern, pressing their bodies together to make one dark heap—then tracked across the river until she located a blob in the water. It was the tall blond *farang* who I'd decided was as good as dead. No one survives that kind of current, that kind of flood. Buddha knew how many tons of violent water would be brought to bear on a frail human form, no matter how much iron those muscles had pumped.

But he wasn't dead or even in trouble. He disappeared from the screen perhaps a dozen times, when it was unclear if he had drowned or if the mist had simply engulfed him; then, with a regularity that became increasingly improbable, the cropped bullet head would reappear a couple of yards nearer the bank. Sure, the flood was taking him downstream, but the fact that he was able to fight the current and remain almost at the same point on the river spoke of an unbelievable strength and endurance. When the Inspector switched back to Goldman, that giant, we watched him walk parallel to the bank to reach a point downstream from the swimmer. At the same time he removed his jacket and let the wind take it. Now Joseph George Goldman stood in a huge dark T-shirt and a knotted rope wrapped just under his gut. This he unwound as he walked. When the swimmer was near enough to the bank for the American to predict where he would make contact with the wall, Goldman secured one end of the line to a steel upright and let the other down the side of the bank. The swimmer reached the wall about twenty yards upstream and allowed the current to bounce him against it until he reached the rope, which he immediately wound around himself. He paused for a couple of minutes before hauling himself up.

Now I was sure he was not human. The swim was impressive enough, but to retain the strength to haul his considerable bulk up the vertical rope quickly and easily for about thirty feet without a pause, even with the help of the knots . . . that spoke of something else.

"Like something out of a superhero comic," I muttered to Krom, who gave me a curious look.

When the swimmer popped his head over the embankment I expected the two Americans to embrace to celebrate the athlete's survival, or at least make high fives, but as soon as Goldman saw that his man was safe on the bank he beckoned him to follow as he returned with long, hurried strides to the first rope that was holding the boat with the Thais on board. I could not help staring at the physical prodigy on the screen who had just swum across our wildest river in a rage. I wondered why he didn't lie down on the sidewalk, or at least lean against the railings breathing heavily. He simply followed the huge American at a kind of warm-up trot until he joined him at the stanchion to which the line was tied fast.

A sudden squall began to tear the mist into floating filigree. The Satnav machine fired up those pixels as it switched automatically to color. The definition of the Chinese gadget was amazing in its precision: every shade, every facial expression, every detail was better than the best HD I'd seen. There was even a touch of the surreal in its precision, as if we had those people in a box right on the dashboard of the van.

Goldman stood upright and seemed to yell something at his Asset at the same time as handing him some object that looked like a Swiss Army knife from his pants pocket, then clapped his hands. I frowned in disbelief. Inspector Krom played with the controls to zoom in on what he was doing.

What I retain of that moment is the precision with which the swimmer cut the rope. He sawed away while bending over it, like a man who is determined to do a perfect job. He stepped back the instant the rope started to fray of its own accord. The strands unraveled: the rope and the boat were gone.

"We'll have to get out of here before they see us," the Inspector muttered. "This isn't meant to be a demonstration. Now it's all over, they might start looking around. It's important they don't know we're here." But she made no effort to move just yet. Instead we watched the huge old American and his young prodigy giving the raging torrent one last glance. "I guess even if they do look this way, all they're going to see is a wet van."

The younger man was stunning in his beauty, with a perfect physique, about six two with Hollywood good looks and cropped hair so blond it was almost white. Still soaked in shorts and T-shirt, he didn't even shiver. When he looked up at the sky for a brief moment I saw eyes of mystic cornflower blue. But he seemed to give off nothing in the way of vibrations or mood, like someone emotionally invisible.

Inspector Krom, her tongue pressing against her front teeth, began to pan across the scene until she found what she wanted and grunted in satisfaction. Now we were looking at a camera team of two huddled on a bridge upstream. Their camera with giant zoom on a tripod was focused like a cannon on the point at which Goldman and his disciple were standing. They were so done up in padded waterproofs that they were bloated spheres; no mistake about it, though, they were both Chinese. What kind of camera could focus in that mist, I wondered. Infrared? Ultraviolet? Laser?

Now Inspector Krom made a sweep of the river where the incident had taken place, then panned inland a bit. I guessed she was looking for Goldman's transport. And there it was, all of a sudden, so perfectly incongruous that she had to return to it a couple of times: a sky-blue Rolls-Royce, with two men standing together, apparently taking advantage of a break in the weather. One of them was a liveried chauffeur, the other was bulky in a light cream Burberry done up to the neck and a tan fedora pulled over his eyes, long hair held back with a clip. There was no mistaking him. Even if the limousine and the chauffeur had not given him away, the Brahmin posture, and above all that famous ponytail, made it as certain as it was strange.

"Lord Sakagorn?" I muttered. "What the hell . . ."

"He's Goldman's legal counsel. Buddha knows why he would compromise himself like this." Krom shook her head. She didn't understand any more than I did.

The weather changed again and visibility dropped to near zero. The Inspector nodded at us. It was time for every cop to leave the scene. The Sergeant and I returned to our own van and Ruamsantiah drove us home. We were silent all the way. I know the Sergeant was plagued by the same thought as me: had some Black Death of the soul stowed away on the ship that brought us Facebook and Twitter?

2

The next morning I'm sitting at my desk in the station reading my usual online newspapers: *Thai Rath* and the *Bangkok Post*. Both carry photos of a hired boat smashed up on the riverbank. (Bear with me here, R: when memory excites I revert to the present tense, which is pretty much all we use in Thai. It's always *now*, after all. FYI, I'm actually in a cell in the police station writing this narrative while my cigarettes are baking in the canteen's oven: I'll explain later.) Ferocious currents carried it downstream at a thirty-mile-an-hour clip before it crashed into a container vessel moored at the port at Klong Toey. Tragically, according to the report, the two women were thrown overboard into the raging torrent when the boat hit an unknown object in the water, while the two men hung on. The drowned female bodies were found a few miles downstream. The two men, it seemed, died in the collision with the ship.

Now Vikorn's secretary, Manny, calls me: "He wants to see you."

I climbed the stairs, knocked, entered, walked across the room to stand near his desk—and waited. The Old Man was standing at a window looking down on the cooked-food vendors on the street below. He might have been one of Asia's richest kingpins and a feudal baron of the old kind, but he never forgot he was a son of the common people. The street vendors had been illegal for three decades, but the Colonel defended them against attack from every quarter of the bureaucracy, from Roads and Bridges to Public Health to traffic engineers and urban planners. By special arrangement he had his *khao kha moo* (stewed pork leg with rice) sent up on a signal from his window. The Isaan vendors would have gladly sent it without charge, or even with a modest bribe of thanks for his support over the years, but he would have none of it. He had Manny pay his *khao kha moo* bill regularly every week plus ten percent for the delivery.

I had spent more than fifteen years bound in medieval service to this man, he dominated my life and mind, and I was as sensitive to his moods as a timid wife; at least that's the way it had been until now. Gossips said it was the onset of senility, the way he had seemed to diminish recently. I didn't buy that. Tyrants like him go raging into the night; the only thing that brings them down is the tyranny of greater tyrants. For the first time in living memory someone or something bigger was winning, and he was losing—that was my analysis anyway.

There were three basic postures he adopted when staring out of this particular window: with cigar (mood climate here ranges from contented to gloating); with hands in pockets (contemplative, confidently waiting the next brilliant, criminal idea to enter his head); and frowning with hands on hips (not a good sign; trouble ahead). To these three mental states, common enough in our species, I must add another, for today he kept turning his face to the sky in the posture of a humble old man begging the gods for help. Here was criminal genius unmasked: ego stripped bare for the sake of survival, all self-love dumped unceremoniously as one might jettison a fur coat to avoid drowning. He knew I was standing near him but allowed a good five minutes to pass before he came back to earth to address me.

"I heard about what happened yesterday," he said and paused. "If you speak of it to anyone, the Americans will take you out. On the other hand, the Chinese want you to continue with your investigation into the Market Murder—that Nong X case."

This was the first official indication that there might be a connection between the Market Murder last week and the events on the river yesterday. In my mind I had tried to connect the unusual strength of the blond young man on the boat and the decapitation of Nong X, but there was no evidence to justify such a theory. After inspecting the crime scene, Sergeant Ruamsantiah had tried to take witness statements from the crowd around the roti vendor. Nobody knew anything. The best lead, if you could call it that, was a remark from the roti vendor to the effect that the house was managed by a middle-aged woman who sold watches in the market. That's all he knew. Despite my detailing a team of ten constables to ask questions all over the market for the past three days, there were no other leads at all. I didn't even have any information as to why the girl was in the apartment at that time. In a last desperate attempt to move the case forward I had the men put up lurid posters all over the market, asking for anyone with information to come forward. So far nobody had.

"Chinese, Chinese, Chinese," I said. "It used to be everything American. Why, please tell me, would the Chinese give a damn about that sad little murder case I'm working on? And more important, why would *you* even think of *forming a sentence* that starts with the words *the Chinese want you to continue with your investigation*? Did the Chinese recently take over District 8?"

"You could say that."

"Why don't you tell me what's going on?"

When Vikorn doesn't want to answer a question, he stares at you, unblinking, like a lizard. "What do you care about the reason they're interested? I thought you were moving heaven and earth to find the perp who murdered that girl in the market square? Didn't you get a witness statement yet?"

"No. You distracted me with a mission that was totally top secret and therefore totally useless for my investigation. Did the Chinese order you to order me to the river yesterday? I'm just curious about who I'm working for these days."

He shrugged. "You are famous. The Chinese hold you in high regard. If you cannot find convincing proof of a connection between the homicide you're investigating and what happened on the river yesterday . . ."

"Yes?"

"Then I suppose that makes the American Asset worth the price."

"Price? What price? There's some kind of investment going on here?"

He grunted. "You have studied history. How did our great country save itself from foreign aggressors in the past?"

"By playing the British off against the French and the Americans off against the British, bending but never yielding. Selling off pieces of the country so the core could remain uncolonized."

"Exactly." He stared at me. *"That boy killed his own mother,"* the old gangster whispered and shook his head. "The Chinese were very impressed." He creased his brow. "But they gave me a proverb: *Pride comes before a fall."*

"That's not Chinese, that's *farang."*

He nodded. "Yes, I think that's what they meant: the proverb is about Americans."

He took a couple of minutes more before he turned and strode to his desk. His ability to step back from despair took longer than usual but was nonetheless miraculous. When he was seated he said, "So, you finally met Inspector Krom?"

He knew very well I'd never heard of her before yesterday, but he wasn't going to explain how or why a senior member of his force had been recruited and kept secret from the rest of us for . . . well, I had no idea how long Inspector Krom had been on our team, or where her office might be. I said, "Yes."

"Good. That's good. You'll be working with her on this."

"On what?"

"I'll let her brief you later. Right now there's something I want you to see."

He stood up with a perfunctory smile and led me out of his room, past Manny who as usual was busy typing at her post, then down the corridor to the large room that was officially called the Main Conference Room, unofficially the Big Interview Room, and, more accurately, the Large Interrogation Chamber. It had been out of service for more than a month, so I was interested to see what kind of renovations Vikorn had ordered for it. As I followed him I noted a slight dragging of his left foot, a way of walking that was not yet a shuffle but perhaps heralded the onset of one. There was no pride or pleasure when he opened the door to the room. He opened it rather with an expression of defeat, like a husband who had reluctantly consented to his wife's wholesale renovation of the home and now had to live with the consequence of his weakness.

When we entered, I found myself slack-jawed with astonishment: everything was Macintosh gray and tinted blue, and there was a huge LED screen at the end of the room, which he switched on, so that now we were looking at Google Maps. Vikorn, who has about ten words of

English, experienced no difficulty in typing *Pacific Rim* on the laptop that controlled the screen. Now we had the entire ocean on the wall along with the lands that border it, from Alaska to Tierra del Fuego on the right, from Siberia to the south of Indonesia on the left. Australia and New Zealand didn't figure in this value system, but flags popped up in unlikely locations in Myanmar, Hong Kong, Jakarta, the Philippines, and northern California. Those all tended to be red and green points, however, with the reds in Asia and the greens in North America. The yellow flags were mostly in China, especially Yunnan and so-called second-tier cities in the southwest and along the east coast, while a few clustered on the outskirts of Shanghai. I scratched my jaw, determined not to ask the obvious question: *what the hell are you up to now?* Instead I went at the issue crab-wise.

"That's, ah, an awful lot of exposure to China."

He nodded. "Correct."

I stared at the map some more, wondering what the deeper meaning might be. Vikorn always has deeper meanings. It was only when I realized the deeper meaning was really a form of confession that I began to develop a fuller understanding. "You have a partnership with them?"

"Joint venture." He shrugged. "They didn't leave me any choice: joint venture or massive bust, abduction up north, bullet in the skull." He scratched his jaw. "They think like me. What I didn't understand is that with them the real business is all mixed up with politics. It's like a merger: you grow but you lose control at the same time."

I nodded, taking it all in. The Earth still looks beautiful on a map. I knew, though, that if one were to zoom in on any town or city and switch to camera view, the gorgeous electronic colors would disappear and the screen would show dormitory towns, pollution, shopping malls, and traffic jams no matter which country you chose; our planet these days is best viewed from space. "All this high-tech stuff—who's running it for you?"

"I thought you'd never ask." He paused in quizzical mode, then added, "But I'm sure you've already guessed."

He picked up his cell phone, pressed a button, said, "Send her in," and closed the phone. He threw me a tolerant smile to show me how far behind his my thinking was. Now there was a knock on the door and a young woman entered.

"I know you've already met, but let me make the introduction anyway," Vikorn said. "Detective Sonchai Jitpleecheep, this is Inspector Krom. Inspector Krom, this is Detective Sonchai Jitpleecheep." He turned to me. "Inspector Krom is our new head of technology," he said.

If he had not spoken her name, I might not have recognized the drenched and hooded inspector in the black coveralls from the day before. Today she wore the regulation white blouse with blue shoulder boards and a navy skirt that reached below her knees. Vikorn normally treated all young women the same way: with impeccable chivalry based on the assumption that his power and charisma would be sufficient to bed her were he crass enough to use them, which he never did. After all, he owned clubs full of women younger, more voluptuous, and less challenging; but Krom stumped him. Part of the problem was that Vikorn was too old-fashioned—and the Inspector a tad too good-looking—for it even to occur to him that she was gay. I had radically to revise my view of the young woman who yesterday had seemed so fascinated by a hunk straight out of Hollywood. It seems I had misread her, for, in the Thai vernacular, it was plain to me that she was most definitely a *tom*. Of course, the requirements of survival in a man-dominated profession in Thailand demanded that she dissimulate: it was a little embarrassing the way she turned girly, to give the impression that the phallic force of Vikorn's power and money were overwhelming her inner command center. (Are there any women who don't know how to do that where you come from, R?)

It was a tired ritual, though, that neither party believed in. I think she would have liked to stand with legs apart, chest inflated, one hand in her pocket, the other brandishing a cigar. Trying to explain the technology while keeping up femininity and deference was quite a strain. Vikorn, on the other hand, looked like he needed to put his feet up in a comfortable chair at home.

"The red are pickup points and the green are delivery points." She looked me carefully in the eye through those very cute black-framed spectacles that sat on the end of her tiny nose. Now she paused, waiting for me.

"And the yellow?" I obliged.

She checked with Vikorn, who nodded for her to answer my question. "They are . . . I don't think there's a word for it in Thai, and my English doesn't stretch that far." She checked with Vikorn again.

"*Listening posts,*" he said with a groan.

"Right," she said. "The Colonel is correct as always. Listening posts."

"But they're almost all in China?"

"Correct." Now it was him and her against me. They both stared into my eyes for a moment, then looked away.

"May I ask why?"

"Because they are Chinese listening posts."

"Listening to who?"

"Me," Vikorn said, then added, "and the Americans. And all the other Asia Pac countries. But it's okay." He shrugged. "The Chinese are our friends." He glanced at Krom and added, "Apparently."

He and Krom were staring at me now, waiting. Why would they be waiting for something from me, the lowest-ranked of the three of us? I looked at Vikorn for an answer.

"Sonchai, what would *you* like to do?"

Does that sound like a normal, civilized question to you, R? Well, over here it's not, it's damned strange for someone like the Chief to ask me in social-worker tones what I would like to do. It's never been my place to do what I like, my business is to do what *he* likes.

"What would I like to do? I'd like to arrest those bastards from yesterday, of course. Especially that damned Asset who somehow induced a Thai boy to kill his mother. I don't have to tell you what that must mean. They've developed some kind of military technique for taking over a person's mind. I don't care what anybody says, no Thai boy that age is capable of killing his mom. Thai mothers instill total and absolute obedience in their children, a dependency that death itself cannot break. Everybody knows an emotionally enslaved male child is a lot more reliable in old age than social security. No, that Thai boy was poisoned by *farang* mind, no doubt about it." I paused. "And most of all I would like to find the perp in the Market Murder case. I want whoever killed that girl and plastered my name in blood all over the mirror."

Vikorn scratched his chin. "You can't arrest the Asset or Goldman. They both have diplomatic cover, and anyway the CIA would never allow it. If you made too much fuss, they would take you out."

"Then I want to arrest Lord bloody Sakagorn of Senior Counsel," I yelled. "He's clearly guilty after the fact and knows what's going on."

I uttered this last outburst quite certain that no one was going to give me authority to arrest the aristocrat lawyer whose connections went all the way to the top of government. To my surprise Vikorn smiled, though a tad wanly. "That's what I thought you would say. Leave it with me for the moment. I'll, ah, have to check."

"With the Chinese?"

He frowned. Then, as if in a senile change of heart, Vikorn suddenly dismissed us: "Well, that will do for now. I'm sure the two of you will catch up in your own time. I'm afraid I have a meeting with the Director in an hour and the traffic is gridlocked on Rama IX. If you'll excuse me?"

Krom and I immediately *waied* and left the room, now known as the Communications and Command Center, or CCC.

The door had no sooner closed behind us, leaving us in the hall together, than Inspector Krom reverted. She hunched her shoulders and lowered her head, giving the impression of serious, if narrow, intent. At the same time she walked next to me slightly bowlegged, like a man with swollen testicles, and used a kind of rolling rhythm with her arms, as if she were readying herself for a fight. She was chummy, though, in her natural form, and chatted to me in a matey way, making use of the latest—and most masculine—street slang.

"What are the girls like over at your mother's bar?" she wanted to know. "Great tits and ass, I bet."

"We pay over the odds." I wrinkled my brow. "You're not a feminist?"

She wrinkled hers in turn. "Do I look that old? Want coffee?"

We left the station to cross the road to the cooked-food stalls. I'd already eaten so I ordered a coffee. Krom ordered extra-spicy *somtam* salad. She stared at me, waiting for me to speak first.

"I'm a homicide detective," I said.

"I know. And yesterday you witnessed a quadruple homicide, and no way will they let you bring in the perps. Like Vikorn said, they have diplomatic immunity."

"Fuck immunity, this is matricide."

She nodded. "I understand. But the key is Vikorn who takes his orders from a ministry in Beijing these days. What did you think of that new high-tech meeting room?"

"I think it's weird, like an alien installation."

"But that's exactly what it is. The aliens are Chinese. That display on the map, that is an electronic gun held to the Old Man's head. It's a naked statement of how much—how very, very much—he owes the Chinese. Basically, he screwed up."

"How's that?"

"They tricked him. He was allowed to move a lot of stuff out of Myanmar—I mean huge loads—through Yunnan and all the way across to Hong Kong and Shanghai. He was already a billionaire, and he doubled his fortune. Sure, he bribed. He bribed and bribed and made a lot of regional bosses very happy—the mistake he made was to underestimate Beijing. Since they never lifted a finger to stop him, he assumed either they didn't know or they were getting kickbacks from the regional bosses. Being a cop and a crook, he didn't quite have the sweep and depth to figure out what Beijing was up to. Now it's too late."

"So what is Beijing up to?"

"Research and development. Of humans. But they're way behind."

Research and development of humans: only a nerdy dyke could come out with a phrase like that and make it sound humdrum.

"And you are what? How come you know so much? How did you know who the players were yesterday, and why were you there right on the spot and right on time? D'you work wholly for the Chinese or just part-time?"

"Can we do me later? I'm sort of classified. Look, you could call this an American Age, or you could call it a Chinese Age, but either way it's a Pacific Age—and Thailand, politically, is Asia Pac."

"So where does that leave me?"

"It leaves you working for a boss who is owned body and soul, head to feet, by certain ministries in Beijing. When Vikorn heard the details of the Market Murder he totally freaked. I was with him. He shook like a leaf."

"Why?"

"Because he's brokering the biggest deal of his life and Beijing is forcing him to guarantee the product. If there's a problem, they take him down for all he's got. He's a very big player for you and me, but to the government that runs the lives of one-and-a-half billion people he's nothing, nothing at all."

"But, yesterday, on the river, that was all American."

"Correct. And the spies behind the cameras were Chinese."

"Americans selling military programs to the Chinese on Thai soil? Is that what you're saying?"

"Yesterday was not a demo, that was the point. Goldman and the Asset chose that terrible weather as cover—they didn't think the Chinese had the technology to penetrate the storm. They were experimenting—what you saw was a dress rehearsal."

"Experimenting? With murder by mind control?"

She looked away, turned her gaze to the street. Beyond the cooked-food stalls where people were sitting and standing, chatting, as on any other day, a knife cutter was calling out from his cyclo on which he had installed a revolving whetstone, another man in long blue shorts and a singlet was peddling brooms and mops from his tuk-tuk, mothers were taking their kids to the local nursery school. It was a very ordinary morning.

"You've never met a cop like me before, have you?" Krom asked.

"No."

She paused as if deciding what to say next. "Very few people know it, but the fact is, we're living in a transhuman age." She glanced at my face to see if I'd understood. I hadn't. In an epoch of constantly expanding vocabulary, I'd never heard the expression before.

She ate some of her *somtam* salad. I sipped my coffee and waited.

"The West is bankrupt in every sense, on every level," she said. "Money is out of control and so are people's heads. Over the next decade technologically empowered civil unrest will force most countries to militarize their police forces even more—much more—than they have already. And when the West goes, the myth of democracy goes with it. It will be dictatorship or chaos, and humans prefer order to freedom when it comes to the crunch. A lot of us feel like slaves anyway: where's the freedom if you're working three miserable jobs to pay off your debts to keep bankers rich? The secret technology we witnessed yesterday is tomorrow's law enforcement, worldwide. It will be every government's must-have, with the blessing of a paranoid population. Those who own it will be billionaires, automatically. Just like the Internet moguls of yesteryear."

"Okay, so Vikorn is a go-between for sale and purchase of highly classified military programs. I got that."

"An unwilling go-between. But who better to use for background checks than the most powerful cop in Bangkok, together with his best detective? If the Chinese were to go through with the deal and the product found faulty—well, they call in the Colonel's guarantee, don't they?"

She gave me a couple of minutes to think it through. "If the product proved faulty, how? You mean, if the product is given to the spectacular murder of young virgins? Yes, I can see that might cause the masters of Beijing to start frothing at the mouth. They would be forced to claim American sabotage, even if it wasn't."

She grunted, then said, "You didn't hear that from me."

She stood up to pay with a hundred-baht note. So far the short sleeves of her uniform had been long enough to cover her arms down to the elbow; now I saw there was a sharp border between the light tan flesh of the forearm and the dense blue of some serious damascene inkings.

"You have full-body?"

The question shocked her for a moment; she hurriedly lowered her hand and pulled her sleeve down.

"It's when you stand up to pay like a man that you give the game away," I said with a smirk.

She threw me a glare and sat down again. "Yes. Full-body." She shook her head, angry at herself for being careless and giving her secret away.

She frowned, laid the hundred-baht note on the table for a moment, and reached into a pocket. She took out a thumb drive. "I knew we were going to be working together, so I brought this in case our conversation went well. A moment ago I thought I'd wait a while. Now you've seen the tat, though, you may as well have it. Just so you know." She handed over the thumb drive. "Share it with your wife. If she needs any reassurance about you and me working together, this will give it to her—big time."

I looked her in the eye as I took it. Then she held out a hand that, I suspect, she would have liked to be bigger and more masculine. As a matter of fact, it was small, slim, and very elegant; no rings, though. I shook it. Now she had one more shock for me.

"Ah, just so you know I know—your little weakness for weed—do I need to say more?"

"What weakness?"

"C'mon, Detective, everyone knows."

"Knows what?"

"Your Achilles' heel, man. Yes, you are straight, honest, compassionate, never take money unless Vikorn forces you, and even then you never keep any for yourself. You are notorious for not being on the take. But that sets up quite a psychological strain that's hard to handle without help. Then there's your permanent search for your biological father. Everyone knows about that."

"They do?"

"Yep."

I scratched my ear. "So?"

"So I have something for you."

She dug into a pocket and took out a vial like a test tube filled with a golden-green liquid. "I made some up, just for you, as a token of our new friendship."

I stared at the test tube, then at her. "What is it?"

"Oil," she said.

"THC?"

"What else? Do you know how to use it? You dip a cigarette in it then warm the cigarette in an oven at not more than a hundred degrees Celsius until it's dry—any hotter and you'll kill the THC."

I shook my head. THC: of course, what else? I slipped it into my pants pocket.

Back at the station I sat at my post in the open-plan office, checked e-mail, checked the news again, went through the usual kind of distractions while another part of my mind scratched incessantly at a couple of key phrases Inspector Krom had inserted into our conversation: *weakness for weed; your Achilles' heel, man; search for your biological father.*

I slapped the top of my desk, causing the cop at the desk nearby to look up and scowl. I rose to my feet.

"If anyone wants to know, I've gone to see Dr. Supatra, the pathologist," I told him. He scowled again and went back to his screen. I had interrupted his game of *Angry Birds.*

———

To know you are a little odd, that you do not possess the full complement of antecedents, complications, traps, and habits that constitute *normal*—that is one thing. To be told by a stranger that your own strangeness is obvious, to have it explained to you that you are one of those with a gaping wound, moreover, that is talked about openly behind your back—that is quite another number to crunch on. My nerves did not begin to relax until I was a good few hundred yards from the station, on the way to the pathologist's laboratory. I liked the anonymity of the street. I always had. Even as a kid I'd been addicted to long walks late at night in the city that never sleeps. In the small hours of the morning it was possible to imagine that those who were still awake were of my own kind: pariahs. I liked Inspector Krom's tattoo. I admired her courage. I feared her ruthlessness.

3

Dr. Supatra also was odd, but that worked fine for her. All medical examiners are weird, it's expected of them. Death is a forbidden country for most people, especially in a superstitious culture such as ours. Supatra, under five foot, slight, long-faced with the intensity of a witch, fitted her profession so well that cops who worked with her saw in her a kind of archetype, as if all pathologists must be cut from the same pattern. She scowled then checked my face with those intense black eyes. There was no point trying to hide.

"You're sleeping? You look exhausted. Are you taking those pills I gave you? Don't take too many, you can't escape nightmares forever. Coming to terms is the only escape."

"I know, it's in the Pali Canon." I let a beat pass. "You saw the news?"

"What news?"

"Those two families who drowned."

"The ones on that boat? What about them?"

"The young man drowned his mother. I saw him. The other drowned his wife, mother of his kids."

She gave me a sharp look. "That wasn't reported."

"No."

I told her what I had witnessed the day before. She listened carefully, absorbing each word and savoring it. Then she shook her head. "This is the tipping point, societies fall so far, then they fall apart. This is known. It's in the literature. Be thankful you're no longer young. Why are you here, anyway?"

"I need to see the body again."

"Which bits? I've put the head and torso in separate drawers. You know what I think."

"You think an extraterrestrial did it."

"What else has that kind of strength? What else gets into that kind of frenzy? Humans can't pull heads off the bodies of other humans, it's impossible, too many sinews, muscles, bones. Maybe you could find an iron pumper who could do such a thing, but it would have been even uglier—the perp here was so strong he pulled the head off almost surgically. It's a terrible thing to say, but this beheading with bare hands was almost elegant—along with the handwriting."

"We don't have extraterrestrials in Thailand. They always prefer the West—name one extraterrestrial who has landed in Asia instead of America or Europe?"

"Siberia," she said without hesitation. "Some landed in Siberia in a spaceship that burned up a whole acre of steppe. There's a clip on YouTube."

"Siberia is thousands of miles north of here."

"So it was a demon beheaded the girl. That's why you have to investigate. How far have you got?"

"Unclear," I admitted. "I suspect but dare not arrest. I need something nobody can argue with. What happened with that one blond hair they found, about an inch long you said?"

"Still testing. All they know is it's not human. It's the strongest damn hair they've ever seen—can't pull it apart. They've sent it to some fancy forensic lab in the U.S."

I followed her to the great wall of steel drawers and stood by while she opened one.

When I had come to terms with the full horror of the case, I had realized that the head, or, to be precise, the face, was the biggest mystery. When Supatra opened the drawer it was exactly as I remembered from last time: the head of a young woman or girl, Southeast Asian, eyes closed, almost serene, like a Buddha image, pale and frosty from the refrigeration. I had ransacked past cases and found nothing relevant. The only case thrown up by research that bore any resemblance was of a religious fanatic in the sixties in the U.K., a gay man who had cut off the head of his guru lover and was found by police cradling it in his arms. He explained that the head was the only part he could respect and revere, the rest was animal. I paused over the long neck and remembered the Long Neck women of the Karen tribe: but they took a decade to stretch their necks using brass rings they added one by one every year. I shook my head, then searched Supatra's grim face.

"Like this," she said. "Don't think I haven't obsessed, too. This is the only way he could have done it to have such a result." In a moment of physical intimacy that was almost alarming, the Doctor placed a tiny hand at the base of my neck and squeezed. "Imagine my hand is like a big steel pincer," she said, "like a crab's claw. So I dig into the flesh with my nails, which are sharp enough to cut skin and minor muscles. Then I snap the vertebra at C5, twist until the head is facing backward, and then simply push." She was now trying to *push* my head off using her second hand under my chin while the first remained clamped to my lower neck and squeezing hard as if trying to cut the sinews with her nails. I experienced not the slightest fear that she could do any serious harm. "You get the picture? That's why the neck is so stretched. But no normal man could do it. It's not just a question of strength; arms and hands are simply not designed for such a feat. It's not how we evolved."

"But the face is not damaged."

"Right. That's part of the point. The only way he could have left the face undamaged is by doing it the impossible way I just showed you."

"Shouldn't she be bloated from suffocation?"

"She didn't suffocate. I think she fainted, then died as soon as he broke her neck. No fighting for air, no bloating. There are no signs of resistance."

"Meaning she knew her assailant?"

"Not necessarily. It could be that the assault happened so fast with an assailant so powerful there was no time or opportunity to resist."

Supatra closed the drawer.

"The video," I said.

She shook her head at me, then took me to her office.

"You're here to investigate or torture yourself? Take a copy, I have a thumb drive you can borrow."

"I don't want it in my house," I said. "I'm superstitious."

"So you're a normal Thai man after all. Have you been to temple? Have you talked to a monk? Did you go to see that *mordu* I told you about?"

"I saw him just for ten minutes—he said to come back."

"What are you waiting for?"

"I don't know."

She clicked a few times on her desktop until she found the video that the forensic team had made. The video shook somewhat at first due to the operator's shock. He was careful, though, to follow the rule: a meticulous panning from left to right, covering the crime scene like a lawn mower so nothing was left out. It took less than five minutes. At the end the video concentrated on the walls, which were bare plaster save for the blood splatter. The video recording halted at the mirror, however, and hovered there. English characters that were not crude or childish, but quite elegant: *Detective Sonchai Jitpleecheep, I know who [smudge] father is.*

I had come to the morgue as a kind of check of myself. I wanted to know if I had hardened enough to carry on. The Doctor, also, was interested to know the answer to this question. In my opinion the experiment was inconclusive. I was shaking, but not quite as much as before. I even managed a grim smile.

"I would like a still of the handwriting," I said.

Supatra clicked on her mouse a few times until her printer produced a copy of the writing on the mirror and handed it to me. "What use is a handwriting expert? It's the one form of communication even the NSA doesn't collect."

"I know. But they can tell likely level of education, cultural origins, even certain character traits."

"Sure, that will narrow it down to a few million. Better you go see the *mordu*. A clairvoyant would be more specific. Okay, I'm a scientist, but I'm still Thai. I've never seen such an obvious piece of black magic in my life. I was joking about extraterrestrials, actually this whole case has Khmer written all over it. Go see the holy man, there's no one else."

"I'm on my way," I said, thanked her, and left.

Out on the street I waited for a taxi to take me across the river. Perhaps it sounds odd to you, R, that in a difficult case one should ask for occult help, but for us it's really not so strange, though we don't normally tell *farang* like you about it. To suppose that humans are rational is a largely Western superstition to which most Asians are resistant. After all, if reason has failed in this case, that must be because reason isn't powerful enough to penetrate the mystery, mustn't it? Clearly, I need something with more chili. I'm off to see the wizard. All the best seers live on the west bank, known as Fangton.

In the taxi I replay those bloody words for the thousandth time: *Detective Sonchai Jitpleecheep, I know who [smudge] father is.* A couple of days ago I put the phrase through a simple computer test. On the assumption that the *smudge* is a word erased and that the writer was using grammatically correct English, there are not many alternatives: in all likelihood the missing word would be an article or a pronoun: *my, your, his, her, their, the, our.* None of them would surprise in an ordinary case of murder by a disorganized psychopath. In the case of an organized mind, though, only two would really make sense; either *Detective Sonchai Jitpleecheep, I know who <u>your</u> father is,* which would not normally be an important enough message to write in blood, or *Detective Sonchai Jitpleecheep, I know who <u>our</u> father is.* That would at least be a revelation worth making; in the mind of a certain kind of psycho, it might even be worth murdering for.

Now as my mind relaxed in the back of the cab it started to gnaw on something Inspector Krom had said with that in-your-face directness that takes no prisoners: *Then there's your permanent search for your biological father. Everyone knows about that.*

4

R, did you know your same-sex parent when you were growing up? If you did not, then my song will be familiar: I never stopped looking for him, from the minute I realized he was missing. All the kids at infant school had a dad, why not me? Therefore the previous thirty-seven years had been rich in daddy substitutes, most of them from my imagination. All I had to go on was Vietnam: a good-looking Yank in his early twenties, face blackened with war (sometimes); a charmer of women (Mum in particular). Because his English was perfect, so mine had to be. Should I thank him for opening my mind to *farang* confusion? I'm not sure, but how else were my fantasy dads going to communicate with me or I with them? He sure didn't speak Thai worth a damn, I had Mama Nong's testimony to rely on there.

Sometimes I made him muscle-bound like those GIs you see in the Museum of American War Atrocities in Saigon (of course I went, long before they renamed it so they could trade again with Uncle Sam—it's still there if you don't believe me). I found one in a photo on the wall of a soldier with arms so powerful he looked incomplete without something heavy to lift. When I realized I wasn't built that way I slimmed my dream dad down a bit. I kept him at average height, calculating that I was going to be tall for a Thai anyway, and who wants to stick out at age thirteen? Then, when I realized how important brains were, I made him smart, really smart. To justify my daydreams I read and read—and did extra well at school and started to imagine that maybe Einstein had paid a visit to Soi Cowboy sometime in the seventies and had an adventure with a bar girl named Nong; until I realized how smart Mum was (Mama Nong learned to speak English faster than me and she didn't even have an American dad); my smarts didn't necessarily prove a thing about him. And so on. I drove myself crazy trying to find some trait of body or mind, anything that I could point to about myself and say, *That's from him.* Did I become a detective in order one day to find him? I'm not sure. Certainly, I was tormented at an earlier age than most by the conviction that it was possible to discover who I was. Did such an absurd idea originate in your hemisphere, R?

Sometimes my search hurt so much I'd confide in Mum. *Tell me,* I'd say, *tell me, just one thing that is definitely him not you?* She didn't answer for years, until the girls in the bars started passing on stories about me. "That," she said, pointing at my crotch. "All men have it, but not all have it that bad. That's him all right."

"He was really as bad as me?" I asked, somewhat troubled by the thought.

"Worse."

"And you put up with it?"

"It was the seventies, there was a war on, I was a bar girl, there were thousands of us, you were grateful even for the chance to compete."

"But you loved him, you told me. I asked you a million times, and that's the only question you've ever given a consistent answer to."

"I was a country girl. In the country you judge the male by its virility and the female by its fecundity. You could say he was a prizewinning buffalo, gold medal, any farmer's pride and joy, deprive him of sex for a night and he'd tear the shed down. Sure I was proud of him. Proud as hell that he stayed with me, took me to America, once — that alone raised me to queen-of-the-village status. And he shared. He was generous. Almost as generous with his dough as with his sperm — and that's saying a lot."

"You were in love with his dick, then?"

"You want a whack?"

She was tough. Looking back, it can make me laugh how she played the fragile Oriental lotus to soak the johns. Like all Thai women, she was master of the art of flattery. Not a customer she slept with whom she didn't compliment on the size of his member, however diminutive: *Wow! Honey, I don't think I've seen one that big before* — was she thinking of Dad as she flicked those flagging phalli back to life? There are questions even sons like me don't ask, but the fact speaks for itself: she only let herself fall pregnant the once. Only one man she so honored. Why him?

So, although I never got used to being without him, I did get used to always having a make-believe *him* to turn to as a role model. In fact I had a whole wardrobe of *hims* who I could wear depending on the need of the hour—e.g., strong, resolute, honest, the best kind of American—especially when I started as a cop. H/we grew partial to weed at an early age, though, and loved stealing cars (just a phase h/we went through, you understand). And when I doubted the historical accuracy of my invented progenitor, I had the brothels to turn to. There I always could find him, so to speak. I knew his excitement when a new, extra-delicious girl appeared on the revolving stages; I understood the profound respect he felt for the way she kept her dignity—and held out for the dough. I experienced that inexplicable compulsion to see just one more naked young woman on a bed waiting for me, like the drunk who needs just one more drink. That, basically, is all I have of Dad.

Now we're stuck at the lights just before the Memorial Bridge, and a monk passes in front of us with an alms bowl and his *looksit* in white behind him carrying the morning's haul of vegetarian food in a bundle of plastic bags tied up together. I almost became a monk; that could have been me there crossing the road. I still believe in enlightenment. It only takes about twenty years on minimal rations, five hours' sleep per night, possessions reduced to one change of robes, one alms bowl, and an umbrella, unlimited concentration on emptiness, then a good monk can return to the Infinite at will. He sees everything, understands everything, is everything. That's what Dr. Supatra's *mordu* did more than half a century ago, but he is Khmer and ordained in Cambodia, which country he had to flee when Pol Pot made life impossible. In Thailand he formally disrobed and hung up his shingle as a know-all clairvoyant named Master Soon.

Soon, by the way, means *zero*. It was typical of Dr. Supatra to recommend him, for he is the most authentic and radical *mordu* in Bangkok, if not Thailand. Almost everything he predicts comes to pass. So, is his daily surgery filled with eager seekers after truth? Nope. People who claim to want to know their future avoid him like the plague. Women especially, who are the chief consumers of clairvoyant products in their endless search for emotional stability and amorous bliss and constitute eighty percent of the market nationwide, generally have nothing to do with him. He really does *see*, that's his problem. His few followers hang around mainly to save him from starvation. Once I realized how unpopular he was, how close to total destitution, how even tough-minded macho types who have been to hell and back, or think they have, find him hard to hang out with, I knew he was the man for me. He just won't tell fibs to make you feel good. No wonder he's bankrupt. Now the lights have changed and we're on our way.

My first conclusion on my earlier visit was that his two decades in the robes in Cambodia did not include training in shack construction. Even I, who have seen more than my share of incompetent carpentry, was impressed by the way the uprights of his hut leaned, the corrugated iron roof sagged, crossbeams seemed to have been chosen for their crookedness, the door was permanently stuck half open, and he forgot windows. Outside a woman in her early thirties was sobbing uncontrollably.

"I hope you haven't come to see that bastard," she managed. "I came for help and advice and he broke my heart in two minutes. He's not a *mordu*, he's a damned demon, that's what he is." More *boo hoo hoo*.

"What did he say?"

A dam broke. "He said I wasted the best years of my life on useless handsome shits who were good in bed and flattered me when I could have married a boring, honest, ugly man who would have taken great care of me and my kids and now it's way too late, and anyway, I still haven't even begun to give up on admiring myself in the mirror even though my looks have melted, my tits and ass have sagged, and self-love has ruined my nerves so no one, not even an honest, boring, ugly man, could possibly live with me for long, and anyway, even if I could find one I'd make his life hell by taking the piss out of him behind his back and to his face because of my insufferable narcissism that even now that I'm no longer cute makes it impossible for me to feel compassion for my fellow human beings, especially if they're not attractive." She paused for breath. "I couldn't believe it, the way he went on. He said what I called love was anything that made my pussy wet, I'd been masturbating since puberty and still couldn't stop playing with myself every time I felt insecure, and the only thing that brought temporary relief was the ruthless lust of a man with a big hard cock." She paused. "I mean, for a holy man he sure knows a lot about women and sex." She wiped her eyes. "If he wasn't so skinny, old, and weak, I would have kicked him in the balls. No wonder he's a failure. Who's going to pay good money for that kind of crap?" She glared. "And he knew it all in less than a second. He didn't even look at me."

"Really?"

"He was trying to fix a hole in his roof with a plastic bag, he didn't get off the chair he was standing on. Didn't even turn his head. What a bastard." She paused for breath. "He's definitely clairvoyant, though. How the hell did he know my tits were sagging when he didn't turn around to look at me?"

When I entered the hut he was standing on a chair, still fixing the hole in the roof. "Daddy, daddy, daddy, daddy, daddy," he said, not looking around. "All your life that's been your mantra. No wonder you're stunted, you haven't even begun to live your own life, you're waiting for daddy before you begin. Get over it."

Now he climbed down off the chair. He was taller than I expected, about five eleven, incredibly skinny like representations of the Buddha when he was starving in the forest. He wore only an old shapeless pair of shorts held up with a piece of string, and his long hair was held back in a makeshift gray bun also tied with string. It had been decades since he'd shaved. As he possessed a mixture of Chinese and Thai genes, his beard was sparse but long, drooping down from the corners of his mouth, which was almost invisible. It ended in a few white wisps. Apart from a black fire in the depths of his eyes he looked as if he had maybe a week left in the body. And his tongue, of course. That was alive and kicking.

He assessed me in a blink. "Now I see you better. That father thing is just a distraction, isn't it? You're like me. I saw you in a dream."

"How's that?"

"A total misfit. You could come from the most stable, loving, chaste, comfortable family in Thailand with a beautiful mum and a wise dad and the very best schooling, and you'd still be all fucked-up. You chose a broken home and a whore for a mother just so you'd have an excuse to be weird. Maybe you're not so dumb after all." An extra voltage of gleam came into his eye. "It's your equivalent of a broken roof." I could see he believed he'd won the battle and was pleased with himself. "It's your great distraction. Anytime you're in danger of having to face the real challenge of your life, you deflect. You tell yourself you're looking for your true identity, which can only happen when you've found your daddy, who, incidentally, will be of no use to you at all when you finally meet him. What a psycho scam. I'm almost impressed." He paused for breath. "It's not entirely your fault. Man has made astonishing strides recently in all things inessential. The price we've paid is enormous. Stuck with an infantile description of reality that cannot come to terms with death or even lesser challenges, the eternal infant must torture himself for lifetime after lifetime, probably without end."

This time when I arrive at the shack I show him the printout of the English words on the mirror. He studies it for a long moment. "Don't you want to know what it says?" I ask.

"No. What it says has no importance. Can't you see what it really says, smartass? It's telling you how big your problem really is."

"How's that?"

"It's not written by a human being. I saw that in a dream last night, but even I couldn't believe it. It's there, though, plain as day."

"What are you talking about?"

"The individual characters. Look at that one, what's that called?"

"It's an *E*."

"Right. There are lots of them. And they're all the same."

"Of course they're all the same. They're all *E*s."

"Idiot. I mean they're *exactly* the same. Same size, same shape, no variation at all. You've meditated, you've studied the Abhidharma, you know how the mind works. Say it takes a tenth of a second to make one stroke of a pen. Then there's a gap in consciousness too brief to notice, but it's vital to your functioning. During that gap the whole history of humanity intervenes in the form of sparks and flashes, your own personal history, the whole cosmos, actually, which of course doesn't exist in time, but when you make the next stroke of the pen you are a different person. After a whole inhalation and exhalation nothing at all remains except the blueprint. No way the next stroke is going to be identical to the first, there has to be a subtle difference. When it comes to a whole letter, well, no normal person possessed of normal consciousness will produce exactly the same letter over and over again."

He stares at me. I take back the printout, hold it close to study, nod, hand it back to him. "So what are you saying? Someone has a template they use to write this stuff on mirrors in blood after they've brutally beheaded a person?"

"No. I'm saying the hand that wrote it was human, the mind controlling that hand was not. It was not a real mind. It was a clone of a mind."

I gape.

"That's a terrific battle you've got on your hands. Try not to win it."

"Try *not* to win it?"

"Sure. If you win it you'll get conceited and start feeling too positive about life, and you'll come back powerful and successful in the next incarnation and totally fuck up all over again and have to start over as a dog or something. If you must win, make sure it hurts so bad you don't ever want to go through something like that again." He shrugs. "But you probably won't win. This is big. Very big. This is the end of the world, what you have there on that piece of paper." He scratches his beard. "By the way, what does it say?"

I tell him. He stares at me and shakes his head.

"What?" I say.

"*What? You ask what?* You're a detective, you told me. Has anything ever been so obvious?"

I take a deep breath. This guy is a master of trying your patience. Maybe it is his teaching method; at this moment it seems like a serious personality defect. "I am very sorry to be so stupid," I say with a smile. "Clearly my modest capacity is so far behind yours it is difficult for you to relate to me. Would you graciously explain what the . . ." I take another breath. "What the hell you are talking about?" I say softly.

He hums tunelessly. Never before has humming filled me with rage. Little by little words emerge from the hum. Finally I realize what he is saying over and over again: "Someone has you on a hook, my friend. Someone has you on a hook." He smiles. "Congratulations. If you survive this karma, you will be close to enlightenment. I almost envy you."

Then he frowns. "Take a look at this," he says, using a dramatic gesture to sweep around his unbelievably squalid abode with the leaking roof, the dirt floor, a mean little brazier, one pot, a plastic bottle of water, a bamboo mat for a bed, a crude Buddha image on a high shelf. "You think this is tough? This is easy." He points to his head. I get the message. He has tranquillity, I have the opposite. When I make to leave he grabs my arm and stares into my eyes. "You smoke weed, don't you?"

"Ah, a little."

"No, a lot. But probably not enough. Next time you smoke, get really, really stoned, then meditate on desolation. Concentrate on the most unpleasant death you can think of, then how it will be at the end, when you realize there never was a heaven or a morality and every single little thing you did to make your life and the world better was a total waste of time."

"Why are you so hung up on desolation?"

"It's where the treasure is hidden."

So much for my brush with the saint. When I emerge from his shack I am surprised to find the woman from my previous visit outside staring at the river. She looks away when she sees me, as if she understands what I am going through. Maybe he puts everyone through it.

5

After I'd given myself time to think about it, I realized there was a reason why Vikorn might be happy to nail the HiSo lawyer Lord Sakagorn, he of the sky-blue Rolls-Royce and the trademark ponytail. The Colonel was from a dirt-poor subsistence farming family in Isaan and no matter how high he rose he carried with him the smoldering resentment of a people bled white by a snotty Bangkok elite who treated them like subhumans, because that's what they honestly believe us to be. Vikorn loved skewering representatives of that class, and although he probably had nothing particular against Sakagorn, there could hardly be a more emblematic child of privilege and exploiter of deference to crucify.

"So how do we do it, Chief?" I asked.

"If you bring his lordship in, you have to justify it. He'll come down on you like a truck, flatten you with the law." He shook his head. "No, you don't bring Sakagorn in without a perfect case."

"Of what?"

The Colonel smiled as he looked down at the street. "He gambles on Colonel Ransorn's patch. There's an illegal casino in the car park area of a condominium block—they've enlarged the security hut to take over the whole of one floor of the underground car park. Inside it's very plush, a Monte Carlo–type setup." Vikorn checked his watch. "He's there most evenings—starts early, after the courts close. His game is roulette. The main point for you is to take pictures. Do it ostentatiously, not only with phone cameras. Have someone with a big old-style camera with a nice bright flash. Little touches like that have an impact on the HiSo mind."

"But there must be a lot of security. Someone like Sakagorn isn't going to use an illegal casino unless it's totally safe."

"Correct," Vikorn said. "But the casino is owned by Colonel Ransorn, who needed quite a lot of help to set it up. I charge only a minimum of interest—but of course, if Ransorn became unhelpful, I would have to charge more—or ask for a return of the loan." He turned to face me. "Leave it with me. I'll tell you when the security at the casino has been suspended. Probably tonight, late."

The operation turned out to be simpler than I expected. At exactly eleven p.m. the casino that lies under the thirty stories of the Shambhala Palace condominium building found itself raided by a small contingent of police who behaved as if they belonged to Ransorn's district but in fact owed their main allegiance to Sergeant Ruamsantiah. Everyone escaped except for the famous, high-flying, brilliant legal counsel Lord Sakagorn. He of the long black shiny hair, the flamboyant lemon waistcoat, the silk bow tie, dinner jacket, and smooth jowls. I sat with him in the back of the car when we returned to District 8. During the ride Sakagorn regained his composure and started throwing out a few forensic hints about how much this was going to cost me, Vikorn, and the police in general, once he got the case off the ground.

"You don't have a chance of making anything stick. You're not even the right crew for the district."

I decided not to cuff Sakagorn when we took him away—after all, he is not the type to make a desperate bid for freedom in the middle of traffic, it would be inelegant. As a result, he was free to gesticulate. His performance was all the more dramatic because somehow in the scuffle he lost his silver hair clip so that his enraged face was now framed by a chaos of long, shiny hair that he smoothed back with histrionic care while he demanded to see Vikorn immediately. This was a matter to be sorted out by money and power—I had neither.

I myself felt the need for a heavy hitter to deal with Sakagorn, so I called the Colonel, who happened to be carousing at one of his clubs. His mood swung from irritation to amusement when I told him about the bust. He especially liked the detail of the lost hair clip. When we arrived at reception they told me the Colonel was waiting in the main conference room, the one with the giant LED screen.

In addition to the thumb drive for the large camera, I had my own phone pictures of Sakagorn at the casino, and also those that Ruamsantiah took. All in all I suppose there were a total of more than a hundred pictures on each of the two smart phones plus the memory card from the SLR camera.

All the time Lord Sakagorn ranted, even citing Aristotle's *The Constitution of the Athenians*, while Vikorn said nothing but merely sat at the head of the table playing with the smart phones until he decided to pick one up and plug it into a cable under the giant monitor. Little by little Sakagorn stopped advocating as the photo gallery appeared in outsize pictures on the screen. After a few minutes of experimentation, which he seemed to enjoy, Vikorn found what he was looking for.

She was in her early twenties, owned the pure white skin of northern Chinese genes, held herself with the grace and simplicity of a virgin protected by power and money, turned to smile at Sakagorn now and then with the respect of a loyal daughter for a father figure, and became confused every time the middle-aged barrister rested a hand on her butt. Her dinner gown was midnight-black, her jewelry silver, her experience limited. Part of her wanted to look on the roulette as a child's game; on the other hand, she would allow Sakagorn to have his way with her sooner or later—perhaps that was why he had made the rather reckless decision to take her to the casino, so that she would be excited, impressed, and perhaps a little drunk when he made his move. Her expression held the question of all young people at a certain point: *Is this what I have to do to be an adult? To have arrived in the world? To be a part of it?*

I have not mentioned her before, because I paid her no attention, assuming she was simply part of the casino's entertainment. Vikorn, though, knew who she was. When he found a photo where her face was snapped at the moment Sakagorn fondled the nates of her ass, he stopped the show and left the picture on the screen. He still had not said a word to either of us, not even a "hello" to Sakagorn, who was technically his superior in the national protocol by a huge margin. Now the Colonel stared at Sakagorn.

"She is over the age of consent," Sakagorn said in a cracked voice that could be a wail of fear or indignation—he perhaps had not decided which.

"By a day or so, perhaps," Vikorn said. "But that's not the point, is it?" Sakagorn stared at Vikorn for a moment, then looked away. "Are you going to tell me her father knows you intended to corrupt her at the casino, maybe slip her something to mellow her, before taking her up to the penthouse? There's a private lift, isn't there, from the casino all the way up to the top of the building?"

"I don't know anything about that," Sakagorn snapped.

Vikorn shrugged. "It doesn't really matter, does it? Her father is in Washington, according to the news. Comes back at the end of the week. I doubt he'll go the legal route to punish you—what d'you think? He can hardly turn a blind eye, with all these photos all over YouTube and Facebook." Sakagorn had paled. Vikorn sighed. "I suppose you took such a risk because you are in love, Lord Sakagorn?"

The idea that Sakagorn could be in love with anyone other than himself caused me to smile, which caused Sakagorn to turn on me in a rage, which caused Vikorn to smile. Little by little, though, the eyes of we three men were seduced back to the screen. That was a very beautiful and very charming young aristocrat. Vikorn cleared his throat. "You haven't had her yet, have you?"

"No," Sakagorn admitted.

"That might just save your life. How did you intend to keep it secret?"

"I don't know. She drives me crazy. She's perfect, perfect. If her father gets heavy, I'll marry her."

"But you are already married, Lord Sakagorn."

"If she doesn't want to be a minor wife, I would divorce for her."

"Tonight was supposed to be the night?"

"Can we talk about something else?" Sakagorn said. He shrugged. "Okay, it's a deal. You keep quiet about tonight, erase all those pictures— I'll give you what you want." He was channeling a quite different persona when he muttered, "It won't make an atom of difference, even *you* don't have leverage in this. It's a lot bigger than you, Colonel. Bigger than the police altogether."

Vikorn seemed pleased that Sakagorn saw sense so quickly and took no notice of the implied threat. The lawyer cleared the hair from his face with both hands and stood in front of the video screen to block the view. Then he had a better idea. "Can you switch that damn thing off?"

Vikorn switched the screen off.

"Goldman," the Senior Counsel said. "Goldman and his Asset."

6

I didn't particularly want him for a client," Sakagorn explained, pacing up and down. "*Farang* are always a problem. Either they can't understand that a system can be different to theirs, or they do understand and cannot stop telling you what's wrong with it. They compare an idealized description of their own catastrophe with a brutally accurate description of ours. In the end one just grows angry and keeps quiet."

"So why did you take him on?"

"I was asked to by a senior member of government. Goldman was doing the high-society circuit and looking for a lawyer. A good friend who is a high-ranking civil servant wanted to know what kind of legal advice a retired CIA officer could possibly need in our country. He suggested I find out."

"You're spying on your client?"

"Who doesn't spy, now we have the gadgets? It's the pandemic nobody talks about."

"But Goldman was special—why?"

"Because he was here before. During the Vietnam War. He was young, but not too young. That's why his Thai is so good—he's been using it on and off for half a century. He's clever, good at languages. The kind of Company man who came into his own during 'Nam. Who was given a super-secret project called MKUltra to oversee in the field."

At the name *MKUltra*, Vikorn raised his eyes for a moment, then dropped them.

"Who became an embarrassment later on. A Cold Warrior from the espionage community of yesteryear. Usually they retired early or took desk jobs at Langley. But there were a few like Goldman who were field men to their marrows, who could not function well stateside—and who could still be useful when run by the right supervisor, someone who knows how to use such men."

"This is the brief you received from . . . someone senior in the Thai government?"

"Yes. That was it. A long lunch with someone very senior—at the Oriental—and someone else. We got through two and a half bottles of Cheval Blanc. It was a good lunch."

I expected Vikorn to pick up on the casual reference to *someone else*. He didn't.

"But even in the context of American wild men from 'Nam, this was a little extravagant, wasn't it? To use our best-connected Senior Counsel to spy on his own client? There must have been something specific."

"A lot of his stuff was done here, in Thailand," Sakagorn said, looking away. "Remember, this goes back half a century. Go back only a little further, to World War Two, and you come to the embarrassing incident when Thailand declared war on the United States. We had reasons to cooperate with Uncle Sam."

"You mean MKUltra happened here?"

"The setup, the drugs, the preparation—a lot of it happened here. The actual violations of human rights happened in Vietnam or stateside. Goldman ran the operation here and in 'Nam."

"But there had to be a specific reason for anyone that senior in the Thai government to be interested in Goldman. Interested enough to involve you."

"The Chinese were keen for us to service Goldman."

Vikorn did not blink at the mention of PRC interests. "You report back to them?"

"Classified," Sakagorn said.

Vikorn had come to the end of his preliminary questions, designed to set the scene. Now he nodded at me.

"And the advice he needed from you—was what?" I asked.

Lord Sakagorn frowned. "One day it will be a question for every jurisdiction: what do you do with transhumans? How does the law apply to them?"

"*Trans*humans? I've only recently heard that term for the first time," I said. "Who are they?"

"They are what we're talking about. What everyone will soon be talking about."

"Why should the law be any different for them?" I asked.

"Because *they* are different. In some ways they are like children. In some ways like animals. Do you expect a four-year-old or an ape to obey the law? To even understand what law is? On the other hand, their cognition skills are more advanced—electrical circuits surgically inserted give them amazing speed of thought. Amazing." He paused to frown again. "Except it's not thought. Not what we normally call thought."

Sakagorn looked miserable, as if it was not the bust at the casino that had ruined his evening so much as having to talk about this new beast, this transhuman.

"They talk well, though. They talk very well. Just like you and me. Actually, with the right programming they talk better than normal humans, no pauses for self-doubt and considered reflection. And they are made of flesh and bone, too. They have normal human bodies—sort of. You can't say they are robots—it would be so much easier if they were. It's hard to get your head around it. Hard to find the words. The more you see of it, the more confused you become." He stared into my face, but seemed not to see me. "They have charm, too. Great charm. That's not part of the programming either. This incredible charm. It's serendipitous. Did you ever meet a really smart person? I'm not talking about computing power or IQ particularly, I mean someone whose mind worked so well they could do just about anything? Sometimes politicians, certain judges—"

"And a certain kind of crook?" I asked.

His mood turned black. He sat heavily on the nearest chair. "Yes. That's what I mean, a certain kind of highly gifted personality can use their gift to charm lesser mortals. When you find some poor sucker whose brain doesn't work as well as yours, you only have to blind him with your superior cognitive abilities and he's putty in your hands. He might say you charmed him, but basically you took over his mind. Made him in awe of you." He paused to gaze at the ceiling. "When he's in the mood he can make you feel like you can't refuse him anything."

"You're talking about the Asset?"

"Yes."

"No matter how badly he behaves?" I said.

"Yes." Another frown and pause. "But not all the time, that's the thing. One minute you're dealing with an Einstein, the next minute with a sociopath. And there's no warning, no way of knowing which bit of him is working from moment to moment." He groaned and sighed. "I suppose they'll fix the glitch sooner or later." He shook his head. "Or maybe they won't. Sometimes, there's a look on his face, as if to say, *Forget it, I program myself from now on.*"

"On the face of the Asset?"

"Yes, of course."

"But Goldman himself—he still runs his 'Asset'? He's in charge?"

Sakagorn shook his head and frowned. The question troubled him so deeply that for once words failed him. Finally he said, "Their relationship has been deteriorating. Sometimes Goldman looks downright terrified." He would not say more on the subject.

I cough. "Lord Sakagorn, I have only one case at the moment and it has nothing to do with geopolitics or the PRC, so far as I know. It is a very local little tragedy, I'm afraid. But it was I who asked the Colonel to invite you to come talk to us . . ." I let the barrister snort at that and make a face, then carried on. "The media have named it the *Market Murder;* we are calling the victim *Nong X.* A local Thai girl, twelve years old, murdered in the market just behind this station." Sakagorn looked as if he was about to yawn: typical of an undeveloped peasant mind like mine to suddenly descend to the squalid and irrelevant. "Someone pulled her head off with his bare hands," I said with a smile. "I wonder if you could help?"

Sakagorn was startled but not particularly shocked. "I don't know. I heard about the murder, but I'm sure I would have remembered if any of the reports mentioned a decapitation."

"We're keeping the details quiet for the purpose of investigation."

The barrister seemed more curious than disturbed. "No other molestation?"

"No. No sexual abuse, no visible signs of struggle, no damage to other parts of the body. Somebody of superhuman strength simply twisted and wrenched her head from her shoulders, probably in seconds, before she had time even to be terrified. I don't have to tell you that simply doesn't happen in homicide cases. Killers do not unemotionally remove the heads of their victims with their bare hands while being careful not to do any other damage or take sexual advantage in any way."

Sakagorn did not disguise his surprise. He stared at me for a moment, thought about it, then shrugged. "Superhuman strength, lack of emotional involvement, a weird combination of extreme violence and total self-control—sure, it's him, Goldman's Asset. Who else could it be? I know nothing about it, however, nothing at all. I wasn't there, didn't know, wasn't invited, this is the first I'm hearing of it."

Now we had an awkward pause in the interrogation. Vikorn changed the subject.

"Tell us more about the background. Goldman and his Asset arrived in Bangkok only last month, you say? What about before that? Give us the history as you know it."

"Goldman ran a CIA program in Vietnam nearly half a century ago. It was basic zombie mind-control stuff that went wrong. There was a big scandal, they pretended to shut it down, Goldman pleaded for them to let him continue in secret. He did some kind of deal and moved the operation to Angkor, in Cambodia."

"Angkor? But the Khmer Rouge were there, they used it as a base."

"Yes, soon after Goldman moved there. He had to move on. But the few years he spent in Angkor were crucial, somehow."

The barrister turned cagey. Perhaps it was embarrassment: he was finding it difficult to come clean. Vikorn and I stared at him relentlessly. Finally he buckled. "I may have been brought up in this country, but until I met Goldman I didn't think I had a superstitious bone in my body. However, I would never visit Angkor again, never." He shook his head. "I went many times as a tourist, loved the huge trees embracing the great stone Buddhas—so romantic. It was a great place to take a girl for a long weekend, in the old days. And so close, about forty minutes by plane door to door."

He looked up. "Goldman got drunk one night and started raving about it. It seems he had the use of one of the lesser temples, not the Wat itself—you know, Angkor was a great city, fifty years ago eighty percent of it had yet to be excavated. He kept ranting about some shrink, some Englishman, some crazy British psychiatrist with a ridiculous British name. I couldn't make out if this Brit was on the team, or running some other team, or what. The whole thing was garbled, he was horribly drunk—scary, a man that size, drunk and crazy. It seemed this British shrink with a weird name I can't remember had persuaded the CIA shrinks to try an experiment. It was the Brit shrink's idea that the Americans were all wrong in thinking that enhancement was a matter of drugs and neurons. The argument was the usual Old World organic versus New World scientific. Basically, he was talking about magic. Black magic." He scanned us. "I don't have to tell you about Cambodia and magic? There isn't a *mordu,* a local clairvoyant or witch doctor in Krung Thep who doesn't claim to belong to some Khmer lineage—it's like the best perfume comes from Paris, the best beef from Argentina, the best sorcery from Cambodia. So the CIA people agreed to try the experiment the British doctor with the crazy name was urging on them. And it worked. Except that it didn't just work on the assets they were trying to develop. It worked on the whole crew. Including Goldman and the British shrink himself."

Sakagorn shrugged. "That's all I can tell you. It came out once only when he was drunk, and he never mentioned it again. I thought it was merely the ranting of a man who had spent too much time in the jungle. Perhaps it was. But something must have sunk in, because there's no way I could bring myself to visit Angkor again. No way. I started to see the whole place in a different light. That huge dark rotting Wat the size of a city block, those hideous stone pyramids like Aztec architecture, that sinister little shrine right in the middle, the whole atmosphere of the thing . . ." He shuddered.

"When you say it worked, what worked?"

"Unclear."

Vikorn and I both grunted. "What else?"

"Nothing. That's all he let slip. They only had a few years, then Pol Pot turned up with his gang of brutes and Goldman had to get out. They went up to Laos." He stared into our eyes, one after another, then shrugged.

I changed tack. "You have spent much time alone with the Asset, Lord Sakagorn?"

"No. Never. Goldman is always there."

"So how are they together? Do they lounge around on sofas watching football and drinking beer?"

Sakagorn shook his head. "No. Not at all. The Asset cannot be without his toy for long."

"What toy?"

"A gaming headset with a screen. Goldman takes it away for the demonstrations. It's like depriving a hunting animal of food—it makes him fierce." He paused again, too lost in his own dread to lie, or to help much either. "You would go round to Goldman's luxury condo off Sukhumvit, and Goldman would be there scheming and brooding, and the Asset would be there in a corner like a troubled teenager totally absorbed in whatever he was playing on the headset."

"Why was that so weird?"

"Because you knew what he could do with that amazing body, that enhanced cognition—all the stuff they'd done to him to make him superhuman—and there he was, like a dumb teen with emotional problems and no social skills."

"But you said he had charm?"

The barrister lost patience. "We're not talking about a human," he grumbled. "Change one strand of DNA in a fruit fly, and you get a different-color fruit fly." He let a couple of beats pass. "But this is not simple genetic engineering. That Asset has received accelerated learning enhancements: ALE in the jargon. Everything I'm telling you now relates to the last time I was with them at Goldman's apartment. That was two weeks ago. Two weeks is a long time in the evolution of a transhuman. His personality is probably quite changed by now."

"But these changes are at Goldman's command?" I was not trying to be provocative. Only now I realized from the lawyer's face what a hot topic that was. Sakagorn stared at me, looked away.

"That's the question, isn't it?"

I decided to pounce. "You said Goldman seems terrified." His hooded eyes conveyed the response: *So?* "Are you saying that Frankenstein has broken free—or knows how to? That sometimes Goldman is the slave and his Asset the master?"

The lawyer recovered and bounced back; it was part of his professional bag of tricks. "I never spent much time with them, how do I know? I simply gave you a passing impression to help—under coercion, I might add. Can I go now, or am I still under threat of blackmail?"

He pronounced the *B* word heavily, giving it full emotional and forensic dignity. I looked at Vikorn for an answer.

"Why has all this come up now, Lord Sakagorn?"

"Because everything has changed. There aren't going to be any more big, expensive, symmetrical wars with tank battles that take place over thousands of square miles. That's all over. How to deal with asymmetrical threats from dispossessed young men and women half-crazed with frustration in one's own country—that is the military/law-and-order problem of the present and future. Everyone knows it can only get worse."

"Why should it get worse?"

"Because the development of a semi-slave class is the only way our species can survive. You see it all over the world, even in the U.S. Some would say *especially* in the U.S. And even in liberal Europe. Social security costs too much, makes the country uncompetitive, leads to more unemployment. France is the example not to follow. But without it, you end up with slaves by another name." He paused. "Why d'you think the U.K. boasts one CCTV camera for every twenty-five citizens? Why have they suspended due process in the United States? I mix with the movers and shakers. They know what's coming next. To be a young or youngish person in a secret service these days is to see Armageddon as a *logical* likelihood within your lifetime. Now take Western Europe and America and multiply by two—you get China." He paused. "You control sheep with dogs and dogs with humans. Who controls the humans? Transhumans, perhaps."

"That's what Goldman is looking at? That's the future he's selling into?"

"That's my interpretation, from a distance. He doesn't share."

I thought from Vikorn's body language that he would end the interview there. So did Sakagorn. We were both surprised when in a fumbling motion that looked almost absentminded the Colonel switched the screen on again. There was our illustrious lawyer with his hand on the young aristocrat's backside. Sakagorn groaned.

"So what did he need from you?"

Sakagorn wrestled with his professional conscience; it didn't take long. "To my surprise, he became interested in the lower ranks of the underworld. I finally realized he wanted some low-life thugs. I thought at first for some dirty stuff. Typical CIA, in other words."

"You *thought*? But you don't think that now?"

He pushed his hair back in extreme irritation. "I'm not a monster. I love life, beautiful things, beautiful women. It's the way I'm made, the way I was brought up. My father had three minor wives and five mistresses, but he paid his way. He was a man, whole. He never hurt anyone unless he had to. He's been my role model all my life. I'm not as good as him and I never will be, but I try—" He had to break off to stifle a sob.

Vikorn and I stared in fascination at this sudden undressing of a baron. He seemed almost to have forgotten us and continued as if talking to himself.

"But when it comes to this sort of thing, this damned hellish new *farang* thing they're springing on the world." He stopped and stared at me, as if I at least retained sufficient innocence to understand where he was going. "Making that boy kill his own mother! Sweet Buddha, if I'd known he was going to do that, I would have stopped him. Even if I'd had to shoot him myself, I would have stopped him, I tell you!" he shouted at me.

"Stopped who?" Vikorn asked.

"Goldman's Asset, of course!"

A pause. "You knew—those two young men?" the Colonel asked.

"Not really. I used an assistant to find them for Goldman. I never met them."

The lawyer's anguish was palpable. Vikorn gave me a nod, which I took as permission to pounce. "So, Lord Sakagorn, may we now return to that lunch at the French restaurant in the Oriental—where the *three* of you HiSo men downed two and a half bottles of Cheval Blanc. You did say there was someone else at that lunch, didn't you? You don't have to tell us who, the nationality alone will do."

Sakagorn stared at me. I guess he was not expecting a murder squad detective to be so sharp in matters of international espionage. He opened his hands as if to say, *Okay, you win.* "Chinese, of course. Very senior in one of the main ministries. Accredited diplomat here in Bangkok." He sighed. "Okay, I was recruited to spy for China, but at the request of the government of Thailand. It happens a lot. Their intelligence services do us favors, and vice versa. I was serving my country by serving the PRC—what's wrong with that?"

"Which is the real reason we find you in such unlikely locations like the river during the storm a few days ago—hardly an occasion for legal counseling, I would have thought?"

Sakagorn waved a hand. He was back on form now and too tough to show how shocked he was that I knew he was there on the river on that wild wet and dreadful day. "Goldman sometimes invites me on his jaunts. My brief is to find out as much about him as possible—so I go along. I hate it, I don't really understand, and I hate it from my gut. But I'm a patriot, I do my duty."

Sakagorn jerked his chin at me and asked Vikorn, "Does he understand? I've heard of him, some kind of monk manqué, they say. The only cop in Krung Thep who doesn't take money."

"True, but he takes orders. You can rely on us."

We watched the Senior Counsel stand and leave the room.

Vikorn bit his lower lip. With Sakagorn gone, he knew I was looking to him for some kind of clue. He played with some controls until the big screen behind him showed the tropical band of the Pacific Rim. He reduced the scale until tiny Laos almost disappeared and it looked as if Thailand shared a border with the PRC. You could draw a vertical line north from Bangkok all the way through the center of China until you reached Mongolia. When he reduced the scale still further, though, the northern direction revealed another player of substance: Russia. He took us on a jaunt through the Taymyr Peninsular in Siberia all the way to the Arctic Ocean, then switched off, stood up, and left the room.

7

BTW, R, are you up to speed on the Higgs boson experiment? You know, all those guys who spent decades looking into the very depths of the universe and finally found the law of symmetry? If they'd asked a Buddhist like me I could have saved them the fourteen billion euros they spent on the Hadron Collider. Yep, the mind works by symmetry. When you think you are looking into the first nanoseconds of the Big Bang, what you are really looking at is the way your own mind works, because that's the only thing the mind can ever discover: itself. Bottom line: the cosmos is an expression of loving kindness; but even symmetry is subject to the law of symmetry. You can't have it without its opposite: asymmetry. It's the law of opposites, good for everything this side of cosmic consciousness.

Once you know the rule, you are no longer surprised by the antics of your head in its unending quest for a smooth ride and a free lunch. For example, here I am in the back of a cab and by all accounts I should be racking my brains about the Market Murder, the atrocity on the river, the tangled intentions of the CIA and the PRC, the huge new game changer of electronic surveillance, etcetera—when in its unending quest for symmetry my mind has counterbalanced into trivia: I am thinking about that thumb drive Inspector Krom gave me. It is still in my pants pocket.

It was clear from her body language that it was not something to check out on my computer at the station; I guessed it was a video of the more explicit kind: with a tattoo like that she had to be a closet exhibitionist. So I called Vikorn's secretary, Manny, to tell her I was stuck in traffic, then told the driver to take me home to the hovel.

When we roll up outside I can see Chanya at her desk working on her computer. She glances through the window in reaction to the noise of the cab, sees me, and waves and returns to her work. It is her new big idea that Western feminism was long ago hijacked by market forces, low-rent journalists, crusader narcissism, and petty-bourgeois judgmentalism, not to mention an unhealthy obsession with clitorectomy as practiced by the Ashanti of South Ghana (I don't know where she finds her Facebook buddies). She decided to found a website that really tells it like it is for Asian women. And that's where her heart is, while I pull off my clothes and pull on a pair of shorts.

"You're taking the day off?" she asks, barely hiding her irritation.

"Just a few hours."

I need a strategy to get her to watch the video. Like many people who don't have much to do, she is fiercely sensitive to any implication that she doesn't have much to do. I think about rolling a joint but decide against it. I also think about that oil Krom gave me, and decide against that, too. I scratch my head and go to the window to think: *What the hell is wrong with me?* I've been beating myself up with that question for years, but every time is like the first beating all over again. Why is paranoia ever green?

"Ah, *tilak,*" I venture. "Listen, I don't want to interfere with your work, but I do have something relevant to show you."

"What are you talking about?"

"Well, your website is dedicated to those good, genuine, strong, independent women who are not eternal undergraduates with personality problems trying to make a name for themselves by endlessly bitching about men, right? The politically correct cannot stand very much reality."

"That's an oversimplification, but okay."

"So, I've met someone you might be interested in. Someone very real in a weird kind of way."

Silence.

"It's okay, she's a hundred percent gay—one of those left out by mainstream fem—" I stop to correct myself. "From mainstream everything, actually. She's really from down your alley—I think. And she has a genius IQ."

"So?"

I tell her about the video. "It's okay," I say. "No need to look at it straightaway, whenever you're ready. I could leave it with you if you like."

"Why, where are you going?"

"Well, nowhere."

"So, we could watch it together, couldn't we?"

"Sure, I just thought you were busy all day."

She sighs, saves something she's been writing, and gives me her full attention. "Okay, let's watch the fucking video. You've got me all excited now."

"Sure," I say, "sure," and take out the thumb drive.

Chanya was intrigued. Lesbianism was only beginning to gain general acceptance in Bangkok when she was in her early twenties. It has taken off quite a bit since then, but she felt part of an earlier generation who didn't really get it. For her, from the start, the mystery, the challenge, the game of life was all about men. She frowned as the video started on her screen. It was obvious, though, that it was mostly song-and-dance, which needed the sound system. Chanya plugged in our rickety old speakers and suddenly the small room seemed to disintegrate under the pressure of that form of rock music called *punk, indie,* or *alternative*— unless you don't like it, in which case it's just plain bedlam. Krom stood center stage wearing her full police inspector uniform, waiting.

I almost never look at YouTube, never check out all those clever amateur video clips that go viral all over the global village and have already been forgotten by the time someone like me thinks about looking at them. So it was a surprise, even a shock, to see how professional the *tom*'s video was.

The scene was some kind of basement. It was less than minimalist: the plaster on the walls was missing in many places, revealing brick-work and reinforced concrete; a large number of luridly colored water pipes emerged from one wall and disappeared into another. There was no stage, but the bare, crumbling wall behind her was effectively the top of the room. She had chosen an old-style microphone so she could use the stand as a prop, but she had a Bluetooth receiver in her ear. The microphone and the Bluetooth receiver already turned her cop uniform into a kind of pantomime costume. At a nod from her the music started. It was something extreme and heavy—I'm afraid I lost track of the counterculture long ago. Now we saw it was a strip video.

Krom doesn't tease when she strips; on the contrary, she rips off her white police shirt with its blue shoulder boards as if to be free of an unendurable burden. She is not wearing a bra. Her small, tough tits form two hillocks in a densely worked tattoo that begins a couple of inches below her neck and takes us on a wild fantasy ride all the way to her shaven pubic region, and farther, to halfway down her thighs. She is both more and less than human, a kind of indigo streak of super energy with seriously animal cravings: a lot of simulated humping in her dance routine. Now she is joined by two young women also dressed as cops. Krom rips off their shirts and skirts; now everyone is naked with close-shaved pubic hair and Krom has found a dildo to strap to her loins, but there is no immediate debauch into group sex. The camera focuses on Krom's face, now, as she starts to sing—I guess *holler* would be a better word—in some kind of rap-style adaptation in Thai. Her two female companions dance on either side of her but are overwhelmed by the force of her superior energy and end by making highly erotic swoons that take them to their knees before her. From somewhere she has produced a huge cigar, which she does not light but uses as a second penis substitute; is it a coincidence that it is the same size cigar that Vikorn uses to celebrate his victories?

When one of Krom's sex slaves began an erotic journey starting with her mistress/master's toes but moving quickly upward, Chanya, former working girl though she is, pulled the thumb drive out of her PC.

"I hate watching dykes make out. It disgusts me." She cast me a glance that was almost apologetic: she was supposed to be our ambassador to modernism, after all, the university graduate who should be closest to the hip gold standard of cocaine, hard rock, and orgies—but she was frowning and looking like she wanted to throw the thumb drive out the window. Instead she handed it to me with one of her psychological insights that are all the more devastating when delivered, as then, in a calm, compassionate tone. "The truth is, she wants to be Vikorn." She gave a pinched smile and added, "A patriarch tyrant with a pussy."

"Okay," I said.

She stared at me in a certain way. I made a face that said, *Well, I've shown you she's totally homosexual, what more security do you want?*

"You're fascinated by her, aren't you?" she said. I shrugged.

After a couple of minutes two arms embraced me, a hand found its way to my crotch.

"That video made me feel horny," Chanya whispered, pulling my shorts down. "When am I going to meet her?"

"Tomorrow if not sooner," I said, turning and slipping my hands under her T-shirt.

Afterward I gave a sigh—actually, if I recall correctly we both sighed at the same time. I had to go back to the station and she wanted to return to the webpage she was designing. There was a twinkle in our eyes, though, as we said goodbye. That was quite a video so early in the afternoon.

"So, I'll tell Krom she can come visit . . ."

"Anytime," Chanya said. Now she was relaxed enough to add, "My schedule is pretty free for the rest of the year."

At the station I found a serious buzz among staff and cops that I didn't have time to inquire about because Manny called me on the internal line.

"The boss wants you, now."

Once again Vikorn was staring out of his window, this time leaning against the frame (a neutral message, this: something happening somewhere else that, no matter how important in the abstract sense, did not rank in his personal value structure).

"You heard the news?" he asked without turning.

"No. I only just got back."

"There was an explosion at Klong Toey Slum early this morning. Somehow it didn't get reported in the media—so far. We heard about it on the grapevine a few hours ago."

"Explosion? As in a bomb?"

"Probably—nobody seems to know yet." He turned to stare at me for a moment. "Not our patch. Not our problem."

"No," I said. I did not say, *So why did you send for me?*

A pause, then: "That moron Lotus Bud called me." Lotus Bud, usually abbreviated to LB, was the sergeant who ran the slum, more or less single-handed.

"Yes."

"He said he found something of yours there, among the debris."

"Huh? Mine? I haven't been to KTC for years."

"Whatever. He says he can't hold it for long but it might be confidential."

"Hold what?"

"He didn't say. But you know what he's like—a moron, but a cunning one. And that's the first time he's called me for about a decade—so I suppose you'd better take it seriously."

"Yes, sir," I said. I did not move, though. This is a tactic I developed years ago to solve the problem of the boss who doesn't answer questions. He returned to his desk and pretended to get on with some paperwork, while I waited. When he engaged my eyes I said, "It's related, isn't it? It must be, or you wouldn't be bothering with it."

He started to say, *Related to what?* then grunted. "You don't want to know, not yet."

"I do."

He sat silent for a long time, looking at me as if he could not decide what I was, a pawn to be sacrificed in a war game, or one of the few people he's ever been close to. He coughed. "I think Inspector Krom told you how sensitive your case is right now." He covered his embarrassment by turning pompous. "A certain power unit north of here is interested in the progress of your inquiry. From time to time they"—here he dumped pomposity to reveal anger—"throw me a little hint or two. Just get over there, will you?"

"Yessir," I said. Such is the nature of the feudal mind that I am saddened my lord and master has been brought under the heel of a foreign power. I ought to be delighted at the possibilities of freedom that are opening up before my eyes, but I'm not. Anyway, foreign powers never really bring freedom, only chaos. Isn't that true, R?

8

A word about Klong Toey Slum, or KTC (Klong Toey City) in the local argot: don't go there. It is not the risk so much as the revelation you may wish to avoid. I speak from personal experience. I was still in my late teens, fresh down from the north after a year in a forest monastery where I purged my guilt after Pichai, my best friend, murdered our *yaa baa* dealer with me as accomplice. As an unconvicted felon I teetered between two futures: the police academy or a return to the robes. I favored the latter and sought advice from an uncle who had spent twenty years as a monk, before succumbing to the siren call of conjugal love (it didn't last). Twenty years is a very different proposition than one year, which anyone can survive with a little grit. His advice was simple: "To succeed as a monk long-term you must become a connoisseur of bitterness. You must live off it the way others live off distraction. I failed." I rented a shack in the slum for ten baht a week to test my appetite for the bitter. Three months later I joined the police.

KTC is, I suppose, much like any favela in Rio or barrio in Buenos Aires, but with Thai twists. It is unusually neat and tidy, even gentrified in certain parts, and there is a clear, communally agreed demarcation of areas. If you arrive from the Sukhumvit direction you will probably see the great slum at its best, with wood-and-corrugated-iron huts neatly set out as if on a grid from ancient Rome, streets well swept, front doors occasionally painted in bright proletarian-pagan tones, all things mostly spick and span; small shops sell basic necessities. This is the upmarket end, though, the Upper East Side of the complex, which comprises five square miles. Press on and you will find a deterioration in the neighborhood: a meth addict lolls unconscious against a hut with no risk of being moved on by a cop, at least not while he's alive; a couple of overweight retired working girls drink moonshine and gamble heavily while they loll on futons outside their front doors. Then you come to the decrepit part of town where old ladies with sparse teeth blackened by betel habits relentlessly bash stacks of aluminum cans into rectangles slimmer than iPhones, twenty satang the kilo. A few yards farther on you reach the heart of the matter: crazies end up here who were never going to bear the rigors of survival out in the world, but are not dangerous enough to be locked up at taxpayer expense in an economy with few taxpayers. Skinny women who could be any age between thirty and fifty, with torn cotton dresses revealing shriveled breasts, faded tattoos, and puncture marks. They are too mad for the discipline of prostitution, too dangerous for rape, too unpredictable to be mules in the drug trade. Their total disengagement from society gives them a license to be wild: rage-filled faces thrust themselves before your nose; harpies sing the epic of mass exodus from the countryside in a tuneless rant free of the need for approval or even company. Their male counterparts are even less social: given to solitary postures of religious intensity in the urban wilderness, fueled by the cheapest of narcotics, or by the narcotic of distilled loneliness itself, they sit on rubbish heaps and screech during brief moments of clarity when the full extent of the catastrophe becomes, for a moment, unavoidable.

And if, before the explosion, you had pressed on a hundred yards or so, to the most run-down set of three shacks, which nevertheless boasted, I am told, an American flag (postmen and visitors needed to know where "the Americans" were living), you would sooner or later have come across the three old *farang* who lived in them.

As for the police, Klong Toey, as Vikorn pointed out, is not in District 8 and does not come under his jurisdiction, but even if it did, I doubt the Colonel, despite his contempt, would have done anything to interfere with the work of Sergeant "Lotus Bud" Satorn, whose nickname derives from his pious habit of ensuring that the house god who sits in the *saan phra poom* or spirit house at the northeast corner of his police cabin is well provided with this floral offering; one assumes the fat and otherwise cynical cop decided long ago that only the gods could save Klong Toey. To this end he has filled with Buddhas, shrines, and other religious artifacts those shelves and cupboards of his hut where less realistic cops might keep files.

(I didn't want to complicate the matter, but in the interests of faithful reporting I have to reveal that the Sergeant has, in fact, erected two spirit houses next to his cabin. One is set on a pillar taller and more elaborate than the other, and receives a double ration of lotus buds: this spirit is an avatar of Brahma and rides Erawan, a three-headed white elephant. The spirit who bivouacs in the second, smaller spirit house is merely a local deity whose peace was disturbed when people began building on the land and who charges rent, also in the form of lotus buds, until he gets his home back at the end of the world.)

LB cheats, takes money from, bullies, occasionally beats up, and generally exploits the community he serves, but not to an exorbitant extent, and even our most avid reformers do not begrudge him the modest profit he is left with once his business associates have been paid off: that he keeps Klong Toey Slum together, one way or another, is enough of a contribution to eclipse his weaknesses. But I'm jumping ahead.

It was a pleasant morning in July, so I decided to approach KTC from the river. We were in the middle of the rainy season, which is the best time in Thailand. It is cooler, mornings can be sunny and balmy, and the rain, when it comes, usually does so at the same time every afternoon, so if you don't like getting wet you can work around it. I took a cab to the port then persuaded the river cops to convey me to the best point from which to enter KTC. When they realized I'd come to meet Sergeant Lotus Bud himself, they dropped me off about twenty yards from the cabin he shared with two young constables.

The trouble with short river trips in speedboats is that you always wish they would last longer. I was exhilarated by the damp wind in my face and the sense of freedom that comes from riding the great, bustling Chao Phraya and in a good mood by the time the Sergeant and I were *waiing* each other. He was of average height, triumphantly overweight with a thick leather belt (a Red Indian on the buckle), darkskinned, in his fifties, big-faced, jovial, a bent cop from central casting who was as crooked as he needed to be to survive and carried no visible guilt or remorse for his contraventions. The great gift he brought to our profession was the common touch: the poor, the uneducated, the downtrodden, the just plain dumb all tended to love him. Ensconced in his cabin, he sat in an old big comfortable chair with huge cushions that billowed on either side, and he gave me a sideways glance as he picked up a mobile phone that lay on his desk and handed it to me. It was an iPhone and looked new. It was almost the latest model, a 5s no less. I switched it on, checked the log and looked for other relevant data, and found none. There were no messages, and only one entry in the Contacts file. It was a full international number beginning with the country code +84: Vietnam. No one had activated the phone's Thai-language application. I looked at the Sergeant and shrugged.

"The photos," LB said. "Check the photos."

I checked the photos. There were about a hundred, and they all featured the same person. Me.

Now I was swivel-eyed and wired, switching between the Sergeant's penetrating curiosity and the pictures, all of them taken on Soi Cowboy. I looked at the date and time on the photos. The dates suggested the photos were taken over a period of about two weeks, usually at around five in the evening, when I open my mother's bar. I guessed Sergeant Lotus Bud was expecting a hasty explanation, perhaps even a confession from which he might one day profit: the suspicion that I, the only cop fluent in English in District 8, was involved in some kind of scam with the English-speaking owner of the phone was inevitable. My starting tactic was to let him see how baffled I was. Those slow eyes narrowed. Greed rode his neurons. He saw an opening.

"Do you want to keep it? I'm supposed to hand it over to forensics."

"I want to keep it for the moment," I snapped. The last thing I needed was for it to disappear into the hands of nerds for two weeks, who were quite capable of wiping the pix by mistake and then denying there were any in the first place.

"But I'm supposed to hand it in," he complained in an exaggerated tone of confusion and despair. When he added, "It's the rule," I knew where he was coming from.

"I love the way you take care of your house gods," I said, taking out my wallet. "Please let me buy a few garlands of lotus buds to help out." I took out a thousand-baht note, held it between my palms while I stood up and stepped out of the cabin to *wai* the two statues. I tucked the money under a can of Nescafé that someone had given as an offering that morning.

The crime scene was also by the river, but quite a way from the police outpost, so the Sergeant and I took a stroll. To our right, the great slum opened to the high blue sky; to our left, the river so sacred to our ancestors and still so important to our rice exporters and their barges.

They are gentrifying riverfront property these days, and I suppose capitalism will knock KTC down sooner or later and declare victory over squalor, but it's a vast area with a lot of people to relocate to somewhere squalor-tolerant, so it's not going to happen quite yet. Not if Sergeant Satorn has his way: he knew everyone. Betel-chewing old ladies gave him the high *wai* as if he were a revered monk; teenage girls on the game grabbed him around his vast stomach: he was the only father figure they had known. Young men about to shoot up saw him coming and disappeared down a dark alley; not-so-young men with serious crime on their minds were shrewd enough to give him big face by *waiing* and half bowing at the same time. Young mothers with dirty faces and screaming infants extracted small sums from him as he passed. Lotus Bud just loved being loved, although some of the attention he could have done without. When one of the crazy women called out, "*Lotus*," he turned to smile, only to have her call it out again, in exactly the same tone, as if he hadn't responded. And again and again, so a shrieked "*Lotus*" followed our steps as we proceeded. He scratched his head and shrugged.

Now the crime scene started to announce itself. It was exactly as the Sergeant had described: as if a great wind from Jupiter came one day and simply blew away three shacks, smashing the wood beams into splinters, spreading the heavier items such as cooking stoves and pots around an area about twenty yards in diameter, and throwing the lighter things like books, toilet rolls, documents, and tubular chairs across a vast expanse. Already we were seeing splinters and papers from the explosion littering the footpath. Nothing lay smoldering, however, and there were no signs of things or people having been ripped up by shrapnel. When we arrived at the epicenter I saw men and women in white coveralls moving methodically over the area, probing with sticks, and occasionally bending down to pick something up. They were serious specialists from the antiterrorism unit, and I could see they had already decided there was nothing of interest to them there. There was a certain disdain in their postures and lack of enthusiasm: *We trained all those months for a little toy bomb like this?* The items they found of interest they laid out on a blue tarp spread on the ground. Automatically my eye checked through the items on the tarp, even as the detective in charge of the investigation came to meet me.

He was young and rendered suddenly insecure to find a more senior detective on the scene. The Sergeant, though, in my pay after accepting my modest bribe, explained about the cell phone, the photos, and why I was there. I was afraid some sinister suspicion would invade his young mind; it was, after all, more than a little strange, even in the context of local law enforcement, that I should have become part of the crime scene. But the detective, too, was overwhelmed by the sense that we were in a private kingdom run by the Sergeant in which anything could happen. On the other hand, those pictures of me on the smart phone needed to be dealt with in some way.

"You don't know who could have taken them?"

"No idea."

"There's no clue in the phone as to the identity of the owner?"

"None at all."

The young detective was too Thai—too programmed by deference, in other words—to ask me to let him keep the phone. He waited for me to offer, but I changed the subject. He shrugged as if to say, *You're more senior than me, I can't stop you.*

I left him to chat with the Sergeant while I walked along the side of the tarp.

I was, as usual, quite solitary in my quest and wondering why this should be a recurrent theme of my life, when I remembered my new friend. Even on my most alienated days I'm never more than half a pariah; from a certain angle, depending on the light, I can appear quite normal and adjusted. Krom was, in a sense, a more pure form of the loner and therefore strangely comforting—even someone to look up to. I also wondered what she knew about the bomb, if anything. I took out my phone and called her. She answered on the second ring. I told her the story so far.

"Photos of you on a cell phone?"

"At the scene of the bomb at Klong Toey." I spoke in a slightly accusatory tone, to indicate that I thought she must know something, then added, "The Colonel personally sent me over here. Way out of our jurisdiction, of course. But then, you and I first met on a matter out of the jurisdiction, didn't we?"

"Klong Toey?" She ignored the provocation and fell silent for a couple of beats. "That bomb was directed at *farang*—Americans, no?" I would classify her tone as wonder and surprise, rather than cynical foreknowledge.

"Correct."

"Where are the Americans?"

"In a government hospital—concussed. Two will definitely live, the third is in critical condition. All three have head injuries. Apparently they are all old men, well over sixty."

"And the phone is set up for English only?"

"Correct."

Silence. "Sonchai, I don't know anything about this."

"Right."

"You're on your own here—it doesn't fit with anything I'm working on."

"Thanks."

"Are you being sarcastic? You don't believe me?"

"You could at least speculate, given all that classified knowledge you're going to share with me sooner or later, once I've been properly vetted—right?"

Silence, then, "You're smart, aren't you? Just like they said you were. But maybe not that smart. I tell you all I can, probably more than I should. Could it be that I'm protecting you as well as myself? Do you think I'm not limited by *need to know*, just like everyone else?"

I groaned. "Just give me a hint, would you?"

"Those old Americans. They could be key, but I'm not sure. If they have connections to anywhere in Cambodia, follow up—but let me know first. That's all I can say." She closed the phone.

I walked around the crime scene to rejoin young Detective Tassatorn and the Sergeant. There was no point in trying to examine any more of the debris, which included a great mass of papers and photos that were soggy from the water used to douse the embers and would probably fall apart if I tried to separate them from each other. Anyway, my line of inquiry had now shifted to the victims. I hailed a cab and told the driver to take me directly to the government hospital where the three Americans were laid up.

They were in a secure ward: standard procedure in case of injury by explosions. You can have yourself shot by five fully automatic combat rifles and still not qualify for the secure ward; just one little homemade bomb, though, and you get the full treatment: metal detectors at the door, grim and very bored security, medical staff not happy that in addition to risking death by disease every day of their working lives they have to risk being blown up by bomb-toting terrorists and—perhaps worse—follow strict government security guidelines.

The first two beds on the ward were occupied by two Buddhist teachers who had been sent to the Islamic south to teach in government schools and within weeks became victims of the troubles down there. The Islamic resistance doesn't like to see its territory seduced by Buddhist do-gooders, so a teaching assignment in Yala, Pattani, or any of the Islamic provinces is a dangerous posting that can amount to a death sentence. I was depressed to see their heads and eyes bandaged and remembered my uncle's phrase, *connoisseurs of bitterness*, but strode onward to the other end of the ward where the Americans lay on their backs.

Question: how do you tell one American from another when they are all over sixty and have their heads, eyes, and half their faces covered in bandages? A male nurse came to find me while I was staring at them. In Thai script, the legend on the clipboards at the end of the bed was strange. It referred to each patient by his hospital registration number, then gave one of three possible names in English: *William J. Schwartz*; *Laurence Krank*; *Harry Berg*. In other words, nobody knew who was who. They were all in comas of various degrees of depth.

"It's not unusual, especially with the old, for people to remain in a coma after traumatic shock for days, even weeks, then recover totally," the nurse explained. "These two," he added, pointing, "have no damage to the skull at all, only the skin. They will recover soon. This one, though," he said, pointing at the last bed, "we're not sure. He was blown back by the blast and hit his head on something hard. There's quite a lot of swelling. If it gets worse we might have to break open the skull to release the pressure." Now he came to the punch line and I understood why he was being so helpful. "That's a long, expensive operation, because after we release the pressure we have to use plates to screw the pieces of skull back together again."

I stared at the implacable mummies lying on the bed. A sentimental fantasy crossed my mind as I looked at them. *No*—I half smiled at myself—*coincidences like that don't happen in real life.* On the other hand, a cynical but inevitable thought slipped past the internal defenders of the soul: *If one of them is* him, *I sure hope it's not the one with the brain damage.* Then a third thought came flying out of left field: *Could that be why the anonymous gray men pulling all our strings are interested in me? Because of him? But why? And if so, which him? And who, actually, is calling the shots?*

"What shall I say to the Registrar?" the nurse was asking. "There are funds for the operation or not?"

I stared at the old man in the bed and allowed that thought to resurface: *Supposing, just supposing . . . After all, one of those guys had taken more than a hundred shots of me on Soi Cowboy, hadn't they? Or had they?* Now was the time to test Vikorn, force him to reveal his hand just a tad.

I fished out my cell phone to call him. I told him of a patient/victim who might need extensive brain surgery and suggested he might like to help out with the expenses. That he even hesitated told me that he somehow knew more about the bomb at Klong Toey than anyone else I'd talked to that day. He said, "Okay, I'll have Manny deal with it."

"What about the other two—they're not thought to be in serious danger, but I guess you'd want to keep them all together?"

A normal reaction would have been for him to say, *No, what the hell for?*

"Sure," he said, "have all three moved to the international hospital at Hua Lamphong. They do a lot of brain stuff there."

"Yes," I told the nurse, "there are funds—but are you equipped for such an operation? Should we think of moving him somewhere else?"

The nurse smiled with relief. "Oh, yes, that is good news. One of the big international hospitals will have all the machines and the expertise. We don't have any specialist brain surgeons here."

I decided to try to clear up one part of the puzzle. "How did you know their names?" I asked.

"They arrived with a money belt containing three passports. We're waiting for the Cambodian embassy to provide more identification, so we can tell who is who."

"Cambodian? But they're all Americans."

"Yes, that's what the passports say: Americans with Cambodian citizenship. I'll show you the photocopies the registration staff took of the passports."

I followed him out of the ward and down to the registration area. He entered an office and quickly returned with three bundles of photocopies.

Khmer script looks quite a lot like Thai, unless you're Thai, when it appears as a collection of tantalizing squiggles and curls—pretty much the way Thai would appear to you, R. Fortunately, the Khmer was translated into English for purposes of international travel. The owners were Americans who had been naturalized as Cambodian citizens. The photographs were taken a long time ago, however, and were useless for identification. The only stamps were Thai visas. It seemed the owners had entered Thailand about ten months before and obtained retirement visas good for a year. They had entered our country together at the same time on the same day.

I thanked the nurse and promised that a team from the hospital in Chinatown would send an ambulance once the paperwork had been sorted out.

From the hospital I decided to use a motorbike taxi to avoid the jam on Rama IV. Like the bike jockeys on Soi Cowboy, my man was a hardbody with a neck like a buffalo who loved taking chances. You become very conscious of your knees when your pilot starts into the close-vehicle work, winding between stationary or slowly moving vans, cars, and trucks. He knew what he was doing and expected me to take care of my own legs. Then my phone rang. I saw the call was from Krom.

"Where are you?"

"On the back of a bike dying from asphyxiation."

"You went to the hospital? Did you find out anything?"

"Maybe."

"Don't do this. Tell me what you discovered."

"The three American victims own Cambodian passports."

It seemed I had finally impressed her. "Interesting life choice," she said.

On reflection, that was my reaction too. I don't want to cause offense, R, but let's face it, there has been a steady exodus from spiritual desolation in the Occident for some time now. *Farang* these days find wives or husbands in many Asian nations, including Thailand, Malaysia—and of course China. Cambodia, though? If they weren't so old, one would assume they were CIA spies as a matter of course.

"I'll tell you more tomorrow when you come by," I said and closed the phone.

9

We started our morning with a row, Chanya and I. She wanted to know exactly why Krom was coming to visit, and if it was a business call, then why did she, Chanya, need to be there at all? She meant she didn't need a social or professional event in which she was merely ornamental. She had a PhD, for Buddha's sake, a Facebook following of nearly a thousand, she had written learned articles for online academic journals—and none of it seemed to impinge on reality at all, as if it all happened on a Google cloud somewhere. She was honest enough to admit that hers was a strange, possibly certifiable form of paranoia—but quite common these days. What she most resented was finding herself in the role of insecure little wife who had to be included in a serious adult meeting so that she wouldn't feel like—well, an insecure little wife.

She was still in one of her rages while she showered out in the yard under a hosepipe, skillfully deploying a towel so no prying eyes could see her private parts, then returned dripping to the hovel, feeling better. She gave me a sheepish smile, laid a hand on my forearm. "Sorry." She smiled.

"It's okay. I understand."

"No you don't. You have a job. That makes you real. I don't, that makes me a ghost. Let's leave it at that."

I guessed that was as good as it was going to get, so I shrugged, smiled, hugged her, and we were about as patched up as we were going to be that merry morning. I guessed she would not let the meeting pass without asserting herself in some way in accordance with online advice from her groups.

We were both showered, soaped, perfumed, and ready for Krom in about ten minutes. I felt tense and excited at the same time. As a cop I knew better than to hope for a sudden big break in the Market Murder case; as a man I hoped for a sudden big break in the case that had my name on it in blood.

Chanya could not resist an irrelevant question. "I wonder what Inspector Krom will be wearing? I mean, she can't come in uniform since it's all so hush-hush. What does a dyke like her put on for breakfast meetings?"

Now that I thought of it, that was a fascinating piece of trivia. What would Krom be wearing?

"It depends if she comes by taxi or on the back of a bike," Chanya said.

"Why?"

"If she dresses up, she won't want to be windblown. Depends how much she needs to impress you." She coughed. "I mean, for her enterprises, of course, whatever they are." Then she added, "She may be a dyke, but she's still a woman, you know."

It was a taxi. The young woman who emerged with a close-cropped haircut and dark glasses wore a fresh-pressed black shirt with cream bootlace tie, a cutaway jacket in black-and-white butcher's stripes, pants with knife-sharp creases and the same wide vertical stripes as the jacket, brogues only slightly feminized with square toes, also two-tone. When I opened the door I was much refreshed by a strong cologne: Fabergé Brut for Men, if I was not mistaken. She carried a slim black briefcase.

"Do come in," I said with a smile. Once in, she made a point of *waiing* Chanya. Chanya *waied* back. She had to acknowledge how impeccably Krom was behaving, giving the woman of the house *big face*, as the Chinese say.

There were no chairs or sofas to sit on, but I guessed Krom was brought up without furniture, like Chanya and me; she had no trouble hitching up her pants, bending her knees, and sitting on a cushion with her back against a wall like a well-dressed gangster. She took a single sheet of paper out of the briefcase. It looked like a printout from the Net.

"MKUltra," she said.

Krom passed the single sheet over to us.

"I just copied the headline. I think that seeing it in black and white on a public document kind of helps with the credibility."

It was a short extract from an article in Wikipedia. We looked at it, then looked up, blinking. Krom read from the extract and we followed, word by word:

Project MKUltra was the code name of a U.S. government human research operation experimenting in the *behavioral* engineering of humans through the CIA's Scientific Intelligence Division. The program began in the early 1950s and officially halted in 1973. MKUltra used numerous methodologies to manipulate people's mental states and alter brain functions, including the surreptitious administration of drugs (especially LSD) and other chemicals, hypnosis, sensory deprivation, isolation, verbal and sexual abuse, as well as various forms of torture.

Chanya and I stared at her with wrinkled brows.

"Ultra was a huge scandal in the seventies, but it went with all the other huge scandals," Krom explained. "The world assumed it was a purely American story all about the toxic mix of ruthless spies and worse scientists. There was a movie: *The Manchurian Candidate*. Naturally, in the film the bad guys manipulating poor innocent Americans are driven by wicked Orientals desperate to take over the world using mind control." Krom looked me in the eye. "I think you know Goldman ran the project in Vietnam as a young—very young—CIA agent. Of course, in Vietnam everyone who was put in harm's way was young, most of the soldiers were under twenty-two. Goldman was twenty-six when he first went out. I guess the CIA also had its Rear Echelon Motherfuckers who didn't want to risk their careers and left the wet stuff to ambitious young men like Joseph Goldman."

I was in shock and had to reread the printout a couple more times. That's the power of print for you. I know the lawyer Sakagorn had hinted at something like this, but to see it referred to in the public space, to be told it had a notorious history that included congressional hearings—that was different. Krom seemed to understand that she had initiated me into a higher level of knowledge—and that was the purpose of the meeting.

When I looked up, the dynamics had changed. I took a clue from the strange look on Chanya's face and switched to Krom, who was staring at her. I had to blink. So far I had seen two sides of the Inspector: the consummate professional cop and the wild humping dyke with full-body tattoo. Now I had to add: seasoned connoisseur of the female form. Chanya was still a very attractive woman (another hurdle to overcome in her quest for respect: *I don't want to be cute anymore*, she would complain while applying moisturizers and embarking on radical diets), and Krom seemed to be concentrating on just how carefully, slowly, and adoringly she would like to undress her. Now I understood the way she was all dressed up and drowned in cologne: did she expect Chanya to fall for her on the spot?

Chanya saw what I had seen and moved a few inches nearer to me. This didn't faze Krom at all. Like a male of the most politically incorrect kind, she appeared confident that she could take what she wanted when she wanted it. Her eyes shone when she looked at me, as if her victory and my defeat were certain. As if she belonged to a superior race. This enraged me, but Chanya's reaction was more complex. Like me she was affronted by Krom's arrogance; on the other hand, in her event-starved life perhaps a little adventure with a crazy *tom* would help pass the time?

I coughed. The moment passed. Krom tore her eyes away from my wife to look at me. "Here's the kicker. After the big Frank Olson scandal, when MKUltra had to go underground, Goldman recruited a young British psychiatrist who had researched psychedelic drugs at Cambridge. How or why he was in Southeast Asia at that time is not known. Some say he was Goldman's original mentor, the brains that made it all happen. For sure, the experiment wasn't going anywhere until this shrink showed up."

"This British shrink made the Asset happen?"

"That's the implication. But the psychiatrist is extremely reclusive. This is all we have, an alleged photograph about fifty years old, and a name you can't forget." She dipped into her briefcase and brought out a sheet with a photograph printed on it.

The photograph seemed to have been taken in a Southeast Asian city, probably Saigon, for there were rickshaws and women in cone-shaped straw hats in the background. It was also long ago; the cars were all models from the sixties. The young man in the picture was unusually tall and skinny, and towered over the brown people around him. He was as improbable as a Greek god who arrived by mistake in the twentieth century in the middle of a war. Long blond hair lay over his shoulders and cascaded down the blinding psychedelic silk shirt. His face was both naïve and triumphant, as if he had found the God particle. He had chemically scaled the heights, solved the problem of existence, and now oozed benevolence, enlightenment, and confidence. He certainly didn't look like an academic, but then those were very different times.

I looked up from the photo. "And his name?"

"Bride," Krom said. "Dr. Christmas Bride."

She stood up quite suddenly, picked up her briefcase, and made her way to the door. She *waied* us, told me not to come out to the street to help her find a taxi, and was gone. Chanya and I stared at each other. I wanted to know what Chanya thought, so I didn't say anything.

"That is one very disciplined lady," she said.

"Yes. I think so too. In what way, though?"

"She came to deliver a message. The message was that name: *Dr. Christmas Bride.* Of course, I don't know anything about the case. Why is that name so important it's worth a special private visit like this? Why couldn't she give it to you over the phone or at work?"

"Because she wants to have you."

"But how would she know that when she's never met me before?"

"Think male," I said. "Among pack animals tumescence is a product of hormones, fantasy, and competition, the lust object itself comes last. Most of the men in the station drool over you, even the ones you've never met—a reputation like yours makes for restless dreams."

When I arrived at work, Manny, Vikorn's secretary, told me that Krom and I had a meeting scheduled with the Old Man later in the day. "It's important," she added ominously.

"What's going on?"

"I don't know. He received a phone call just now and he turned serious."

"Where did the call come from?"

"I think Beijing."

10

Krom and I sat next to each other on the wooden seats Vikorn kept in his office, opposite his desk, while he sat in his padded executive chair. When he took out a Churchillian cigar and lit up, the familiar ritual was accompanied by sidelong glances at Krom, as if he were engaged in an act of defiance. He blew dense gray smoke out of his mouth and waited for it to diffuse throughout his office before he spoke.

"The Americans are in a hurry," he said. "At least Goldman is. I don't know why, and nor do the Chinese, who are suspicious. Why the rush for a security system that will take a decade to develop after purchase? Anyway, Goldman has promised some kind of show."

He stopped and waited for questions. Both he and I were intrigued about how much Krom knew, how networked she was with Beijing. The Chief studied her for a moment, while she obligingly offered him a three-quarter profile without engaging his eyes. She did not respond, and my guess was that she was not aware of what Vikorn was about to tell us.

"As you would expect, there's plenty of documentation on this Asset thing, but it's hyper-secret. Goldman claims he used influence and a lot of dough to *borrow*—his word—a certain *proof* that his Asset is the real deal." He drew on the cigar, exhaled, stared at Krom. There was perhaps a note of anger when he asked, "Do you know anything about this?"

She shook her head. "No."

"But it has to do with the murder in the market, doesn't it?"

She shrugged.

Now he had my complete attention as he spoke directly to Krom.

"The Market Murder has given Goldman one huge credibility problem, but the origin of the problem so far is suspicion and innuendo. The Detective here has almost nothing to go on, no way of proving anything definitive either way. No one has come up with any convincing proof that the Asset did it. On the one hand, the crime is so bizarre it is difficult to think of an alternative suspect. On the other hand, that makes an ideal setting for anyone who wanted to sabotage Goldman's sale. Therefore, the Market Murder has forced Goldman's hand. Does he have a game-changing product that will bring more or less total control to those governments who can afford it? Or has he spent over fifty years producing some kind of out-of-control freak who can perform a few circus acts but could never be a team player in a disciplined security service? That's probably the issue. But why the rush? Isn't haste suspicious in itself? What's he afraid of?"

"Another murder like the one in the market," I said. They both looked at me.

"Right," Krom said with a smile.

The Chief took a long toke on the cigar and stared at Krom. "Perhaps. What I'm not sure about, and would like your input on, is why would the Chinese continue to be interested? Isn't this the kind of product where the potential purchaser simply refuses to go ahead if there's the slightest hint of a defect in the product? It isn't just a question of money. The credibility of the PRC government is at stake if they buy a defective asset of this kind—don't you agree?"

Now both the Colonel and I stared at her. She nodded as a kind of acknowledgment that she did have further thoughts. "There's a rumor—I don't know because it arises from Goldman's side so it could be counterintelligence—anyway, a rumor that it's not any extracurricular activities by the Asset that is making Goldman panic. It's the relationship between him and his Asset. The beat on the street is that they're no longer getting along so well. It could be just rumor, but it relates to something else, something Beijing is very interested in. As a matter of fact, something that every specialist in transhumanism is passionate about."

The Colonel and I both raised our eyebrows. Now Krom revealed herself by standing and pacing, just as if she were the Chief. It was a curious performance, because she was wearing her regulation uniform with white shirt and shoulder boards, blue pleated skirt that reached below the knee: the essence of subjugated womanhood in a man's world. She compensated by putting her hands in her pockets as she paced. "This thing is more important than blind military obedience. It is the essence of the project: the gold ring. If Goldman and his people have got it right, Beijing might be prepared to overlook a little recreational killing. Any government would put up with a lot to have Superman on its side—especially if there is only one such in the world. Goldman is rushed because he needs to prove this very special quality of the Asset before a whole shitload of suspicion, innuendo, and negative publicity make the purchase impossible, even for China."

Vikorn frowned at her. "What do you have in mind, exactly?"

Krom went to the window and looked out and spoke to it, exactly as if she were the Old Man himself; as if she had taken over already. "The product is fitted out with some high-tech circuitry that improves cognitive function by more than a hundred percent. This in itself is not revolutionary. All over the world similar experiments are being conducted in secret. Goldman's original and totally exotic approach is inspired by the British psychiatrist Christmas Bride. You see, the result of artificially introducing performance-enhancing circuitry directly into the brain has always been, without exception, crippling mental illness resulting in clinical depression, catatonia, and ultimately suicide. The problem is the personality itself—or, if you like, the psyche. That was the problem with MKUltra from the start."

"And Goldman has found a way around that?"

"That's his claim. That's really what he's selling. But *he* didn't solve the problem, *he* didn't have any idea how to go about it, until he teamed up with the Brit shrink."

"Can you tell us a little more?"

"You have to bear in mind that this is just speculation—I don't have a very high security clearance. As far as I understand it, the point is *learning and adaptation*. If through training from birth you can produce a mind at once robust and flexible enough to cope with the enhanced cognitive power, then you really do reach a kind of grail."

"How so?"

"Because there is really only one way a personality can cope, and that is by riding an extraordinary learning curve. It's a form of self-evolving AL—accelerated learning—that achieves the gold standard of infinite evolution at speeds hundreds if not thousands of times faster than anything our species has achieved so far. ALE in the jargon: accelerated learning enhancement."

"From human to god in one generation?"

"Or to monster." She turned from the window, smiled formally at the two of us, and resumed her seat.

The Colonel and I let a good five minutes pass. Finally Vikorn cleared his throat. "So, Beijing is sending an expert who works out of a laboratory in Shanghai: Goldman has to reveal his hand, and fast. He is insisting on airtight security. The two of you will entertain him— Sonchai, I want you to take your wife to make it look like a social event. I already cleared her with Goldman. The expert is one Professor Chu." The Colonel allowed himself a flicker of a smile. "He has visited Bangkok before. He will show you what an evening out in Krung Thep means to him. Let him control the moment. Sooner or later, when Goldman is ready, the Professor will receive a phone call. Just follow his lead."

Now *he* stood up and went to the window. Somehow he had retrieved control. "That's all," he said and remained with his back to us while we filed out.

Back at my post I check out the reports of Ruamsantiah's men who took statements from the market vendors and others who were in the square at the time of the murder of Nong X. Our constables tend not to be of the most motivated kind, but here, perhaps out of pity for the victim, they have done their best. Instead of the usual, *Witness stated he/she was not too clear about the event, could not remember anything relevant,* type of report, I have more than twenty lengthy statements, which go into detail about the witnesses' private lives, domestic disputes, religious convictions, feelings of sadness for the victim, rage fantasies of what they would do to the perp if it were up to them, conviction that some kind of negative occult force is at work in our country at this time: all useless, in other words. My phone rings.

It is young Detective Tassadorn, still working on the Klong Toey bombing. His tone turns a little strange when he says, "Detective, we found another cell phone at the bomb site. It was buried under a pile of debris, mostly lumber and trash."

This does not strike me as strange. Everyone has cell phones, even *farang* down-and-outs. "What condition is it in?"

"Well, that's the thing. It was a cheap local make and looked totally destroyed, but the forensic people took it and managed to transfer all the data to a hard disk."

I am beginning to feel insecure here. Why doesn't the young detective come to the point? "Yes?"

"Yes. Most of the contacts and recent calls are to known cannabis users, small-time dealers, and birdshit *farang*, mostly British and American." I wait. I have heard enough of his tone now to realize he is excited and disturbed. "There were photos, too."

My heart gives a little leap of foreboding. "Photos?"

"Yes." He lets the moment hang. Perhaps he is not as new and naïve as I thought.

"And?"

"Three are of you."

"Of me?"

"Yes. We're pretty certain they were taken on Soi Cowboy."

I stare at the phone. Ever feel your insides quake for no good reason, R? I cannot understand where I put my cool, all of a sudden. I have to let a few beats pass, then say, "I see."

"Yes. I thought you ought to know right away."

That is an incomplete sentence. The unstated part would be something like, *Before I tell everyone else.*

"Thank you, Detective. Thank you. I appreciate it. I appreciate it very much." He is so much younger than me, it is not difficult to sound as if I have it all under control.

"What are you going to do?" he asks.

"Leave it with me," I hear myself say in a confident tone. "I'll get back to you."

When I close the phone I'm shuddering. I have to stand up and take a walk before the cop at the next post sees what kind of state I am in. Outside on the street, I stride toward Sukhumvit at quite a clip until I'm out of range of the station's psychic orbit. One anxiety a cop in Krung Thep doesn't normally have is fear of perps. Our rules are quite strict: no matter how unpopular you might be with your colleagues, no gangster is ever going to target you, because the boys would close ranks and take him out. It's not quite as rigid a law as gravity, but close. Now I don't feel so protected. How much evidence does a person need before they're entitled to own their paranoia? The bloody mirror with my name on it could have been an aberration by a psycho. An iPhone with a hundred photos of me on it is not so easily explained, but not necessarily sinister in itself (Chanya tried to cheer me up by suggesting it's because I'm so good-looking: probably some *katoey* with a crush on me took the pix). It's always the third clue that clinches it, both in madness and in law enforcement: *another* phone at the scene of the bombing with pictures of me in the photo gallery? And taken on Soi Cowboy, just like all the photos on the iPhone?

Naturally, I need a smoke, and, to be honest here, R, I am on the point of going home and leaving the planet on Air Cannabis for a while, when that curious blip called duty drives me in another direction. Obviously, I need to pay a second visit to Sergeant Lotus Bud at KTC. There is a detour I need to make first, though.

11

The best place to buy carved wooden religious objects was on Petch-buri Road. In a shop surrounded by Buddhas, bodhisattvas, monks, angels, fairies, gnomes, and demons, I scratched my head. Personally, I was partial to the old Burmese carved monks, for the workmanship (you buy them in pairs: skinny with walking sticks, bent, devout, cheerful, at peace). In the old days the carver meditated until he saw the subject in the crude wood before he started chiseling. I found a couple of teak monks that would fit beside me on the seat of a cab and haggled over the price until I lost patience and paid up. I carried the monks to the cab, where I carefully set them down in the backseat, according them all dignity.

When I arrived at the police post in Klong Toey, I saw that a supper of rice whiskey and noodles had liberated the sweetness within the middle-aged cop. What a lifetime of self-denial and contemplation had done for the monks, a quarter bottle of Mekong had done for him. With alcohol, though, it's all about timing. If I'd arrived earlier, he might have retained some resistance; later and he would probably be incoherent or belligerent. I'd bought a flask of my own to top him up if necessary.

I carried the monks out of the cab and set them down on his desk as he watched. At this moment it did not matter, according to the theology, how I treated the sculptures, because they had not yet been consecrated, but I showed respect anyway. The Sergeant stood back to assess them.

"Burmese? Nineteenth century? Will you look at those heads . . . The model the sculptor used—must have been a child or a young woman—perfect. What a wonderful image of innocence! Reminds me of the kids here, before they go wrong."

He saw no contradiction between innocence and the hundred scams he was up to his ears in; his contemplation had long ago taken him beyond such false distinctions. Nor did it matter that I was bribing him with religious objects: it made him feel all the more devout.

He had placed his great chair with cushions outside his cabin and invited me to grab one of the tubular chairs inside. He placed the flask of Mekong I'd brought on a small collapsible table between the chairs. We drank out of plastic cups and talked about Klong Toey, the slum and the famous market of the same name.

He particularly wanted to talk about the market, how it was the closest to the port and received goods brought from overseas via the Gulf of Thailand, but also, because the port was on the river, goods are brought there from the interior. True, he explained, "It's not a wholesale market, but most restaurants, especially the thousands of cooked-food stalls, buy a lot of food in detail rather than bulk." I knew that to be true. Come between three and six in the morning and you'll see a representative of just about every major restaurant in the city, even the very top end, which send the chefs themselves to find the choice sea bass, snow fish, fresh chicken, rabbit, beef, every variety of chili, lemongrass (gross or in detail), and every other herb, vegetable, meat, fish, or poultry that hit the tables of restaurants and private homes throughout the city every day. Italian chefs in particular valued our basil, which we cultivate in a number of varieties: sweet, holy, and hairy.

But I didn't understand why we were talking about basil when he knew very well why I'd come. I was wondering if he was not just too drunk, too old, or too decadent to be of use, when he said, "It was an accident, you know."

"What? The bombing? How can a bombing be an accident?"

"Not the bombing, the casualties. It was the first Thursday in the month."

"So?"

"First Thursday in the month, those Yanks were normally up before dawn—usually about three-thirty a.m.—to visit the market."

"They were in the catering business?" He grunted and wasn't going to speak until I'd at least started to work it out. "There's a delivery—a special delivery—first Thursday in the month?"

"Sure. A rice barge brings it from the north. The kingpins are Lao. Everyone in the business knows. I bet your Colonel Vikorn knows. It's basically cottage-industry stuff, though."

I was trying to decrypt the story, which was not difficult, and at the same time trying to fit it in with what little I knew about the three Americans. It seemed they had only been hanging out in Bangkok for ten months. I had no information about where they were before that, but ten months is not long enough to set up a fully protected trafficking operation from scratch all on your own, not if you want to be secure. You would need local input, local operators you trusted. I figure there is only one plausible explanation.

"They came to you when they first arrived? They were old Southeast Asia hands who were naturalized Cambodians, so they would know the form if not the local language."

"They came to me for help. They said they'd had to leave Cambodia, but they didn't say why they were in Cambodia, or why three Americans their age could not return to the States. But they were sincere, I could see that. I felt compassion for them. Obviously, they needed a trade, some way to make dough. And they learned Thai much quicker than most *farang*, because they were already fluent in Khmer. After a couple of months they were part of the furniture. Very unusual."

I'd been trying to keep my sipping of the Mekong to a minimum, but I was starting to feel a tad tipsy. "You set it up for them?"

"I never set up anything. I told them a certain wholesaler who brings sacks of jasmine rice down from the north occasionally brings something else in the bags. He is very discreet, a careful man, almost as old as them. I like dealing with old men, they're safer and they don't have ridiculous ambitions. It turned out fine. The rice producer would hold a monthly auction among, say, ten trusted dealers, usually dividing the produce up between them. They each have their own patch, so there's no fighting. The Americans would buy just enough to sell to American tourists they felt they could trust. They would hang out in Khaosan Road, checking out just the right *farang* who wants to get high in Asia, but is old enough and cool enough to keep quiet. That's what I knew they would do and it worked out fine."

"But how did the wholesaler know to trust them? And I bet they have safe passage with the dope anywhere in Klong Toey. And I bet that cost them at least ten percent. And I bet you charged a setup fee as well."

"Win-win," the Sergeant said, lighting a Krong Thip 90 and sipping some more whiskey. "One of them told me there are *farang* books about it. *Economics*, they call it."

"So what happened this month? Why weren't they at the market on the last Thursday?"

"'Cause they didn't need to be. These are not ambitious empire builders. They did so well in their sales the previous month, they had enough money to last them. There was a group of oldies passing through, relatives of vets missing in action, just come back from Vietnam. Bought up all their stock. They always worked on a sufficiency basis. They were careful never to take too much."

I sipped the Mekong and nodded. It was important not to rush him. "You mean, whoever planted the bomb was relying on them being out, at the market, when it went off?"

"Why else choose that morning on that day of the month? There are no coincidences in Thailand."

I scratched my chin. "So the bomb was just to scare them?"

"Yes, that's my theory."

"But why?"

He shrugged. "In Bangkok it could be anything. Maybe the bombers thought the Americans had cheated them. Maybe they were just Thais who don't like *farang* moving into the business. Or it could be something else. Like I say, those old men have only been here less than a year. They would have a lot of history from another country, wouldn't they? And what kind of history, when you consider they chose to live in the lowest kind of third-world slum?"

I let a couple of beats pass. Atmosphere is important for intuition, and that's the faculty I wanted the Sergeant to exercise right now. "You're right, dead right. Why did they need Klong Toey? Those old men, the three of them—there must have been something different about them that you noticed. There aren't any other *farang* living here, not even birdshit *farang* like them. And, frankly, I've never heard of Americans becoming Cambodian citizens. The traffic tends to be in the other direction."

He took a deep toke on his Krong Thip, sipped some more Mekong, and nodded. "That's right."

"So, what about them?"

"At first they seemed just like old *farang* men, you know, kind of charming, steady, very likable, been in the East a long time, smart enough to be polite like Thais instead of aggressive like *farang*."

"Then?"

"Then, when you watched them carefully, you realized they were all crazy. In a very specific way that's hard to explain and not actually out of control in the way of most crazies. But they were all nuts."

"Could you be a little more specific? You call someone crazy, you have to have a reason."

"Ask anyone who knew them around here."

I lost patience. "But what were the symptoms?"

"You don't have to snap. I know what you want to know, but there's no way to tell you what you want to know, because it's so hard to explain. If one of them recovers, spend an hour with him and you'll see what I mean."

I grunted, leaned back in the chair, tried to tune in to his long, slow waves. "In what way crazy? Give me an example."

"In the middle of a conversation they would break off."

"Old men's minds wander."

"This wasn't wandering. They would break off and think very intensely about something for as long as five minutes, as though they were in a different world, then return to the conversation. They all did it. They were aware of it and tried to cover up. That's what was crazy."

At the moment I had no way of absorbing Lotus Bud's psychoanalysis of the three old men. I was as drunk as I needed to be to bond with the Sergeant, who was quite drunk himself. I figured it was now or never with my killer question.

"Sergeant," I said softly, in a tone I'd not used before. Even in his inebriation he noticed the nuance, laid his head back, closed his eyes, then opened the left one to glance at me. "The smart phone you found after the explosion." He grunted, closed both eyes. "Sergeant, it was in exceptionally good condition for a phone that had been thrown up in the air by a bomb and landed on concrete. It was not only brand-new, it was an Apple 5s—a luxury, almost like jewelry, costs over twenty-five thousand baht new, when anyone can buy a cell phone for just a few thousand. I bet there's no one in Klong Toey who owns an iPhone—not a legal one, anyway. Everyone around here buys fakes or secondhand or stolen. And that place where you said you found it, that was quite a way from the bomb site. A delicate thing like a phone, especially a sophisticated one like that . . . Well, it was operating perfectly, wasn't it? Those photos of me were clear and bright, just as if the phone had not been through an explosion. And it was brand-new."

A long pause during which LB took a slug of rice whiskey. "He said I had to let you figure it out for yourself. He didn't really care if you found out, but I wasn't to tell you unless you figured it out first. He's playing some game with you."

"You mean someone came to see you? Before or after the explosion?"

"After. A few hours after."

"And gave you that iPhone and told you to call Vikorn?"

"Yes."

"Who was he?"

"An American."

"Huge, old, a giant?"

"No. He wasn't old. He was tall. Slim. Young. Very fit like an athlete or a military man. His hair was very short and so blond it was almost white. A killer."

"How would you know that?"

"How would I not know that? I've been a cop in Klong Toey for three decades. How could I survive if I didn't know men? And women too. Pimps, whores, pickpockets, burglars, car thieves, murderers for passion, murderers for greed: each one has a different signal, a different smell."

"How was his signal?"

"Flat. Only killers for fun have that signal. What do you call them?"

"Psychopaths."

"Right."

A pause while I absorbed this wisdom. "That's all—he came, gave you the phone, and told you to call me but not to mention him?"

"Yes. He said you would be very interested. It was very private, very personal. Between you and him. He said you and he would be meeting soon. He said you and he are going to be very close." Lotus Bud turned his head. "I thought about that. You're working on that murder of a young woman who lived in the market square behind the police station in District 8, right?"

"Yes."

"Have you thought about where that is exactly? I checked on a map after he left."

"Of course I know where it is."

"I mean geographically."

"How's that?"

"It's the exact geographic center of District 8. If D8 is a chessboard, that murder happened on the center squares. Your district, with your name on the mirror. What could be clearer than that?"

We stared at each other. Now my cell phone started to ring. I fished it out impatiently, afraid that the Sergeant would change his mind about confiding his thoughts to me. It was the young Detective Tassatorn again.

"Khun Sonchai? I have news. Do you want the good or the bad first?"

He was a little breathless, and at first I supposed it must be because he'd cracked the case and, like a good Buddhist, was trying not to sound too proud of himself.

"The good first."

"I've found them."

"Who?"

"The two young thugs who set that bomb."

I let a couple of beats pass. "Really?"

"They were seen. Two separate witnesses saw them running from the explosion and recognized them. They're low-grade crooks, lowlifes who do small crime to get by, not real pros."

"They have form?"

"Tons of it. One has a sideline in bomb-making. Not big terrorist stuff, you know, just local intimidation work. He specializes in settling scores. I don't need to tell you how the mafia likes to use explosives. They scare more and can be hard to trace. He was also involved in that car-parts scam, you know, Red Kim's gang were bringing in spare parts and assembling high-end foreign cars from them to dodge the tax."

"So what, you found prints?"

"Not prints. The bomb experts were able to find traces of liquid petroleum gas. I organized a raid and there were traces on their clothes."

I glanced at the Sergeant, who was developing deep religious feelings for the two carved monks I'd brought him and listening to the conversation at the same time.

"That's pretty good news. Wow! You really work fast. You did all that in less than forty-eight hours." I heard the purring of an ambitious young man on the other phone. "So where is the bad news in all that?"

"They retained Lord Sakagorn."

"*Sakagorn?*"

The Sergeant perked up for a moment, then returned to his reverie. "Yes."

I let a couple of beats pass. "I see. So did you get a confession, any kind of statement?"

"No. Sakagorn found holes in the way I obtained the warrant. It's true, I cut a few corners—how was I to know they'd instruct him? He thinks up legal points even the judges have never heard of. He sent one of his assistants to the station to argue, orally and in writing, that there is no power in any of the police statutes and decrees that enables us to hold those suspects. All our evidence was obtained illegally, according to Sakagorn. What do I know? Everybody skipped those courses at the academy. The instructors didn't know the law either."

I scratched my jaw, remembering my own year as a cadet. Law was not big on the syllabus. "I see."

"Detective," the young detective said in a low tone, "should I be scared?"

"Yes," I say.

"Please advise me."

"Let's look at it both ways. Say you decide to take on Lord Sakagorn and prosecute. You will be bombarded with offers of wealth and rapid advancement if you play ball, and threats of dire consequences if you don't. In the unlikely event that you win against him in court and get a conviction, he won't rest until he has used his influence to destroy your career. He'll find a way to discredit you and win on appeal. If, on the other hand, you play ball with Sakagorn, then kiss your freedom and integrity goodbye, he will own you for life."

On the other end of the phone I heard the sharp gasp of a young man who had just entered the last initiation, the one where you finally admit there is no way out. My mood altered when he started to cry.

"I knew it would be like this. They warned me, but I believed in my karma and the teachings of the Buddha. They said that I was like a white sheet that would be dipped in black dye every day. From white I would go to dirty white, to gray—in the end, I would be pure black. But I didn't want to believe them. How have you managed, Khun Sonchai, all these years? You are famous for not taking money."

"Even preserving one's soul requires a certain amount of wriggling, Khun Tassatorn. Innocence can't save you all on its own, it needs help from experience."

"Yes. I can see that. Do you want the bombing case? Are you saying this to enhance your career?"

"I don't want it at all. My career cannot be enhanced. I have a reputation, like you say, for not taking money, career advancement is blocked for me. You still have a chance, you're young and ambitious, it's just bad luck you got landed with this. You are more than welcome to keep the case, if you like."

"I'm not crying for my career, Khun Sonchai, I'm crying for Thailand."

"I know, Khun Tassatorn. What would you like me to do?"

"Take the case, Khun Sonchai. My chief will find a way of transferring it to District 8 if Colonel Vikorn wants it. Colonel Vikorn gets what Colonel Vikorn wants, everyone knows that. Now we've talked I know you are so much stronger than I. Perhaps only you could take on a case like this and survive. But please answer one question: why are you so interested in this particular matter? To tell you the truth, I never would have worked so hard if you had not inspired me with your overwhelming passion, rushing off to the hospital like that to visit those old men. I've never seen anything like it. When I asked people if Khun Sonchai Jitpleecheep was like this on all his cases, they told me no, normally you were not the kind of cop who always gets his man. Normally you were very reasonable and laid-back, they told me."

I was not sure how to answer. Why did I rush off to see those three unconscious men? It was the photos on the cell phone of course. Someone takes a hundred pictures of you, the hungry heart assumes it must be love. Curious how the spirit moves.

"I'm not especially interested in the case, Detective. I'm just putting one foot in front of the other, plodding along. I've always found that to be the safest."

"Is that what you advise?"

The trouble with innocence: it tries to recruit someone who has lost it to help retain it. "I don't advise anything at all, Khun Tassatorn. War is always a balance between wanting to win and needing to survive."

A long pause. "War. Yes, that's the one thing they don't tell you in the academy. From the first day on the beat, you're at war. And you start thinking like someone in the middle of a battle that never ends." His voice turned bitter. "You start to think like a cornered rat."

I let the moment pass.

"It's not only police work that's like that," I said. "My wife is an unemployed academic and she feels pretty much the same way."

He grunted. I gave him time to recover. Now he changed tack.

"Yes, please take the case. You are braver and tougher than I'll ever be."

"There's no need to talk like that, Khun Tassatorn. Get some sleep. You'll feel better in the morning. I was in the same position as you once."

"No," he said with some finality. "In the morning I will not feel better. In the morning I will resign and ordain as a monk. It was the vocation I should have chosen in the first place. I was not made for this world. I'm not built of steel like you. What do you say to that?"

"If you really do it, I shall envy you."

"Then I will do it," he said, and closed the phone. I put my own back in my pocket.

"You didn't talk about those photos of you on the cell phones," Sergeant Lotus Bud said out of the corner of his mouth.

Throughout my conversation with Tassatorn, the Sergeant's head had sagged farther and farther to one side until it was resting on his shoulder and he had appeared to be asleep. I shook my head. My street smarts simply did not compare with his.

"He didn't mention it."

"Scared," LB said. "Those pix I found are the real reason he's giving you the case."

"Those pictures of me on that iPhone? So how do you explain them?"

"I don't know exactly," Lotus Bud said. "But that young blond guy knew all about those old guys, who had been dealing dope for a year. In that time you learn a lot about the business." He raised a droopy eyebrow to look at me. "You learn what a lot of us have heard over the grapevine."

"Like what?"

"Like stories about a certain respected detective with a weakness for weed who helps to run his mother's bar on Soi Cowboy. You would have been the answer to their prayers if they could have first taken you on as a client, then maybe persuaded you to help with sales contacts. That way they would have had cast-iron protection—that's the way they would have seen it. It's the way Asia works, and they knew that. Don't tell me that didn't cross your mind?"

I sighed and took out a five-hundred-baht note to slip under the can of Nescafé on the shrine to the household gods.

"Of course it crossed my mind," I lied.

The Sergeant used his cell phone to call a cab. I heard him tell the driver to put the ride on the Sergeant's own bill. He was quite emotional when we said goodbye, I assumed because we'd bonded while drunk. Or perhaps he thought I didn't have much time left in this body. Just before the cab drew away he said, "Of course, that wouldn't explain a hundred photos. It would explain the connection but not the photos."

"That's right."

He grunted. "And it wouldn't explain why the phone came to me via that young *farang* killer." He scratched his beard. "Not every mystery has a solution—which is okay, solutions can be dangerous."

"Yes."

"There's one other thing, though. I'm surprised you didn't ask about it."

"What's that?"

"Well, I don't speak English worth a damn and that young American only had basic Thai."

Now I knew I was losing my skill set. Why didn't I think of that? "So how did you communicate?"

"Khmer. Same as I used with the old Americans, before they mastered Thai. I was brought up in Surin. Khmer was the local dialect."

"He was fluent?"

"Spoke it like a native. Better than me. The Surin dialect is pretty basic, but he spoke the real thing without accent."

In the back of the cab on the way home, with no fellow human to distract me, the mind returns to primal chaos. I am like a tower of billiard balls that miraculously remained verticle for a moment and now collapses as I knew I would. *Why me?* is the question everyone asks at this point in a breakdown. I go over the three curses for the thousandth time: Nong X, murdered, my name on the mirror; an iPhone with one name in the Contacts application and a hundred photos of me; another cell phone with three more photos of me. None of this should have destroyed my sense of self were there not the haunting possibility that one of those Americans in the hospital, all of whom are naturalized Cambodians, may be my father and the looming conviction that we are all implicated in something bigger than a murder and a son in search of a dad.

When I arrive at the hovel Chanya is awake and working at her desk. I enter and press my back against the door before succumbing to the tremble-and-blurt phase of mental disintegration. At first she wants to carry on working; then she decides that as my lifelong companion she may have a part to play in my despair; then, as I blurt with ever greater rapidity, trying to pierce her shell, she gets up, takes my hand, and has me sit in her chair while she squats in front of me.

"But these are two totally unrelated issues, work and personal issues, all mixed up," she explains in a tone that scrupulously avoids sentimentality. "You need to distinguish them."

"How?"

"Well, work is real, and all this lost-father stuff is just something that's been hanging there rotting in the back of your mind forever."

I stare wild-eyed at her, failing to comprehend her total lack of comprehension. Then she remembers she once did a course on what might be termed first-response therapy: *Cries for Help and How to React to Them.* She suddenly assumes a care-and-concern expression (wide and worried eyes, furrowed brow, social-worker buzzwords, physical contact to provide the illusion of warmth, nauseating patience). When she starts to wipe my brow, hold my hand, and gaze earnestly into my eyes, it pisses me off so much I pull out of it and push her away. Am I alone in preferring madness to therapy? She now stands up in a flash of anger.

"So, have you spoken to your mother about any of this?" she snaps.

"Any of what? Decapitation? Transhumanism? Geopolitics?"

"That's all professional stuff, that isn't what's bothering you. It's the illusory connection between you and those three Americans: you have transferred your personal id onto what should be superego preoccupied with work and contribution to society—I'm using old vocabulary here, but the ideas are basically the same today as in the time of Freud."

"Huh?"

"*Of course none of those old* farang *are your father.* That's a classic transference from fantasy to reality. The reason there were photos of you on that old cell phone was just as Lotus Bud said: they heard you were a smoker and a cop and wanted you as a client."

"So what about the hundred pictures on the iPhone? What about my name on the mirror in blood?"

She waves a hand. "Stuff like that can always be explained, once the whole picture is clear." I see from her face that it is quite a while since she did the course. She is not totally sure she is following the right tack. "Clearly, the father thing is at the root of all this. I'm going to speak to your mother tomorrow. Perhaps some kind of intervention is what you need."

That seems to have exhausted the twenty-first century's reservoir of compassion. I'm happier when she reverts to a more primitive technique. She gives me a big smacker on the lips, jiggles my dick in a friendly way, grins right into my face, and says, "What about that oil Krom gave you? How are you supposed to smoke it?"

I sag with relief: whatever the issues between us, we are both big fans of self-medication. Now Chanya is intrigued by the idea of dipping a couple of cigarettes in the oil, then baking the cigarettes at hundred degrees centigrade for fifteen minutes until the solvent has burned off, leaving, in theory, pure THC stuck to the tobacco fibers. Neither of us have smoked this way before and we have no idea what to expect. We bake two Marlboros, one each, lie on the mattress with a makeshift ashtray on either side, smile at each other, and light up.

So far as I can recall I was a third of the way through my own little ciggy when I found important information to share with Chanya. *This stuff is really strong,* is what I wanted to say, but the words came out so garbled that even I could not understand them. It didn't matter, for Chanya was lying dead straight, arms rigidly by her side, her eyes firmly fixed on the Invisible. Eventually she roused herself enough to say, "Krom's oil is very strong," and returned to heaven. For myself, while I felt in full control of my mind, my facial and tongue muscles were a different matter. The couple of syllables I attempted seemed garbled; I could not understand what I was trying to say. And so we lay on our backs, the two of us, for quite a few hours, our bodies touching, our souls a cosmos apart. From time to time during the course of the night I returned to earth to take a glance at Chanya, who remained rigid, bug-eyed, and enthralled by my side.

12

Krom sent separate SMSs to Chanya and me to remind us that we were invited to supper tonight. In the cab on the way to Heaven's Gate Tower, generally known as the HGT, Chanya suffers from an attack of nerves. Despite her former success as a hostess and escort, it has been a while since she worked.

"It's going to be awkward, isn't it?"

"How so?"

"You must have thought about it. This invitation comes from on high, through Vikorn's PRC connections. Vikorn has let this Professor Chu think he's going to lay a dazzlingly attractive inspector who is also a high-tech whiz kid—a woman totally up his alley—all on the Colonel's tab. It's one of those male transactions in which women are the currency, don't try to pretend otherwise."

"Women aren't the currency, lust is. It's like the Buddha said, it's lust, fear, or indifference with humankind."

"That's right," she says with a grin. I still admire the way she can flip her moods in a second. She has flown across an internal abyss like a lama, now she's on the other side, laughing. "On that retreat I went on two years ago, we turned it into an exercise. We used the imagery of a clock face with an arrow and three positions: attraction, aversion, indifference. In our meditations we had to observe which one the arrow was pointing at, from second to second. Then from split second to split second. The arrow moves automatically according to the thoughts in your head, there's no control. In the end the whole universe amounts to that: lust, fear, boredom. Unless you're enlightened."

She looks me in the eye. "I called her. I forgot to tell you?"

"Krom? Today?"

"Yes. After you went to work. There have been rumors. There were a bunch of cops from your police station at the *khao kha moo* stall when you were having that intense little chat together that lasted quite a while. I called to tell her about the gossip. She apologized and said there was nothing between you. I said I knew that. It was one of those totally civilized girls-being-tidy things."

I'm amazed and stare at her. "How the hell—?"

"Pi Tai told me. You know, she runs the typing pool. I'm not totally without sources."

"Really?"

"Cops are just amazing gossips—the men more than the women." She looked me in the eyes. "It's okay, I know she doesn't fancy you, she probably couldn't get wet for a man anyway. Lust, aversion, indifference. When she looks at you her arrow points to indifference. When she looks at me it points to lust. When you look at her your arrow points to fear. You're scared of her."

"Why?"

"She's smarter than you."

I let that pass. "And you—where is your arrow pointing, these days?"

She holds my hand for a moment, as if to soften a blow. "I've been stuck on indifference for too long, Sonchai. I've done it for you. You marry a man to tame him, because his virility scares and unsettles you. Allowing yourself to be tamed in turn is only fair, part of the deal. So you end up with two very tame humans. Apparently Mother Nature set it up that way. But I can't keep it up, darling. I really can't. And neither can you." She removes her hand and looks out of the window. "You do know where your arrow points when you look at me?" It's my turn to look out the window. She pronounces the word softly, tenderly, kindly, deftly: "Boredom." The moment hangs. "There is something about Inspector Krom that seems to offer a cure, isn't there?"

"She's dangerous."

"That's what I mean."

Sometimes the only way out of a conversation is to take it somewhere else. "I don't think I've come across a brain like hers before," I say. "I'm going to feel sorry for the Professor if he thinks he's going to sleep with her tonight—or ever."

"Should I give him the come-on instead? Would it be good for your investigation? I wouldn't have to fuck him, I could just string him along until you told me to stop. Maybe that's the only contribution I can make."

I groan. "For Buddha's sake, Chanya. Please."

She laughs again, that free and troubling lama laugh from the other side of the abyss.

We emerge from the lift lobby and look up: Orion and his belt; the Big Dipper; bit of Moon; Pegasus. Whichever poet first called it a *black velvet canopy encrusted with diamonds* was right: you can't improve on that, although in the tropics it can also resemble a wet blanket with holes in it. Chanya is charmed. She stares into the heavens, willing a crew of aliens to send a ladder for her to climb up.

We were the first to arrive. Stars aside, it was a bar so expensive and successful it could afford to place its tables far apart. Baristas—all men—wore quick-draw holsters where electronic menus and credit card machines nestled. They were intense, focused, professionally polite, and quite ruthless in pursuit of a place in the mixologist's (do *not* call them barmen) hall of fame. Trained by aliens and very un-Thai, in other words. We ordered a couple of piña coladas, because that's what we order in bars like this, checked out the other customers: a group of young upper-middle-class New Yorkers getting louder drink by drink; a blond couple sipping white wine who looked German; a Chinese couple probably from Hong Kong; a British family, obviously wealthy, with a teenage son and daughter. Now a single Chinese man appeared and the maître d' ushered him to our table. Chanya and I stood up.

First thing I have to report, R: he was tall. No one was expecting *tall*. Well, you don't, do you, when you're told you will meet a Chinese professor who works out of offices in Shanghai? Let us be honest here about our species-wide addiction to stereotypes: short, plump, mid-fifties with male pattern baldness was the first image that came to mind, not a five-eleven northerner in his early forties, lean with strong harmonious features like a film star and a full head of jet-black hair coiffed by an expert. This only created another layer of complexity. Suddenly Krom might not be the victim of cynical male humor; she might be the evening's big winner. Except that she was a dyke, of course.

"Detective Jitpleecheep? I'm Chu." He turned chivalrously to Chanya, to whom he offered a Hollywood smile, circa 1950. This was going to be an interesting evening. Chanya mastered herself to return a finely honed smile designed to acknowledge his beauty and importance without in any way compromising her status as a chaste married woman. Of course, it was just a posture and we were not legally married and her pupils were opened a little wider than was entirely appropriate considering she had known the newcomer for less than a minute, but *face* is everything in the East. When we sat and he looked expectantly at the empty chair, Chanya, now on her best behavior, told him that "Ms. Krom will be here any minute."

Now our vulgar piña coladas with the great hairy lumps of pineapple sticking out of extravagant glasses with cocktail sticks sporting white paper hats seemed *bannock*, or country bumpkin, especially when he ordered a *coupe* of Dom Perignon—vintage, naturally.

Then it was nothing but small talk until the other star arrived. The Professor had studied trivia, probably as a survival skill essential in cultures without depth or mahjong, and was horribly good at it. He tried us out with politics, philosophy, and economics, then slipped naturally into Chanya's preference for women's issues: is the West actually *behind* China?

Chu was too sophisticated to give a standard-issue critique of the hypocrisy and double-talk of the Western model that had never done better than half deliver on any of its promises to anyone, ever, especially its own people—although he hinted as much. He dealt instead with the conflict in China between the modernizers, who are the survivors and inheritors of Mao's revolution, and the closet imperialists who secretly assume that China will return to its former splendor, decadence, and inequality; indeed has already done so in Shanghai and Beijing and all along the east coast. Did we know there already existed a breed of wealthy merchants who have stopped cutting their fingernails to prove they never do manual work, just like under the Empress Dowager? Chu balanced the various arguments skillfully, taking care not to omit anything relevant even if prejudicial to his case, then concluded that, yes, China is streets ahead of the West in terms of women's issues—and most of the other issues, too, although he conceded a certain attitude problem when it came to pollution. Now Krom arrived.

Who ever would have guessed? She came as Charlie Chaplin. Well, that was my first thought, because of the hat. It was not a bowler—not quite—but that kind of shape, pushed rakishly back. I had to admit it went well with the pearl satin shirt and trademark bootlace tie, the black pantaloons and the laddish lace-up black boots, but it was the hat that said, *Careful, I'm different.* I was proud of her. Chanya, though, felt upstaged. The exclusive eye contact she had enjoyed with the handsome professor had now to be shared with this startling and fascinating newcomer. She tried, but could not compete with the hat. Our eyes met. She looked away.

To make matters worse, Krom, who I'd considered incapable of small talk, immediately opened up the conversation by referring to the Jade Rabbit. BTW, R, *Jade Rabbit* was the Chinese Moon buggy who kept a diary on the PRC's social media sites. The poor thing ran out of energy while stranded on the Dark Side and left his two billion fans in Greater China with a touching farewell message:

> If this journey must come to an early end, I am not afraid. Whether or not the repairs are successful, I believe even my malfunctions will provide my masters with valuable information and experience.

That did sound a tad like the heroic self-sacrifice of early communist mythology, and I was waiting to see how the very urbane Chu would respond.

"Believe me," he said to Krom with a smile, "I despise Chinese infantilism as much as you probably do. But Jade Rabbit has been a great success with the masses—like Mickey Mouse in the West. Except that JR is doing a real job. That must constitute progress, no? Imagine a world where Donald Duck, Tom and Jerry, Mickey and Minnie actually do something useful instead of mindlessly beating each other up?"

"That's so true," Chanya said.

"So much depends on how technology hits the private citizen," the Professor explained. "Computing power among the masses is already extraordinary—there was a degree of paranoia about that in the Party, but it turns out the little people prefer to share porn, gossip, and insults and listen to junk music. It's a fantastic way of shutting them up, like a voluntary electronic gulag. No danger at all except from organized Islamists."

Chanya had now decided she didn't like the Professor after all, and took this last statement as clear indication of his male chauvinist totalitarian soul, which, she had already intuited, was not attracted to her anyway. Krom, though, looked at it differently. She agreed that the amount of computing power out there among the people as a whole was amazing—like a source of uranium nobody has yet seen how to harness. Suppose, for example, a village of a couple thousand people all linked up their computers in pursuit of a common cause? Of course, when that does happen, the world will cease to be recognizable.

It was conversation as cover, in other words. Krom had the attention of the alpha male that Chanya had lost, despite the fact that Krom didn't want it. For my part I did not banish from my mind the possibility that the irresistible Professor might be hors de combat by reason of being gay. He didn't give a single clue about which way he swung until, at the end of the meal when the ladies went off to the bathroom together, he changed seats and shifted closer to me than is normal at this kind of supper and began to whisper sweet nothings in my ear.

The sweet nothings, though, were yet another cover in this hall of mirrors. In between seductive smiles along with a hand placed on my shoulder, he managed to convey a quite different message. I confess I had not noticed the arrival of two Chinese men during the course of the meal who had installed themselves at the far end of the restaurant on seats facing us.

"They're from the ministry," he whispered. "I wonder if you would help me lose them?"

I used my best quick flick to take them in. My mind went back to that morning on the river. "Are they photographers?" I asked.

"They've been using miniature video cameras all night. They're the latest, better than anything the West has. Quite invisible unless you know what to look for."

"Where do you want to go?"

"Pat Pong—but I don't dare with them on my tail."

"No problem," I said and took out my cell phone to call Sergeant Ruamsantiah.

"No problem," the Sergeant said. "I'll call Colonel Wanakan. He'll have a couple of his boys check their passports when they leave the restaurant. Where are you?"

"Heaven's Gate Tower."

"I went there once. Hated it."

"The food?"

"No. The height. It gave me vertigo."

But on the way to Pat Pong the Professor received a phone call that altered all our plans. I watched the change in his expression as someone spoke on the other end of the line: playtime postponed, this was a work moment; adulthood returned with a thump. "Tell the driver to go to this address," he said to Krom in the back of the cab, using a stern tone we'd not heard before. "We're going to a demo," he told us.

13

The address was a condominium in an upscale building on Soi 24, probably the most expensive street in the city outside of the business district at Satorn. According to the property pages of the *Bangkok Post*, units here sell for just under two million dollars. It sounds a lot until you compare similar properties in other capitals. In Bangkok that kind of money buys four thousand square feet of habitable area including maid's quarters with a plunge pool on the terrace, guards at the gate who cut sharp salutes and click their heels Prussian style, and a house god who lives in a small palace atop a stone column and looks in four directions at once. To judge from the offerings as we passed him on the driveway he was partial to oranges, bananas, and Pepsi-Cola.

I was not entirely surprised to see the two Chinese cameramen from the ministry in the lobby, waiting for us. They had brought a modest movie camera with tripod that they carried into the lift. A woman from reception took us all to the top where the entire floor led to a magnificent entrance with alcove. Just inside the alcove, on either side of the double front door, two burly white men who had to be ex-marines, or serving marines co-opted for the night, stood at ease. They raised machine pistols and politely asked us to wait before coming any closer, then spoke into their shoulder mikes. Goldman appeared at the door with a Chinese woman in a business pants suit who told him that Chu was one of them, that Krom and I had to be let in because we were from Vikorn and the cameramen had to be let in because they were with the "other" ministry. "That camera stays outside with the guards," Goldman said, then turned to us with a smile.

"Good evening. Please come in." The tone said, *Quickly, fast now,* but it was to be a gracious soiree: the giant wore a silk paisley smoking jacket, puffed on a cigar, stood by the door like a good host while we trooped in. Then he said to the guards, "That's it, you see any apes coming out of those lifts, you shoot." The ex-marines grunted.

I wasn't expecting rows of seats as in a small movie theater, all pointing toward a back wall with a white screen. It was a long room that lay between us and the blue plunge pool on the other side of glass sliding doors. You couldn't miss the state-of-the-art sound system or the large photograph of Goldman in a dinner jacket high on a wall. A polished pine staircase led to bedrooms upstairs. Krom took in the sound system while I scanned the framed photographs that took up the length of one wall. I paused at one of the Asset with a racing bicycle and a famous American cyclist who had won the Tour de France. Both he and the Asset wore identical high-tech shirts featuring the Stars and Stripes and looked so happy they might have been in love. Most of the other photos showcased the Asset's sports achievements: swimming, fencing, karate, and especially cycling. At the far end of the room a blackwood Chinese temple table held cups and trophies; I guessed he came top of the league in all those challenging sports.

The chairs were filled mostly with Chinese, men in gray business suits, with a couple of Chinese women also dressed in monochrome. Sakagorn, in a tuxedo, sat next to one of the HiSo Chinese women who might have been the head of the delegation. Everyone was looking serious but relaxed, polite but not convinced. *Buyers in a buyer's market* was the impression I took away on my first glance. And now Goldman looked nervous.

"Okay," he said, "we can start. Just a couple of words first. What you are going to see I have not stolen." A pause to let his joke sink in. It didn't. The word *stolen* did not invoke any response at all, one way or the other. "I would love to have stolen it for keeps, but then all hell would have broken loose. So I borrowed it. That's the reason for the rush. Within a couple of hours from now this tape has to be back where it was borrowed from. They deliberately made it nondigital to make it harder to copy. This is strictly a tape of a dress rehearsal that didn't go perfectly. So why am I showing it? Let's be frank. I have the most fantastic product in the world, but it is not perfect. Buy now, in its imperfect state, you have the opportunity to modify and improve. You buy him, you get me, too, and I will train anyone you like. I will train others to train trainers. In five years you have a viable unit. In ten you have the beginnings of an army. With me you get the complete program and the opportunity to make it all your own. Wait another couple of years, though—" He held up his hands. "It isn't a question of money, I know you can afford it. But what would you prefer to be, the second country to get the Bomb, or the fourth, or the tenth? Why not the first? Anyway, I present myself to you tonight as an honest broker. This is what I have, warts and all. And I know there is one thing above all you'll all be looking for, because you are all professionals in the field. The key, I don't need to tell you, to this particular kind of product, is the *accelerated learning enhancement*: ALE. And this is what the echolocation exercise here is really testing. I invite you to take out your timepieces to do a check. I am confident the learning curve will astonish you. Okay."

At his signal the lights dimmed and a projector began to whirr. And there he was, the Asset himself, perhaps a year or so younger, on the screen, beaming, a tall young blond in mouse-gray open-neck linen shirt, navy pants, and running shoes. He was standing on a stage empty except for a single chair and holding a microphone and cross-referring to people invisible to us. His English was strangely mid-Atlantic, as if he spent a lot of time with a British grandfather. This was a key moment for me, R—a first flash of full enlightenment. The memory is vivid and present as I write.

"Okay," the Asset says. "I just walk on like this—and what? I make it up? I've never done this before, this wasn't part of the program. What do I do in this type of real-life nonmilitary situation?" His voice is light, buoyant, silky, freshly washed. Kind of preppy, I guess you could say.

A pause. Then a quiet, scholarly kind of American voice says, "You ad-lib. And you learn."

"What shall I say?"

"At this stage you are telling them who you are."

"Who I am?" For some reason that raises a laugh somewhere in his audience, which causes him to grin. "Yeah, right. Hey, hello humanity, I am your worst nightmare—how about that?"

"C'mon," the voice says, "this is sales practice we're doing here. You're selling yourself as a product. You knew you'd have to in the end."

"Oh. Okay. These are ordinary people I'm going to be speaking to in this scenario? I mean, people who don't know? But they must know something, or there'd be no reason for them to be here—or should I say *there*?"

A sigh. "Just do your basic public image performance and follow the exercise. It's gonna be echolocation."

"But I've only just recommenced echolocation after a five-year lapse."

"That's the point. How quickly you pick it up. That's what they're going to be looking for. Do an intro first, off the bat."

"Well, here I am," he says, smiling into the camera. "This is the *me* show"— another smile—"any questions you have, I'll be only too happy to answer." Smile three. "Unless the answer's classified, of course." He laughs.

"Who the hell are you?" one of his minders asks, by way of a prompt.

"Classified." He laughs, showing brilliant teeth. "Okay, since you have the clearance, I guess I can tell you I'm first and foremost a military asset whose activities are top secret. I don't want to sound pompous, but you guys are pretty much the first civilians to get this close." He pauses, frowns. I don't think he was listening to a receiver grafted onto his inner ear, he just looked as if he was. "My locations are top secret. This one is temporary, naturally."

He smiles, stands straight, tall, flat-stomached, broad-shouldered, beautiful—takes a breath. "First and foremost, let's avoid the word *super*, shall we? I'm not made of steel. You pinch me it hurts, you kick me in the genitals I double up in fetal position and howl like a baby—and so far as I know I'm not vulnerable to Kryptonite—ha-ha." He smiles again. "Anyway, it's an overused word that sends the wrong message. *Enhanced* is better, less threatening anyway, but still giving an impression of superiority that alienates ordinary people. To be frank, there was a time when I favored *posthuman* as a serviceable tag, but it's been hijacked by the sci-fi community. In the end we at the base have come to favor *transhuman*, abbreviated to *TH*—let me ask you, how does that sound? No one here overly disturbed by that? That's great, I'll report back. After all, *trans* something means beyond but not necessarily *superior*, right? And it's democratic, too. In our great country, once the technology is in place I personally don't see any reason why every citizen should not one day acquire at least some of the talents, abilities, and mental enhancement that certain great men have, through a lifetime of effort and sacrifice, made available to the community in the person of, well, myself. There always has to be a first man on the Moon, right? Some may even go beyond what I have achieved. It just isn't practical or desirable that one person should take every potential all the way. Eidetic memory, speed reading, and calculating—sure, I have some of all that, but you don't want to get cluttered or unbalanced. I can do ice baths for over an hour, but I can't compete with Wim Hof, who holds the record of over two hours. I can engage eighty percent of my muscles through brain command, but Dr. Mak Yuree can do ninety-five percent. My team thought long and hard and decided to give the cardiovascular aspect priority, after all we're talking here about defense of our great country as the original objective. Now, I know it sounds like showing off and I don't want that, but with sixty percent more red blood cells—well, some of you have seen me fight, right?"

He pauses and remains silent for a minute, then resumes.

"Echolocation: listen." A few beats pass. "Did you hear me clicking? Probably not, we've found ways of taking it out of normal human range, although some children can detect it faintly. What else? I have an excellent visual memory, but we agreed to keep me a grade or two below savant level. When it came to sound, though, well, even before I was selected I loved music, and now I can truthfully say without exaggeration that there is not a tune or musical sound, piece of music from pop to classical that I cannot reproduce at will. Computing power? I'm not quite at Shakuntala Devi's level—she can do the twenty-third root of a two-hundred-and-one digit number, while poor me can't go beyond the eighteenth of a hundred-and-fifty-digit number. Even so, I get by. I can speak backward, which is useful in intelligence work, and naturally in military training my ability to go without sleep for five days at a stretch is invaluable."

"How about sex?" someone in his audience calls out. "Do you fuck? If so, boys or girls?"

He falls into confusion for a moment, but recovers quickly. "You're just testing, right? I'm afraid that's, ah—shall we say another program? One I'm not at liberty to discuss at this time?"

"Could you click, please?" the provocative voice says. "Beijing wants to hear you click."

"Beijing is watching this live? They want me to click? But I thought I'd just made it clear—"

"They say how can they check echolocation if the clicks are inaudible?"

"Okay. Okay. Audible clicks are fine for exhibitions. No use in a fight, though."

"All you need to do is reduce by an octave or two, bring it into the human range."

Confusion again on that pinup face. "Ah, okay, look, I haven't done audible clicks for maybe five years, the whole training was to take them out of the audible range for humans. We did pool training with dolphins—you can't always hear them click either." He frowns. "David's clicks were especially high—I couldn't hear them until the fifth enhancement."

"David?"

"He was my friend. We were allowed to play together every Wednesday. I was sad when that particular program came to a satisfactory conclusion."

"He is your friend but also a dolphin?"

"Was," the Asset says. "I was so depressed, they had to postpone one of the implants."

"You have to learn not to press the sentiment button," a preemptive voice yells. "That's where they're going to attack. When you go public everyone is going to want to prove you're soft and human just like them. Do you want to be just like them?"

"No."

"So, don't let it happen."

"Okay," the Asset says, nods contritely.

"Were there any other animals in any of the other programs?"

"David was not an animal, he was a wonderful, magical being."

"Don't you hate them for destroying him? Was he a threat to the security of the great nation? Did he suffer?"

Bewildered, the Asset sits down on the chair and closes his eyes. The moment passes, he loads another program and stands again. Smiles. "Naturally there will be those who object to the whole idea of transhumanity, but progress cannot be stopped. No doubt there were those who saw the wheel as an invention of the devil, but we need to maintain a perspective. Artificial enhancement of human beings is not new, although we are the only species that practices it. Already there are so many artificial extensions of our senses: hearing aids, false teeth and breasts, buttock implants, tattoos, the motorcar, spectacles, telescopes and Moon landings, fertilizer and GM foods, everything. It may well be true, although I hate to brag, that I am the leading edge in a new phase of this evolution, but as I believe I have already made clear—"

Someone yells a word that must mean *cut*.

"We've lost Beijing," someone says.

"You see, isn't technology wonderful?" the Asset says, triumphant again.

The movie stops abruptly, people in our audience shift around and whisper in Mandarin, then it starts again. Now the Asset in the movie is onstage blindfolded with a thick black band and using his hands to bat back tennis balls that are thrown gently at him. The camera focuses closely on the balls as they reach the Asset in high lopes and the careful way he bats them back in pretty much the direction they came from. There is also a close-up of the band across his eyes.

"That's okay," a voice says, "that's pretty damn good, but we would like to hear the clicks. This is science, right, and sport, it's not magic. People don't hear the clicks, they're going to think you're cheating. That's just the way the mind works. The miracles have to be explicable, even when they're not."

Suddenly as each ball approaches we hear a series of clicks from the Asset so rapid they are like a single sound. "Great, that's just great. Is Beijing getting this?"

"Yep," a voice says.

"Okay, so increase the speed. Keep the clicks audible. Increase the speed steadily, when he starts to miss *do not slow*, keep at that speed until he gets his mojo back."

There must be a machine hurling the balls at him. The speed increases until he can no longer react fast enough. The cameraman does not need to be told to focus on his face at this point. The struggle there is titanic, filled with rage and madness barely under control. Still the balls keep flying at him, still he keeps missing them. Then little by little he masters his own technology and is able to echolocate each ball at amazing speed. The clicks rise in pitch until they become inaudible, however.

"Okay, that's great. Look, you can't click that fast at audible levels, that's okay, we'll use a machine to show you are still actually clicking. But this time we're going to use smaller, more solid objects going faster. Golf balls. Okay?"

"Okay, fire away."

There is confidence in the tone. He has conquered the new game and is able to accelerate at will. Finally, to show his total mastery, he deflects one of the golf balls back into the audience. "Ouch," someone says. It is the voice that has been giving the orders. Laughter.

"Okay, cut," Goldman says and turns on the lights. "That's it, timed out. I have to get this back to where I borrowed it before the next security shift. Everybody out. Hope you enjoyed the show. You all know where and how to contact me. Good night."

14

In the cab on the way to Pat Pong with Professor Chu, Chanya and I cannot decide what it was we just saw: a sales pitch, a military demonstration, a game, a home movie show? Somehow the inferior and amateur quality of the video made it convincing. No one does poor photography anymore, we're all pros these days. It is Krom who sets the tone.

"So, the Asset is definitely close to escape velocity, if the video tonight was genuine." She looks at Chu.

"I think it was genuine," Chu says. "I'm convinced. Of course, it could have been a mock-up, but I doubt it. The first thing a serious potential buyer will do is test the echolocation for himself, so there isn't really a chance to cheat."

"Goldman must be desperate to break all the rules like that."

"I think he has clearance," Chu says. "I don't think he really 'borrowed' that tape surreptitiously."

"How come?"

"The gap is narrowing," the Professor says. "The others. The competition."

Krom turns to us to explain something important that the Professor already understands: "If that echolocation exercise was the real thing, that demonstrates much more than a capacity to catch balls blindfolded. That pretty much demonstrates accelerated learning capacity no one else has yet reached. Anywhere, ever. It's the grail of the TH community: ALE. That's why Goldman was willing to take the risk to show it to that ministry."

"Professor Chu's ministry?" Chanya wants to know.

"No," Krom says with an affectionate smile, "another ministry."

"The other ministry the cameramen come from?"

"No," Krom says, the smile wearing a little. "Yet another."

"I don't get quite why the learning capacity is so important. I mean, on an abstract level, sure, it's what humans are better at than animals, we learn quicker. But why does it get that kind of respect?"

"Because it's not just a demonstration of physical coordination of a high order. For him to learn to catch the balls that fast he had to tap into accelerated evolution. It involves not just physical response mechanisms but the intellect as well—and computing capacity. Personality. Everything, but especially personality. That is not a totally human human anymore."

"What is it then?"

"Is it okay to use the word *spiritual*?"

"You mean he's become like a Buddha?"

"No. Like a demon. A pre-Christian, pre-Buddhist god. Pagan. Like something out of a Hindu temple, or pre-Roman Europe." She pauses to think for a moment. "Once you get into this technology all kinds of things start to make sense that didn't before."

"You mean this technology is not totally new?"

"They're starting to think all the great ancient societies had it. It's what we refer to ignorantly as magic. A superior science that led to catastrophic hubris—all the ancient cultures have that folk memory."

"So we're starting back on the road to catastrophe?" Chanya says.

"Personally, I think we're at the end, on the brink."

"That's why we all find the Asset so fascinating," Chu says as we reach the bars.

"So what is *escape velocity* in this context?" Chanya asks, too late because we are all distracted getting out of the car. Then we are distracted by Chu. We remember the formerly most intriguing question of the night: which way did he swing?

The answer was, with hindsight, inevitable: *katoeys*. I'm afraid the Professor turned quite coy about those bars he most wanted to visit, which led Chanya to put him in her *Total Jerk* file even before he turned giggly. It was amazing. Krom and I finally decided to try him out in one of the tranny bars after seeing no serious spark of desire generated in the gay or the straight bars. In the Love Me Tender, however, the quality of the surgery together with the unnerving beauty of its products was damned impressive. Chu grew a beam on his face that quickly developed into an attitude of gratitude and generosity toward us for bringing him to paradise. He insisted on paying for round after round of drinks, while round after round of exquisite products of the gender reassignment industry came to pay him close attention. By the time he had settled on three that he wanted to take home, Krom had already disappeared to the lesbian bars on the other side of Surawong. Chanya and I caught a cab.

"Krom made a pass at me," she said to the window in a soft mutter.

"She did? When? In the bathroom at the restaurant?" That was the only time they were alone together, as far as I could remember.

"Yes. It wasn't aggressive and I'm not even sure she wanted to do it. I mean, something like that could ruin this little partnership she has with you, couldn't it?"

"So why did she do it?"

"Because she couldn't help herself." A pause. "I turned her down, of course."

15

I decide that the evening with Professor Chu definitely constituted work and I am therefore entitled to take the day off. But I have to visit the station that evening to clear the backlog of e-mails, which turn out to be a good few hours' work. I stroll home and find Chanya still awake and watching an old Thai soap on YouTube.

"Did you switch your phone off?"

I check my phone, see it is switched off. "Yes. Shut it when I was trying to clear the e-mails. Forgot to switch it on again."

"Uh-huh."

She wrenches her eyes from the movie. Now I see it is not a soap but a comic version of the Nang Mak ghost story, about a Thai woman so devoted to her husband that she manages to return from the Other Side and serve him as a ghost—until he finds out and she has the kind of destructive tantrum only ghosts can do well (half the village dies from her curse in this version). Chanya pauses the movie in order to speak in a gentle voice. I have a feeling we are about to have a serious conversation about me.

"Sonchai, Krom called earlier."

"Ah-ha!"

"She said she was looking for you, but maybe she was looking for a chance to talk to me."

"To chat you up?"

She scowls. "No, to talk about you."

"What about me?"

"Your mental health."

"Really."

She turns from the screen to give me her full attention. "We had quite a talk, but it kept coming down to the same thing. I told her what kind of state you are in. Sonchai, now that you've at least come out with your father obsession—we both agreed that's a good sign, so much better than having it festering away inside—surely you've got to see your mother about it? About him?"

"I will. Soon. A good detective doesn't question the key witness until he has his ducks in a row."

She grabs my chin and turns it until I'm looking at her. "You're scared, aren't you? It's Psychology 101: people are plagued by two opposing drives—the drive to know and the drive not to know."

I break away from her to go to the window. On the road all is still under the streetlights. "You spoke to Nong?"

"Yes, after Krom called."

"And?"

"She said she'd be in her bar tomorrow at about nine in the morning—there's some inventory she needs to check on. She said you could stop by then, if there's something you need to say or know." She lets a couple of beats pass. "Frankly, Sonchai, how likely is it that she doesn't even know his name?"

"His name's *Jack*," I say plaintively.

"C'mon, Sonchai."

"Are you sure Krom wasn't using me as an excuse to get close to you? You're the one said she made a pass at you at the Heaven's Gate Tower."

"Maybe I was mistaken. It was ambiguous anyway."

"Or did you make a pass at her?"

She slaps her desk and glares at me. "Okay, you win. You don't want to talk about it, that's fine." She turns back to her soap. I figure she's going to watch the movie all through, and I can't sleep with the light from her screen blazing away, so I decide to smoke a joint—I'm not sure I'm strong enough for more oil just now. I'm pretty mellow when she comes to bed. I assume she is still pissed off with me after our little spat, but instead she curls up beside me and starts to play with my dick.

"I'm not in the mood," I say.

"So why is it getting bigger?"

"A man lies down to relax, the blood in his head makes its way downwards. Not every erection is a tribute to the love object."

"Really?" She jiggles a little more at exactly the right calibration of touch and rhythm. We've been together a long time, after all.

"Okay, I'm persuadable."

She disappears under the sheet to go to work on me. When she pops up again she has reverted to manual labor, but very skillful. "Sonchai," she says in the cozy voice she uses for moments like this.

"Yes?"

"Suppose I did have a little fling with Krom. Would it upset you very much?"

I freeze for a moment, then relax and scratch my jaw. That's quite a question. "I'm not sure."

"It wouldn't be the same as if I went with a man, would it?"

"Maybe not."

"I mean, it wouldn't be like some rival had usurped my womb and thereby threatened the survival of your line, your DNA? The sort of thing male lions get het up about."

"I guess not."

"But you would be hurt?"

"I'm not sure."

The hand goes on strike. "Sonchai, I'm trying to have a mature adult dialogue here. You're my number one relationship, that's final. I don't want to damage us by being selfish."

"I hate it when you do this soft, liberal, middle-class stuff. It's so condescending. Like you hold all the cards and aren't you great for not acting like a fascist bitch."

Now the hand has relinquished the love object altogether. This has the effect of making me feel lonely. Under the guiding influence of cannabis I grab the hand and put it back. I hold it there in a viselike grip. "Why don't you admit that was what her call was all about? You discussed having an affair, didn't you?"

Instead of pulling back, because I won't let her, she tries to strangle it. "Okay, yes, we did kind of touch on the subject when she called. You were definitely the main point, but then we talked about it."

"And?"

"I said I would want you to be okay with it."

"Okay with it? What does that mean?"

She sighs. I release my hand. She relaxes her grip and returns to the traditional up-and-down motion. "It means if I had the fling with Krom would you use it as an excuse?"

"To do what?"

She pauses and grips tight again. "Screw that new girl at your mother's bar. I've seen the way you look at her."

I honestly hadn't thought of that. Her name is Katrina, a *leuk kreung* like me with a Russian absentee father, twenty-three, stunning, with everything still firm. Now my dear wife has really given me a hard-on. "You bet," I murmur.

"Bastard," she murmurs back. She lets go and withdraws the hand, leaving me desolate and lonely. Then she jumps on me. That's okay, we don't have the crime of marital rape over here; basically, you get into bed naked with someone, you take your chances (am I being a tad too robust for you here, R?). Anyway, if she's channeling Krom, I'm definitely fantasizing that she's Katrina.

Afterward we are relaxed rather than blissed. The tension is gone. Chanya curls up against me. In the silence and the dark I wonder about my lover. For her the thought of doing anything new and challenging, like sleeping with a woman for the first time, is a welcome cure for an extreme numbness. It could just as well have been base jumping.

Now, in the way of all humans, especially stoned humans, my mind switches to something completely different. A memory that hitherto had no relevance to the present pops up in perfect clarity. It went like this:

I heard the first whisper one hot humid afternoon on Soi Cowboy. The Isaan lingerie vendors were selling bras and panties from their stalls through oral hire purchase agreements, the cooked-food stands were doing a roaring trade, and the motorbike taxi jocks were practicing kung fu while making lewd offers to every female who passed. The *soi* boasted its usual abundance of attractive women under thirty and not a one of them looked more *fatale* than any regular country lass in shorts and T-shirt, yawning, eating, and gossiping al fresco on a sultry day. The sorcery of sex and money would transform them into irresistible succubi at exactly seven p.m., not a minute before.

They all knew me and I knew them, mostly because they all wanted to work for my mother, Nong, at the Old Man's Club. Mama Nong paid better than all the other bars because Police Colonel Vikorn owned most of the business. She didn't need to bribe cops so she had a wider profit margin; therefore she could be choosy, and she was. She chose girls like a seasoned wine taster chooses wine. Sometimes she surprised even me, taking on a girl who didn't come close to a rival in looks and body, but possessed a certain extra something that Nong herself had owned in her day: magic that could turn a poor girl into a rich one overnight. All you needed was the talent to make a man believe with all his soul that he couldn't live without you, even though you were, well, an article for sale among thousands. That's all. I understand you call it capitalist democracy, R, over there in the West.

Now O called out from across the street: "Hey, Sonchai, some old man was asking for you last night. Said he saw you on TV."

As the respectable face of Police Colonel Vikorn's pharmaceutical empire, I was often on TV, giving the kind of glowing account of our district's law enforcement record that *farang* like to hear. Naturally, I speak in English. No Thai would believe a word, but I didn't feel guilty or impure about this particular duty. If the world currency is hype and hypocrisy, then hype and hypocrisy it must be. Survival has always been the guiding fundamental on these shores.

"Really? So, what bar are you working in now?"

"Rawhide."

"How is it?"

"Oh, it's okay. Bit quiet. Any room at the Old Man's?"

"I'll ask, okay?"

"Thanks, Sonchai."

Like the bite of a mosquito—how are you supposed to know it's malarial?

It happened the next afternoon too. This time it wasn't just hot and humid; the heavens opened when I was halfway between Country Road and Suzy Wong's, so I dived into the Pink Pussy where I'd misspent much of the sperm of my youth. Some of the girls who really were girls then are still there, mostly as entrepreneurs introducing customers to new arrivals from Buriram (there's a saying: *Are there any pretty girls left in Buriram?*). "Hey, Sonchai," Lalita said, "some old man was in here last night asking about you."

"Really? Did you tell him to look for me at the Old Man's Club?"

"Of course. He said he knew that."

I shrugged. "That's all?"

"He bought me a drink."

I waited for the punch line. When it didn't come, I said, "So, did he take you upstairs?"

She smirked. "For an old man he was really cute. Kind in bed and very funny. Very generous, too—we only lasted thirty minutes and he gave me two thousand baht."

"Anything else about him you noticed?"

"Just the way he was—kind of hard, but knew all about sex. Different. He wasn't your usual wick-dipper, that's for sure."

I didn't think any more of it until the next day when it happened again. The reportage came from Superbar this time. And then from Blue Balls. It finally dawned on me that he was playing some kind of game, this mysterious old man who claimed to be looking for me, but never looked for me in the Old Man's Club, where he would surely have found me. Then one evening, at about ten p.m., I was strolling down the *soi* to grab some fresh air, having been on the go at the Old Man's since five in the evening, when I saw an aging *farang* leaning against a wall at the end of the street, staring at me. What impressed me most was that he was standing under some exterior air-conditioning that split the light into a joyful spectrum of colors, which were raining all over him.

I wondered if this was the old man who had been asking about me—and should I be thinking about personal security? To avoid any kind of problem I deliberately averted my eyes, turned, and walked back to Mama Nong's bar. Only then I allowed myself to reproduce the image of him in my imagination: he reminded me just a tad of Brando in *Last Tango in Paris*. In Europe or North America he would have been wearing a sweatshirt under a gray raincoat open at the front, disclosing once-impressive musculature—and showing signs of alcoholism. That night he was in long shorts and T-shirt, like me, and drinking from a can of iced lemon tea. An old man, sure, but a dangerous one. And there was something else that only returned to me with hindsight: a look in his eye unmistakable to any cop who has had to do with the desperate and the damned. This man had firsthand experience of what shits the gods can be and, unlike the timid majority, intended to tell them so face-to-face when he met them.

That was it. I never saw him again and there was no reason at all to keep the memory in the foreground—until now. I am quite certain that old man is one of the old men in the hospital ward. On the other hand, throughout my life absolute certainties have turned out to be misleading products of despair, so I'm probably wrong. It would be nice to know, though, for sure.

The memory of the "Rainbow Man" continued to haunt me into the next morning. Nowadays there is a way of finding out who your father is, of course; or, to be more precise, who he is not. For a while I thought about enlisting the skills of the forensic team at the station, but decided it would have been too embarrassing. The news would have spread like a computer virus.

A quick search in YouTube using the key words *DNA Paternity Testing Kit* revealed that there existed a quick, shame-free solution provided at low cost by Know the Father Laboratories Incorporated, based in Kentucky. Part of the sales strategy of Know the Father involved a clip from a reality TV show where a sobbing, torn-apart young woman swears on every holy book she's heard of that the child is *his* (pointing at the image of a man on a ten-foot video screen beamed in safely from another county), while the putative father on the screen darkly mumbles that he doesn't believe her and she is a lying whore.

In the video clip the presenter ratchets up the drama and illustrates the power of the product by pushing the distraught mother to her limits: "We need the truth now, Jeanie, if you have any doubts, anything you want to say, honey, that you haven't said already, any little indiscretion you've covered up till now, this is the moment."

"I swear by Almighty God I've been faithful and true, may I be struck by lightning and go to hell if I lie."

Groans, cheers, and great roars of empathy from the audience. Everyone's on her side, including me. Cut back to the giant screen where simmers the jealous bastard who is in the process of ruining a perfect marriage and losing a faithful caring wife along with his beautiful bouncing baby through Stone Age possessiveness (it doesn't help that he's a three-hundred-pound slob with a black walrus mustache and shaved head): "I'm tellin' you the kid ain't mine. That ain't my nose, it ain't my chin, and they ain't my eyes." Boos and jeers from the indignant audience.

Now a drum roll while the presenter unwraps the lab results: "DNA does not lie, ladies and gentlemen: the man you see on the video screen over there is . . . *not* the father." Astonishment and incredulity from the audience (*Man that bitch can act! Sure had me fooled*). The guilty mother collapses prone on the stage, sobbing her heart out: there goes the child support. Voyeurism that ancient Rome would have been proud to indulge at the Colosseum. At the bottom of the video clip: *Know the Father, it's YOUR right.*

After the clip came the demo: you send for the package, it arrives within days wherever you are in the world. There are two envelopes and a number of swabs like Q-tips. You take one of the swabs and roll it around inside the cheek of the putative father, then you take another and roll it around inside the cheek of the child. The envelopes are clearly distinguished with capitals, one with an enormous *PF*, the other with a *C*. Naturally, you need to make sure you put the right ensalivated swab in the right envelope; this is emphasized three times. Before you send off the envelopes you pay the fee using a credit card. In my case I sent off to Know the Father for three packs, just to be sure. Swabbing would be a cinch, since all three suspects were supine on hospital beds and not in a position to refuse. Anyway, at my age there was no risk of a claim for child support, and none of them seemed to be in long-term relationships, so they had nothing to fear. Best to do it while they were unconscious, though, just to be on the safe side. I took care to use Chanya's PC and her e-mail account to order the kit.

16

My mother was slightly drunk by the time I arrived at her bar. She, who rarely drinks during the day, sat at a table where four empty bottles of Chang beer stood like soldiers and she was sucking at a fifth when I walked in. A Marlboro Red was sending a spiral of blue-gray smoke up from an ashtray. She was still a good-looking woman, but for me, right now—well, this might have been the first time she looked old.

She threw me a guilty look when I entered. That in itself was a first. She brought me up in the old way: I owed her my life, period. Any transgressions by her were automatically discounted by that unbeatable trump. Like most Thai kids, I took in this subliminal message without argument. Now she looked guilty.

We sat in silence for a moment.

"Tell me about him—all of him," I said.

She pulled out her smart phone to call her driver. "We'll have to do it at my house." She waved a hand around the empty bar. "It would be too depressing to talk about it here." We sat in silence together while she finished her beer. A few minutes later we heard a horn outside the bar.

Nong's Mercedes is large, black with tinted windows. It was Vikorn who insisted on it: a gangster's chariot would scare off most of the local mafia, especially since they would assume it was a gift from the Colonel. In the car I sit back to enjoy the sheer comfort of this masterpiece of German engineering; you hardly hear the engine, hardly notice the wonderful acceleration; what you appreciate most is the silent, gentle, seductive air-conditioning: it's nothing like a Toyota Sienna. At the same time I'm thinking, *What really is going on?* Am I on track to find my father, or am I merely a pawn in that global no-man's-land where international gangsterism meets geopolitics?

Now we were turning off Sukhumvit in to a narrow side *soi* that was unexpectedly lined with ficus and other trees, not to mention a lot of big houses behind high walls and gates guarded by CCTV cameras.

When Mama Nong had accumulated enough savings from her European tours, she bought this piece of land in downtown Bang-kok. I vaguely remember a time of great excitement combined with extreme stress: somehow, without documentation and handicapped by an unblemished fiscal virginity—she had never paid tax to any rev-enue department in any country anywhere (she still has not)—she per-suaded a bank manager to grant a small mortgage over the land, but, given the nature of her trade, she was not sure she could always meet the monthly repayments. Somehow she managed, and the purchase turned out to be shrewd beyond her wildest dreams. Over the past thirty years land prices in the city have shot up more than a hundredfold and my mother had no difficulty in mortgaging the quarter acre in order to build a house on it. Personally, I would have preferred an old-style teak structure on stilts with a general hanging-out area under the house, a big garden with a Bodhi tree or two, plenty of flowering shrubs, tropical succulents, and vivid plants with weirdly shaped blossoms. But Nong had been to America and had other ideas. I did get the big garden, the plants, and—a reluctant concession since it made her feel *bannock*— the Bodhi tree. The house, though, albeit on stilts, was essentially a reinforced concrete imitation of something out of American suburbia, with a giant swimming pool, the dead chlorinated blue mass of which was rarely, if ever, pierced by a human form—least of all my mother's, who never swam.

You can take a girl out of the country, but you can't take the country out of the girl. Quite simply, once the house was finished, she reverted, called some female cousins and childhood acquaintances to form a rotating circle of *puans* (friends) with whom she liked to lie on futons and gamble with cards for small stakes, smoking Marlboro Reds, sip-ping a modest amount of beer and rice whiskey, and sharing gossip that provided reportage in extreme detail of the private lives of fel-low villagers whom she had not seen for decades and probably never would again. No hypocrite when it came to exploiting her wealth, as soon as she could afford to she hired a maid from her home village whose lack of initiative and low IQ made it easy for Mum to underpay her at the same time as keeping her cooped up in a small room next to the kitchen where she slept, ate, watched TV, and did the ironing. Fortunately Maymay, the maid, was also devoid of sex drive, for not only would the owner of the Old Man's Club forbid any kind of hanky-panky on her private premises, but she would likely forbid it even in a short-term hotel on Maymay's day off, for Nong was quite Confucian in regard to slave control. As I've said, though, my mother knew how to pick women, and the faithful Maymay generally spent her free Sun-days in her room sleeping, watching TV, eating, and ironing. I had a strong sense that for the first time since my birth, Mum was about to drop her tough, indomitable front and share something of her inner life. I was right. She did and the memory is present and vivid.

When we reach her house we ignore the main entrance and instead use a gate at the side that leads to the garden. Maymay is there, stand-ing still, facing the Bodhi tree: a pure soul in a religious trance, or an idiot with a vacant stare? Nobody knows. Nong calls her softly, though, to be on the safe side, and orders an ice bucket with a bottle of Mekong and some glasses, then excuses herself and goes into the house. She emerges a few minutes later in a baggy housecoat and slippers. She is as happy squatting as sitting on a chair; now she descends to a rush mat set next to a low table, sits cross-legged, takes out a box of Marlboro Reds, and lights up. After a couple of tokes she says:

"So you have questions. Where would you like to start?" I shrug. "The question you haven't asked, which I expected you to ask—which you should have asked by now, Detective, is—?"

"What?"

"Why didn't I cut his dick off when I had the chance?"

I splutter. The punishment to which she refers is less common than it used to be in Southeast Asia. Nong, though, in her younger years, was just the kind of Thai girl capable of exacting that kind of revenge from a man who did her wrong, the logic being that he would not repeat the error in this lifetime. "Okay," I croak. "Why didn't you?"

She stares out over her garden, sighs. "A child is born, the first thing you worry about is how to keep it alive, feed it, take care of it, live with it for the next fifteen years. You don't worry about unimportant points of history."

"So, what are you saying?"

"That it was just easier to let you believe the simple version—the version everyone else also believes. That way you wouldn't grow up confused. All along Soi Cowboy there are women around my age who had *leuk kreung* kids with *farang* men who disappeared as soon as they fell pregnant. All those women were on the game at the time. It was just easier to let you see it that way."

"I don't follow."

She nods. "Naturally. That's the whole point. If you can't follow now, after fifteen years as a cop, how would you have been able to follow at age seven, or ten, or even fourteen? And after that there was no point, you were off having sex and stealing cars and doing drugs—you'd lost interest in your personal history. Like all teens you were only interested in your personal present."

"Will you just get on with it? I have no idea what you're talking about."

"Think about it. I had only just started in that bar in Pat Pong. The *mamasan* was going to hold an auction for my virginity, as was the custom. She expected to make a fat profit, half of which she would share with me—or one of my uncles would have killed her. It was that kind of arrangement. Considering my good looks, she was going to ask one hundred thousand baht—there are always men with a virginity fetish willing to pay that kind of money, not all of them Japanese. Then your father walked in. Fresh-faced, tall, handsome to die for, weirdly innocent, on five days R&R from Vietnam. He'd never hired flesh, least of all taken part in an auction for a virgin. He wanted me, though, without actually realizing what wanting me might mean. Just like America had to save the world from communism, so he just had to stop the *mamasan* from selling me, and the only way he could do that was by buying me himself. I'd never seen a man in such a state. All I did was sit with him for an hour, holding his hand, wondering when he was going to take me upstairs to the cubicles, while his face went through all those weird moods: you know, when men have the hots and feel guilty?

He kept eyeballing me and telling me very earnest things in English which I couldn't understand. All I could think of was how big he was and if his dick was in proportion, it was really going to hurt and maybe I should send out for some painkillers and K-Y Jelly in advance."

Her cigarette has gone out. She lights another and contemplates her garden.

"He certainly seduced himself, though. By the time he was through with the eyeballing he was sobbing his heart out. He found another girl to interpret and said he'd never set eyes on a woman so perfect in body, face, and soul. Buddha knows where he got the *soul* part from. I think he was blown away by my being a virgin—it hit him in some special place. He told the *mamasan* that if she would only hold off for a couple of days, he would find the money. He went into the big performance and the *mamasan* agreed to wait for him to come back with the dough: there weren't any immediate offers for my body from other customers at that price. So a couple of days later he's borrowed the money, most of it from Bobby da Silva, his best friend. Now he pays the *mamasan*, and everyone, including me, assumes he's going to take me upstairs to the cubicles, but when the *mamasan* tells him he can have a room without charge for an hour considering what a good customer he's just become, he gets upset all over again. You have to bear in mind, Thais at that time had very little exposure to Western thinking. We had no understanding of the kind of man who would hire a girl just to gawp at her, like an exotic pet. As you know, the fee would have given him the right to have me whenever he wanted for a month afterward, any way he liked."

Nong takes a long sip of Mekong and stares out over her garden. It is one of her contradictions that this consummate businesswoman never thinks of redeveloping her land to build an apartment building on it and make a big fat profit. She loves simply owning it.

"Even today it's kind of unreal to me, how he wouldn't touch me without my permission. But now I understand he was acting honorably according to his culture. There were times when I wished he'd just get on and screw me, instead of that sickly self-restraint they use to make themselves feel virtuous." She sighs. "But that's the way it was. After a couple of days, I had to ask, 'What are you going to do with me?' I couldn't very well go back to the bar, after he'd paid all that money.

And he had to return to the war." She takes a toke on the Marlboro Red. "Screw me? Bust my hymen?—oh, no, that would be exploitative. So he has me undress in front of him ten times a day. He loves to take pictures, but he's especially creepy about nude photos. He lets me see how he tortures himself about me. I am the sex toy he daren't have sex with. In his fantasies he exploits every inch of my young body—but no sin is ever committed, apart from masturbation. Perhaps he wanted to be able to say that he never had sex with a prostitute. He even tells me that if I like, I can remain a virgin until the day we get married."

I pause over my Mekong. "Married?"

Nong calls her maid again to ask for *that box.* Maymay returns with a container like a portable safe or a large jewelry box made of steel with a small key in the lock. I have never seen it before. Now she digs out a pile of yellowing correspondence and some old faded photos. She hands me one.

My mother, still very young, is standing wearing a sarong between two men. Her hair—and demeanor—are in the way of old Thailand, for the devastation of the late twentieth century had not yet ruined our culture. She is projecting fierceness and courage as she stands between two young American soldiers on R&R—one of them towering over her—who could have been on a jaunt to Coney Island to judge from their dumb grins. Bobby da Silva is a smooth-faced handsome young man with Latin features.

And now I think I understand the message Nong is trying to convey to me: *Imagine these three young people. Nothing they have done or suffered so far has really touched the innocence of their souls. If these two young men have killed, it must have been from a distance, under orders, with no real awareness of the darkness that is about to overwhelm them.*

Now she chooses another photo from her collection and hands it to me. Two big male hands hold a newborn infant. There are signs that it was taken in a hospital, but the main point seems to be the date when I was born, which has been typed onto the picture in large characters at the top. Now she hands me another.

At first I do not understand the next photo. Unlike the previous two, it has been taken in haste, under battle conditions. With some effort I recognize the tall American in the first photo. His face is so distraught that even from this distance of nearly forty years I feel a pang that anyone of my blood should have suffered such a devastating blow. Now I can make out the scene a little better. There is plenty of smoke, but it is obvious that my father's company has suffered a terrible defeat. Uniformed men are caught by the camera while they run to and from a helicopter whose tail can just be made out. And those two bloody objects in the foreground, with some of the cloth still clinging to them, are the legs of one Roberto Eduardo Santos Tavares Melo da Silva: there is a caption to that effect.

In the next picture, Nong and the tall American stand on either side of a wheelchair holding Bobby da Silva, minus his legs. On da Silva's face there is a cripple's look of extreme contempt for the world and its bitter disappointments. On Nong's face is a grim determination that this, too, was something to be endured and overcome. I look up and stare at my mother, whose mood has changed now that she has begun to remember.

"Your wife practically begged me to talk to you about this, which is why we're here, but I didn't think it would hit me this way." She gestures toward the picture with the amputee. "You don't realize how soft you get—I could take it when I was twenty, but not anymore." She looks me in the eyes. "And you have to think about my strategy as a mother. How easy would it have been to show you a picture of a man you would never meet?"

She is right. I really cannot get my mind around the idea that the man in the picture is my father, and yet remains unreachable. I try to think which of the old men in the ward he most resembles, and realize the attempt is useless. Even without bandages a man of seventy or so does not necessarily resemble that same man aged twenty—the distance is too great, the changes wrought by a harsh world too extreme. Maybe some kind of clever isometric software would do it, but I feel helpless. Maybe Chanya was right after all: in some part of me I really don't want to know. Nong is watching my features, reading me effortlessly.

Despite her reluctance, she hands me another photo. Unlike the other pictures, it has been taken surreptitiously and seems at first to make no sense. It was taken through the open door of what appeared to be a hospital ward or activities area, but there is only one human figure. I cannot say for sure who it is, for it could have been any man—

which was just another way of saying it is *him:* a man still evidently young sitting in a tubular chair, bent forward, turned slightly to the camera with both hands pressed insanely against his ears so that his whole face is squashed as if lamenting the loss of his soul. There are a pile of medications on the table next to him.

Now I really cannot take any more. Nong nudges me and shoves under my nose the photo of her and my father and his friend in the very early days together.

"Look, will you!" She puts her finger on my father, aged about twenty. "Is that an angel or an alien, I never could decide?" I look at the bright—*too* bright—face, that full smile that seems like an exaggeration to non-Americans; the expression suggests he was wired more into the higher cosmos rather than the Earth. "See, Bobby da Silva is innocent, too, but it's a different kind. He's in his body and sex is not a source of torment for him, it's a thirst he knows how to quench."

I borrow a cigarette from her, which she lights for me. I lie back on the futon, take a toke on the cigarette, and then raise myself for a good long slug of the rice whiskey.

"So, you were living with my father but not screwing him?"

She shrugs. "Living with? He and Bobby were staying at a cheap hotel while he was on R&R. This all happened in the space of a few days."

I nod. "Okay. So what happened?"

"What happened? What always happens when a man is confused in that way? All of a sudden, the night before we were supposed to say goodbye, he snapped and jumped on me. It was totally clumsy and he was finished in less than a minute, the whole buildup of the past five days popped in a single spasm. Blood, pain, and sperm is what happened. Then he was gone. But he'd come inside me. Good boys are always the most dangerous. A whoremonger would have banged me the first night and used protection and we all would have lived happily ever after."

Of course, that makes me feel just great. She catches my forlorn eye and leans over to pat my head. "But then I would never have had you, would I?"

I grunt.

"And I thought afterward the bump that was growing in my womb was a kind of claim of ownership by a man who didn't want to admit he was made of flesh and blood."

I cannot say I am overly thrilled to be the product of an incompetently managed spasm that lasted maybe ten seconds—exactly the kind the girls in the bar make fun of after they've been paid and the john's gone home. On the other hand, I wonder who on earth is not the end result of an unsatisfactory beginning. Were you planned, yourself, R?

"So he left you like that? Did he send money?"

"Sure. This was an honorable white boy, sure he sent money. He sent the little money the army gave him, and he even found a close friend in the States who wired me five thousand dollars, which was a huge sum for a Thai girl at that time—and of course I had half the money he'd paid the *mamasan*. And he wrote every day. Promised he would come see me the minute they discharged him—or the war ended." She pauses and stares into space. "I couldn't believe it. Every single day he tells me he's totally crazy about me, keeps my picture next to his heart, I'm the only reason he can carry on fighting in the filthy war. To a Thai country girl, this is Hollywood dreamland stuff. I couldn't believe he was serious."

"But you replied?"

"Sure."

"But you told me you didn't know his family name."

She makes a scoffing noise. "Don't turn into a junior detective all over again. I had enough of that when you were at the academy. Listen: I didn't know his family name because I didn't know about *farang* family names, and anyway I couldn't write in English any more than I could speak it. You know very well I still don't write it. I had someone read me the letters."

"Who?"

"I took them to the Wat and asked Phra Tatatika—you remember that *farang* monk?"

I remember: her favorite monk was an American former marine, almost the first in a trickle that became a steady stream of *farang* men looking for a way of escape in a Thai monastery. I guess a former marine would not have been shocked by my father's letters.

"But you said you replied?"

She takes a pen out of her box. Carefully and slowly she writes down one of the few phrases she knows in written English on the back of one of the envelopes: *I miss you.* I smile. It is a translation of exactly the Thai phrase she would have used. We tend to say *I miss you* where *farang* might say *I'm crazy about you.*

"That's all you wrote, each time?"

"Once a week. There was no use writing in Thai, was there?"

"And during that time, were you—"

"No, I wasn't. So long as he sent money and paid my bar fine after the down payment ran out, I didn't work. I was a good Buddhist girl, a deal is a deal."

"But the envelope," I exclaim triumphantly. "How did you write the address?"

"Huh! Some detective after all! You need to check your facts. Nobody in the world could remember such an address, with all those military numbers, codes, stuff like that. He sent stamped addressed envelopes, the military stuff was already printed on the front."

"Every day?"

She opens her arms. "Maybe there was nothing else to do. You know what they say about war, ninety-nine percent boredom, one percent terror? He couldn't keep writing to his mother to tell her not to worry and that he'd be home soon."

"But he did write, just like he said he would. He did love you?"

"Was it love? I don't know. I'm not sure either of us was mature enough to use that word, but we were very excited by each other. And of course I thought I'd escaped the poverty trap for life on my very first night on the game. I was in a kind of dream."

I give her time to review the memory. When she fails to continue, I say, "So, I still don't understand. You had everything you wanted, you scored the jackpot in your first week, he thought he'd bagged the most fantastic woman in the world. It doesn't sound tragic. He was writing to you every day, telling you how much he adored you." I raise my hands and shoulders.

She takes the wad of photos from her box and flips through them until she comes to the one with Bobby da Silva in a wheelchair. "That happened."

Now she shows me the inside of the box where letters are neatly stacked. "See, this is before." A pile of jagged envelopes where she had opened them. "And this is after": perhaps as many as a hundred unopened envelopes.

"You didn't open them?"

"I got sick of what he was saying. I couldn't stand it." She looks me in the eye. "You have to remember, I couldn't read English. I was embarrassed to have someone else read me that junk."

Now she is finally ready to deliver her punch line. "It was a different man with a different name. He told me I may as well keep calling him *Jack*, but in fact he had changed identity. I may have been a no-good bar girl with poor karma, but I was still a Buddhist. I couldn't take all that hatred, that endless poisoning of his mind, all those promises to 'get back at Charlie for me and Bobby.' And the killing of the 'gooks' and the 'slope-heads.'" She stares at me. "He didn't seem to notice the Vietnamese were almost the same race as me. He had volunteered for Special Forces. When I say he was a different man, I mean totally different, unrecognizable. I had the instincts of a new mother. I didn't want my child contaminated. I told him he wasn't going to see you anymore. I told him I didn't want you to inherit a murderer's karma."

It is a hot day here in the garden. A cold shiver shakes me to the bones. "But he visited you afterward—or not?"

She has straightened her back and is sitting cross-legged like an Isaan girl, her strong chin jutting, her eyes closed. "This is as much as I can take, Sonchai. I don't want to talk about it anymore today. You have enough to go on for the moment."

I see that she has made up her mind to say no more. But when I prepare to leave she starts talking again. It is strange behavior. She does not look at me and could have been complaining to the Bodhi tree.

"So, Roberto Eduardo Santos Tavares Melo da Silva lost his legs, this was tragic, a catastrophe, very, very hard to look at. But in war men lose limbs. Thai men don't totally give up on who they are just because their best friend lost his legs. It's because something happened that the white man couldn't control. The gooks were winning—that's what he couldn't stand. The one thing that never occurred to any of them until it was too late, that they might actually lose the war."

"What happened to da Silva?"

"Bobby? I'll tell you what happened to Bobby. He borrowed money from his family to come back here to Bangkok, where he drank and whored himself to death—deliberately. But by then he and your father weren't talking. See, even da Silva hated what your father turned into. He never wanted revenge, he only wanted his legs back, and when he couldn't achieve that, he decided to go out with a bang. Lots of them."

There is no point trying to press her for more information; when Mama Nong says *no*, it means just that. I will have to return for more answers when her mood has changed. I hardly need to point out, R, that the man she has just described bears no resemblance to the "prize buffalo" who would "tear the shed down" if deprived of sex. I seemed to have at least two natural fathers, according to Mum. But by the time I reach the end of the *soi*, my passion for more knowledge overcomes me. I buy an iced lemon tea at the 7-Eleven on the corner, down it, and walk slowly back.

She is waiting for me. I snuck around the side, using my key to the garden door, but she is not surprised when I appear before her, blocking her view of the pool where she sits cross-legged on her mat. She looks up to stare at me, sees something in my eyes that was not there before, and nods.

"You're not leveling," I say. "There's something else. There has to be. Something direct and personal that made you ashamed. That made you not want to tell me the truth. That made you want to break with him totally. It must have been serious—this was the guy who took you to America, right?"

"Did you bring dope?"

"No."

"What are you going to use for anesthetic?"

"Nothing."

She raises her eyes, then gestures for me to sit with her. "Of course, you've guessed he came back?"

"Yes."

"Okay. So he came back."

She pauses for so long, staring at the Bodhi tree, a gnarled triumph of persistent life that hangs over the dead blue pool, that I have to say, "Yes?"

She grunts. "It is all so long ago." She stares at the pool. "He'd changed, but so had I. The war was coming to an end. You were about eleven months old, growing fast. Obviously, only a year had passed, but that's a long time in war and people change quickly when they see their loved ones shredded. He wrote to me, but I had stopped replying. A woman in the position I was in then is interested in hearing from the father of her child only if he has something practical to offer. Money would have been great, but even a reliable presence might have been helpful. I wasn't interested in confessions of guilt and how bad he felt about leaving me and how he still had such strong feelings for me." She checks my eyes.

"I thought you didn't read those letters."

She smiles. "Only one in ten. A girl gets curious, after all. And there was some small gratification that he felt so bad—that he was still think-ing of me at all. Frankly, a Thai man in his position would not have stayed in touch." She lights a Marlboro Red, inhales gratefully, exhales.

She swallows. "He came back after about a year and he was exactly the kind of man I had expected him to be on the first date. Oversexed, tough, willful, physically incredibly strong, wired, hyper-alert—a killer. We had the affair we should have had the first time round, but neither of us had known how. I'd been selling my body and he'd been hiring flesh in Vietnam—lots and lots of it. So we both knew everything there is to know about sex. I was still young, in my early twenties, he was only a year older, but you could say it was an affair made in hell. We simply went wild. Like all such things, it lasted maybe a month, then when we cooled down we didn't like what we saw. We didn't like each other and we certainly didn't like the face in the mirror in the morning. The passion died like a damp firework and it was all over. At least as far as anything physical was concerned."

"This is when he took you to America?"

"Yes. You wouldn't remember, but your aunt Mimi looked after you for a month."

"But how was he over there?"

She pauses and then nods. "Stressed, I suppose, although I was too young to look at it like that. He was angry as hell at the way vets were being treated." She looks at me. "He kept getting into fights—except that other men could see what he was and were scared of him. At least five times I had to hold him back—beg him, even. I knew in my bones how easy it would have been for him to kill. I kept telling him I was a Buddhist, I didn't believe in solving problems that way. It was one of the things that broke us up." She gives me a shy look. "That and sex."

"How so?"

"He was voracious. Even with my background I found it hard to cope. Three, four times a day, no letup. Amazing."

She looks at me. It is as though she is challenging me to ask the last big dangerous question. I have no idea what that might be and stare back at her, puzzled. Then it hits me.

"There was another change in him, wasn't there?"

She looks away at the Bodhi tree. "Yes. The wired psychopath who volunteered for Special Forces could not survive—I could see that. To tell the truth, I began to assume he would end up murdered or in jail. But something else happened. He volunteered for some super-secret military project he said had been officially closed down, but was still going strong in secret locations. He said I might read about it one day. I didn't know what he was talking about. All I know is there was some kind of initiation—and he never contacted me again. I assumed he was dead. He is for me, anyway."

I nod. I'm a cop, I think I know when I've got the full story. Without another word I stand up and leave. While I am walking away I am sending a text message to Krom: *Roberto Eduardo Santos Tavares Melo da Silva*. On the one hand, I'm feeling optimistic: that is one very unusual name; if Krom can find his records, then she must be able to find out the names of the other men who were in his squad.

On the other hand, I have at least five images of this strange man, my father: the classic naïf who believed the lies his country told him; the Special Forces psychopath; the MKUltra volunteer—perhaps; the vet locked in vengeful nostalgia for those terrible, intoxicating years four decades ago; the man who, somewhere in all this, really did once love my mother.

17

The parcel from Know the Father Corporation arrived promptly with my DNA sample collection kits. It was quite large because I'd ordered three packs, and came with instructions the tone of which swung abruptly from kindly parental (phrases began with *We at KTFI want you to be comfortable with* . . .) to the fanatical when it came to preventing contagion.

I'm excited about paying a visit to the upmarket hospital in Chinatown to which the three old men have been sent, but when I reach the station there are over three hundred e-mails with my name on them and at least ten percent are urgent and need answering. Then, when I've waded through the e-mails, one of the sergeants wants me down in the cells to interpret for a *farang* couple: Brits who have brought in about ten thousand Ecstasy pills expecting to make a small fortune. Now they are going to spend a few decades in jail and are hysterical and hard to understand. It's about eleven-thirty in the evening when I finally retrieve my pack of DNA sample collectors and grab a cab.

The hospital is crowded, despite the hour. In Asia we are much attached to our traditional cures for common diseases; after all we have been using them for thousands of years and, generally, they all follow the principle that the body should be treated holistically. Acupuncture, Ayurveda, meditation for healing, Chinese herbal remedies all follow this impeccable ideal, and we embrace one or more of them, depending on the case, with faith and reverence—except if the disease hurts like hell or threatens death, when we opt for the quick, artificial, life-denying fixes of *farang* drug-and-cut cures. Sure, we Thais have plenty of folk remedies for gout, for example, which we believe comes from eating too much chicken, but try living with the agony of a swollen knee joint for a month (or have the metatarsal-phalangeal joint at the base of your big toe swell to the size of an orange), while your revered herb master guides you majestically through the Four Natures, Five Flavors, and the Meridians before finally arriving at the Specific Function, when you know that colchicine will fix it in a day. In other words, the international-class Western hospital in Chinatown is always busy—and not only with Western medical tourists (drugs average twenty percent of the cost stateside and the atmosphere is much less militarized). The department for intestinal diseases, for example, is perpetually crowded with Thais who are unable to curb their chili habits despite the holes the pepper burns in their intestines.

It is close to midnight by the time I arrive at the special ward to which they have transferred the three American vets. The huge hospital is as alive and vibrant as the go-go bars at this time; many of the patients are on Western time schedules, especially those who have popped over from California to change sex on the way to the beach. A guard takes me up to the ward in a special lift; there are two more guards at the door to the ward, which is very small and at this time contains only three beds and as many patients. A large sign in Thai and English says: SILENCE. It seems the Registrar sent the fingerprints of the three oldies to the American embassy, who maybe checked with Veterans Affairs, or the U.S. military, and came back with their names within the hour. Now I read the names at the ends of the beds upon which three men lie unconscious: Willie J. Schwartz, Larry Krank, and Harry Berg.

Harry Berg is the closest to death, but I don't pay him much attention. His breathing is shallow, there is very little brain activity. There is no sign that he will ever resume command of his body, or even want to. Larry Krank is still unconscious but the machines are recording bouts of rapid eye movement, which might prefigure a return to the world. Now I fixate on what I consider my best bet: Willie J. Schwartz, whose middle name is John, but he might be known as *Jack*. I noticed when I entered that he moved his eyelids a few times and may be ready to emerge from his coma. I don't want him to recover just yet, though, and start to open the large envelope into which I've slipped the sterilized envelope with the two swabs. I'm just about to open the seal when one of Larry Krank's machines starts buzzing. It's not an insistent emergency kind of buzz, more like a friendly *hey this guy's waking up* kind of signal. I see that Larry Krank has opened his eyes and is staring at the ceiling. Now a nurse enters, a Thai woman in her forties who looks like one of those devout Buddhists whose life direction was always to help others. She sees me but has no time for me just now. Her nametag says she is Nurse Silapin. She's a pro and only needs one look at Larry to call a doctor. When the doctor enters she doesn't ask him what he wants to do, though. She tells him what drugs she wants to give the patient and the doctor apparently agrees. Now she is calling the hospital pharmacy. Now she is looking at me.

"Detective Jitleecheep," I say, flashing my ID.

"Why are you here, Detective? It will be days before any of these men can speak. Perhaps not even then."

"Just checking," I say, holding the envelope behind my back.

A junior nurse arrives with a drug concoction from the pharmacy and gives the package to the senior nurse, who takes out the vial with the cork top and the disposable syringe. Meanwhile the male doctor leaves the room. I watch in fascination as she plunges the needle into the cork, turns the bottle upside down, withdraws the piston, and fills the syringe with a colorless liquid. I think she is going to inject him in the arm; instead she pulls the sheets down, bares a part of his chest, and stabs him with the needle in the solar plexus at the same time as pressing down hard on the plunger.

It is like watching a resurrection. The big old man opens both blue eyes wide as if he's seen God, sits bolt upright, lets out a scream, then allows himself to descend gracefully back to a lying position.

"Adrenaline and testosterone," the nurse says. "The combination works better with men than women. It's like they're made for the big crude blast. Then they fade on you." She spares Larry Krank a long look. He has closed his eyes again. "He'll pull through, though. He's strong." She offers me a celestial smile. Now she turns to Willie J. Schwartz. Apparently he is the subject of a different experiment. She keeps her eyes on the patient as if she has a keen intuitive understanding of where his mind is at; then, at a given moment, she caresses his bare forearm in a blatantly sensual way. His eyelids spring open. She smirks at me. "It works in fifty percent of cases. It's like most human beings don't really want to return to the world unless there's some love waiting. A tender touch can stimulate the will to live better than any drug."

If old Willie was dreaming of an erotic welcome back to the world, though, he is disappointed. He groans as one glance at the ceiling confirms his worst fear: he's still alive. Now he turns over on one side to go back to sleep. The nurse isn't happy with this idea and asks me to sit and talk to him while she goes to find the doctors. I'm tempted to break out the swabs and stick one in Willie's mouth, but decide against it because I have no idea how long the nurse will take to return. I think there will be more windows of opportunity and with luck I'll be able to do at least two of them. I'm a little nervous about Harry Berg, the one still on the critical list. I don't suppose a swab can be life-threatening, but that kind of fragility is scary—and perhaps there's that cynical thought that I don't really want it to be him, not if he's going to die on me. I decide to wait. After all, none of them are going anywhere, I can return again and again. If the worst comes to the worst, I can find some excuse to swab them for forensic reasons when they're recovered. It is impatience that drives me, though.

The nurse's instruction to keep Willie J. Schwartz's attention is not as easy to follow as one might think. Despite that he has just emerged from a coma that has lasted many days, his overwhelming instinct is to return to it. When I sit on one side of the bed to stimulate him with conversation that will prevent a relapse, he turns over again, leaving me with his back. When I walk around the bed, dragging my chair, to attack from the other side, he turns over once more. At least I can be sure he is fully awake and, apparently, an antisurvivalist of some stature.

"Your friend is awake, he needs you," Nurse Silapin tells him when she returns with two doctors. She has to repeat it three times before he turns his head to look at Larry Krank. At the same time the doctors are forcing Larry to look at Willie. Finally, the two old men recognize each other despite the copious bandages around their heads and chins and start to grin. Apparently the doctors are satisfied with Nurse Silapin's unorthodox methods and the three of them leave the room together, discussing another case.

Now the old men begin to speak in a language that I cannot follow. It seems to be a mixture of English, Vietnamese, and Khmer, with a few Thai words thrown in. My eyes are fixed on Willie J. Schwartz, waiting for a chance to find out what the *J* stands for. Using my English and Thai, with just a smattering of Khmer and no Vietnamese at all, I try to understand some of what they are saying. I want to know what names they use for each other. After a couple of minutes I am able to decipher a scrap of conversation:

"Where the hell are we, Mitch?"

"In a hospital in Bangkok. It's okay, it's a good hospital. The Thais are taking care of us."

"What the fuck happened?"

"He bombed us, Brad. The bastard bombed us."

This news takes a while to penetrate the mind of the man I've been thinking of as Larry Krank, aka Brad. After a while, he turns his head in the other direction, to look at Harry Berg for a few moments. Then he turns back to Willie. He makes a slow kind of jerk of the head in the direction of the other man. Now he utters his first full English phrase.

"What happened to Jack?" Larry asks Willie.

"Looks like he got hit bad, Brad, real bad. I don't know if Jack's gonna make it."

My pulse has doubled. How strange is the human heart! Now I am filled with compassion for the man who I'm certain is my father. *Don't die, Jack,* I mutter. *Whatever you do, don't die.* I stand up, suddenly reckless. The two old men have assumed I'm part of the administration and paid me no mind so far. They look at me. "Did you just call him *Jack*?" I demand.

They look at each other. Willie, aka Mitch, shrugs. I make a quick assessment and decide they're both too old, too vague from drugs and injury, too past it to care. Anyway, if it comes to the crunch, who would believe their word against mine? I break open the first envelope, pull out the second, grab the swabs by the stems, careful not to contaminate the heads, and I'm approaching Harry Berg, aka Jack, when an alarm goes off. I turn to see Willie J. glaring at me in senile outrage. It is only then I notice the big red button on the wall next to his bed and the light flashing above it. Larry Krank, too, is suddenly in a state of military alert.

"He's a fucking cop," Willie says, then reverts to what sounds like expletives in their private language. Then in English: "Trying to fucking bust us when we're —"

The nurse bursts in, sees the swabs, and comes to the same conclusion. Her outrage is of the kind exclusive to the pure of heart. Blood rushes to her head. Guards and doctors appear. Now they're dragging me out and frog-marching me down the corridor to a small room without windows. They lock me in there. Five minutes later a cool Chinese man in a dark suit arrives with two guards. He is the Deputy Registrar.

"Do you have a warrant to take DNA samples from these patients?"

I take a deep breath. "No."

"Please let me see your police ID."

I show him. He nods at one of the guards, who snatches it. "I'll need three photocopies," the Deputy Registrar says.

We wait, staring at each other until the guard arrives with the photocopies. The Chinese gives me my ID back. He nods at the guards, who jerk their chins at me. I stand up. At the door the Deputy Registrar says, "No doubt you will be hearing from your superiors. Our group's legal department will decide how far to take this." He pauses for a moment. "We like to keep on good terms with the Royal Thai Police Force. And the RTPF have good reasons to keep on good terms with us."

My companions and I take a private lift down to reception, where they throw me out. I'm trying to shake myself free from an embarrassment that attacks like a pinching demon, causing me to twitch, and at the same time feel a strong need for further evidence. I hire the first motorbike taxi that passes.

"Where do you want to go?"

"Soi Cowboy," I say.

I have the jockey stop outside the Pink Pussy. Lalita is there sitting at her favorite spot, in shorts and T-shirt. She watches as I get off the bike, pay the driver, and turn to her. She smiles. When I join her on the bench outside the bar, she says, "Are you going to buy me a drink?"

"Sure. Make it a lady's drink if you like, but I'm not here for your body."

She disappears for a moment to fetch the drink, a spoonful of Coke with a dash of rice whiskey, which costs a fortune, half of which she will keep.

She sits next to me again on the bench and says, "I bet I know why you've come."

"Why?"

"You want to ask more about that old man."

"How did you know?"

She shrugs. "Just like that. I know you don't fancy me, so there's only one other reason."

I cover my surprise with a cough. "Okay. You're right."

"What else do you want to know?"

I scratch my jaw. It's a question that occurs regularly in detection. How do you know what you want to know from a witness when you have no idea what the witness knows? She's a smart girl, though, famous for her commercial success.

"You said he was kind with you."

"Kind and clever. Even though he was old he managed to turn me on. He was romantic. Once a year or so you find a customer who wants his sex served with a little romance. I liked it, even though it was pretend romance. Isn't all romance pretend anyway?"

"Sounds like it was promising. Couldn't you find a way to tempt him back?"

"That's what I was doing—making more of an effort than usual."

"And?"

"When he was about to come he called me *Nong*. He'd been calling me Lalita up to then, now he switched. And after we'd finished he burst into tears. He saw I was disappointed, that's why he paid double."

I let a few beats pass. "That's it?"

"Yes. That's it. Nong's your mother's name, isn't it?"

"Every third girl on the street is called Nong."

"I know. But you came back to ask about him. That's why I mentioned it."

18

Obviously, the Asset killed the girl in the market apartment. With his superhuman strength he twisted her head, snapped the vertebrae between C4 and C5, and pulled until it detached from her body. Then he wrote my name on the mirror in blood, including a reference to my father.

As you know, R, normally in police procedurals you are given the identity of the perpetrator one-third of the way through the narrative and have the pleasure of watching the sympathetic, humble, hardworking cop (but s/he's a dead shot with a forty-five) plow their way through the clues in a frenzy (*must stop the bastard before he kills again*) until the cop finally discovers what you the reader already know—whodunit— thus clearing the decks for a nice little orgy of vengeance at the denouement. Here it's different: I-the-cop am now certain *he* dunit, and *he* did it to reach me in a way that hurts the most. That innocent girl with the head of a Buddha died just so he could get my attention. The mystery is *why*? In theory all I have to do is wait. Except that he has disappeared. A week has passed and no trace. Goldman also has disappeared. All I have to play with is that smart phone. Therefore I call over and over again the number of the single entry in Contacts that begins with the Vietnamese country code. If I wake up in the early hours, unable to sleep, the first thing I do is press autodial for that number. No answer. Then, one fine night, around three-fifteen in the morning, I try it and there is an answer.

"Hello?"

The accent is very British, very cultivated, from a more authentic age when such vowels could be uttered without fear of ridicule. For a moment I'm stuck for words. I don't want to wake Chanya, so I get up and take the phone out into the yard. The voice becomes impatient and suspicious: "Yes? Hello?"

There is really only one person it can be. "Dr. Christmas Bride?"

A pause. "Who wants to know?"

"Detective Sonchai Jitpleecheep, Doctor, calling from Bangkok. I was given your number in connection with a case I'm investigating here."

A longer pause while he adjusts his attitude. Then he says, "Bullshit."

I think he is about to close the phone on me. I need a key word to hold him.

"Goldman," I say, "Mr. Joseph Goldman," and let the silence speak for itself. He is in no hurry to rise to the bait.

"I see," he says slowly. "You have my attention. How did you get my number? Who told you to call me?" The tone now is incisive, peremptory, imperial.

"A colleague handed me a telephone in connection with a murder inquiry."

Silence, then, "I don't think that answers my question, does it?"

I decide to risk the truth; half of it anyway. "This number was in the Contacts file of a telephone that may be relevant to a bombing at Klong Toey, here in Bangkok."

A sharp intake of breath.

"You knew about that bombing?" I ask.

"Yes."

"How?"

"Never mind." A pause. "I'm afraid this is all a surprise to me, though frankly not a huge one. I'll have to think about it and call you back."

I have the feeling he will call someone else as soon as I close the phone.

I walk around in circles, waiting for him to call me back. He takes about ten minutes, and now I am certain he has had a hurried conversation with a third party: his attitude is quite different. The Old World courtesy has returned, but he is businesslike, as if I am a task he has agreed to take on.

"Look, thinking this all through, I suggest we meet."

"Do you want to come to Bangkok?"

"I don't think that would answer our needs. Yours, anyway."

"I don't follow. What needs?"

"The story I have to tell is the strangest you'll ever hear, that I can guarantee. It is frankly beyond anyone's credulity, except that it's true. I wouldn't dream of sharing it with you unless I can show you the evidence at the same time. Seeing is believing. Thomas was the only disciple with a brain."

I wonder if the biblical reference has anything to do with his name. "So, what? Shall I come to Saigon?"

"No. There's no evidence here either. I'm afraid we'll have to meet in Phnom Penh—I'm going to have to take you up-country." He utters this last sentence with a sigh, as if under constraint. "How soon can you get there?"

"Phnom Penh? The flight lasts about one hour, there are flights about every hour or two. Give a couple of hours either end, plus time to reach the airport—I suppose I could be there by early evening tomorrow."

"I'll fly from Saigon. Stay at the Foreign Correspondents' Club. I'll do the same." A pause. "I suppose you've begun to have an idea of how big this is, Detective? You're like a man who went fishing for trout and caught a whale."

PART II

THE
JUNGLE

19

In Phnom Penh Dr. Christmas Bride has booked us into the Foreign Correspondents' Club, with splendid views over the river, just before it joins the Mekong. Actually, it isn't a foreign correspondents' club at all, although the old colonial mansion (long verandahs, high ceilings, slow fans) looks the part. It is a private hotel named by its owner in honor of those intrepid reporters who used it as a base from which to file stories about the Khmer Rouge catastrophe, after Nixon and Kissinger destabilized the country with blanket bombing—as in Laos.

The riverside was wild and dangerous at that time, a great place to buy opium, heroin, and as many M-16s and AK-47s as you could carry before you got mugged by a gang carrying even more. Rape was the local sport, along with prostitution, child abuse, and knife fights. Now all that color has moved upstream somewhat, and loud, threatening posters proclaim in English draconian penalties for anyone caught with underage children. There's not a lot of enforcement against local transgressors, however: the campaign is targeting Western men in the hope of jailing them before they return home and abuse European kids; the posters are paid for in euros, after all.

Despite that Cambodia is only an hour by plane from Bangkok, once you add on the rituals of security and state control (they take a mug shot at both ends, you are not allowed to smile or wear glasses) you end up with half a day of travel, which is why the sun is going down even though I left home this morning.

It's still hot, though, hotter than Bangkok, and despite the fans an overwhelming lethargy pins me to my wicker seat in the bar of the FCC, so that all I can do is watch a fisherman with a throw net stand in his boat on the river and cast away just as if the city has grown up around him over the past few hundred years and will no doubt crumble in due course without any effect on his fishing style, or indeed any claim on his attention at all. I order a glass of cold white wine and give myself a moment to think. Travel is a stressful bore these days, and I've spent most of the last few hours checking my passport, completing visa applications, checking that I've not contaminated clothes or luggage with powder from my gun, which of course I could not take (they can pick up a single molecule of saltpeter with those floppy wands they wave all over your bags; if they find any they torture you with interrogations for the next few days). What I am wondering now is, so to speak, merely a lowercase version of my life's most constant theme: *What am I doing here?* I have come on the strength of a single phone call with someone in Saigon. But his name is *Christmas Bride.* Now an old *farang* man enters the bar.

He who I have come to meet is over six foot and skinny in khaki walking shorts, money belt, and T-shirt. Long white hair springs out from his head in all directions. Polar-blue eyes. I am sure much vigor remains in that eighty-something body, but it is the long mobile face one fixes on. Tragic craters transform into blooming smiles that fade into whimsy; a gaze of half-focused benevolence tightens into an interrogator's stare; the mouth taughtens and looks vicious, only to relax again into a grin, which replays every nuance of every kind of grin from sardonic, cynical, cruel to naïve, happy, vulnerable—and back again. The mind behind it all has known and lived every major event in the history of the human psyche from Adam to Mickey Mouse. He is a walking history of consciousness, starting with reptiles and including congress with angels. He is the kind of man you assume is insane until someone tells you he is a psychiatrist from the sixties, when you say, *Oh, right, one of them.*

As he strides toward me with the purposeful grace of yesteryear, hand outstretched, his expression now is deeply and gratefully welcoming, promising hospitality and sensitivity of the highest order.

"Thank you so much for coming," he says in that same tone I first heard on the phone: cultured, clear, beautiful, without the snobbery an inferior soul might express with that Brahmin accent. "Awful bloody trip, isn't it? What are you drinking? Wine? I think I need a double scotch on the rocks." He calls for a waiter using fluent Khmer.

The charm works. I am relaxed, impressed, instantly well-disposed without being intimidated. I am charmed into leaving the narrative, and the explanation, to him. We sit opposite each other at my table on the terrace.

"Names are important, so we should not dispense with the ritual. I am Christmas Bride, at your service."

"I am Sonchai Jitpleecheep."

He bends his head to grasp his chin with a large ruddy hand, frowns. "Hmm. I don't know much Thai, but why *Sonchai*—not *Somchai*? *Somchai* is the common name, no?"

"*Somchai* is the common name. *Sonchai* means to think or dream. Apparently it arises from a mistake my father made."

"Ah-ha! *Sonchai* means to dream? And Jitpleecheep is pretty much unpronounceable for the Western tongue." I smile. "So you are a dreamer camouflaged from one half of yourself—not to mention the world?"

"Got it in one," I say.

Bride takes out a packet of Camel cigarettes, knocks one out, fits it to an ivory cigarette holder, and lights up with a Zippo. He speaks through the first burst of smoke. "Oh, no, please. I'm not being clever here. I'm admiring *your* clever labeling. You've used the barricade to grow behind it beautifully—and in secret—that's the key. Just imagine being lumbered with a moniker like mine." Now the cratered face descends into tragedy tinged with rage. "The bitch was a Catholic of the old school, you see? She'd probably be illegal today." He glares. "Christmas? And coupled with Bride? She thought she was nailing me to the cross at the baptismal font for the duration. I promise you, with a name like that you either crawl under a rock at age twelve and stay there, or you—" He stops himself and smiles.

"Drop acid more than a thousand times and kill God?"

His face is transfused with delight. "Excellent. Excellent. You play the apostate inadequate, then, when the timing's right: *wham!* Fantastic life ploy—wish I'd known of it when I was your age. You must be one demon of a detective." He drops his voice and leans forward. "So, you met dear old Joe Goldman. How was he with you?"

"I watched him through radar for about ten minutes. He was rather involved with the task in hand. He didn't pay me any attention. Then we met again when he showed a promotional video at his apartment in Bangkok. That's all."

He nods. "I have the feeling this is a new field for you. Let me tell you, spies are fascinating, one of those professions like prostitution that has never been properly studied, perhaps because of what it reveals about the world we have made. Goldman is a more or less standard example."

"But your relationship with him is what? How do you know so much? What is going on? Why am I sitting here talking to you in Phnom Penh?"

He takes a long toke on his Camel while he eyes me shrewdly. "Since when has the acquiring of knowledge and experience been that simple, Detective?"

I make signs of frustration. He turns his head to one side and lets some beats pass. "It really is just as I said over the phone. There is no technique for explaining all this in a way that anyone would believe, let alone a trained detective. I beg you to allow me to narrate the thing in my own way." I do not ask, *But why would you want to explain it at all to a total stranger from Bangkok?* I nod instead. "Good. Tonight the prologue, tomorrow the story and the evidence." He orders another double scotch, leans back in the wicker seat, stares out over the river for a good few minutes, takes a long toke on the Camel, then begins:

"Let us go back in time by half a century. We are somewhere in the late fifties or early sixties, our sample subject has been brought up according to the old WASP catechism: it's basically old-fashioned sexism and racism, but the takeaway message is that democracy only works when it is undemocratically controlled by fat wise old white male Protestants. Socialism is the ultimate evil, which you must be prepared to die fighting against if you want to call yourself an American. Oh, yes, I forgot. There's also the best-friend syndrome. A best friend is of the same WASP background as you to the point where he is indistinguishable from you. You will not at any time feel the slightest sexual attraction to your designated best friend, but you will be prepared to die for him if necessary."

He pulls on the cigarette, inhales, exhales with relief and gratitude.

"Don't believe what they tell you about tobacco. Without it I'd have died of boredom twenty years ago. It's just a question of not overdoing it—we need *wisdom*, in other words, and there's precious little of that left in the world." He points to the pack he had placed on the table. "A habit my American friends taught me in the jungle. Do you see, the animal on the front is not a two-hump Bactrian camel as one would have expected, but a dromedary? The manufacturers knew that, of course, but were advised by industrial psychologists that one hump was somehow easier for the average Joe to take in than two. A primitive example of mind control—we've come a long way since then." He sighs. "Not that we Brits are in any way innocent, you understand? I don't mean to imply that. Every dirty trick in the book they learned from us." He muses. "As a matter of fact, there are very few serious geopolitical problems today that were not created by the Foreign Office in London in the eighteenth and nineteenth centuries. Kashmir is probably the best example, after Afghanistan, Iran, Pakistan, Tibet, sub-Saharan Africa, and pretty much the whole of the Near and Middle East. In Tasmania we annihilated a complete race of humans. That all happened when we were civilized Christians, of course."

"What are you saying, Doctor?"

"What am I saying? I'm saying that when we consider a case like— well, let's call him Private Jack Doe as a twenty-year-old GI—we need to strip out a few erroneous assumptions, like he gives a damn about democracy or the plight of third-world Asians, or even has an idea of what those words might mean, or even has a precise idea where Vietnam is. Or is even aware of the excuse for being there at all, except that Uncle Sam knows best. You see, in a nutshell such a background is essentially tribal and shamanic. A lot closer to the mind-set of Crazy Horse or Red Cloud than anyone cares to acknowledge."

"But who exactly are you talking about when you refer to this hypothetical Private Jack Doe?"

He pauses, waves a hand, says, "Later," and continues. "Then some truly world-class idiot grabs Jack and half a million like him and sends them to the other side of the world to kill as many fellow humans as he can manage. If he wants to know why, it is explained using a metaphor from infancy: dominoes. Almost from the start Westmoreland and the

CIA turned it into a body-count war, which is to say a war of extermination.

"Naturally, since Jack has already been initiated he hardly needs to be told that the people he is killing are inferior. The way he has been taught to see it, not only are they socialist, but they are brown-skinned slope-headed communists who have Stone Age technology and eat on the floor. Of course it's okay to kill them. You have to kill them to save them, obviously."

I am upset. The implication of blatant genocide is a little hard for a half-caste like me to take. I try to control my thoughts.

"Right. Then something happens to change his head around? Fall in love with a local girl, for example?"

He looks at me with the curiosity of a man who expects little of life but can still enjoy the thrill of busting a fool's naiveté. "Well, that might do it, temporarily. But it's as easy to fall out of love as it is to fall into it. Very often we fall out of love as a defense against threats to our core identity. I doubt such a boy as I've described could be in love with a communist, for example, for very long. No, I'm thinking of a more radical experience."

"Death? The death or mutilation of a close friend?"

"Certainly, the presence of death is the essential factor in any initiation of depth. But what I'm talking about is something that blows the whole shooting match out of the water. Something so radical it really can break down all that tribal programming in one fourteen-hour period."

I can guess where he's going so I shrug and stare in expectation.

"Lysergic acid diethylamide." He chuckles. "Oh, they were so right to be scared of it, with that uncanny instinct of theirs. Of course, it never came close to screwing up as many lives as alcohol, but it was infinitely more threatening to WASPs." He shakes his head. "I'm not a religious man — as you correctly pointed out, acid helped me kill God — but there was something quite uncanny about the way it appeared at exactly that time."

"How do you mean?"

"I mean just when it was so desperately needed." He catches my eye. "You know what I'm talking about of course?"

"I have an idea, but please tell me."

"Omega Unit 197 of the MKUltra project, to be precise. LSD was my specialization. They were pretty much forced to recruit me, because no one had done as much research on it as had I. Mostly on myself. Acid was universally available in Vietnam, thousands, perhaps tens of thousands of the men took it. For many it was simply a psychedelic trip experienced purely at the level of sensory distortion. For others, though, who happened to take it at exactly the wrong, or, according to my perspective, the *right* moment—particularly those who volunteered for Ultra, or were volunteered *by* Ultra, so to speak—you ended up with an absolutely fascinating case of psychic nudity. A human soul stripped to its very variable essentials. A cloud of consciousness that suddenly *sees*. All too frequently, American servicemen who received such sudden wisdom could no longer function."

"As soldiers?"

"As people. It was a terrible scandal. The military and the silent majority can only tolerate demons they are familiar with. The tribal programming allowed for all the usual battlefield psychoses and could even tolerate the extremely high incidence of heroin addiction among the men, not to mention alcoholism and suicide. But when the hippie movement threatened to spread to 'Nam, the idea of sending boys out there who would have their heads totally turned around by LSD supplied to them not by Charlie but by subversives straight out of Haight-Ashbury—what would be next, love-ins with the Vietcong?"

He pauses and rubs his chin. "But there was a parallel narrative. The CIA maintained a low profile because they were the ones who inadvertently caused the acid craze to spread by experimenting with it on human guinea pigs, most of them military personnel and not always volunteers. The public got the truth in tiny drops that precluded scandal, and all was going well until the news of the murder by the CIA of Dr. Frank Olson, more than twenty years after the event, hit the fans. Olson was a bacteriologist and CIA officer involved in the Company's LSD experiments. Hell broke loose."

He smiles. "You see, I was famous professionally, because of dozens of papers I had written on the subject of LSD. Famous, too, in the subculture, for singing its praises. They needed me even more than they hated me." He frowns, takes out another Camel, and lights up. "I think it was my long hair they most resented. Their in-house shrinks were all gray men in suits with crew cuts. I was psychedelic, big time."

"Why did they need you so much?"

"Collateral damage." He taps his head. "Right here. And we're talking thousands of souls. Uncle Sam doesn't screw up by halves." He sighs. "It really is a miracle drug. D'you see, it acts like an electron microscope—and that's the problem. The teeniest, weeniest neurosis is magnified ten thousand times—and that's merely with recreational use in favorable circumstances among friends. Imagine how it might affect one—" He stops to stare at me, as if unsure of the wisdom of continuing.

"What?"

"If some bastard is butchering a child in front of you, for example, as part of the experiment? Or ordering you to do so?"

I stare at him. Blood has drained from my face. I feel gray.

He remains quiet, giving me space. When he thinks I've recovered, he continues. "All their own shrinks wanted out pronto. The thing had gone horribly—and I mean *horribly*—wrong. The reputations of upward of a hundred psychiatrists was on the line. Not to mention the Company itself. I was an ideal scapegoat, a grinning clown with a doctorate in hallucinogens. Confident, too. Stupid, I suppose. But not so stupid that I didn't realize how much they needed me. This was my moment. As it turned out, my nationality worked in my favor. They could blame everything on an alien—as usual."

He looks at me as he coolly takes a toke. "I told them I needed a very big space where no one could find us. They said, 'Not U.S. territory.' I said, 'Okay.' They said, 'How about Cambodia, we'll buy a chunk through a shell company. We'll do a secret protocol with the government so they leave you alone.' Usual thing. I said, 'Okay, but I need money.' They said, 'Money is no problem.' I said, 'I mean funding for the next twenty years. You don't fix heads the way you fix broken legs.' They said, 'Funding for the next twenty, okay.' They weren't so sharp when it came to bargaining. They'd let me see how desperate they were, so I said, 'No, funding for the next forty.' They said, 'Look, just make the problem go away. Whatever you need, you've got it.' I said, 'Seclusion. Absolute seclusion. Most of these guys and gals are never going back to the world. They need a special space to live and die in.' That made them very happy. They even smiled. 'How about dense jungle, twenty acres, only one way in and out, land mines all around?' They were particularly generous with land mines. I said, 'Yes.' They said, 'We'll send in the engineers to do the earthworks for you. Army huts good enough?' I said, 'Water? Electricity?' They said, 'No problem. As many army generators as you need. Wells as deep as you need. Pumps and pipes.' I said, 'Fuel?' They said, 'We'll bury linked ten-thousand-gallon tanks for diesel, you'll be self-sufficient for decades.' I said, 'Food? Cooking?' They said, 'Your problem. No normal person is allowed in. It's you and the crazies. Grow what you need.'"

Bride draws another long toke on the Camel. "Of course, I saw what they were up to. They thought I'd never last more than a few years, but that was enough to pass the buck. They'd find a way of saying it was all the fault of this crazy Brit shrink: 'Only have to look at him to see how mad he is. Don't know how he got away with it for so long, trying to build some kind of LSD utopia in the middle of the Cambodian jungle.'" He smiles. "Actually, they were quite right. The man I was then would never have lasted. I had to become someone else, didn't I? I had to go further with the LSD initiation. Further than anyone ever went. Much further than Leary would have dreamed possible." He gives a wan smile. "Poor Timothy—I knew him well—so much talent, but he fell prey to the vice of evangelism." He closes his eyes for a moment and allows a sardonic smile to bloom. "I'm talking about the early negotiations. Once we were settled they found reasons to take a deeper interest in us. But we'll save that story for later if you don't mind."

Now he gazes over the river: mostly wet-look black with some reflection of city lights. "Most of them died, of course. Beautiful boys and some girls too—the women who had volunteered at Langley. Heads all fucked up. Know that poem 'Howl' by Allen Ginsberg? *I saw the best minds of my generation destroyed by madness, starving hysterical naked, / dragging themselves through the negro streets at dawn looking for an angry fix*'? It was worse than that by a thousandfold. Make that a million." He is quiet for a long moment. "Suicide usually. I knew it would happen. What you will see tomorrow are the survivors. The best of the bunch. The toughest, anyway. The remnants."

I am put in mind of a weekend seminar where the first evening is spent on introduction of the topic, prior to more serious learning the next day. After a few more minutes it becomes clear the Doctor has delivered his welcoming talk and now descends to entertaining anecdotes about life in Southeast Asia over the past forty years, how much has changed and how much has not. It seems he survived Pol Pot's brutal regime, but he does not explain how. He is a gifted raconteur, though, and keeps me fascinated until it is time to go to bed.

20

I'm still at the Foreign Correspondents' Club. Doc Bride called just now to say he has checked out already and is downstairs with a car and driver. He is impatient because the journey into the bush is long and slow at the other end and he wants to arrive at our destination by early afternoon. I'm throwing my toothbrush and shaving gear into my overnight bag, checking my money belt for passport and cash, dashing down to reception, paying in baht at a ruinous exchange rate, humping my bag out to the white Toyota four-by-four with a Khmer driver that is waiting at the curb. The Doctor and I sit in the middle seats, but at opposite windows. He issues an instruction to the driver in Khmer without saying hello to me.

Phnom Penh is a small town and it takes only a few minutes to reach the suburbs, which quickly degenerate into shantytowns with dirt roads between shacks with tin roofs. Quite often there are homemade elevated walkways to enable people to keep out of the mud during the rainy season. Kids have fun in tin cities like this; I catch sight of big, round, mischievous faces, small gangs with monkeylike mastery of the maze in which they live. On the other side of the glass it is already hot, of course, but not yet unbearable. I know these slums will be asleep before noon and stay that way until sunset. I have a feeling that where we are going may not have great satellite cover, so I make my early-morning call to Chanya.

"Hello, darling," I say.

She grunts sleepily. "Where are you?"

"Phnom Penh, we're in a van on our way to the jungle."

"We?"

"I'm with Dr. Christmas Bride."

I thought the name would amuse her, as it did the first time, but she merely grunts again.

"You okay?" I say.

"Yes. Except that I'm suffering from event starvation, Action Man."

"See you in a day or so. There might not be any satellite cover where we're going."

"Take care," she says.

I turn to look out of the window: scrappy bits of land, some huts, a brand-new part of a highway that says *foreign investment* all over it, some brush and paddy fields, a boy following a buffalo with a switch. I try to work out where this Englishman is coming from. In repose, when he is not making full use of his mobile features, there is much of the gargoyle in the way he stares malevolently into space.

At about noon the driver turns off the road, which is now bare concrete, onto the shoulder, which is an outreach of jungle remains. There are no tall growths and the scrubby bush looks unhealthy and primitive, as if something has poisoned such advanced life as trees and flowers, leaving only primeval vegetation that hugs the ground and crawls like something cowed and persecuted. I know that we have been traveling steadily east since we left the suburbs of Phnom Penh and that it was in the east that Nixon dumped his thousands of tons of bombs in a secret operation that was supposed to destroy the Ho Chi Minh Trail, but succeeded only in destroying Cambodia. I suppose we cannot be in that area yet; even so, the suspicion adds a kind of poison to the moment. When the driver opens the back I see a wicker basket piled up with sandwiches and two bottles of wine. The driver finds a collapsible table and even a tablecloth, wineglasses. The Doc and I sit opposite each other on folding chairs.

The sandwiches are well made, with enough of the juice from the tomatoes softening the white of the bread without compromising the *craquant* of the crust; the cheese, a buffalo mozzarella, makes, with the olive oil—and the hint of basil— a delicious soft multitone motif in the mouth, and the authority of the ham completes the symphony. The wine adds the frisson of narcotic essential for a complete culinary experience. This is all thanks to French influence in Cambodia. We eat in silence.

A couple of hours later the road turns into a mud track, then stops at a wall of jungle. Now we are staring at those huge exotic Asian hardwoods of the same kind that embrace giant stone Buddhas at Angkor. The only gap in the overwhelming vegetation is filled by a truck with a wheelbase at least five feet off the ground, with giant tires. Without a word Doc Bride gets out of the van and gestures for me to follow him to the truck, leaving the Khmer driver to turn around and go home.

We approach the truck from behind and it is from the passenger side that I first catch a glimpse of the man in the driver's seat, a silhouette that reveals a mop of negroid hair so huge it is like an exotic bush. I would have expected it to belong to a lithe young fellow from the 'burbs, circa 1968, except that it is gray. When he turns around to acknowledge me, I see he is in his early seventies. Bride climbs in before me and the three of us share the bench seat.

"This is Amos," Bride says. Amos and I exchange greetings. "Tell him about your hair, Amos. He needs to start to understand."

"The development of a young person is very delicate," Amos says. "Interrupt it violently with a powerful mind drug, and that young person will return to certain events again and again throughout their life. Some part of them will fixate for the duration. I was a good black boy in the sixties, never grew my hair long, did drugs, or got into trouble. My dad was obsessed with keeping my hair short, those hippie blacks disgusted him, like they were betraying their Negro Christian identity. But I wanted to grow my hair long. Then I volunteered for MKUltra." He gives a huge, heaving sigh with a glance at Bride. "Don't make no difference knowing what the problem is. The passengers on the *Titanic* knew the problem was a huge rip in the hull, but they still drowned. That's why the great religion of psychology failed utterly." He gives me a quick look, turning his vast gray bush to do so, then says, "Right, Doc?"

"Amen," Bride says.

"I can't do nothin' about this obsession." He turns again to stare at me intensely for a moment as if his personal history has absolved him from normal social restraints. Dr. Bride waits patiently while Amos loses himself in some kind of inner speculation that continues for about five minutes and involves gazing at me in clinical fascination. Only then does he start the truck and we move off.

Once we're on our way I see why we need a truck like this. Huge ruts in the track from the wet season would destroy any other kind of vehicle. And the jungle is so dense, you'd probably need a gallon of napalm for each square foot to clear it. Progress is slow, therefore, and nobody speaks for an hour or so. Little by little the mood of both my companions changes. Mine changes, too, but in the opposite direction. They relax somewhat and Amos shares his chore by saying things like, *Damn close, wow that weren't here last year.* Doc Bride grunts back in a friendly tone. I, on the other hand, feel the oppression of the jungle just as if I were bouncing around on the bottom of a green ocean on an alien planet with extraterrestrials as companions.

21

Finally the truck stops at the end of the track. An iron arc forms a vault over an entrance and carries the legend:

I AM IS THE PRISON THAT MAKES YOU FREE

I look at the Doc, who looks embarrassed. "*'I was so much older then, I'm younger than that now,'*" he quotes.

"What does it mean?"

"Don't remember."

Amos jumps out to open two heavy iron gates while we wait with the engine running. "The gates used to open automatically, but that was before the last generator packed up," Bride explains. "Somehow the natural evolution of our community caused us to give up on fixing things." He points to a water tower on iron scaffolding. "We used to have an electric pump, now they use the emergency hand pump that's been repaired a dozen times. A lot of work, but it's something to do."

Once inside the compound I see there are no walls or fences other than the impenetrable jungle. The three of us jump out and the Doc helps Amos close the gates behind us. Now that we have entered the camp this wizened old man takes center stage like a king who has returned to his castle.

We are inside a large flat space comprising a closed village of long single-story wood huts on concrete pillars to keep them off the jungle floor. Many have been joined together longitudinally to make a kind of railway carriage fifty yards long or more. Streets are formed between them with overhead awnings to protect from rain and sun, and there are elevated boardwalks to keep people above the mud during the wet season. The compound suffers from a sense of neglect and decay; jungle grass has sprouted around most of the huts, gravel pathways are overrun with weeds. Only a few of the huts have the appearance of habitations; the others are run-down to the point of collapse. One near the jungle wall has succumbed to creepers and the roof has caved in the grip of a vegetable boa constrictor. There doesn't seem to be any people around.

"They'll arrive one by one," Bride whispers, scanning the compound. I am put in mind of a nature documentary where the wildlife expert whispers into the camera with religious reverence. "They've seen *you*, that's what's holding them back. It's not fear, exactly."

"What, then?"

"Shyness. Very few strangers come here, we lost the knack of talking to outsiders pretty soon after we started. Naturally, now I live in Saigon I've retrieved my social body." He checks my face to see how I react to the phrase *social body*, which is a Buddhist concept, used mostly by Tibetans. "Also"—he scratches his face—"we're all conscious of being weird. You can be sure they're watching you. They won't come out until they're sure you're okay."

"What do I have to do?"

"Nothing. They'll read you from a distance."

"You lived here full-time?"

"Certainly. There was no other way. It was the valley of the blind and I owned one good eye."

I shiver: here live souls who were inches away from total destruction by the ones they most trusted. Aggravated rape of the mind. No one has ever been punished.

Now I notice there is an empty circle in the middle of the compound, the interior of which has been carefully cleaned and scraped and covered with gravel. The Doc indicates with his chin that I should stand there while he and Amos go off behind one of the huts.

After about five minutes a man in denim dungarees appears: a few wisps of white hair that must once have been blond, broken veins in a sensitive north European skin, a posture of deep humility bordering on meekness, a straggly white beard. I would put him in his mid- to late sixties. He looks deeply at me but says nothing. He continues to stare at me from watery blue eyes without speaking while, one by one, other inmates appear from different directions. They emerge from behind the cabins, or perhaps out of them, it's impossible to say.

There are seven of them, not including Amos or the Doc. In each case they walk slowly, warily, but at the same time with a sense of propriety: this is their space. They are all between the ages of sixty and seventy, dressed similarly in denims, with jungle attitude. Those with hair have grown it long and tied it in a ponytail. Most have not shaved for decades and have acquired long, unkempt spade beards not dissimilar to those of holy men of the Himalayas, but to me they most resemble rednecks from remote hamlets somewhere in Alabama. They stare and wait about ten yards away from me without speaking or moving. Behind them I see the Doc and Amos watching from some distance, leaning against a hut. Now one of them steps forward and starts to sniff me. He steps back after quite a few inhalations in which he seems to be examining my odor. Now another steps forward and does the same thing. One by one they all have a good sniff, then retire to the edge of the circle: I guess identity is established by odor here in the jungle. When I check their faces I see in each the same tormented speculation on some problem of inner space.

There are no words exchanged at all between this close-knit community, but a decision seems to have been collectively taken when the first old man steps forward. He looks into my eyes. Without offering a hand he says, "I'm Ben."

"I'm Sonchai," I reply, squinting at them in disbelief. Now they take a single step forward, one by one.

"Casey."

"Herman."

"Jason."

"Jerry."

"Frank."

"Mario."

Ben starts to speak in the wavering voice of someone who rarely uses words at all and seems to be delivering a set speech in a language half forgotten.

"I had a vision. She was a combination of Sophia Loren and Marilyn Monroe. Doesn't matter if you think of her as Marilyn Loren, or Sophia Monroe, doesn't matter at all. That's the way with wormholes.

It doesn't matter, see? My vision encompassed the beauty of both those women, and all the other good women in the world, it was just a perfect, glowing female love, two kinds of woman in one body, and Marilyn Loren was standing at the top of an iron staircase, a kind of platform at the top of the staircase, and I climbed up to it, driven by pure love I climbed up to it, to that platform where she was waiting, then I realized I'd made a slight mistake, she was actually on another platform, a little higher up, but when I got to the next platform I saw I'd made the same mistake, and so on. Over and over. And this obsessed me. Long after they'd done screwing with my head it obsessed me, this pure love that had come to me while they were training me to kill people. But without Marilyn Loren, life had no meaning for me—none at all. She was the only thing left in my head that I had put there myself. It took the Doc to explain that I'd gotten stuck in infinity. In his system infinity is a thing you can get stuck in. Just as your body can get stuck in a doorway, so your mind gets stuck by—" He stops himself, begins again. "It turned out that Marilyn Loren was my wormhole. That was the living agony at the center of the corpse."

He steps back to the edge of the circle to let a brother step forward.

"Hi, I'm Casey." His hair is tied back with a piece of string and his Amish beard extends to the center of his chest. "I loved dogs, so they made me kill one, slowly, when I was on acid," he says, tears streaming down his face and wetting his beard. "That's how they got me. Dogs were my wormhole. I killed lots of people, too, but only after they made me kill the dog."

Another steps forward. "Hello, I'm Jason. Want to know why I stayed in the body? I saw this was not life, but death. This sojourn in the body is death. So why be in a hurry to die? We'll all soon be free anyway. But I can't stand to be with people who don't know they're dead. It fucks my head up so bad, I have to run away. Do you know you're dead? I can't tell. You kind of look like you do and you look like you don't, both at the same time."

One by one they step forward to deliver their harrowing stories, then stand back. Now it is my turn to speak.

"I'm just a beginner here," I say, almost paralyzed by the sense of weirdness. "I've come to learn. I would like to know more."

This gambit has a strange effect on the group. They stare and stare at me as if I'm crazy and they scratch their heads. Finally, Ben says, "Really?"

"Yes," I say. "Really."

Small talk has no place here. It seems I've said something with serious implications that I cannot myself unravel. They frown and study me. When discomfort makes me walk around the circle holding my chin, trying to come to terms with the weirdness of the camp, they follow me with their eyes and hold their chins, as if I am a stage act. As if I have an answer. I finally exclaim, "Will you stop staring at me, please?"

Instantly they drop their eyes, as if ashamed of themselves. "We're sorry," Ben says. "See, for us you're something very special."

"Yep," another agrees. "Very special."

General murmurs of agreement.

"Would you mind telling me why?"

"'Cause you said you wanted to learn. Nobody else ever said that to us. Anyone who visited didn't want to know scat—they just wanted to get the hell out."

At this they all nod their heads gravely.

"What is a wormhole?"

The question has the effect of making them laugh and grin. "Didn't the Doc tell you?" Ben asks.

"No, the Doc didn't tell me."

"Well he darn well should have," another says.

"Doc's messin' with your head if he didn't tell you."

"So why don't you tell me?"

Ben scratches his head. "For us, it's not verbal." More nods of agreement. "No way a man with an active wormhole can talk about it."

"And we all got them."

"Even the Doc."

"Even you, probably, or you wouldn't have come."

"That's right. And you sure wouldn't want to learn from us if you didn't have your own wormhole."

Silence. I wonder where Dr. Christmas Bride has hidden himself. The men speak in mutters inaudible to me, then Ben steps forward.

"We can't explain wormholes, but we can show you the original."

"Right," they agree in a mumble.

"We call it the Great Wormhole, but it's not really."

"Right. The Great Wormhole is life on earth."

"But that's too big an idea for us. So we stop the investigation at *our* great wormhole, even though in reality it's only local to us."

"Exactly."

Now I've lost the plot entirely—or they have. "So," I say, "let's go. Let's go find the Great Wormhole."

"Really?" Ben says.

"Sure," I say.

They mumble together some more in their impenetrable dialect. "We're scared it might totally freak you out," Ben explains. "They demand that I warn you it might freak you out. Not the same as the way it freaks us out, but just the same . . ."

"I'll take my chances. My head and I have been through a lot together."

This makes them chuckle.

"He says his head and him have been through a lot together."

Now they are all looking at me fondly and chuckling.

Without another word Ben leads me to one of the huts at the far end of the compound. It is just about intact, although it looks as if it might succumb to the jungle within a year. Above the door someone has painted in crude letters the legend *Great Wormhole*. Underneath are the words *Museum of American War Atrocities*. I stop to stare at Ben.

"We copied the one in Saigon," Ben explains. "All the exhibits are from original pictures, but we couldn't reproduce the glass jars with ground stoppers they keep the Agent Orange fetuses in, so we just took photographs. It's pretty much a faithful reproduction—except for the name, of course. You go to Saigon now, it's called the *War Remnants Museum*." He pauses before entering. With a gesture of resignation, as if to say, *Here, you might as well know it all,* he slips a hand into an inside pocket and takes out a very worn snapshot. "The Doc encourages each of us to carry one, so we can remember who we're not anymore. He keeps a snapshot of himself just the same."

There are plenty of creases in it and the color has faded, but it is still possible to recognize the muscular and rather beautiful young man with long blond hair tied back in a ponytail, holding an M-16 and looking stoned. He is not in uniform, however; his magnificent shoulders and biceps are left bare except for the straps of his dungarees.

"Special Forces?"

He stares at me with such stress that I wonder if he is going to explode. Then he starts to relax again. "Yeah, that's right. I was the kind who volunteered for everything. Volunteered once too often. Special Forces, then MKUltra. Ultra liked to recruit from Special Forces. Never thought it would be my head that caved, though. Never thought Uncle Sam himself would do that to me."

His features go through a complex rolling ritual that ends with an expression of psychotic wonder. It is a war, certainly, that is playing across his face and, I suppose, the rest of his body, nerves tensing and relaxing, the left fighting the right, one side of his face malevolent, the other retaining the gentle resignation of old age. Old age wins. The violence subsides. It was as if I could experience his demons, watch them do battle with angels, lose the fight, and slink away: Armageddon shrunk to a few ivory cells in one man's brain. Now he looks up at me.

"We can go in now. I'm okay with it now. I think."

22

Memory, of course, is notorious for its power to deceive. Neverthe-less, I am certain Ben and his brothers have faithfully reproduced the museum that I first visited in Saigon with my mother, Nong, all those years ago. Walking ramrod straight, and a little too fast, Ben takes me to what I suppose is his favorite exhibit: a photograph of a giant thousand-gallon tank of Agent Orange, which carries the legend *The Giant Purple People Eater.*

"This is where we turned Nazi," Ben announces loudly. He has become suddenly officious, a different person entirely; stress works all his features. His words pierce the somnambulant state I seem to have slipped into. "Did you know we had to refine napalm to make it better stick to human skin? It stuck especially well to the tender skin of young children."

"No," I hear myself saying, as if underwater. "No, I did not know that."

A kind of panic overcomes him, like someone who suffers from claustrophobia. He marches us through the rest of the exhibits at a fast walking pace—the My Lai massacre; victims of Agent Orange; the picture I saw on my first visit with Nong all those years ago (exactly as I remembered: an athletic-looking GI, an M-16 in his left hand, his right holding the torso of an enemy fighter, which is hardly more than skin plus head hanging upside down; the GI is laughing hysterically).

Now Ben is glaring at me. I am put in mind of crazies who throw tantrums for no apparent reason: a sudden resurgence of uncontrol-lable rage waiting for a trigger.

"You gotta blow them away, you have no choice. You can't be who you are and let them be who they are. It don't work. Someone has to die." He raises his voice again, making it crack. "We coulda won, you know?"

"Won what, the genocide?"

He blinks rapidly. "Yeah. The genocide. Why not? It's only the first time you kill that you feel bad." He stamps his foot. "So, why didn't we just drop the Bomb on Hanoi?" He stares at me, distraught. "I could have been standing here a winner, instead of a loser."

I am afraid of him, this crazy old man, so I say nothing. The suffering of a crazy possesses an unnerving authenticity that can make you feel like a fraud in your fragile sanity. Is it because we know deep down that a divided mind is perhaps the only honest reaction to a cleft world? Sorry, R, these are jungle thoughts, I'll be okay once I'm out of here.

Or will I? There's an atmosphere of finality in the camp that creeps up on you, as if this were the hidden endgame I have been postponing all these years.

A groan starts somewhere deep in Ben's chest, and ends with a scream. "You trying to fuck with my head, boy? You trying to fuck me up all over again? We weren't supposed to lose." Now he weeps. "We could have had a victory parade just like after World War Two. The whole of New York would have turned out to honor us."

Now I cannot stand any more. I am pulling him toward the exit by grabbing the strap of his dungarees. He forces a halt in front of the "Napalm Girl," who is running naked toward the camera, her body burning with the chemical that has stuck to her. Ben bursts into tears. Now *he* is running toward the exit. I race after him, but when I pull open the door of the hut, there is no sign of him.

I have to go back in. I stop in front of a photograph of an eighty-five-year-old woman in a wheelchair leading ten thousand people in a march from Berkeley to Oakland on November 25, 1965; she carries a banner with the legend *My Son Died in Vain, Don't Go to War, Go to Prison.* Black-and-white pix of marches and demonstrations from Chile, Argentina, Mexico, Canada, Cuba, France, Britain, the USSR. Now I see close-ups of Hugh Thompson and Lawrence Colburn, two helicopter pilots raised to the level of superheroes: they saved the lives of ten Vietnamese civilians at My Lai. In November 1965, Roger LaPorte, Norman Morrison, and Alice Herz soaked themselves in gasoline and set themselves on fire outside U.S. government buildings. Here is the wall of the intellectuals, led by Bertrand Russell of the U.K., giving finely articulated reasons why the war must end. A telegram sent by Ho Chi Minh to "American Friends" on the occasion of 1968 New Year's. Finally, a distraught young woman, on her knees, weeps over the dead body of a fellow student at Kent State University.

The one that grabs me the most, though, is a highly colored, deliberately amateurish poster by vets who opposed the war: *Don't go, the U.S. Government will turn you into a psychopath.*

Outside the hut it has started to rain with the sudden violence of the tropics. I stand in the downpour and shiver. Now a tall, wild figure, also without protection from the rain, appears from behind one of the other huts, cupping a lighted cigarette.

"Ben flipped, didn't he? Captain America took over, I suppose? You must forgive him—and forgive me, too," he says. "I hope you understand why we had to do that?" He gives a good strong pull on the Camel.

"What is a wormhole?"

"I'll tell you in the truck on the way back. The point was that you should see where everyone is coming from."

"Everyone?"

He looks at me. "Yes. The Asset included."

23

I follow Bride down a narrow path through the jungle opposite the
main entrance. We stop on the edge of a clearing where crops have
been grown in the past, but not recently: another long hut on blocks,
but without windows and with locks more serious than those on the
other huts. The Doctor points at it: "That was my lab, for four decades."
He shakes his head. "Four decades. The first ten years are about adaptation, organization, hierarchy, the sophistication of food gathering
and preparation and water retrieval. After that people need something
beyond mere survival. And that's normal people who haven't been
severely damaged. In the Middle Ages in Europe nearly half the year
was taken up with religious holidays, which often degenerated into
orgies. We needed a structure, d'you see? But what? There were no
examples we could use from modern times. Or even medieval times.
Or even ancient Roman times." As he ticks off the millennia he studies
my face, searching for the light of understanding and finding none.

"One had to reach right back to the very wellsprings of the human
psyche."

"Eleusis?" I ask.

He gives a tolerant smile. "A good guess and, I confess, the thought
crossed my mind. But you have to remember ancient Greece was an
upstart civilization patched together with half-understood philosophies
stolen from Egypt and Persia. Greece was the New World of the time,
the older cultures laughed with contempt at the superficiality of clowns
like Plato."

He leads me from the hut to a footpath, where we surprise Amos of
the big hair. I saw him out of the corner of my eye as we emerged. He

was standing behind a tree. The tree was too thin for his hair, though. Now he comes out, smiling, as if trying to pretend he wasn't spying. Dr. Bride grins.

"See what I mean about espionage?" He jerks a chin at the black man. "Amos is an artist. He's excited that you're about to witness his masterpieces—and he's also shy. Is that not so, Amos, my dear friend?"

"Once a shrink always a shrink," Amos says, shaking his head.

He leads away from the camp, along a well-worn path that brings us to some karst formations that perhaps once amounted to small limestone hills, but have been eroded so that the mineral outcrops are no higher than the trees. The karst, though, has produced a cave system with an entrance at ground level behind a Bodhi tree. We pause for a moment.

"Caves are where we started. We must put ourselves in the bodies of our most distant ancestors. Imagine a brain just as efficient as our own, probably more so since it had to be more alert to survive. Now consider how this brain developed expertise in cave management and technology over more than fifty thousand years. According to some, as long as two hundred thousand—that's a hundred and ninety-six thousand years before recorded history. What were we doing all that time, with those marvelous big brains of ours?" Bride stares at me, waiting for a response.

"I guess we got pretty good on caves."

"They're in our DNA. If we're honest and relaxed, merely entering a cave does something to our heads. I'm not talking mysticism, just the basic law of programming. There's no way caves don't evoke something from deep within. Right, Amos?"

Amos nods and moves his gaze from Bride to the mouth of the cave, then back to me. "He's right. It really started with the cave."

"But before the rituals could be established, there was work to be done. Hard work."

"Had to shovel shit for six months before we reached the end," Amos said.

The black man shares a glance with the Doc, who nods. Amos leads us into the shadows. Once we cross a certain line, though, I see there is illumination.

The cave is so deep we cannot see to the end. Indeed, it gives the impression of infinity because there are oil lamps set at about ten yards apart that form a double line like the lights on a landing strip; the lamps seem to continue, endlessly, into the bowls of the earth. My mind flicks through available references and produces a memory of the caves of Cu Chi, dug mostly by women.

"Did the women also work here? You said some of the casualties of MKUltra were female?"

A strange look comes over Bride's face. "Yes," he says gently, as if he feels sorry for me. "But not much. You see, most of them fell pregnant within the first year. They were keen to work, they were good American stock with the Puritan ethic still operating, somehow, but we couldn't allow them to risk the babies, could we?"

While I look at him I am aware of my lips forming words, then discarding the words, because no sound comes. *Are you ready for this?* his expression asks. *No, I'm not ready for this*, I signal back. Something in me carefully covers up the reference to the women and their babies.

When Amos hands me an oil lamp so I can explore for myself, I discover paintings. I think of the cave paintings at Lascaux, which had so impressed one of my mother's French clients that he insisted on taking us there. These paintings are fresh, though, and do not depict animals. They are more in the tradition of urban graffiti, with stylized fighter planes, begging Southeast Asian kids, barrels labeled *Napalm* and *Agent Orange*, even a street of brothels that could be Soi Cowboy.

Amos leads us a dozen or so paces forward before we are joined by someone who emerges out of the shadows. It is Ben, the Special Forces vet who showed me around the museum. I guess he must have slipped over here after he ran out of the museum. He exchanges a few words with Amos in that language I do not understand. Bride joins in the conversation, speaking the strange dialect in that plummy accent of his. Now we continue.

One by one the other vets emerge from the shadows to greet us. After a few minutes, they have all arrived: Ben, Casey, Herman, Jason, Jerry, Frank, Mario. There is a feeling of a religious procession as we move in a group slowly down into the earth. The cave narrows after about a hundred yards and seems to be tapering before it ends altogether. The frescoes have changed their character; instead of recognizable objects from the modern world, they have become more abstract:

serpentine coils twist in and out of each other in ayahuasque patterns. Deeper still, and the snakes grow wings.

I am wrong about the cave coming to an end. It narrows to less than the width of a door in a house, so that we have to turn and squeeze past, but it immediately widens again into a spherical space with a ceiling so high it remains invisible. This is the end of the journey into the center of the earth. A sheer wall of limestone faces us across a space in which a single naked male human body lies on a slab. I'm fighting the need to vomit and staring at the Doc, speechless.

"Mat Hawkins," Amos says. "He died two days ago." He turns to let Bride speak.

"As I said," Bride continues, "I had to go back to basics." He coughs. "We all did it, of course. I mean *Homo sapiens*. Cannibalism is our primary loss of innocence and at the same time our primary sacrifice and the food supplement that saved us from annihilation in times of famine. Not one early society of humans did not practice it, especially when in pioneer and pilgrim mode. Without it there would be no human race. Naturally, if one is to rebuild the psyche from scratch, one has to return to that moment."

"Naturally." I stare at the part-eaten cadaver. "You only ate bits of him?"

"The purpose is sacred and ritualistic—that's how you purge necessary sin, d'you see? Like eating the body of Christ—a relatively modern and ersatz imitation of the real thing such as we have here. We ingest the dead flesh, give it life again in our own bodies."

Bride is using a quite different personality as vehicle to convey his mood. He is beyond solemn; it is as if the gargoyle I saw in the van had found its voice.

"Right," I say, "right," unable to take my eyes off the long wounds where someone has carved steaks out of Mat Hawkins's thighs.

Amos has come closer to me and seems to represent the group, who is staring hard at me. *Does he get it or not,* their eyes demand to know.

Now my mind slips back again to the women and their kids. *Were the children brought up here, to this?* Something in me doesn't want to know the answer. I close my mouth.

Bride speaks in a slow priestly tone. "You could say it was a kind of sorcery, one might as well use that word. As the great Carl Jung pointed out, the material world might yield to reason, but the human psyche does not. We are hardwired by the laws of magic, which we desecrate with every logical thought we entertain. Hence the agony of modern man. It was reason got us into this mess, reason that sent half a million to serve as psychopaths over here in Southeast Asia. What could have been more reasonable: *We are right, they are wrong, the President is facing an election, our people love war and it makes us rich, so let's kill them all the way we did the Indians.* Only a return to the most basic, magical, reverential springs of human consciousness could heal my damaged band of brothers."

"Radical," I say, trying hard not to sound like a reason-crazed modern. "Radical."

"Yes," Bride agrees. "Quite right."

He is still waiting for something to click in my brain. I am still bewildered. What more could there possibly be?

Bride coughs, I think to hide his frustration with me. "It was always a ritual carried out with the utmost respect, a consecration and a sacrament, a literal sharing of our brothers who having given their lives to the community ended by sharing their flesh—the ultimate in selflessness, you might say. The very opposite of narcissism." I nod. "And to a large extent, it worked—did it not?" The question is addressed to the group.

"Sure did," Amos says. "We might not look like humanity's finest, but we're sure as hell a lot more straightened out now. If it weren't for all those man steaks, I don't think we'd all be able to walk and talk at the same time." A chorus of agreement from the old men. And still the message conveyed by stares and tightening of the lips tells me that I'm just not getting it.

"That's always the final question, then as now. Does the magic work or not?" Bride is insisting, coming closer to me and towering above me in his need for me to understand. "Even the most reasonable men and women of the Central Intelligence Agency would agree with that. After all, they are in the business of being effective: *whatever works* has always been their secret motto."

"Goldman," I say.

"Correct." Everyone seems to sigh with relief. For some reason I had to be the first to utter that name.

"Goldman—he followed what you were doing. He got it. But he had no scruples?"

"Keep going," Bride says.

"The children." I've finally said it, but feel no catharsis, no relief. Neither does Bride or his men. Now that I've burst the balloon they look at the floor in shame.

"We had no facilities to bring up kids," Amos says, his voice sad and angry. "How could we? We were cavemen struggling for survival. You need first-class hygiene for a newborn infant. You need drugs. Not every mother can breast-feed. In conditions like this, in ancient times, only a small percentage of kids survived the first three years."

"We didn't want to see the children get sick and die. That wasn't going to help the therapy," Bride says. "We'd silenced enough villages where children once played."

"Goldman took them," I snap. Amos turns away and Ben begins to whimper. Even the Doc cannot look me in the eye. "You were like a Nazi stud farm, breeding humans for war purposes. How else was the CIA to get its zombies, now the program was in deep cover?" I blow out my cheeks; I am red-faced as the revelation sinks further in. "I think he encouraged you. I think he wanted you all to screw yourselves silly. What a gift for his program: babies no one knows about, with no social identity, invisible kids growing up in a totally controlled environment. *Militarily* controlled, with guidance from military shrinks."

Dr. Bride looks up at the ceiling of the cave. "He promised our girls first-class health care, prenatal and postnatal, he brought in military doctors who had practiced obstetrics—there weren't many of those, naturally."

"You have to remember these girls already had their heads turned upside down," Amos says.

"Marilyn Loren," Ben sobs, "she was the best, the most beautiful—and the most fucked-up."

"A certain kind of mental breakdown makes women especially voracious," Bride says. "It's quite well known. Vivien Leigh had it. Used to pop out to the park for quickies. A lot of the girls were like that. And at the end of the day, if the girl wants a baby, she gets one."

"No way they could have taken care of the babies, though," Amos says.

"They were taken away from their mothers—at birth?" I ask. "Soon after? They never knew maternal love?"

"He wanted to start with clean slates," Bride says. "And he got them." He shakes his head. "What could we do? As Amos said, no way the girls could have stayed here and taken care of their own kids, and neither could we. We were all already crazy."

I nod. Once you enter into the logic, things fall into place. "A dozen or so young women horny as hell among more than a hundred men— and no contraception?"

"The women didn't want it. Most of them wanted to give birth at least once. The instinct doesn't respect difficulties like jungle locations—not with women like that whose heads have been tampered with. And they knew their lives were over. Giving birth was the one remaining human thing they could do." He sighs. "Giving birth is a woman's trump card, you have to let her play it, you really have no choice in the matter."

"It must have been one big baby factory."

As I cast my eye over the huge vault of the cave, the slab with the half-eaten cadaver, the ragged faces of the old men, I see ancient connections. It is as if we had all been in this space before, many thousands of years ago.

"I need to get out of here," I say.

The journey back to the light is all uphill. A romantic streak in me expects catharsis; what I experience when we emerge from the cave is an attack of depression. Bride seems to understand. He even seems worried about me.

"I don't want you to get sick," he says. "That's always a risk at moments like this. Let's go back to the future."

"So where did it happen, the other side of the experiment, the indoctrination, the black magic?" I asked, trying to sound casual, as we made our way back to the camp.

"Where do you think?" Bride said.

"Not Angkor?"

"Why not? For a brief but sufficient moment Goldman was able to grab what he needed. Pol Pot didn't take it over until the mid-seventies—by then Goldman had refined his technique. He could reproduce the conditions elsewhere."

"I still find it hard to understand, a modern American military man like him delving into superstition."

"Sorcery works. Human sacrifice is behind all great powers. Look at the U.S.: twelve million native Americans slaughtered, that's more than Hitler or Stalin—and look how well they've done. The entire nation is testimony to the efficacy of the practice." He throws me a glance. "It's simply a matter of dumping the delusion of reason and seeing the human condition for what it is. In reality there is nothing reasonable about us at all—and very little that is humane. One would have thought two world wars proved that. We dream we are rich, happy, and good while the economy is healthy. It only takes a terrorist bomb or two to pop the bubble, however, and we're back to cave mentality."

I began to speak. Perhaps it was a reflex of shock, because I was mumbling mostly to myself, working it out: "The Asset, that's why he kills and terrorizes. It's not an unfortunate by-product of his programming, it's built into his training—from birth. Goldman overcame the zombie effect by creating a voracious psychopath. He has to have his red meat. That's what Goldman was doing on the river that day. It wasn't a mere demonstration, it was feeding time for his tiger. That's why they needed Sakagorn—someone with that kind of authority and charm, an aristocrat who commands deference in a feudal society, and with tons of slush money to keep people quiet."

24

"There were two hundred and thirty-three of us at the peak," Dr. Christmas Bride says as the truck trundles slowly through the jungle tunnel with Amos at the wheel. "Including a dozen American women, all of them white."

His somber mood has quite dissipated; he is a scientist again, fascinated by his life's work. Now the plight of the women and their children doesn't seem so sad to him. On the contrary, the circumstance was serendipitous, looked at from a scientific point of view.

"It was before your time, of course, a distant epoch when men were men and women were women." He smiles. "I have nothing against gender equality, nothing at all, but as a psychiatrist I have to say that if you go about it by degrading the sexual identity of both male and female, you end up with infantilism. After all, in nature the only humans without developed gender identity are infants. Haven't you noticed how childish the West has become? Just when it most needs men and women of mature judgment it seems there aren't any. Such a society is vulnerable to the most radical manipulation."

"Why so?"

"Think about it, what do dissatisfied children do? They complain, they cry—but it never occurs to them to rebel effectively. In the end they grumble and obey. Infantilism and slavery go hand in hand. It is almost as if the West has been softened up for that very purpose by forces beyond its control."

"You got that right," Amos says, at the wheel and concentrating on the track.

"So what about the others, the GIs in your care? Where did they all go? You surely didn't eat them all?"

"*'Some flew east, some flew west, some flew over the cuckoo's nest,'*" he quotes. "Natural wastage—people without hope die young. Many were too far gone for anyone to save them. One used whatever drugs would keep them calm, if that was what they wanted. I never discouraged them from taking their own lives, once I was sure that's what they intended. The simple truth is that mental pain may be as unendurable as the physical kind—indeed, it may be much worse. I was working in uncharted waters, I had to take each case as it came and after a year or so make a decision. Some simply wandered off into the jungle. One assumes they died, but not necessarily—after all, many of them were skilled jungle survivors. One heard rumors from time to time about crazed vets wandering the jungle and using crossbows to hunt for food."

"So now there are eight?"

He hesitates, then looks at me, waiting for something. "Eight plus three."

"Those three derelicts living in Klong Toey Slum?"

Dr. Bride sighs. "It's really very simple. The man who believes he is your father led two of his chums to Bangkok. It was a kind of last adventure before death, and a bid to reach back to his personal history before Ultra. For him you exist on the far shore of the sea of madness." He stares at me, then looks away. "Someone had brought news of a Eurasian detective in Bangkok, just the right age, with a mother named Nong." His eyes examine me again for a second. "He took Willie J. Schwartz and Larry Krank, to use their official names, who were the three most able to appear normal in public, and they all went off to see if they could find a way of making a living in the world. They wound up doing a little trafficking in Bangkok, in the slum of Klong Toey. They kept very little for themselves, sent most of what they made back to their brothers in the compound. Jack was shy about contacting you, though. He was biding his time. He found out where you worked and spied on you there. He asked about you, but you have to understand he was like a jungle animal: cautious, shy, given to scuttling away at the first sign of psychic danger. He took a few pictures of you, I'm told, on a cell phone, and stared at them for hours on end."

"Which cell phone? There were two," I ask. Bride seems not to understand the question. He shrugs. "So who planted the bomb? Why?"

"To be frank, I'm not sure. It is certain that Goldman saw a security threat to his program just when it was gaining commercial traction. On that theory the bomb was intended to send them scuttling back—remember how fragile are their mental states. They weren't supposed to be in the hut when it went off."

"But there's another theory?"

"Well, as we both know, there's another player, isn't there?"

"The Asset ordered the bombing?"

Bride doesn't answer.

"None of this explains why I'm here, now, today. Why would you spill the beans on a whole secret operation like this, just because one old derelict thinks he's my father?"

Once again, the Doctor seems disinclined to answer. He stares out of the window with that gargoyle expression on his face, as if he hasn't heard.

The long slow journey through the tunnel is over, and the truck emerges first onto bumpy cleared land, then finally onto a paved road where a people mover is waiting. The Doc explains that since we are not only nearer to Vietnam than to Phnom Penh, but, as a matter of fact, nearer to Saigon than Phnom Penh, it is easier to drive across the border than take a plane from Phnom Penh to Ho Chi Minh.

The border guards let us through even though I have no visa: the Doc speaks fluent Vietnamese and bribes them as a matter of course. I guess he must use the crossing a lot. Once we are in Vietnam the road is pretty clear. I am silent all the way.

25

The colors of Vietnam are gold and green. Mix them together and you have the muddy waters of the Mekong Delta. Keep them separate and you have the baize green of the paddy and the bright yellow dust of the elevated causeways between the fields. The French, with their legendary good taste, used those colors lavishly in their sumptuous villas, with the occasional dense blue to set them off. Oh, yes, somehow Vietnam manages to be more stunning than Thailand; she is like a beautiful sister, who was always going to be the most savagely raped. Of all the invaders, though, Big Money has perpetrated the greatest violations of a rural culture. You don't see so much paddy or old colonial villas these days as you near the outskirts of HCMC. Capitalism has emptied Hanoi and sent everyone down to Saigon where the work is. The endless overhead cables, building sites, cement batching plants, construction cranes, and the raggedness of an entire country dug up and cemented over to make it fit to compete in the twenty-first century have quite extinguished arcadian innocence. During the journey the Doc used his cell phone to book us rooms at the Continental: "Where Fowler liked to have breakfast—you remember, in *The Quiet American?*"

Now I am thinking: *The Quiet American.* The name of the book awakens something in me as if I have been bitten by a snake. It was that book I ransacked more than any other in my search for *him.* That haunting portrayal of a country at the mercy of alien idiots was, for me, all about him. That tale of a middle-aged man who falls for a bar girl (who looked in the movie just like Nong in her youth) was where I sought *him* more than in any other book, simply because it was better written than the others.

There are fewer trishaws these days, but still plenty of old women in black trousers, the Chinese quarter is still called Cholon, and nobody refers to the city as Ho Chi Minh. Of course, the Continental is still there, set back a few hundred yards from the river and just behind the Opera House, still surviving and thriving, quite as if there never had been a communist victory. I order a pastis at the bar and sit outside. When the waiter arrives with the clear liquid in a glass along with a small jug of iced water, I watch with pleasure while I pour the water into the pastis and it turns cloudy, and I invoke the first words of that book: *After dinner I sat and waited for Pyle in my room over the rue Catinat.* A few more sips, and I'm feeling as if I've been in Saigon forever.

I have time to kill because the Doc said he needs to "recharge his batteries" after the road trip. The clerk at reception shows me on a map the shortest route from the Continental to the War Remnants Museum: left at Ly Tu Trong, across the barbecue park, then up one block to Vo Van Tan; a thirty-minute stroll, maximum, the clerk says.

In this city people like to sit outdoors on ledges, or squat, or sit on low plastic stools in the shade of a building or Bodhi tree, and take over that spot for whole days at a time. Young women chat together, men drink beer and play a form of checkers with crown bottle tops; when hungry they send for takeaway that they consume in the space they have adopted as their daytime home. On most side streets there is at least one barber with his mirror hung from a tree or railing, a chair with a customer all soaped up and ready for the cut-throat. The barbecue park is a good-size place where both trees and people wobble in the heat and you wonder if they're real or not. It took me an hour to reach the museum, which is unmistakable with its forecourt littered with small fighter planes, massive ordnance, khaki tanks, and bomb casings as tall as me. With so much firepower, how did they lose?

I buy my ticket at the kiosk. When I enter the museum, though, something happens to my ears. I know that there are other tourists here, indeed there is a group of about twelve Vietnamese schoolchildren in blue uniforms who are assiduously noting the names and numbers of weapons on display, which were used against their country in the war. There is an elderly American couple, the wife supporting her tearful husband, who after only five minutes loses control and has to leave. Three French men in their forties stand stunned and uncomprehending before the guillotine that their country used before others took over the task of torture: perhaps they had expected to see evidence of American bad behavior only? But I cannot hear anything. It is as if I am viewing the place from a different dimension, where the other visitors are merely shadows.

I do not examine the exhibits except to confirm they are the same as in that replica museum in the Cambodian jungle, then leave and cross the park again. It has been over four hours since the Doc and I checked into the hotel and I've not heard a word from him. He still has not told me what wormholes are. When I use my cell phone to call his room, the operator tells me he has blocked all incoming calls and left strict instructions not to be disturbed.

I have a theory as to what "recharging his batteries" might signify. The main clue was a change in the Doctor's mood on the final leg of the journey from Cambodia. He became impatient with the traffic, as if there were an urgent matter in the city awaiting his attention. Now I have no more doubts: it wasn't Camel cigarettes alone that kept his head together all those years in the jungle.

When I arrive back at the Continental I talk to the clerk, who calls the manager. I explain that my elderly companion, while exceptionally fit for his age, does have one or two health problems that need constant checking. While I'm talking I'm peeling off a great wad of dong that I changed on my way back from the museum, which doesn't amount to much in dollars but quickly impresses the manager. When the bribe has reached a sufficient level, he holds up a hand, smiles, and selects a key from the rack. I do not ask why the manager would need a key to open a door of a room that is legally occupied. The manager slides the key gently into the lock, opens the door sufficiently to peep inside, nods at me to enter, then closes and locks the door behind me.

The reason for extreme caution lies in the Doctor's hands: a pipe about a yard long with a bowl sinuously emerging about a third of the way up the stem. The room reeks with the sweet smell of opium. Despite the clues, I am surprised. Why would this master chemist use an old, addictive, and toxic drug when he could have used LSD?

The accommodation is a suite in the style of grand hotels of yester-year: a generous sitting-out area with two chaise longues, brocade wall-paper, a bust from ancient Rome, and an arch that leads directly to the double bed. Dr. Christmas Bride reclines on one of the chaise longues.

He faces the street although his eyes suggest his mind is elsewhere. When I pull up a chair to sit next to him he blinks and smiles. "It's okay, we can talk, I've only had the one," he says slowly in a dreamy voice. He nods at the pipe. "Admitting you need help is a sign of sanity," Bride murmurs. "After a certain age, though, the help tends to be chemical in nature. People don't really ease the psychic burdens of others and talking makes it worse."

The voice remains dreamy, but the mind behind is sharp enough.

"Wormholes," I say. "You were going to explain them."

He makes a lazy gesture with one hand, as if he is too blissed out to actually wave it, although that's sort of what he intends. "Just some crazy idea I thought up when I was young, ambitious, and pretentious. I first suggested it in a paper I wrote for an academic journal. One was allowed so much more imagination in those distant days. I made the wise-ass observation that the cosmos is a creation of human imagination, having all the characteristics of a Rorschach test: the ancients saw gods and goddesses, we see black holes." He warms to his theme. "What is a black hole? It is the ultimate destroyer, it rips up suns, planets, and galaxies, shreds and destroys them, not even their light can escape— isn't that exactly the psychology of modern man who produced two world wars and enough weapons of mass destruction to destroy humanity many times over? 'Nam itself was a black hole from which, back in the day, no light escaped." He pauses for a number of minutes. "But it is also the way out. Perhaps the only way a materialistic consciousness can escape: through total annihilation."

"Go on."

"So I decided the only solution was to find one's own wormhole and follow the path of destruction all the way through the tunnel to the other side. Only one direction was possible, one must allow oneself to drown in the vortex. That, broadly, was my healing method. It was the opposite to everyone else's. My premise was that after a certain amount of irremediable damage, the mind will never return to factory settings—it has to self-annihilate and rebirth. It needs the wormhole. It needs to disappear like the Cheshire Cat and reappear at another spot in space-time. We needed the jungle."

"You used acid to probe and heal the damage already done by acid?"

"Yes."

"Did it work?"

He has reentered his secret world and does not hear the question — yet. It hangs in the air while his eyes glaze over, then become sharp and focused on some inner vision that causes him to tense his body for a moment in concentration. His expression is ruthless, hard and cruel. I'm put in mind again of an ancient gargoyle. All this takes about five minutes, so I'm surprised when he finally says in an affable voice:

"Heartbreaking. Of all of them. What else is there to say? For forty years I witnessed, lived through, the whole catastrophe created mostly by the white man. There was really no other way of looking at it, after a while. It is as if we conquered the world through a brand-new kind of idiocy which the world is now able to reproduce without our help. But it was the white man who through his genocidal madness made possible the great revelation: modern humans do not reacquire undifferentiated consciousness through sitting on our backsides in a lotus position for six years. We're much too far gone. We have to blow ourselves up and hope someone will put the fragments together again." He sighs, closes his eyes. "Buddhism is too difficult for most people and Christianity is an incoherent jumble of largely Roman superstition that has nothing to do with the Jew called Jesus. Materialism is dreary: every healthy little girl or boy knows there is a heaven. Goldman and his gang are terrified that Islam will prevail in the end, being the only system offering completeness. I told them if you think like that, then you need a Second Coming to defend yourselves."

Something has happened in that vast unfathomable mind of his. He is like a boat that hit an invisible rock and is shuddering from the jolt: "D'you know, they took me seriously?"

After a few moments he opens his eyes again and lays his pipe on a small glass table with a wrought-iron base on which all the opium paraphernalia is laid out. I watch him scrape the bowl clean, then prepare the opium. He uses a toothpick to gather up a small amount of black viscous matter from a piece of stiff cellophane and mixes it with some ground-up aspirin, heats the mixture with a butane lighter at the edge of the bowl, and sucks. He is certainly an experienced smoker, to judge from the way he is able to consume the whole smudge of opium in one long inhalation. He tenses himself to concentrate on preparation of the next pipe, which he hands to me at the same time as exhaling his own smoke. Now he relaxes with a long complacent sigh.

"But you already know all this—and much, much more. I'm not being spiritual—just stating a fact. We absorb so very much more than we are conscious of."

I am looking at him while I fiddle with the lighter. The smoke is smooth and sweet and relaxes the lungs rather than causing me to cough. I close my eyes and there it is: *Detective Sonchai Jitpleecheep, I know who [smudge] father is.* I hear my own voice as if far away: "You're saying my father was—is—also the father of children born after me, there, in the camp, to Western women?" The logic comes slowly, fighting my resistance all the way. "So this Asset, he could be related to me?"

"Half brother," Dr. Bride says in a matter-of-fact tone.

I take a good five minutes to process the information. "It was he who set up this trip? That's why he left your number on the iPhone. He wanted me to know . . . everything."

"I had no idea what he was up to. He is in an important transition phase and close to escape velocity, psychically speaking. Your phone call shocked me. In the end he left me no choice. He is driven, d'you see? In spite of everything, he has one very simple human need."

"For what?"

"Love, of course."

26

Next morning I rejoined Dr. Bride in his suite. Given his repertoire of personalities, I was curious as to who he might be after his opium binge. What I found first was an elderly and kindly sage, in awe of the life he had led. As an identity it was not particularly convincing; as a posture, though, it was highly attractive. I was put in mind not of the man he really was so much as the man he might have been if not for 'Nam.

"I've ordered breakfast," he said. "Shall we have it on the balcony?"

We shifted chairs around a small marble table, then the breakfast arrived: stainless steel coffee and milk pots, Danish pastries, croissants, *pains au chocolat*, cheese, eggs, and cold cuts. The waiter poured the coffee and left.

"Myths," Dr. Christmas Bride said. "One really cannot do without them. How are you on Faust?"

"Faust? Pact with the devil?"

"Exactly," the Doctor said.

"Oh, Buddha."

"Yes, quite," Bride said. He waved a hand at the assorted clumps of humans down below in the square in front of the Opera House. "Look at them," he said, "What do they all have in common?"

"Not a lot," I muttered.

"On the contrary, they have one vital thing in common. They are all more or less innocent. The tourists, the beggars, the cyclo riders, they all look out on the world with innocence and bewilderment. The poor are bewildered by their suffering, the wealthy by their privileges, but none really want to do harm, in their own way they all want to return to the same heaven you and I visited last night. We inherit a quite manic certainty that such happiness is possible, indeed it always seems to be just around the corner. All great thinkers have wondered at this mystery—except the modern ones. Something about industrial societies causes us to despise innocence at the same time as encouraging everyone to pursue happiness, when it's perfectly obvious you can't have one without the other. It's very odd."

"I'm lost. What are you talking about?"

He gazed out over the street, his jaw working. "In dismantling human beings, chemically, socially, psychologically, we made the same discovery, Goldman and I. Without this obsession with achieving happiness, without the carrot an inch or two out of reach but tantalizingly close—you end up with dispirited zombies, useless for operational purposes. Fit only for YouTube disinformation."

"Okay."

"So both Goldman and I found ourselves working at the same problem, from different perspectives. I was intent on healing, he on developing a human war machine. In both cases we came up against the same mystery."

"Yes?"

He chuckled. "Goldman is not a philosopher or a psychiatrist or a deep thinker. In the end he came to the only human being who was in a position to help. Me."

"Yes?"

"The answer was simply too much, too terrifying, too awful in the style of Oppenheimer's terrible quote from the Bhagavad Gita—'I have become Time, slayer of worlds'—only infinitely worse. Oppenheimer only destroyed bodies and buildings. What I had discovered destroyed souls." He let a long time pass, during which I sneaked looks at him from the corner of my eye. He seemed racked by a spiritual torment that would not let go. Finally he shook himself like a dog and stared at me. "When they realized there were going to be children born in the camp, they changed their attitude," he said.

As if that constituted a full and final confession, he sagged back into his chair. I was left none the wiser. He raised his ancient head that now looked something like that of a vulture with spare skin hanging at the jowls.

"I would never have consented, d'you see? I held off until I saw what they were doing to the kids."

"You mean after they took them away?"

"It was a gift they had only dreamed of. Young people without any national or cultural identity, with no legal existence at all, who if they belonged to anyone belonged to the CIA, in a country where children were looked on as chattels anyway. I told them, 'No, no, you don't make functional people like that. Not with sadistic exercise, enhancements and war games—too superficial, children are deep.'" He moaned softly to himself; I was not sure if he was expressing pleasure or pain. "They cited the Spartans. That's when I seized the moment. I said, 'Are you crazy? D'you have any idea what intricate and extensive mythology filled the head of a Spartan lad? In exchange for a grim material world, he lived in an inner world of gods and heroes, another kind of consciousness. For such a warrior the only purpose of life was to provide the opportunity for an honorable death. You have to start with the mind, the psyche—the body will follow. Enhance the body by all means, but don't meddle with the mind, you're simply not qualified.'" Another moan. "The first of their very sad and pathetic failures had come to light. A kid with an enhanced body who was too confused to get out of bed. A head case for life. A disaster. They said to me, 'Okay, do it your way.' They were scared because of what had happened to their star zombie. I said, 'It has to be the archetypes, gods and heroes, a Jungian education. Magic is part of it.'" A pause while he worked his jaw. "They literally stopped up their ears: 'Don't tell us, keep your mumbo-jumbo to yourself, we'll make a contract, you take the kids, you deliver them at age sixteen, we take it from there.'" He raised his hands and dropped them.

There was no point trying to goad him on. I waited. He took a deep breath. "So I worked with Goldman. He played General Groves to my Oppenheimer. We both realized independently that trying to capture or define the human spirit was a pointless exercise. The way forward was to indulge it."

"Indulge it? Like indulging an animal in its favorite food?"

"Exactly. I'm afraid it was exactly like that. Except that we are here talking about psychic food. A kind of nourishment peculiar to human beings." A pause. "A form of nourishment well studied by those societies we are taught to despise in modern times. A form of nourishment someone like Hitler or Himmler might have understood, although they were no more than beginners, dark clowns nibbling at the edges who quickly became victims of their own meddling." He looked at me. His voice shook. He was a quite different kind of old man when he said, *"We discovered the rage of fragments cut off from the whole and the way to harness it."* He could not keep the triumph out of his voice.

Now he stared at me like a madman. "The awful thing was that it worked. D'you see? I think even Goldman hoped it was not so. Unfortunately, we had found the God particle on the psychological level, which is the only level that matters. Suddenly the whole of human history fell into place, human sacrifice by another name: Aztecs, Romans, Nazis, European colonists, American imperialists, video games, endless holocausts." He shook his head. "Goldman went mad. Even now he is only sane fifty percent of the time. That's why the CIA tries to keep him at a distance. But they cannot do without him. He is the only one they have who fully understands the new weapon system."

"So why not dump the new weapon system?"

He smiled wryly. "D'you know, I think they would like to do just that. But they cannot. Competition, d'you see? You can't stop arms races once they start—the logic is irresistible."

"But a race with whom?"

"Do you really think the Americans are the only ones working on this? Experiments on helpless humans is universal wherever there is an absence of democratic surveillance, which is everywhere because democracy is failing. The Japanese did it in World War II, the Russians did it led by Professor Ilya Ivanov under Stalin in the twenties and carried it on in secret after Ivanov died: the so-called *humanzee* project. Now the new player is China. They have made a lot of progress, but they're coming from way behind. They have no comparable program, but their need is great. This kind of weapon is more suited to homeland security than war. Soon there will be two billion people in the PRC, just when food and fuel start to run out, worldwide. Keeping the peace, putting down riots with muscle—that's the policing and soldiering of the future. A normal man who has been trained to kill cannot manage more than a few hundred slaughters without breaking down. Himmler discovered that."

A long pause during which his gargoyle returned. His expression was pop-eyed, triumphant and vicious now. "In fact, that was the main problem they wanted me to solve: how do you kill relatedness between humans so that a single warrior can go on killing without any psychological fallout?" He smiled. "It was such an intriguing puzzle, I couldn't resist the challenge. Then I came up with the answer. Do we worry unduly that literally billions of animals—cows, sheep, chickens, pigs—are killed on our behalf every day? It does not trouble us because of the differentiation of species." He stopped to check I was following. He was eager to share his brilliance. "I said: 'I will make them gods, for the gods never care how many little humans they destroy.'" He shook his head. "And that's what I did. After all, what is identity other than a subjective certainty based on no evidence at all? A manipulable fantasy, in other words. Descartes didn't dig deep enough. It would have been smarter to say, *I think therefore I am not,* since honest thought destroys identity. A Buddhist like you knows that."

"So you created a new species?"

"Yes." He warms to his theme. "Naturally, I gave them many of my own tastes in music, history, cuisine, and the arts—perhaps went a tad too far with the Counter-Reformation and the French Revolution, which are my favorites, along with metaphysical poetry and Renaissance choral music—but I was careful to give them a wide range of religions to choose from. Or they could be atheists, it didn't matter. What mattered was that they were too different, too superior, ever to relate to normal people." He let a couple of beats pass. "Even Goldman and his gang realize that seven billion people living on credit and surface tension is not a goer long-term. The transhuman has to be higher and deeper than that."

My cop's mind processed what he'd said despite myself. I, too, felt a terrible reluctance to see something that, I guess, many people sense but will not acknowledge. I thought again about that incident on the river. "It's not actual killings that . . . feeds these . . . products?"

"No. It's the destruction of the souls doing the killing. That's what it feeds on. And you do have to feed it, regularly."

"But feed who or what exactly? Something that is no longer human? So what is it?"

"Ah! How difficult it is for a modern man to answer that question, which a medieval man would have answered with confidence in a second."

"You're talking about the devil?"

"Aren't you?"

I thought about that and decided to change the subject. I was on the point of leaving, after all, with the most pressing question still unanswered. "Doctor, may we now talk about the elephant in the room? Why have you gone to such lengths to help me understand all this? Surely not on the strength of one phone call from a Bangkok cop in the middle of the night?"

"I was asked to," he said with a smile.

"Who by?"

He cocked his head. "Well, if we stick to the terminology, I suppose I would have to say the devil." He stood up and disappeared into the interior of the suite for a moment, to return with his Camels, his ivory cigarette holder, and his Zippo. I watched and waited while he lit up. "Of course," he said, coughing out a stream of smoke, "one has always to bear in mind that in the more sophisticated forms of Christianity, the devil is simply Christ seen from a different angle."

An English gentleman to the last, later that morning Christmas Bride accompanied me to the airport, where I took the next flight back to Bangkok. While I was waiting airside I called Chanya to tell her a little about my adventures. She said she had had lunch with Krom while I was away, but did not elaborate.

PART III

THE
MESSIAH

27

It is a busy night at the Old Man's Club and I am on my own: Mama Nong complains that I've managed to avoid my bar-minding duties for over a week already and she did not see why a couple of days in Cambodia should excuse me from my obligations as junior shareholder, which, she pointed out, pays better than my cop's salary. When I've finally kicked out the last drunk and locked up and am looking forward to going home to my wife, my phone vibrates in my pocket:

*Darling, I'm so incredibly f##**g bored and Krom just called to ask if I wanted to go see a show—so that's what I'm doing. C.*

The message hits me in a place that suffered collateral damage during the war of adolescence: nobody loves me and I feel lonely. My jealousy is of the self-pitying kind: I was looking forward to telling her all about my adventures in the jungle; but she is with Krom and our contract of intimacy has been compromised. I don't want to go home to an empty hovel, so I decide to stroll instead while suppressing a voice of rage against Chanya for leaving me all alone late at night. *And she's with that dyke Krom!*

Sukhumvit has changed. Most of the bars have closed after the one a.m. curfew; those that have remained open have locked their doors and will only allow entrance to *farang* or those Thais with the correct password. The luckier girls found customers and are either in a hotel bed somewhere if the deal was for "all night" or snug in their own beds if it was merely *chuakrao* or short time. The rest are hanging out at a long line of collapsible tables and chairs placed around makeshift bars on the sidewalk that have suddenly appeared and stretch, with intermissions, for over a mile. Fortune-tellers also have emerged from whatever underworld they inhabit during the day: a square of dark cloth on the ground, some Hindu diagrams of the body, some Buddhist diagrams of the mind, a couple of packs of well-worn tarot cards, a guide to palm reading, and you're set up as a clairvoyant, or *mordu*, of the night. It's a clever piece of targeting: almost every girl who is still around at this time is feeling down on her luck and needs reassurance. Generally, though, the ladies of the night resort to the more reliable relief of a bottle of rice whiskey shared among friends. At the same time I'm wondering in some dark alley of the heart, *Are they having sex together right now, Chanya and Krom, this minute, while I'm walking along?*

Nothing like self-regard to strip you of your street smarts: I do not hear the car roll up, or the door open and close, or quick steps behind me. I do not even realize I am no longer alone until a feline caress begins at the base of my spine. Even then I assume it is a girl risking all on the last chance of the night; I turn with a *Sorry, darling* smile on my face. It is him.

He is taller than me by about four inches with a proportionate advantage in body mass. It is his superhuman fitness, though, that intimidates. I do not feel threatened—I do not think he is about to kill me—but I am unmanned. He walks beside me with effortlessness grace, while I immediately begin to sweat and my pulse rate increases. When he takes my arm I'm unsure how to react: to pull away might be offensive; on the other hand, that gentle but firm hold on my right forearm is freaking me out. Now he leans over to me to whisper a sweet nothing in my ear:

"'Twice or thrice had I loved thee before I knew thy face or name, so *angels affect us oft.*'"

He smiles into my shock. It is important, though, to keep walking. "I know you're a compulsive, like me," he whispers. "You've read everything in your search for self, haven't you? But it's time you realized something very important."

"What?"

He wants me to look him in the face again, but I am unable to. That pale skin, slightly tanned, those cornflower-blue eyes, that short hair so blond it is almost white: the eerie beauty that came over in the video clip is tripled in real life. A trillion dollars of *farang* brainwashing from Hollywood is telling me how perfect he is, theoretically. I need to keep walking with my eyes focused on the pavement, like a woman proposi-tioned by a strange man late at night.

"That old man in the hospital, our biological father, he can't tell you anything about yourself," he whispers in my ear. "He is the past. He has no relevance anymore. We are on our own in the world, you and I. We need to bond." He speaks gently, as if to a child. "Don't be frightened of me. I wouldn't hurt you for anything. You're all I have, my love. All I have on this great wide earth." He hesitates. "This *sterile promontory*, as the poet said." He leans around as we walk to produce a caring, loving smile right in my face. I cannot do other than to give a half smile back. Fear aside, the sense of being trapped in a submissive female role is profoundly irritating, but even if I had not seen what that superbody can do, his superior training and strength are too obvious, too much a part of his reality to ignore.

He sighs. "It's okay, I understand, this is all very new to you. How did you like the camp, though? What a dump, huh?" He makes a face that I suppose is intended to be nonchalant. "Oh, how I wish you could have seen it at its height, with us kids running around, everything ship-shape, spick and span, every day a holiday. Football, baseball, fencing, athletics, classical music, poetry—we were all so smart, you see, junk culture could not seduce us, for the Doc had inculcated us with his own tastes in the arts—cries of joy, our little souls overwhelmed by our great good fortune all the livelong day. It was our holiday camp long, long ago. That's where I met our daddy for the first time . . . I wanted so much to be there with you when you visited, but they told me, 'No, it's too soon, the poor love has to catch up with things you've known all your life.'"

He stops to hold my shoulders and turns me to face him full fron-tal, smiles again with tolerance and patience, like a lover who does not doubt his wooing will win out in the end. "Don't you want to thank me for setting it all up for you? You do know it was me all along, don't you?"

"Ah, yes, I think I worked that out. The iPhone was yours, there was only one entry in Contacts, I called it. Yes, you set it all up brilliantly."

He smiles and looks as if he is about to pinch my cheek, so pleased is he with me. "I can wait, oh yes I can wait, but you have to let me share my little treats with you. One by one, not all at once, naturally. The *last* thing I want is to freak you out."

I am focused on his voice now; light, silky, freshly washed, not a trace of blue-collar masculinity; not a soldier's voice at all. It sings a song of vacancy. Is that a howl I hear behind it all? Is this really my brother? I feel his antiseptic need like a steel band around my head, tightening. This must be the demonic motivation Dr. Bride spoke of: the vacuum from which all life flees.

Only now I become aware of the car that has been following us. It is exceptionally quiet because it is a sky-blue Rolls-Royce. Now it slides up to stop with the rear near-side door perfectly aligned with us. The door opens. "Please, my dearest brother," he says and jerks his chin.

I enter a HiSo world of aromatic leather, discreet perfume, air-conditioning at a pleasant twenty-three centigrade, and the famous barrister Lord Sakagorn dressed in a dinner jacket with plum bow tie, his long hair held back in a new silver clip, sitting in the front passenger seat, his liveried driver at the wheel.

"Are you excited?" the Asset asks me. "You're going to see your kid brother strut his stuff—not all of it, just a little exhibition to help with sales, isn't that right, Lord Sakagorn?"

Sakagorn is almost dumb with embarrassment. "Yes," he manages and sags. "Yes, that's right."

Next to me in the backseat the Asset stretches out. He flashes me a smile. "Forgive me, my brother, I need to go into a different space now. I have to prepare. I might not have time for you until it's over." He closes his eyes and psychically disappears, leaving only that extraordinary body.

Silence as the limousine rolls through Chinatown. Normally there are gold shops with glittering lights and Sikh guards in turbans with pump-action shotguns on just about every corner, and hundreds of small clothes stalls that take up the sidewalks and narrow the road; now, though, it is too late even for gold traders. We pass a couple of Chinese Christian churches that were founded before Constantine converted, a huge gaudy Taoist shrine, the Temple of the Gold Buddha, then a glimpse of the river. Fangton, the other bank, is the downmarket side where murders are more common and less expensive: I take comfort from the fact that this is Sakagorn's Rolls-Royce and all the people we pass give it a second glance. A kidnap is unlikely. Now we take the bridge to cross the river.

"It's a fight?" I ask Sakagorn. It is the obvious conclusion, after all. The Asset is quite still and appears not to have heard the question.

"Yes."

"A kind of exhibition match?"

"You could say that."

"Who—" I stop myself because I almost said *we*. "Who's *he* fighting?"

"Rungkom."

I gasp. "Oh no."

Sakagorn doesn't say anything, merely stares ahead into the night.

Rungkom retired as unbeaten Muay Thai national and international champion about five years ago. People wondered why he didn't keep fighting for another few seasons, considering the amount of money he was making; there was a hint of moral weakness, whether women, drugs, or alcohol is unclear, although most gossips cited all three as probable causes. Everybody knew that Rungkom, a great bashful hulk from Isaan when he first started on his career, just loved to party with Krung Thep's fashionable elite. The usual dark stories abounded, implying a dependency on cocaine and indebtedness to loan sharks. What I remembered of him in the ring was an incredible high kick with speed and feints that seemed to come out of nowhere. It was so fast and so hard, no one could figure out a response. Most of his fights ended in the first or second round. His face, rocky with scars, appears vividly in my mind as we drive to the fight. I recall that his path has taken a certain predictable turn since his retirement and drug dependency. He is by far and away our most popular and expensive private boxer: the kind rich men hire to fight bare-knuckle in secret locations where the betting starts at a million baht.

Sakagorn's driver slows the car when we reach a ragged area where not much has been done to separate the land from the river, which flooded a few days ago, leaving a lot of mud and uninhabitable dirt between building projects that were ruined by the water. The driver knows where to stop thanks to two large halogen lamps that have been set up on the wasteland where a single white Lexus people mover is waiting with the lights on.

The barrister Sakagorn shakes his head. "Such a shame, such a sacrifice—but what can you do?" Suddenly he loses control. "Fuck you, Jitpleecheep, fuck you to hell." I stare at him. "It didn't have to be Rungkom, any bunch of hoodlums would have done. He could take out ten no problem. This is to impress *you*." The Asset remains in deep meditation, oblivious.

We stop about a hundred feet from the Lexus and Sakagorn gets out of the Rolls. At the same time the sliding door of the Lexus opens and Goldman emerges. The halogen lamps catch the catastrophe that seven decades have wrought on the agent's fat face. Unlike Sakagorn, though, he seems in fine fettle: a man in a rare mood eager to rock and roll. He waits for the aristocrat to approach him. I watch Sakagorn cross the waste ground. Lord Sakagorn seems to diminish in stature with each step. The two men do not *wai* or shake hands. Goldman sneers down at him while they speak.

Now I become aware of another vehicle, a huge Toyota Carryboy at the opposite end of the clearing, which I had not noticed because it sits in darkness. The internal lights flash on as doors open on either side. The mighty Rungkom and his trainer emerge, with two bodyguards. The athletic figure of the former Muay Thai star stands out, a superior being in his own right. When the doors shut and the light goes out, the fighter and his entourage of about six or seven are almost invisible. They stand near the truck and wait. Rungkom folds his arms and stands with his legs apart, steady as a rock in the shadows.

It becomes clear we are waiting for someone else. Lights of another vehicle arriving at the edge of the wasteland light up bits of ground, then pick out bits of the night sky as it bounces over debris. The new vehicle is a people mover, a Toyota that looks hired. Music and laughter burst from it when someone opens the sliding door at the back. The music is a mixture of Thai and Cantopop, the laughter both raucous and effeminate at the same time. Now Professor Chu emerges; both Goldman and Sakagorn rush to welcome him. While they are doing so, three exquisite *katoeys* also emerge, giggling and rasping simultaneously. They recognize Rungkom across the clearing lit up from the lights of their vehicle and *wai* him like a hero. Then they spot his opponent, the silent Asset who has emerged from Sakagorn's Rolls to lean against it negligently. Who will die tonight? The *katoeys* give way to frivolity, as if the tense mood is something to be tasted like wine, then spat out again. But they follow the discipline of the bordello: their job is to take care of Chu; that is what he is paying for and those are seasoned professionals behind the baby-doll faces. They gather around him, searching his body language for clues as to how he wants to play this very exciting game.

Chu handles the social challenge by switching between personalities, one for the trannies, the other for Goldman and Sakagorn. I don't think either of them were expecting the *katoeys*, but the Professor is a rep with enough spending power to buy an infinity of patience, assuming his anonymous client is the PRC; or, to be precise, one of its ministries. Sakagorn gives him the full *wai* that he normally only reserves for very HiSo locals; even Goldman is able to control himself enough to demonstrate a degree of charm. He bows to the Prof at the same time as taking one of his hands in both of his, as if making some kind of betrothal, then welcomes him in Mandarin. Chu accepts the homage without reciprocating. On the other hand, he responds to jokes, prods, and caresses by the *katoeys* like a teen on a first date. It is like watching a light go on and off, depending on whether he is addressing the *katoeys* or the two high-powered salesmen. The party pauses, though, when more headlights precede another visitor. The vehicle is a police van. As soon as it comes to a halt, the rear door slides open.

Krom is in her black tailored boiler suit. I'm not sure if it represents the latest in tomwear, or a signal that she is on some kind of special duty. The emergence of two Chinese with a high-tech video camera does nothing to dispel the ambiguity. Her van has stopped about fifty yards away from what must be the arena and sits in darkness once the driver has switched the lights off. Chu, the *katoeys*, Goldman, and Sakagorn fall silent and strain their eyes in Krom's direction. Chu blinks at the two Chinese cameramen. I am not sure if it is the same two who were at the Heaven's Gate Tower, nor if they are the same as the team at the river that day. Do we have a total of six, four, or two video specialists in the plot? Three ministries, or two or one? Chu, his face flat as a mahjong tile, watches the team silently carry their camera and tripod across the waste ground and focus it. There can be no doubt, now, where the fight will take place. Goldman's van, Rungkom's four-by-four, and Sakagorn's Rolls mark three points on the circumference of a circle. Krom and I have seen each other, but she didn't wave and neither did I. Right now I have no idea what side she's on. These are fast-moving times. Two days ago we were close, now we are alienated. I'm already feeling strange enough when the door to the police van slides open again and a woman emerges. I recognize the striped red-and-gold leggings, the white Spanish leather belt, the pearl blouse, and the long earrings, because I paid for them. Chanya doesn't acknowledge me either. When Krom and I finally make eye contact, hers are cold as ice. No time or opportunity to make a scene, though. Something heavier than a troubled heart is at issue this night.

Now Goldman has switched his attention from Chu to the cameramen. It seems he was waiting for something that hasn't happened, so he strides over to them. He speaks to them in Mandarin; one nods, the other shakes his head. Both of them return to the police van to bring back a second camera and tripod that they plant at the opposite end of the arena to the first one. Now the team is split between the two machines, one man each. Goldman wants a professional two-camera video, not a functional evidence-gathering exercise. Once the cameras are in place the show can go on. He nods at Sakagorn, his sidekick. The Senior Counsel nods back.

"Okay," the giant says in English, facing one of the cameras. "These are the rules. Rounds will last one minute. To compensate for unfair advantage, my Asset will not respond aggressively in any way during the first round. That means he will conduct a purely defensive fight for that round. He will not punch or kick. During all subsequent rounds, he will have right of reply with fists only, while Khun Rungkom can use fists, feet, shins, head—what the hell he likes. Breaks last thirty seconds. Okay?"

The question seems directed at me. I deflect it by looking at Rungkom, who nods. Goldman doesn't ask the Asset if he's happy to be a punch ball for sixty seconds at the mercy of a world-champion kickboxer. The Asset rouses himself, though, and begins a few warm-up exercises that include stretching his arms laterally and making small circles with his hands while he runs gently on the spot. I try to decipher the body language between these two men. There isn't any. My impression is of a marriage on the rocks.

Sakagorn takes a whistle and a stopwatch out of a pocket of his dinner jacket while Goldman guides the two fighters to the circle of open ground between the three vehicles. Sakagorn is about to blow his whistle, but someone yells *stop*, first in Thai, then in English. It is Krom, holding her smart phone. She strides over to Goldman and looks up at him. "Someone else is expected."

Goldman stares down at her. "Listen, lady, if that's what you are, this is my party, okay? No one else is expected."

"It's classified, that's why it's last-minute. I received a message." She holds up her phone. So far she has spoken in Thai. Now she adds in English, "You will wait."

Goldman looks as if he is about to explode, then calms down. Perhaps he has guessed who the mysterious guest may be. He shrugs. "Whoever it is gets five minutes, no more. We don't need unnecessary exposure."

A minute later the lights of another vehicle appear from the road, then bounce around as the car hits the uneven ground. I seem to recognize the old battered red Mitsubishi. It stops near the imaginary circle of the boxing ring, the lights die, and Sergeant Ruamsantiah emerges from the driver's side, Colonel Vikorn from the other. I might have guessed. Both of those Isaan boys are fanatical Muay Thai fans and were passionate about Rungkom in his day. The Sergeant earned himself a lot of street cred at the station by claiming he was a personal friend of the famous fighter. Both men are dressed in the same outfits they have worn to boxing tournaments since they were kids: worn T-shirts and jeans. The Colonel also sports a cloth cap. He scans the scene, absorbing its essence in a blink, while the Sergeant walks over to Rungkom and *wais* him with deep humility. I cannot make out the words, but by the gestures and the expression of extreme concern on the Sergeant's face, it is not difficult to guess. Rungkom responds also with a *wai* and a gracious smile. He is expressing compassion for Sergeant Ruamsantiah, who is reduced almost to tears. *Don't worry*, the fighter seems to be saying, *this is my choice, my karma, thank you for your kind concern.*

The Sergeant leaves him, shaking his head. Meanwhile the Colonel has summoned Krom and spoken to her. Whatever he said seems to have impressed her. She walks back to Goldman. "The Colonel bets ten million baht on Khun Rungkom."

"This isn't—" Goldman stops himself in midsentence. Perhaps he has remembered how important Vikorn's agency is to his project. He starts again. "We're not taking bets. We're not set up for it."

"In that case, if Khun Rungkom loses, the ten million will go to his family." She has spoken loudly enough for the fighter to hear. Rungkom walks over to Vikorn, gives him the high *wai*, and thanks him. He returns to his corner. Goldman nods at Sakagorn again, who blows his whistle.

Now the fight has officially begun. In Muay Thai, however, there are protocols to be observed. Rungkom first kneels and *wais* to make homage to the master who taught him to box and the spirits who have helped him so far in his career. Now he nods at Sakagorn, who has returned to his Rolls-Royce and wound all the windows down. The unmistakable notes of a Thai oboe, called a *pi chawa*, emerge from the limo's first-class sound system and Rungkom begins his warrior's dance, which lasts only a few minutes. The Asset continues his mild limbering-up exercises.

The open area of ground is quite small and the fighters have to remain under the lamps in order to work. A second blow on the whistle means they can start the action. Now they face off.

The Asset hardly pays any attention to Rungkom, who begins to dance around him, feinting with both fists and feet in order to make a full professional inventory of his opponent's strengths and weaknesses. Rungkom is puzzled because the American makes no effort to evade kicks that come within a millimeter of his face. It is as if he can measure distance down to nano level and guess the feints by some kind of telepathy. Then when the Thai finally lets loose with a head kick from an unexpected direction, the Asset simply isn't there. He dodged at exactly the right moment, leaving only a split-second margin to avoid a blow that would have broken his cheekbone.

So it went on and I began to feel despondent. It's true there were two strikes from the champion that left the Asset shaking his head and bleeding from cuts above and below his eyes, but those were blows that should have ended the fight, and the Asset merely staggered. Sergeant

Ruamsantiah has covered his face with his hands. I want to yell, *Run, Rungkom, run for your life.* But I see from his face that he has reached a very personal conclusion. Perhaps he isn't so fond of his HiSo lifestyle as the media claims. Perhaps he is somewhat disillusioned with success and feels a certain nostalgia for the early days when he was the hottest kid in Muay Thai and every fight was a personal statement of his quest for freedom and glory. He really is a champion, for already he has understood that he cannot win, that he might not leave this wasteland alive, but Sakagorn will have to give his family the agreed price and pay off the loan sharks, or someone will come for Sakagorn one fine night when he is least expecting it. And of course, there will be ten million from Vikorn, who always honors his debts. As for the fight, the best he can hope for is to damage the Asset so badly that he will be crippled for the next round.

The Asset is tiring, too, though, there's no doubt about that. Rungkom sees it and delivers a full power kick that was designed for the Asset's jaw but—even better—lands on his Adam's apple. Even a fully trained CIA zombie needs air, and for a moment the Asset doubles over coughing violently, as if he is about to fall. Rungkom sees it and comes in for the kill. But this is where training tells. The Asset not only manages to recover with astonishing speed; he has also prepared his posture so that when Rungkom delivers what he had every right to believe would be the killer kick, the Asset is able to twist around so that the force of the blow is lost on the muscles of his shoulder, and Rungkom now is close to exhaustion. A blow as heavy as that drains the fighter who lands it. I cannot describe the brief look that came over the Asset's face when Rungkom hurt him; a snippet of conversation with Dr. Bride flashed across my mind:

You're talking about the devil?

Aren't you?

Sakagorn blows his whistle. That was a very long minute. Now I am muttering out loud, "Run, Rungkom, run for your life."

Thirty seconds have passed and Sakagorn blows the whistle again. Rungkom doesn't care so much for his life, that much is clear now. I think he has decided that a damp and desolate piece of wasteland by the river would make an appropriate place to die and he is looking forward to fighting all the way to the end. He is especially clever at dodging the Asset's punches—at first. It only takes one body blow under the heart to hurt him, though. I cannot doubt that a few ribs broke when that elegant fist landed with sickening force. Now the Thai moves awkwardly, favoring his right side, all too obviously trying to protect the left. Then, crunch: the Asset lands another punch in exactly the same spot under the heart and Rungkom can hardly believe the pain. It is only twenty seconds into the second round, but it's all over for the Thai. Now I can't help it. I yell at the top of my voice, "Get the hell out, Khun Rungkom, for Buddha's sake, it's not worth dying for."

Rungkom is a warrior, though, and knows different. He must have considered many times how it might be to die at the top of his game, under blazing lamps, in the ring of honor. Sakagorn must have promised a fortune to his family or he would never have accepted the challenge.

The Asset stops fighting, turns to Goldman with a sneer on his face, as if he, too, thinks it bad form to have set him against a mere human. Goldman, with an ugly look, gives the thumbs-down. The Asset turns from Goldman to Rungkom with a kind of curiosity. He is like a tiger making a decision as to the most elegant way to destroy his prey. He walks up to Rungkom in a casual way, easily dodges the champion's last sad kick, and puts the full force of his extraordinary body behind an open-palm blow to the center of the fighter's forehead. Rungkom collapses like a sack of cement. As he lies stretched out in the dirt, it is obvious to me that he is dead. I feel only disgust and sickness. Of course, it is impossible not to hate Goldman and his Asset. *That was just a tiny little taste of what we can do*, the expression on the agent's face says.

I watch, stunned, while Rungkom's people carry him to their truck. Two have to enter the vehicle and pull while the others hold him up. Not a chore that can be done with elegance, but they try.

I am sad as hell and pretty much obsessed with what I have just witnessed when I feel a gentle hand on my arm. "Let's go home," Chanya says.

Startled for a moment, I stare at her. "Did you have sex with Krom?" I ask. She takes out her phone to call for a taxi.

28

can only have sex with a man," Chanya says in the back of the cab. "But that's not the most important thing I learned tonight." I raise my sad eyes. She lays a hand over one of mine. "Krom's been enhanced, Sonchai. She's one of them."

An invisible spider crawls up my spine. "Huh?"

"Not like that monster tonight, that Asset—but down that road. Her body is incredibly strong. Not like a woman's at all." I stare at her. She looks away, out of the window, at the silent street. "It's like something has been going on, maybe for decades, behind the backs of ordinary people. While we've been amusing ourselves with our little human issues that have to do with love, sex, and freedom, and the quality of life and democracy and pollution and stewardship of the earth—little minor things like that, which will turn out to be mere distractions— something else has been happening. Something that is about to change everything suddenly and forever—and despite myself I can't wait." For a second a convulsion shakes her body and she emits something between a laugh and a shout. "It all really is going to be over, all of it." She waves a hand to include the world. She seems genuinely relieved.

"What are you talking about?"

She raises her arms dramatically, then lets them drop. "Whatever it is, it's out of control. Forget about human rights, that illusion is about to be squashed by something too big to care—or even notice." She sees the look on my face, squeezes my hand. "Don't be jealous, Sonchai. What is one woman going to fuck another woman with, an inanimate object? How would that satisfy me, given who I am and what I've done? I'm not scared of men and I don't hate them, I spent a career manipulating the hell out of them. I adore the poor weak cuddly things." She lets go of my hand. "She wanted intimacy, let's put it like that. It was fun, for a moment, to be charmed by such a . . . person. She's very funny when she wants to be. Incredibly versatile. She seemed to spill her guts a bit, just like a man would—but now I'm not sure about that. I think there was a lot she told me that she expects me to pass on to you. Stuff she wouldn't tell you directly. I'm a kind of firewall. Coming through me everything is deniable, especially since we were supposed to be having sex at the time."

"What kind of things did she tell you?"

"Well, this Christmas Bride you visited with, she knows a lot more about him than she let on that time she came round to see us. She holds him in awe."

"Krom, in awe?"

"Yes. And she hinted that they're mainly interested in you because of your father."

"*They?*"

"She didn't go into detail. That's the word she used. It's like she belongs to some splinter group that lives off crumbs that the main group throws them. It seems at that camp you visited, in its heyday, well, there was an awful lot of sex and no contraception. Your putative father was particularly active, a real alpha male. A lot of the enhanced kids were from his stock. They didn't know how to bring up freaks. Most died—this Asset survived. That makes them interested in you."

"For my genes?"

"Maybe. Or maybe something else. Maybe for who you are. You see, I saw it tonight with Krom, and I'm sure I'm right about this. They have a problem with their product. Those creatures can switch their programming at the drop of a hat. It's impossible for them to have any lasting allegiance to anything. That's the weakness in the program. They're too smart and accomplished to take ordinary humans seriously, including the ones who created them. And after a certain tipping point they evolve much quicker than us." She shuddered again. "I know they're taking over, I can sense it."

"So how can I help them?"

"They think that with your genetic and emotional connection to your father, and since you're a mature man . . ."

"They want to enhance me?"

"I don't know. That was my first reaction. Krom can be subtle, she dropped little hints and left me to put it all together. After tonight and what you witnessed before on the river, we know that there exists a technology arising out of the LSD experiments fifty years ago that actually works."

"So it seems."

"Think about it for a moment. You insert such people into key positions, just like secret services use moles. But these people rise to the top in everything they do, whether commercial, industrial, military—they *have* to, because they really do leave the rest of us behind by a very long stretch, which gets longer with every breakthrough."

"So you end up with a whole world controlled by talented psychos— where's the change in that?"

"The talent—it's just monumental. Wasn't that the point of the fight tonight? A world-class Muay Thai fighter swatted like a fly?" She lets a few beats pass. "She said something else, I'm half-afraid to tell you because you just won't believe it."

"That's one hell of a tease, Chanya. What did she say?"

"That certain world leaders were already enhanced—not like the Asset, but in minor ways, using spin-offs from the new technology."

"And?"

"Well, one of them lives very north and very west of here in a country that has a history of similar experimentation."

"Why so coy about it?"

"That's how she put it. She wanted you to know that, I'm sure."

"So we're talking north?"

"Northwest. Very far."

"Russia?"

"She wouldn't specify."

I'm watching the night go by out of the cab window, trying to take it all in. "You think Krom is a product of the Chinese version of the experiment?"

"Maybe in a mild way, yes, that's my guess. While I was with her she had to answer a call. She speaks fluent Mandarin, Sonchai—she was just pretending to be at intermediate level that evening with Chu, so as not to make you suspicious. Why would a Thai cop be fluent in Chinese?"

"So she finally admitted outright that the Chinese have foisted her on Vikorn—muscled him to take her on, a spy in his camp?"

"Sort of. Like I said, she used deniable hints, avoided specifics."

"But why is Goldman so keen to sell his product to the Chinese? Shouldn't he be all secret about it, like in a nice old-fashioned arms race?"

"Not race. Think arms *sale*. When my enemy needs to buy my technology to fight a third party, he becomes my friend—but don't tell anyone. Think maybe the Chinese already have a product of their own, but perhaps not so advanced. So the U.S. has a super-smooth version that can just about go to cocktail parties and run multinationals and attend Republican conventions without eating people's livers for hors d'oeuvres. Better they sell that to the Chinese than have the Chinese continue with their own R&D—or buy from someone else."

"The Russians?"

She shrugs. "Krom made it clear the PRC is in a hurry. It has to do with the U.S. dollar. It's a mathematical certainty that it will collapse within the decade—the inevitable consequence of a planet-wide Indian rope trick called quantitative easing: those are her words. There will be riots and chaos worldwide. And China controls a quarter of the world's population. In the West the tightening has already started, even today there's a greater sense of personal freedom in a third-world shantytown than a modern first-world state—sooner or later people will start to notice. The captured elephant doesn't freak until it feels the chain."

"But still . . ."

She inhales deeply. "It's like I said, something big is about to go down. I have no idea what, except it will include a lockdown on individual freedom. She hinted that oligarchs and world bankers are on the committees that run these programs." She paused. "You know, there must be something extra they do to their assets, some form of higher consciousness, like they've learned how to steal a measure of enlightenment."

"What are you talking about?"

"Krom. When I made it clear I couldn't do sex with her, I thought she was going to explode. I actually feared for my life. I suppose she thought that by going back to her flat I was consenting."

"What flat? Where?"

"That's another mystery. She owns a one-bedroom apartment on Sukhumvit at On Nut, but it was clear she doesn't live there. Probably just uses it for pickups."

"So where does she really live?"

"She didn't say. Pretended not to hear the question. Anyway, as I was saying, she had to make a huge effort to control herself. I really thought I was finished. Instead she went into a kind of trance and started to talk." Chanya smirked. "Know what? She started to sound like you."

"How?"

"This is what she said. She said the human being is the only creature aware of death, which is another way of saying our consciousness in its true form is a product of the tension between the two, life and death. If you can't go down to the wire with your own annihilation, then you're never fully human. That used to be what religions were for. The hidden purpose of modernism is to offer a cop-out that turns us into manipulable dolls. No one grows up anymore. Everyone is immortal. When the entire species is stuck at the mental age of thirteen and a half with heads full of noise and football, that's when *they* take over. Not long to go. Pretty much there already. That's what she said."

"What else?"

She shrugs again. "She kept referring to that *batch*—she used that word. They have fierce, childish emotions. According to her, it wasn't Goldman but the Asset himself who ordered the bombing of those old men. The Asset doesn't like it that your mutual father left the camp. To him it's like a violation of some sentimental value, some idealized childhood that probably never happened—they just programmed him that way, not realizing what the consequences might be. To him your father has to be some old tough jungle guy from out of a Stallone movie, not a small-time dope hustler. The Asset chose a moment when he thought those old men would be out at the market to have those kids plant the bomb. He wants the oldies back in the camp."

The cab was turning into our street, and I leaned forward to tell the driver to stop outside our hovel. I was reaching for my wallet to pay him when Chanya came out with her last bombshell.

"Do you know the name Roberto da Silva? She said you'd mentioned him in a text message. She said it's not true that he died. She said he's here in Bangkok, owns a bar on Pat Pong."

I freeze for a moment. It's not the information that has thrown me so much as the incongruity. "Why did she suddenly start talking about that?"

"I don't know. She went into yet another personality. She became very serious and confidential—maybe a last attempt to get me into bed. Or another ploy to reach you. As I said—these creatures, they're shape changers like you wouldn't believe."

If Chanya's ploy was to share confidences as a way of reestablishing intimacy, it worked. By the time we reached home both of us were experiencing the same sense of relief: we belonged together, we would protect each other faithfully from the big scary new *out there*; it was very childish and almost thrilling. Then, just when we were in a deep forgiving embrace that would certainly evolve into the kind of wholesome, tender, unselfish, fantasy-free, loving coupling that, if it exists, rarely survives prolonged cohabitation despite being monotonously recommended by marriage counselors of the old school (I can't recall our ever trying it ourselves), my phone rang.

29

It is Nurse Silapin, using a conciliatory tone.

"Detective, your Inspector Krom explained everything to me. I think I owe you an apology regarding the other night. We all thought you were trying to collect evidence for a criminal investigation. Now I know the real reason you wanted to take a DNA sample."

"Yes?"

"Detective, something extraordinary has happened to the man you think may be your father. In view of the fact that you may be the next of kin, I think you should come immediately."

"Okay."

"Detective, I'm sorry, but the administration has requested me to insist. There can be no swabs, not even for the most intimate of reasons."

"Right. I learned my lesson."

I pull my clothes back on and run down the *soi* to Sukhumvit to find a cab. I tell the driver to take me to the hospital, and as we flash down a black and empty street, I think about that word: *extraordinary*. Not negative, exactly; not necessarily positive either. Do I really need ambiguity right now?

At the hospital I knock on the door of the special room and Nurse Silapin lets me in. Willie J. Schwartz and Larry Krank are standing together at the far end, next to their beds. I think I understand the problem when I look at Harry Berg, aka Jack, who is in the nearest bed, his eyes wide open and staring at the ceiling, a beatific expression on his face. No matter how long I wait, he does not blink, but that does not faze me. I am in a state of intense excitement, for they have changed his bandages and removed those that covered most of his face. There is no longer any doubt, this is the Rainbow Man who stalked me on Soi Cowboy, Lalita's favorite customer of the month.

"How long has he been like this?"

"About five hours."

"He can't talk?"

"Can't or won't," Nurse Silapin says. "I thought at first of catatonia, but it's definitely not that."

"How do you know?"

"We did a CAT scan." She frowns.

"And?"

"Basically with a CAT you're looking for parts of the brain which normally show neural activity but are unresponsive due to trauma."

"Yes?"

"Well, his brain is all lit up in dozens of places. It's not that he isn't conscious, it's as if he's suddenly super conscious. I've done some research, but there are only a few anecdotes, no real precedents for something like this. The doctors are scratching their heads. They want to leave him alone for the moment. All his vital signs are excellent."

I look from the nurse to the two old vets at the other end of the room. Willie is staring at the floor, while Larry Krank is fixated by a speck on the wall. I ask the nurse if she would mind stepping out for a moment while I talk to these old men. She seems confused but complies.

I walk up to the two of them, hands on hips, leaning forward, outraged. "You gave him *acid*?"

Both old men avoid my eyes.

"He wanted us to, Sonchai. We could feel it."

So they know my name. How?

"If he comes down, he'll explain himself. We've all been together so long, we kind of know what the other is feeling."

I splutter. "Doc Bride gave it to you?"

"He sent some."

"After the damage that drug did you?"

"Wasn't the acid, it was the way they used it. See, we had to go back past that, and the only way there was more acid. We made friends with LSD, you might say."

"The Spirit. It's what we call it."

"That's how we knew Jack needed it."

I take a step back and assess them coldly. I shake my head. There is no way to read these guys.

Willie, though, seems to understand there is a gulf between our respective grasps of reality. He tries to remember how normal people behave and talk, so he can adapt his argument.

"We became experts," he says. "Not on the level of the Doc himself, but pretty good."

"The Doc's something else. He's a real scientist, a genius."

"A mad genius, but a genius."

"He has a scale of levels. Jack is on level seven right now, the highest."

"That's why we're not worried. Nothing bad can happen to anyone on that level."

"The whole cosmos is open to him right now. Just look at his face if you don't believe me."

"The Spirit rules," Willie says.

"Amen," Larry says.

"How's that?" I ask.

"It's what we say when someone is on level seven: they have ascended, they are not the same person at all."

"It's like with the Doc. When he's on seven, well, watch out, that's not a human anymore, that's something from a higher realm."

I have to admit Harry Berg, aka Jack, looks pretty happy right now. Considering how stressed and confused I feel, I guess you could say he's better off.

"You're really Sonchai the detective?" Larry asks, smiling warmly. "That's great. That's just wonderful." I stare at him; clearly there is more. He looks at the floor shyly. "You could say you're the reason we're in Bangkok. We could have made a lot more money in Pattaya or Phuket, but Jack insisted we stay here in the city, so he could be near you."

"Really?"

"He worships the earth you walk on, Sonchai. To him you're some kind of miracle. He expected you to be in jail or dead from an overdose long ago. You're a Buddha to him. He keeps telling us how beautiful you are. He took pictures of you on some cheap cell phone he bought for a thousand baht. Sometimes he visited the street five, ten times in a week, just to see you, just to watch you walk past him. One time when he was falling around drunk in the street you helped him up and asked where he lived and helped him to a cab. You remember that?"

I shake my head. "No."

"Look," Larry says, "we're real sorry about how we reacted last time. We were sure you were going to bust us."

"So we figured out a way of making it up to you," Willie says.

I wait while Larry goes to his bed to pick up something from under his pillow. It is an envelope of the kind hospitals use, with plastic lining. He has me look into it: two cotton swabs, like Q-tips. He grins at me. Willie nods at Jack on his back, still beaming. I look furtively around the room.

"I'll do it for you if you like," Larry says. He goes over to Jack with the swabs, pulls open his jaw with one hand, swabs around inside his mouth with one Q-tip then the other, pops them in the envelope, and hands it to me. "There's no doubt who you are, of course. But everybody likes to be sure about stuff like this."

I leave the hospital with dark misgivings. I just don't know how I feel about Jack permanently high on "level seven." It would be the ultimate irony if, as a good Buddhist boy, I have to go into trafficking to take care of my elderly father who is incapacitated due to enlightenment. Never mind, I have the swabs now, I'll send them off to Know the Father in the morning.

30

It does not take a great feat of detection. I used to know the names of all the bars in Pat Pong because Mama Nong still worked there from time to time while I was growing up. When I tick them off in my mind, one name in particular hits me like a truck. I take a cab to Pat Pong.

It's a discreet little pub, less than half the size of the great sex palaces that line the street. It looks as if it caters to a regular clientele and has no need to advertise: the sort of bar that remains a favorite with oldies, Vietnam vets in particular. And of course, bars like this where everyone pays cash are second only to casinos as facilities for laundering money.

Exactly as I remembered, the legend in italics above the entrance reads simply *Silver's*. It is late afternoon and the cleaning staff are at work making it all shipshape for the evening's festivities: aroma of pine cleaning fluid; women with bamboo brooms sweeping; a supervisor in her late forties checking the register. There is a platform for girls to dance in bikinis, or in their birthday suits; it's small, though, with hardly room for more than three girls. All in all the bar is a little money box that would not cost much in terms of bribes to keep it operating.

None of the cleaning staff want to bother with me, which allows me to walk up to the woman at the cash register and ask, in the most casual of voices, "Is Khun da Silva around?"

She does not look up. "No."

"Can you tell me how I can contact him?"

Now she looks up. "No."

"Why not?"

She pauses in her work to assess me. "Look, if you're law enforcement, we already paid this month. You need to check with Colonel Wanakan."

When she tries to go back to unpacking paper tubes of ten-baht coins, I place an arm across the till. She stares at me, more in contempt than fear. "You don't have to tell me where he is. You only have to call him, then pass me the phone." At the same time I am flashing my cop ID.

She shrugs. "Who shall I say wants to speak to him?"

"Tell him Son of Jack."

"Son of Jack?"

"Yes. Son of Jack and Nong."

I watch while she picks up her own phone and presses an autodial number. She repeats my message into the phone, then hands it to me. Silence, then: "Yes?"

"I need to see you."

"Impossible. Why?"

I try to think how to play it. What do I have that a man like that could possibly relate to? "Desolation," I say.

The address is less than ten minutes' walk from Silver's, a midrange apartment building with underground parking and a three-man security detail in the lobby. When I explain I'm here to see Khun Da-Sil-Va (you need to pronounce it in a singsong if you want to be understood, with the *Da* high, the *Sil* low, and the *Va* high), the mood music changes. The security makes a call to someone who must be fluent in Thai, then gives me a high *wai* when they close the phone. With a deference usually reserved in our culture for money and aristocracy, they show me to a private lift that serves the penthouse.

Penthouses are special worldwide. In Southeast Asia they tend to be almost unbuyable, because the developer reserves them for himself, either to live in or let, or as a safe repository of wealth. I'm holding that thought when the door opens and a Thai man in his early forties opens the door. He doesn't need to pump iron, this guard, nature and a childhood in Isaan built him like a tank. Once I'm over the threshold, an American voice calls in Thai.

"He's here," the bodyguard says, and shows me into a reception area with upscale furnishings. I'm guessing the apartment is at least ten thousand square feet. The man in the wheelchair is looking out the window at the cityscape of Pat Pong and Sarawong. From another angle it is just possible to glimpse the river. Even from the back I can see how huge his head is, how developed those arms and shoulders. He tells the guard to leave us, and only after the door has shut does he swing his chair around. He is old, of course, well over sixty. I don't know if he kept his hair color or if he dies it black; everything about him gives the impression of latent power—except he has no legs. He offers a hand; I shake it.

"So, you found me."

"Did you expect me to?"

He shrugs those enormous shoulders. "It was always a possibility." He frowns. "But I don't know where he is, don't want to know, haven't wanted to know for four decades." He makes a grimace. "We had a falling-out."

"How's that?"

He nods in the direction of where his legs once were. "He couldn't handle it. You could almost say it was worse for him than me. He filled his heart with rage and a lust for vengeance. Joined Special Forces. They mangled his personality, he went through a total change, hundred and eighty degrees. I had enough to cope with, my own head wasn't so strong after the grenade, but my mother was a good Catholic who brought me up to avoid feelings of intense hatred. The way I saw it, we invaded someone else's country and got what was coming to us. I felt unlucky, but not unjustly treated—at least not by Charlie. I told him I couldn't handle seeing him anymore. Then he volunteered for something else—something even worse." He pauses to stare into space. He whispers hoarsely, "The first five years after the attack are a blur to me. It was all sex and drugs on the way to oblivion."

"What happened to change you?"

He smiles. "My mother came to see me. She figured I wouldn't be able to stand her heartache. She was right. She was also no longer young. I promised to go on living for as long as she did—but I wasn't going back to the States." He raises his great arms then lets them down. "No way she really understood what that meant in the seventies, coming from a vet who had settled in Bangkok."

"What did it mean?"

He scowls. "That woman managing the bar told me you're a cop. Do you have to ask?"

I let the question hang for a moment. "You had no start-up money to open a bar?"

"Now you're getting close."

"You're not known to law enforcement in Thailand—I checked."

He nods. "So, I don't need to spell it out for you, do I?"

"Some non-Thai agency heard about you. CIA or FBI? One or the other. They came to see you." I wave a hand at the enormous room. "Owning a modest bar doesn't buy this kind of accommodation. But they must have had more than suspicions."

"They had a scandal is what they had. Sending young American men to get themselves killed and mutilated in a lost cause was bad enough. To compound that with stuffing the bodies of heroes with smack before flying the bags home—that had to be dealt with, and seen to be dealt with. But I was lucky, they had nothing at all on me. On the other hand, it would have been easy—very, very easy—to fit me up." He scratches an ear. "I don't know how the name of your father came up. They kind of inserted it into the conversation, it seemed for no reason. Then I realized they wanted something from me."

"What?"

"Silence. It was the late seventies, the great scandal of Frank Olson was still in everyone's mind. The war was long lost. They knew I knew your father had volunteered for that program. Far more important to the agency than violations of the bodies of heroes was the containing of MKUltra."

"Go on."

"Naturally, I promised on my honor not to participate in or in any way become involved with that particularly despicable form of private enterprise that so desecrated the bodies of the fallen. And I promised never to talk about your father and MKUltra."

"In return, it seems they left you alone?"

"Yes. I would have preferred they hadn't gone and lost me my legs in the first place." He makes a gesture to include the whole penthouse. "This is just a consolation prize. There were quite a few vets who took the same route. At one time half the bars on Pat Pong were part-owned by vets. Some of them are still around."

"You said they 'inserted' the name of my father into the conversation."

"Yeah."

"What was that name?"

"Jack."

"Jack what?"

He stares at me. "You're kidding, right? Or are you deaf?"

"He's my father, I have a right to know."

"And I have a right to go on living in crippled luxury. If and when you report this conversation, there's only one conclusion that matters: I refused to tell you the name of your father. End of story." He stares at me. "Maybe you are desperate, but how am I supposed to test that? You could be working for them, trying to set me up."

"Why would they want to do that?"

He shrugs. "If I knew why the CIA do things I would have detailed knowledge of why the world is so fucked, wouldn't I?"

"But why would my father's name be an issue? When you knew him you were both FNGs, hanging out together, doing R&R in Bangkok. You must have known his family name? You must have heard it every day at roll call."

He swings his chair around to stare at the distant river. Now he has his back to me and seems to be talking as much to himself as to me.

"He called you Sonchai. Is that still your name?"

"Yes."

He gives a dry chuckle. "It took me five years of learning Thai before I realized he'd screwed up. The standard name is *Somchai*—with an *m*. *Sonchai* means to think or dream. It kind of symbolized everything, that little mistake of his. Like no matter how hard we tried, we were bound to screw up out of sheer ignorance." He swings the chair around again to face me. "I cannot tell you his family name because they disappeared him, airbrushed him out—with his consent."

He is not without compassion. He has to take a deep breath before he is able to say, "He doesn't exist, Sonchai, except as a ghost, a memory. That was the deal he made when he volunteered, and they expect it to stay that way."

I stand still, frozen. He turns away from my gaze. "Think it through, Detective. You leave this building knowing the family name of someone who was volunteered for Ultra. Now you or someone working for you starts to make inquiries over the Net, using that name. Within hours I receive a visit. Maybe this time they'll come with local law enforcement and a file full of evidence, real or false, it doesn't really matter."

"Linking you with the smuggling of heroin in the body bags?"

He stares at me until I break eye contact. "You're smart, but maybe a little naïve, and that leads you to miss the point."

"What's that?"

"We're living in a giant Ponzi scheme. The Fed buys Treasury bonds without spending money because it doesn't have any. Currency is created on a computer—it's totally notional. There is nothing at all to back it up. The system was never designed that way, we're in a virtual universe."

"What the hell has that got to do with anything?"

"The black hole is massive and it's eating the world. Even ordinary Americans have started to feel it. Government has come to mean papering over the abyss with fairy tales. Politicians know those fairy tales are the only things people are still willing to vote for. But it's very fragile. Anything can pop the balloon at any moment. There's no morality in government service, except the duty to keep covering up. No one wants to be the whistle-blower who destroyed the world. Even sleeping scandals from long ago have the power to bring down the seawall. So what do you think the intelligence services of the planet are really planning for? Not sabotage by a foreign power, but massive civil unrest. A super police force manned by supermen and superwomen is the only way to go." He stares at me as if sorely tempted to say more. Then he shuts up and turns away. I think, *Black hole*, that phrase again.

I give it one last shot. "He must have come to see you *after* he was in the Ultra program. At least once, or you wouldn't know all this."

He looks me in the eye. "He wasn't the same man, Sonchai, he really wasn't the same man."

31

Next day I'm at the cooked-food stall opposite the station, my gun jammed down the back of my pants, eating *khao kha moo* and continuing to absorb my meeting with Roberto da Silva, who looms in my memory like a crippled hero from a time of giants. Then my phone vibrates and I pull it out of my pants pocket. The message from Chanya is simple enough: **HE'S HERE. FOR BUDDHA'S SAKE HELP.**

For a long moment I blink at the phone, unable to take it in. Now I realize who *he* is and I'm trying to get *her* on the phone. No answer. I'm sweating, I can feel my face twitching with fear and rage. I put money on the table for the food, stand in the street to stop a cab that already has a passenger, a *farang*. I flash my police ID: "Emergency." The *farang* gets out grudgingly at first, then speeds up when he sees my face. He starts to say, "I'm not paying—"

I cut him off, push him out of the way, tell the cab driver to ignore the rules, just get me there. I sit beside him, frantically trying to get someone on the phone, anyone who knows her: my mother, *her* mother, her closest friends. Finally, I have the brilliant idea of calling our next-door neighbor.

"Someone came about half an hour ago, I happened to be looking out the window."

"Man or woman?"

"Man."

"So what did he look like?"

"No need to shout. He was tall, young, a *farang*." A snicker. "Very good-looking, blond, a real pinup."

"Is he still there?"

"I don't know. I only looked out for a moment. I'm not a nosey person." She adds, "Don't worry, she's a good girl, you know, very kind and devout, I'm sure—"

I cut her off.

At the hovel I throw some twenty-baht bills at the cab driver, run to the front door, knock, ring, and fumble with my keys at the same time. It doesn't help that someone has closed the drapes so I cannot see inside. When I enter it's quite dark. I switch on the lights. A flood of relief: Chanya is there, sitting on her chair by her computer. A flood of terror: she isn't moving. A flood of relief: I can see she is breathing. There is something strange about her, though. She is rigid. When I touch her I feel a vibration. She is shivering in a way I've never seen before: a constant shaking of her whole body, but high-frequency shortwaves as if she is plugged into some machine. I turn her face to look at her. Her eyes are open windows to the terror within. I tap her gently on the shoulder, grab a bottle of red wine I've been meaning to drink one happy evening when this damned case is over, open it, pour her a mugful. She opens her mouth, allows me to pour some in. When it starts to drip down her chin she snaps out of her coma, swallows, reaches for the mug, downs it. I pour some more.

"He was here," she gasps. "That thing of yours. He came."

"What did he do?"

She shakes her head. "Nothing. Sonchai, that's what is so incredibly scary. He didn't need to do anything. He just stood there. Oh, Buddha, I've never known anything like it. This big, slim, gorgeous man with the most beautiful hands and Hollywood good looks simply stood there and scared the living shit out of me. He's not human. Whatever it is he gives off, it's not human. You can't be around him. I saw that at the fight, but I was too far away to understand. I thought he was just some super soldier the CIA had created—I had no idea what it really meant, that something like that could actually exist. *His eyes.*" She gulps some more wine.

"He didn't say anything?"

She shakes her head. "Oh, yes, he did."

"What?"

She stares at me and starts to shake again. I try to hold her, but she pushes me away. She is not shaking with terror, but with a kind of high, disbelieving laughter. "He said, 'Happy birthday to you.' For tomorrow." She shakes her head at me as if to say, *Can you believe this?* "You forgot, so did I. *He* remembered."

"Did he say anything else?"

"That you had to meet him for your birthday lunch. You must not tell anyone else. And you must not bring a weapon. If you told anyone or brought a weapon, he would know. But otherwise you would be perfectly safe. He did not want to hurt a hair on your head."

"That's all?"

"Then he said, 'Tell my brother I'm sorry if I've been rude.'" She looks at me. "That was the weirdest of all. Like he just appears from nowhere, scares me to death, then worries that he might have offended *you.* Like he's broken some minor social rule, when he's, you know, the living walking image of something totally alien that doesn't belong, like something that just got off a spaceship—and he says it again, in a polite tone, quite apologetic as if he was really concerned: 'Tell my brother I'm sorry if I've been rude.' But at the same time the psychic gouging was deliberate, he started to feed off my terror and had to control himself. I could feel him doing things to my guts, just by staring, boring straight into my womb. He knew what he was doing. He kind of paralyzed me with perverted lust that twisted my guts. He had to literally snap out of it, or he would have had his fun with me. I would have been like that poor girl whose murder you're investigating, body parts all over the house." She poured herself some more wine. "That's beyond screwed up, Sonchai, that's way beyond psycho. And I could tell, he has perfect mental organization—I bet he would come out sane and well-balanced in any test. Probably a model citizen."

"A *model citizen,*" I repeat, grabbing the bottle and swallowing some wine before she drinks it all. We stare at each other.

"I forgot," Chanya says, drunk now. "He left you this."

She takes a packet from the table. "I wondered if it was a bomb and if I should leave it outside. But he's not like that. He's much more intimate than that. He fucks you with his mind before he tears your head off." She hands it to me. It can only be a book, a paperback, wrapped in satin with red, white, and blue stripes. I pull off the wrappings and show the book to Chanya: *The Gospel of Judas.* I heft the gift for a moment while Chanya watches. When I open it the inscription reads:

> *Shall I compare thee to a summer's day?*
> *Thou art more lovely and more temperate.*
> *To my dear brother, long lost, found now.*

I show Chanya the message and open the book. The central argument of *The Gospel of Judas* is that it was Judas Iscariot, not John, whom the Christ loved most. Judas, the only disciple with any worldly sense, is set up by Jesus as the fall guy for the most brilliant piece of theater of all time called the Crucifixion. In other words, it turns Christianity on its head.

Now my phone bleeps:

Birthday lunch tomorrow, Dear One? Do you know Nandino's? It's
on the river. They have a private room. I'll book. Twelve forty-five for
one o'clock? Smart casual.

"You won't go, will you?" Chanya asks. "He could just kill you on a whim, rip your head off like—"

"Of course I'm going," I say, staring at the book and the neat handwriting. "How can I not?"

"Because you're a cop?"

"No. Because I'm a lost soul."

32

"Please, do have some *grissini*," the Asset says. "Freshly baked this morning. I told them I want the highest standards, no shortcuts, for I have a very special guest." I take one of the breadsticks Superman is offering me. We both crunch for a moment. "Hmm, they baked them with rosemary. Excellent, don't you think?"

"Ah, yes, very good," I say truthfully, "very, very good."

As an expression of his good manners he has seated me in a chair facing the panoramic window. I have a perfect view of the Chao Phraya River behind him: rice barges, tourist yachts, long-tail water buses, sampans, rowboats. It's busy.

"Do you love Italian food as much as do I?" he asks in that silky, well-washed voice.

"Actually, yes, I do enjoy it more than any other *farang* cuisine."

"Let's face it, everything worth having in Europe originates in Italy. Especially the food. French is basically Italian with a truckload of butter and cream thrown at it. Of course, the word *Italian* covers a thousand dishes. I don't mind the poverty cuisines of Sicily and the south, but it doesn't have the finesse or variety of the north. No, it's got to be Tuscan or Piemonte." I blink at him for a moment and continue munching. His blue eyes shine. "Shall I tell you what you are thinking? You are thinking my, my, what breadth of education and culture they gave him, this Asset. Am I right?" I cough. "But let us return to the small talk. Italian, yes, basically, the whole of modern Western culture originates in my hometown." He smiles and crunches on another *grissini*.

"Your hometown?"

He shrugs. "One of them. I can't say I'm exactly proud, but there you are." A pause. "We'll come to that shortly."

I shake my head. The frightening thing is that he is not crazy. It is just as Chanya observed: a perfectly organized brain of the highest intelligence. Now the waiter brings a full bread basket with seven-cereal rolls and a tapenade of anchovies. Every Thai loves anchovies; they taste like the sauces we make from rotten fish.

"Could you tell me—I mean, I'm very flattered—but, why, exactly, would you want to celebrate my birthday, at such short notice?"

"Orders from the Doc. He got stoned with you, didn't he? Just like him, goes on one of his opium trips, spills his guts, still high the next day and still spilling, then a couple of days later he's paranoid about security. He wanted me to check you out. I told him not to worry, the detective is my half brother, I trust him implicitly with everything."

I don't know how to respond to that, so I let a few beats pass. "So how are your—our—brothers and sisters?"

He frowns. "If I gave the impression they are still alive, I'm afraid I misled you for sentimental reasons. They all took their own lives. I'm the only one left. They pushed us too hard, you see? It's the way they are, destructive testing is all they know."

"I'm, ah, sorry to hear that."

"Yes. I was the only one willing to go all the way. *They* had no idea what *all the way* meant, of course. Clumsy fools. But, as you see, it all worked out brilliantly in the end." He gives me an assessing smile. "Now *they* are wondering if there is something special in our genes—the ones we inherited from our father." He shrugs. "But it's just speculation. Personally, I'm not convinced genes have anything to do with our mutual survival. After all, as I told you, our siblings all failed."

"Who is *they*?"

He pretends not to have heard my question. I'm in a dilemma here. If I simply continue to humor him, he will become irritated. On the other hand, how else can I handle it? In normal social intercourse one breaks through a level of basic politeness to something more intimate. But with *him*? As usual he has read my mind. It took one flash of those unreal eyes.

"Shall I tell you what the problem is? You will be surprised at how simply it may be expressed."

"Okay. Tell me."

"My name. You have not asked me and I have not offered. In your head you still think of me simply as *the Asset*, do you not?"

"Yes," I confess.

"Ordinarily you would have asked how you should call me—but in my case a name like Jack or John, or even something exotic like Ermenegildo or Bartholomew, wouldn't do it, would it?" He giggles.

"No."

"And you think the reason is I am not like others, I'm too different, too weird to deserve or be capable of carrying an ordinary human name—correct?"

If he had used a different tone I might have been afraid of some kind of paranoid outbreak, but he is relaxed, in control, and even slightly humorous in his manner. The waiter brings two tiny langoustine cups as *amuse-bouches*. We devour them in one swallow and call for more *grissini*.

"Shall I tell you my real name—at least insofar as any name can be said to be real? Let's put it another way—would you like to know who I am, really?"

I realize I must answer each of his questions with total honesty. "I'm not sure," I say.

He grins. "Excellent. Yes, you are quite right. And the reason you are not sure?"

"I don't know."

"Because the answer is quite daunting. I know you sense it, though, for you are very intuitive, like me. I'll give you a clue. It is fortunate that you are a Buddhist. Someone of a more Western persuasion might have a nervous breakdown. So, can you guess?"

"No."

"Tut-tut. I think you can. But you are too polite. Or afraid of being laughed at. You must not be. I won't have you anything but frank and open—so much do I love you, my brother."

"I'm lost. Okay, tell me."

"I am Jesus Christ, of course." The *grissini* sticks in my throat, I cough. "Oh, I don't mean in some ridiculous way of the mentally ill. I can see that thought just flitted across your mind. No, I mean as a matter of pure cultural logic, that is what I am: the Second Coming. Think about it. Two thousand years of unmitigated lies, nauseating superstition, mental and physical torture, genocide, corruption culminating in two world wars which were *Christian* wars—and nothing but war and exploitation ever since—in the end the West must produce the living image of its own twisted path. *Me.* I am the alpha and the omega, but more importantly I am the Thing Itself." He smiles. "After all, one does need an identity of some kind—at least for the moment. Oh, you must not think of me as that poor jerk on a cross. That was, shall we say, the give-them-a-chance phase. No, if anything I'm more the guy in the middle on the back wall of the Sistine Chapel. Why shouldn't I kill and send to hell those who have failed me so badly?"

There is indignation in the stiffening of his spine and the flash of his eyes. I decide to plunge into the asparagus crepes, which are really very good, before taking the matter further.

"That's why you said Rome was your hometown?"

"I said one of them. I do go there a lot. I have a frequent visitor's pass for the Sistine Chapel. Jerusalem is still hard for me, and as for Bethlehem—have you been there?"

"No."

"I can assure you that these days it's not at all the kind of place where you'd expect to find three wise men and a virgin." He gives a great chesty guffaw.

I stare, openmouthed. What kind of monster is this?

"Actually, it always was a squalid little dump." He laughs some more. "Is this difficult for you? But as a Buddhist you are aware of the basic truth of rebirth, are you not?"

I hesitate. "Yes."

"So, you know that in this body one finds only a segment of the whole person, who is, by the way, androgynous. To find the whole being you must add in all the previous lifetimes. Well, someone has to be Jesus, don't they?"

"I suppose."

"And don't tell me you are not aware that my message two thousand years ago was basically Buddhist with a few politically correct references to the Old Testament to keep the Pharisees off my back?"

I cannot eat anymore, appetite cannot survive such conversation. I give up and put down my knife and fork.

"It's quite true that I did ten years in a Buddhist monastery in Kashmir two thousand years ago." He frowns. "I had a wonderful time, but all the while there was this awful sense of doom, you know, because I had to go back and get myself crucified. Put rather a dampener on the experience." He smiles. "But not to worry, it's all over now. Revenge is mine, I will repay." He pauses to look me full in the face. "And you will help me."

The confession that he is God has relaxed him the way a good confession relaxes some perps. It is as if we have exchanged vows of loyalty and now he can speak freely. I decide to try to obtain an admission to the crime of murder by God. I do not have any recording equipment, it would be only my word against his, I would probably not get a conviction, but it would bring some kind of closure.

"Naturally, as Christ you rely entirely on the Father."

"Naturally."

"You would not kill without his . . . direction?"

"He feeds me, like any father. I owe him everything."

If only he wasn't sane, there would be no threat to my worldview. I take three folded pieces of paper from my jacket pocket and smooth them out in front of him. One is a fish-eye view of a murder scene in which a young woman has been beheaded. The second concentrates on her head, which has been wrenched from her shoulders. The third is a shot of a mirror on which someone has written in blood, *Sonchai Jitpleecheep, I know who [smudge] father is.*

Up to this point I had no idea what my next move would be. I had to know how he assimilated his past actions. How does God deal with his own bad behavior? Will he wrench my head from my shoulders? I am using crude but well-tried tactics here. Now that I have confronted him with hard evidence that a savage killer lives in that splendid body of his along with Jesus Christ, will he explode? Collapse in remorse? Find some theological way around it? But this is a totally new breed of *human* and he doesn't do any of those things. His training takes over. He turns the pictures around under his hand, examining them curiously.

"This happened where? Why wasn't I told? Okay, you won't tell me because I did it. Let us form a plan. We'll try to catch me together. Let us work it out. You were assigned to the case, so it has to be District 8. The killer—me—has a connection with you, therefore any repeat crime will happen in District 8. That's got to be where I strike next, and I *will* strike again, because my purpose is to obtain and retain your attention. Why?" He frowns. "Because of the way I was conceived, brought up, enhanced, and trained—I am a killer freak from B movies, a kind of Frankenstein, in desperate need of normal human love and kindness, of a family. I desperately want and need to impress you because in my mind you are all I've got, being of close kin. In reality I don't have anyone at all, I'm deceiving myself that you are in the least interested in me as a brother. All you want is to solve the case, make the streets safe again for young girls, lock me up for life. I am this pathetic fellow so riven by madness he dares not acknowledge the total contradiction between two halves of himself. As in classic psychosis, the one half of the personality is hermetically sealed off from the other. What it all points to is that I not only will kill again soon, but it will be in this same market—the one behind your police station, is it not?"

He pauses to look at me. "That's the obvious reading, anyway. Have I got it right?" He doesn't wait for an answer but frowns deeply as if he is consulting himself on where he plans to strike next. "A little *too* obvious, perhaps—you are not entirely convinced, although I'm sure your colleagues would fall for it. But, yes, it will have to be the market again—if I'm so smart, strong, and powerful, I would naturally want to taunt you in the most provocative way." He looks up at me for a moment, says, "Don't worry, we'll catch me," smiles cheerfully, then returns to the documents I gave him.

I have shifted back from the table, forcing my chair against the wall. This is revealing behavior on my part. If I were physically afraid, I could easily have run out of the restaurant. But you cannot run from this kind of fear. The end of the world does not need any component of violence to terrify us. Here is a man of superhuman powers who wants to recruit me into hunting himself.

I make an excuse to break off the lunch. He looks up, nods at me briefly, and returns to his study of the scene of the crime. He does not seem surprised or offended. I feel an intense frustration that he didn't break and confess. I want to yell at him, rub his face in the evidence: *No, you are not Jesus, you are a psychopath.* I guess every shrink has wanted to do that from time to time. But I'm not a shrink, I'm a cop. Until now the weirdness of the world has been clearly defined by law and practice. Outside of those definitions I'm as lost as you, R. I stand up, make my apology, stare at him in disbelief. Already he has made those pieces of paper his own. He *will* find the perp. Using his training and enhancements he will track himself down sooner or later.

What kind of insanity is this? *Is he telling me he will murder again, in that same market, as a way of relating to me?* When balance fails the mind can go on twisting forever, it seems.

33

If another child dies at that monster's hands it will be my fault. Fear of future guilt drives me now. At the market I stand among a confusion of people, wild-eyed and mad. Fruits, vegetables, and cheap clothes from China and Vietnam are everywhere for sale along with downmarket cell phones and a lot of plastic covers for iPhone and Samsung products. There is a phone repair stall at one corner, a knife sharpener at another, a seller of red and yellow plastic buckets at a third, and dozens of cheap clothing and shoe stalls in between. The stalls being lawless, no one has the authority to impose order, so that every last inch of the disputed land is occupied rent free. I am wondering how, exactly, I might try to protect every kid in sight. I am sweating in the morning heat. *This is stress. Oh, yes, this is stress.* I am thinking how much I hate transhumans when my cell phone bleeps: *Shit hits fan, Goldman ballistic, meet KKM, food stall now.*

There are no customers at the *khao kha moo* stall, except one who is staring into space. When I draw up a chair at her table she flashes me a momentary glance then continues to gaze. I am instantly irritated. I cough: no reaction. Wearily and shaking my head I pull out my phone and read the SMS aloud: *"Shit hits fan, Goldman ballistic, meet KKM, food stall now."*

Krom remains staring dull-eyed into the distance. I try to remember from my teens what gambit works best in reply to this opening. I get up to leave. As I do so, she finally speaks: "She told you I made a pass at her and she rejected me and we didn't have sex—didn't she?"

I scratch my beard, stunned, for the moment, at the disconnect with the SMS and my mood. "Yes."

"You believe her?"

"I'm not sure. I don't even know if I care."

"Really? That's unusual, a man generally cares very much what a rival does with his wife. When the rival is a dyke it makes men crazy."

She takes out her smart phone and shows me a video that lasts less than a minute. The naked woman on her back is certainly Krom, that is obvious from the full-body tattoo. But as for the tongue that elegantly begins its homage at her feet and leads us up the *tom's* right leg all the way to the moist, parted, and panting labia—the identity of its owner is less clear. All I see is some jet-black hair from behind that could be Chanya's but might just as well belong to another Asian woman. True, there is a momentary quarter profile in which I catch a glimpse of a cheek and nose that look familiar—but there is no certainty. I study the clip with some intensity, though, and replay it a couple of times before handing it back.

"Who was holding the camera?" I ask. Krom looks away. "Chanya never mentioned a third person."

Krom takes back the smart phone. "Do you want to see the whole video? I'll e-mail it to you if you like."

As she speaks she is flashing me little sly glances full of schaden-freude.

"No," I say. "If you had a clip of Chanya that was recognizable you would have it on your phone. You're bluffing." Then another word comes to mind, one that has acquired a special significance recently. "*Feeding*, aren't you?" I say.

It is an unusual word to use, but accuracy can startle. Krom blinks several times, and for a moment looks confused, as if she has been called out doing something everyone does. *Don't we all love to see the emotional pain of others? Aren't we all voyeurs at heart?* her look says. Then she sees that I disagree. *No, not everyone gets off on that,* I signal back, *not everyone is a predator of the heart.* And now she does that special thing I've come to associate with the enhanced: she snaps out of it, goes deep within herself, and in a few seconds she has changed mood and personality. Now she gives me the big welcoming smile. She wants to ignore completely the last few minutes—not to mention the evening she spent with Chanya—so we can be buddies again, quite as if she has not seduced, or tried to seduce, my wife. It seems like a good moment to strike.

"So, Krom, tell me more about being enhanced, how did it happen in your case?"

"Can't tell you. Classified, for the moment. You're not ready yet."

"Something happens, doesn't it, to people, those very lucky special people who belong to the club?"

"What club?"

"The only one that matters anymore—at least, that's the sense of the story so far. The club of the enhanced."

I don't think it is a particularly brilliant question, so I am surprised when it has the effect of changing Krom's posture. For a moment I think she is finally going to open up.

"Yes, I guess you could say that. *Special* is a dangerous word. Different, though. I'd go along with that." She smiles. "We humans all have a distant folk memory of a time when we could fly. You could say this memory makes all of us miserable, but some more than others: we are the species that fell to earth and lost its wings out of sheer stupidity. But if something happens and by some incredible piece of luck you get your wings back—yes, then when you look at other people you're looking at what you used to be—"

"A lower form of life?" She purses her lips. "You have the same relish for the sufferings of others as *him*, don't you? You are the new aristocracy, you transhumans. Inwardly you are the billionaires in your limos driving through a slum and despising everyone and everything you see."

She seems to think hard about that. "Yes," she says brightly. "Yes, that's quite true. How clever of you to see it so clearly."

"But you also have the fatal weakness of all winners. You need to feed off emotions you no longer feel, to which you no longer have any right. You are no longer in the human family—love is shut off for you. All that's left is to despise and destroy the happiness of others. You are a vampire."

She snorts. "Love? You and Chanya are bored to death with each other. I brought you both fun, danger, knowledge. And I found out about your father's buddy, da Silva."

"Yes. Why exactly did you do that? Because you knew how much pain lay down that road?"

"I try to help you when I can—we're friends, aren't we?" She lets a few beats pass, gives a bright smile. I think, *Feelings have no currency in this community.* Then she says, "So, have we had the catharsis already? Can we be friends again now?" She giggles. "Maybe vampire isn't such a bad rap. With seven billion humans full of blood, it's a smart choice of food source. Let me be your very special tame vampire, I'll protect you from the competition."

"Why are you laughing?"

"Because you have this little problem with me—aren't you leaving out a crucial piece of evidence?"

"How's that?"

"Your own brother, man. Sonchai, you are closely related to the biggest vampire of all. You must know that?"

I let my frustration reach a kind of head, then I exhale. When I inhale again I am able to say slowly, "Krom, just tell me as much as you can for now. Just so I can at least start to get a grip."

She nods, as if I have at last pressed the right button with the right attitude. "I was recruited. It was like a mutual search. It was as though I was tunneling from underground, trying to reach the surface, and someone else was tunneling down from the surface, trying to save me. The kind of thing people used to associate with religious experience, but there was nothing religious about it. Except I finally found the guts to have the tattoo I'd been dreaming about since age twelve—*that* was a religious experience." She flashes me a glance. "When I think about it now, it seems obvious, even ordinary."

"What does?"

"At the jungle camp you visited, very few of the kids had any Asian blood. Maybe three, four at the most, fathered by Vietcong who had been forced to participate in MKUltra. The Chinese needed Asian genes in their products. They couldn't very well have a super police force of blond blue-eyed Caucasians. So, they were looking for volunteers. Naturally, the program I entered had to be adjusted to accommodate my age and background. They didn't have me from birth, so I was never going to be as advanced as Goldman's children. I spent two years at a special facility in Qinghai. We shared it with some kids who were going to be the next generation of Olympic athletes. It was entirely voluntary for the first few months, then I had to make a decision: leave or commit for life. There was someone there I related to, someone I wanted to stay close to, so I committed for life. In return they made certain adjustments to my brain. Very minor compared to what you've seen from Goldman's program, but enough to make a difference. Here, there's something I've been waiting to show you, when you started to ask the right questions."

She takes out her phone again, swipes a few times, then shows me a photograph. At first I cannot see the relevance. I have to flick from it to her and back again quite a few times. "That's really you?" She smiles. The more I look at the photo the more I understand. The young woman on the tiny screen is exactly what I might have expected from someone of Krom's background. There is the obvious intelligence in her eyes, but she wears the sullen, resentful face of any young person who has no intention of adjusting to or participating in her society. She is unkempt, her hair an orange-and-green mess, her T-shirt looks as if she has picked it up off the floor, her head droops and she is scowling. An unhappy, even tragic outsider: lost, utterly lost, and about to tip into something sad. There is no direction in that soul, none at all. I am stunned at the then-and-now comparison and find myself nodding while I try to take it all in.

"How many . . . I mean, how many of you are there?"

"On the Chinese side, only a few hundred. But each one of us will train at least ten, so you get an exponential curve. The program takes decades to complete, but a recruit can return to society and operate within five years. It wasn't difficult for them to pull a few strings to plant me in the Thai police. The Americans have fewer trainees, at the moment. They went too far too fast—you can see the results. The Chinese have been less ambitious in the talents they've implanted in us." A pause. "With a few exceptions. As with any advanced technology, it's generally more efficient to buy, borrow, or steal the other guy's research than work it all out from scratch. But you must always be on guard against double-bluffs: maybe the technology you're buying is flawed, even deliberately sabotaged. Basically, that's what your case is all about." She gazes at me. "The Market Murder with your name on it." She takes her phone back, gives the photo a quick glance, and deletes it. I wonder if she's kept it there just for me. "Like any applied science, once it's seen to work it can't be stopped. It becomes inevitable."

"A new kind of human race?"

"Why not? Once we were mere *Homo sapiens:* apes who could think. Now we're *Homo sapien sapiens:* apes who can think about thinking."

"And the next phase—your phase? How would you define that?"

She thinks about it. "Depends. The Americans learned a lot. They started to think of it as a return."

"A return?"

"Something weird happened in Cambodia, in Angkor, while Goldman was there."

"A return to what?"

"Exactly. That's the question, isn't it?"

She takes a few bites of her food, chews thoughtfully, then says, "Be ready, my friend. I know you hate me right now, but I'm still your friend and my advice is *be ready.* I don't know exactly when or where, someone will call you. All I can tell you is that the intelligence is pretty good this week and the listeners are picking up signals of intense activity. Someone is going to make a risky move, because they're desperate. Sorry to be mysterious—but I really, sincerely, lovingly recommend you *stay alert.* And get some sleep, you look awful."

"But your SMS . . . You said Goldman has gone ballistic? Was that just a ploy to get me out here?"

"No. Actually we are talking about a sideshow, but he has been caught bugging the station." All of a sudden she starts to cackle. "He had devices all over the building, he bribed the tea lady because she serves rooms on every floor. You'll see." She consults her watch. "Vikorn has called a meeting. The FBI legal attaché will be there. I would like you to meet him. If there's no chance to talk with him before the meeting, we'll do it after."

"FBI?"

"The Chinese made a sophisticated sweep yesterday, using the latest antisurveillance technology. It was just a gambit, though, because we've known about the CIA listening to us for months. The evidence is overwhelming, however, and therefore very embarrassing. The CIA decided to let Goldman take the flak. They've washed their hands of him and left everything to the FBI attaché at the embassy." She spoons up the thick brown sauce and skillfully includes the half of the boiled egg, chews, swallows, and smiles. "But like I say, it's a sideshow."

"How's that?"

"The Chinese are creating a smokescreen to cover the fact they've finally broken one of the CIA's most challenging telephonic encryption systems." Now she allows a crooked grin to build as she stares at me. "We have some of Goldman's most intimate conversations with his controller at Langley. So, time to raise hell about CIA bugs at the station." She shrugs. "Apparently it's basic diplomacy—not my field."

When she stands up I notice her laptop case, which she hoists over her shoulder. While I have her in a communicative mood, I decide to ask something I have been curious about for some time. "Krom, tell me, why is your name Krom? Isn't that Cambodian?"

She cocks her head. "The Krom are a Cambodian tribe, from the south." She grins. "Full marks for asking, Detective. It's sheer coincidence, though. My father called me that because I was conceived over there, when they were on their honeymoon."

In the couple of minutes it takes to reach the station and walk up to the big conference room, Krom morphs into the super-efficient police inspector for the day, hardly looking me in the eye. When we enter I see that the high-tech monitor is switched on and showing a screen saver with fractals of narcotic color and intensity. Goldman, that giant, is already seated and gives us a look of aggressive curiosity as we enter. There are two other men waiting: Colonel Vikorn slouched at the head of the table, and a pale slim man with jet-black hair about five ten in dark suit and tie, in his late thirties or early forties. He interests me because he is a *leuk kreung:* a half-caste like me. The non-*farang* half of him is not Thai, though: I would guess his Chinese genes originate in the north where people are pale and tall. I give Vikorn a high *wai*, which he acknowledges with a nod.

Now I turn my attention back to the *leuk kreung*. When he gives me his card, I see he is legal counsel to the American embassy here. I remember that legal attachés are invariably FBI, which doesn't have a great relationship with the CIA. The lawyer's name is Matthew Hadley-Chan.

Matthew Hadley-Chan sits to Vikorn's right. Krom and I take up the seats farther down the table.

"Well?" Vikorn says, looking at Goldman, then at the FBI.

Goldman is not looking well; indeed, he is seriously haggard. "The first thing I want to say is how sincerely my government and I regret any misperception that may have arisen—"

"Cut to the chase, Goldman," the lawyer Hadley-Chan snaps like a man who has been waiting to pounce. "You bugged a friendly power on whom the U.S. depends for support and intelligence in a region which grows strategically more critical every week as tensions rise. You have abused one of our most important relationships in Southeast Asia. If you want the Bureau to help clean up your shit, stop pretending you are capable of regret or sincerity. In this room we all know what you are. Let's start from there."

Goldman stares at him, incandescent with rage, then controls himself as military programming intervenes. "You want to take that line, okay." For once he is nonplussed. He stares at the lawyer as if there's something about him he has trouble coming to grips with. "So, okay, you want straight talk, this is it. Yes, we did a little eavesdropping, and guess what we found out?" He sticks out his jaw and glares at Krom, me, and Vikorn in that order. Then he addresses himself to the FBI. "It's true we did not find any activity against American interests in Southeast Asia. What we found was a massive conspiracy to control the Afghani heroin trade in alliance with Russian and Pakistani kingpins." He glares triumphantly and folds his arms as if to say, *Okay, so go public with that.*

Matthew Hadley-Chan scratches his jaw and speaks a few words to Krom, who picks up her laptop case from the floor, opens the case, and takes out the laptop. It is a roomy kind of case, though, and it is clear that it holds more than the shiny Apple MacBook Pro, which now sits gleaming on the table.

"These are not U.S. government offices, Mr. Goldman," the lawyer says. "And we don't plant bugs on our closest allies anymore. You should have retired twenty years ago, Goldman, while the world was still going your way. Your worst offense, though, speaking off the record, is to underestimate our hosts."

Now Goldman starts to lose what is left of his self-control. "Don't bug our allies? What the fuck do you think the NSA spends half its time—"

He stops speaking because Krom has taken something else out of her laptop case. We all acquire mystic concentration. Goldman is ashen. It is an extraordinary-looking machine about one inch long with both wheels and feet, a short antenna, and what must be a miniature camera on a swivel. She matches it with three more of the same from the briefcase while Goldman's ashen turns to purple. Now she takes out a glassine bag filled not with an illegal substance but illegal gadgets; at least, that's what I assume they are: tiny black oblongs about an eighth of an inch in diameter and half an inch long, more than a dozen of them. Inserted in a hole in a wall or door they would look like nails. Goldman is swivel-eyed trying to read each of our faces in turn.

Krom attacks her laptop, manipulating keyboard and mouse at great speed, looking every bit the supersmart ambitious Asian female police officer with those black spectacles on her tiny nose. The spiderlike contraption on wheels starts to stir. Now that she has mastered the controls she can make it shoot off in any direction. At the edge of the table it breaks out a set of tentacles with miniature suction pads that allow it to run down the table leg like a mouse, straight across the floor, and up again until it is sitting in front of Goldman, pointing its camera at him. Now on the giant LED screen we have Goldman's head, about two feet tall, staring at a miniature mobile covert surveillance device, or MMCSD as the jargon has it.

"It's a very old tactic, Goldman," the lawyer says. "Didn't you attend that class at Langley? I believe they call it *turning the bug.*"

Now Krom uses the sound system to air part of a recorded conversation.

"*How long have they been bugging us for?*" It is Vikorn's voice.

"*I don't know. We've found about twenty devices so far.*"

"*Who's doing it?*"

"*There's a character called Goldman at the center of it. He's CIA.*"

"*Are they allowed to?*"

"*No way. Interference in the policing of a friendly power—that's strictly no-no.*"

"*We wouldn't want to offend them, though, would we?*"

"*No. They might come looking for weapons of mass destruction and destroy our country.*" Krom giggles.

"*We'll do a recording using my voice. Make like we're thinking of moving into the Afghanistan trade soon as the Americans have left that country. Then we embarrass them by proving it's not true and get them off our backs—hopefully forever.*"

"Yessir," Krom says.

"Where is Afghanistan, by the way?"

"Somewhere west of northern India," Krom says.

I watch a smile bloom and fade on Vikorn's face as Krom replays the recording, just in case someone missed the point.

Goldman, slumped in his chair and staring at Krom, is not embarrassed by the double-shuffle; he is fixated on something else. "You broke the codes to work an M245X? You may be brilliant, but not that brilliant."

"Of course not. It would take a supercomputer and twenty skilled operators to break those codes."

"So, how did you do it?"

"We sent one of the M245Xs you let loose on us to China. They used a supercomputer and twenty skilled operators. Took them a week. The Colonel has excellent contacts in the highest ranks of the PRC. They kept the original model for research and development." Krom offers him a girlish smile.

Goldman is bothered by the sight of his huge head on the screen and the surveillance device on the desk. He figures if he swats the M245X the problem will be solved. He is a big man with a big hand. Naturally, he would not come down on the metallic object from a vertical direction, but why not just sweep the damn thing off the desk?

I guess he was in the field when the capabilities of the M245X were demonstrated to Company officers. He passes the back of his hand across the desk with some vigor, and now the iron spider has snapped open a pair of pincers with which it is clinging to his hand. He doesn't want to show how much it hurts, so he flies into a rage, which is inarticulate at first, with the blood turning to crimson under his fat cheeks. He wants to be rid of the gadget without providing us with the spectacle of a six-foot-four, three-hundred-and-fifty-pound man in a fight to the death with what looks like a child's toy, but those pincers are mean. Now the floodgates of articulated rage open wide, the politically incorrect resentment of five decades or more going back to the first tightening of lips, swallowing of rebellion when, as a cadet, he found that even in those days Company rules imperfectly expressed his own idea of the America he had volunteered to defend with his life. He stands up.

"Now you listen to me," he says, "and you listen good. I'm no slick lawyer but I have leverage here. So, they screwed us by turning the bug—that's a damn sideshow and you know it." He is addressing the FBI lawyer. "I don't give a shit if I seem like something from ancient history, what I have nobody else has in the whole of American covert operations. I have the most special product in the world. So cut me a little respect, okay?"

Matthew Hadley-Chan snorts. This is no ordinary spat between two giant American egos; this is a battle between the divorced hemispheres of the American mind. Now Goldman really lets go.

"I don't give a shit what it takes, my program gets priority. I'm not interested in any bleeding-heart liberal crap about democracy, civil fucking liberty—" He has shifted the pincers from the end of a pinkie; now they are buried in the soft flesh of his palm near the thumb; blood drips from two puncture marks like a cobra bite; his frustration is reaching ballistic level. "From World War Two onward we have been and are the only true guardians of civilization in our time, the greatest country the world has ever known, that has brought the highest standards of living to the ends of the earth—and who was it who created, fought for, developed all this? *The white man*, of course."

Like most Thais, Krom has an inbuilt reflex in times of rage. She goes very quiet and attacks her laptop with some rapid keywork. Goldman is too far into his tantrum to notice until the other M245Xs have crossed the floor and run up the legs of his pants. Whether they reach the apex simultaneously or one by one is unclear. Certain it is that the meeting ends with Goldman staring at Krom and Krom staring back with her finger poised above one of the keys.

"Adam and Eve were niggers," Krom explains. "From Africa."

Goldman blinks and nods in submission. Krom releases the devices, which fall down his pants to the floor. He thinks about stamping on them, but decides discretion may be the better part of valor and storms out, slamming the door.

Now I realize there is one vital element to the meeting that has quite passed me by. Maybe you saw it coming yourself, R, but frankly, my mind has been boggled enough recently and I must have blocked out the clues. There is no denying it, though, that very special thing between Matthew Hadley-Chan and Krom, which has nothing to do with sex or lonely hearts, even though the glance they share can only be called intimate. And there is something else, too: the FBI dealt with Goldman's outburst by switching off entirely and retreating deep within. Once you've seen a TH do it once, you never forget.

My jaw hangs open: *They've infiltrated the FBI already?* The Eurasian lawyer coughs. "Sorry about that," he says, and adds, looking Vikorn in the eye, "I don't think we'll be bothered by him anymore. He won't be bugging anything for a while." He turns to Krom. "You got all that on video?"

"Sure," Krom says.

"I'll make sure it reaches the right levels," he says, nods again at Vikorn, and leaves.

I notice that Krom, also, is in a hurry to leave the room. When she has packed up her laptop and the surveillance gadgets she makes hurried apologies to Vikorn and me and also leaves. I decide to give her a couple of minutes before I follow.

Neither she nor the FBI are anywhere to be seen in the corridor. The obvious place to look for them would be in the smaller interview room next door. It is locked from the inside. When I put my ear against the door I am able to hear a conversation between the two of them. I cannot understand a word of it; it is in Mandarin. Perhaps one of them has attended an enhanced hearing class, though, because suddenly the door opens and Krom and the FBI are staring at me. They exchange a glance. The lawyer seems to be waiting for Krom to speak.

"Can we let him in?" she asks.

"Certainly," Matthew Hadley-Chan says. "The Messiah has given his half brother full clearance, even up to the highest level."

He pronounces the word *Messiah* in exactly the cringe-making way of any evangelist. I am shocked, but not so shocked that I lose curiosity in Krom's reaction. As usual, I have no intuitive understanding of her mind: I just never seem to know where she is coming from. I am fascinated by the unforced reverence in her face.

"You've been with the Messiah recently?" she asks with naked awe.

"He has done me the extreme honor of including me in the next step of the project," he says with nauseating piety. He turns to me. "Here," he says, dipping into his jacket pocket and taking out a thumb drive. "All you need to know is on this drive. The files will self-destruct within the next six hours—and cannot be copied. I think the matter speaks for itself."

I see from the body language of the two of them that it is time for me to leave. The point, apparently, is the thumb drive. I shake my head. That cannot be sexual attraction filling Krom's eyes when she looks at the FBI; it's an awe more radical than that. I exit and close the door as quietly as I can. In my pocket I carry the thumb drive. *Six hours,* I think, *six hours.* I better take it home. If Chanya's working I can listen to it on earphones.

It is the FBI legal attaché who fuels my speculation as I make my way back to the hovel. In my mind's eye I trace his probable life path. A smart Eurasian born, perhaps, in disadvantaged or lower-middle-class circumstances to a mixed couple, the Chinese half probably his father with the traditional Asian immigrant's drive to succeed in a society more mobile and fairer than the one he was born into, which is not necessarily saying very much. His dutiful son passes exams at or near the top of his class, absorbs law at Harvard or Yale with relentless ambition, then joins the great benefactor, Uncle Sam, to serve honorably as living proof of the loyalty and dedication of a *leuk kreung* who knows all about the sneering racist forces ranged against him and is forever grateful for the protection built into the system. Like me, though, he suffers from an internal contradiction: the rootless *I* needs more than status to be sure it exists. Then a fateful meeting occurs: as in the book of Luke, Christ shows up at the lawyer's office one fine day, whether in Bangkok or Washington, and the lawyer turns evangelist. My mind boggles.

34

At night when I'm working on a heavy case I switch to the vibrate function on the smart phone before I sleep. I leave the ringtone on, but turn it down low so as not to disturb Chanya. Even so, when it goes off it makes quite a display, lights flashing, the vibrations sending it on a circular navigation of the floor and, of course, the subdued ringtone (the Stones: "You Can't Always Get What You Want"). I block it before it vibrates its way over to the bookshelves, then I pick it up. I am only one-third awake. The screen tells me it is two twenty-four in the morning and that the caller is anonymous—except that the freshly washed voice is familiar to me.

"A car will be outside your house in three minutes. It will wait thirty seconds. Do *not* bring your gun, you will be protected." He hangs up.

Three minutes, as it happens, is exactly how long it takes to pull on some shorts, grab a T-shirt that I hold in my hand, slip on some flip-flops, leave the house, remembering to bring my wallet, keys, smart phone, and police ID, and walk to the road. The car is rolling up to our front door as I'm pulling on the T-shirt.

The driver is none other than Matthew Hadley-Chan of the FBI, looking very fit in shorts and sweatshirt as if he has been jogging. He owns a gun, a large combat rifle made of high-tech materials lying across the backseat. I sit in the front. We do not speak but drive off at high speed toward the police station at District 8. We do not stop there, though, but penetrate farther into the market area. I am aware that we are only one street away from where the Asset wrenched the head off Nong X, so that I am casting more and more glances at my driver.

"Can't tell you anything, sorry," he says. "Looks like they're gonna bag the big one tonight. The Captain will explain soon as you're there."

"Captain?" I say.

"Yeah. The bright shining star himself."

I am puzzled by the casual reference made in the offhand American style. "You don't mean the *Messiah*, do you?"

His expression turns serious. He puts a finger to his lips.

The market is not open at night, but the framework of iron poles that provides support for tarps during the day is left intact, along with the bare wood boards. As I look I see that there are men and women with blackened faces under some of these stands, all with combat rifles, all lying very still on their stomachs. As I pass I count eight humans—some are Caucasian, some are black, a couple are Thai, three are female. The FBI leads me quickly to a corner where an alley leads onto the square. It is quite dark. At the same time as the FBI whispers, "Here he is, Captain," a fine, slim hand reaches out, grasps my upper arm with unexpected strength, and pulls me into the darkness.

"We're about to catch me this time," he whispers. "I'm two minutes away," he adds with a giggle. "Watch." In the darkness I can just make out those perfect teeth when he smiles. "You do still think it was me who killed that poor girl and wrote your name on a mirror in blood?"

"Yes," I say. Then, looking around at the carefully laid trap: "Okay, no." I must be confused, because then I say "Yes" again.

"Watch. The perp will be heading for a specific building about thirty feet from where we stand, where the bait is waiting."

Bait? I want to know if the bait is a professional and a volunteer—or not? Now that fine manicured hand grasps my arm again and a faint nod causes me to look across the silent market. A tall figure has appeared, a *farang* with hair so blond it could almost be white. He is young, springy on his legs, at an unusually high level of physical fitness. His face is obscured by a baseball cap. I think, *Two? There are two of them? Two Assets? Identical twins? Why didn't I think of that?* Asset II sniffs the air a lot, sometimes bending down, sometimes reaching up nose first to catch whatever olfactory information is hanging around.

"He's had the olfactory App," my half brother explains with a sneer. "Guides himself through his nose, like a dog. Disgusting."

We watch while the intruder works swiftly, moving from side to side but always heading toward one particular front door. He tries it, it is not locked. He turns the handle. I feel an urge to rush him, but a hand restrains me. He is allowed to enter the building. Seconds later there are two bangs that are too loud and too special to be shots from an ordinary gun. A child or young woman screams. We all move in a rush toward the building. A *farang* woman in combat dungarees emerges running with a young Thai girl in her arms, about twelve years old, horror in her eyes. The woman takes her to a van parked on the other side of the market. Everyone else makes for the front door. There are about ten of us now, entering one by one.

Inside, it is a typical local shop house, with cheap electrical and household goods for sale on the ground floor, family accommodation upstairs. I am thinking this is not like any rescue I can remember. Everyone is focused on the body of the perp.

Two shots from marksmen waiting in ambush inside the house have brought him down. Their guns are propped up against a wall, high-tech and capable of firing exotic shells. The body on the floor with two big holes in it has everyone's attention, but no one wants to preempt the *Captain*. He is behind me as we enter; I am aware of everyone looking toward us.

"Listen up," the Asset commands. "The three scientists—using our color coding that's Drs. White, Black, and Pink—will have exclusive use of the body for exactly eight minutes for preliminary research. Sergeants Purple and Violet, you did the shooting, you stay with the doctors in case they have questions. During that time, the women lieutenants, that is, Gray and Cream, will form the first line of resistance: anyone coming within fifty yards of ground zero is warned off. Use polite feminine firmness on local people, any nonlocals are to be treated with suspicion. Your line is: *Please accept our apologies, we are protecting American government property for the moment, and we will release the area in less than ten minutes.* Soldiers Brown, Blue, and Charcoal, you are the second line of defense. *No outsider gets to look at this body.* Lethal force is authorized as a last resort. At the end of eight minutes an old black Toyota covered van will arrive. Do *not* shoot at it. It will be traveling fast. If you keep to the timing, at the moment when the body is being rolled up in the tarp, the van will arrive, and the body will be placed in the back of the van, which will drive off. There will be no American personnel within a hundred yards of ground zero after two minutes of the van being gone. Understood?"

The Asset in this mode has a natural authority. Everyone holds him in awe; at the same time, he is polite and friendly. I cannot tell if this group has worked with him before or if they have come together for this case alone. He is so polished in his performance, so much the highly trained pro, that his people simply follow his orders. The three scientists do not wait but instantly start on an examination of the body. I'm left wondering if this *Captain* really is the crazy I had lunch with only days ago. I think the Asset tonight is neither acting a part nor being himself; I think transhumans learn to select personalities to fit with the moment and cover the void that way. Like humans, only more so.

Blood-splatter patterns and large dark deposits on the floor show how the perp was shot twice before he could reach the girl: I think the first shot was a hollow-nose bullet of large caliber, and the second an exploding bullet that destroyed his chest. He lies facedown with arms and legs spread in classic shot-man position, his face pointed away covered by a forearm and invisible to me, his bright blond hair catching the light.

Sorry, R, it looks as if I've misled you: I've been wrong all along. *He* didn't do it after all. I turn to the Asset and say in disbelief, "It really wasn't you who killed Nong X here in the market ten days ago?" Not the most elegant question I've ever asked; he graciously ignores it.

"Let's get this straight," Dr. Pink, a woman, says to the gunmen. "You shot him through the gut with a hollow-nose round?"

"A JHP, ma'am, jacketed hollow-point forty-five with high-velocity propellant. Right through, hit his spine round about L1 or 2, but he kept coming on. No point giving him a warning. Something like that, you don't give margin, you just shoot while you're still alive. Sergeant Violet then hit him with an HE, ma'am."

"HE?"

"High Explosive, ma'am."

"I had no choice," the other shooter said. "Never seen anyone recover from a JHP before."

"I'm not interested in legality, soldier," Dr. Pink says in a gravel voice. "It's the technology that's sending green balls down my pants leg."

"Me, too, ma'am," Dr. Black says. "He was still walking after you cut his spine in half?"

"Still running."

The three scientists kneel over the body. "Damn it, will you look at this."

"It's a graphene sheath," Dr. Pink says. "I saw it right off."

"They've learned how to encase the nerves in graphene?"

"Might be worse than that," Dr. Black says.

"Yeah, that thought crossed my mind too," Dr. White says.

"How's that? What could be worse than that they've worked out how to encase nerve fibers in graphene sheaths?"

"That they've worked out how to make the nerve fibers *out of* graphene rods," Dr. Pink says. "That they're about a decade ahead in nanotechnology."

"Oh," Black says. "Oh no. That is bad news, if it's true. That puts us way behind."

"Of course we're way behind," Pink says. "They get to do vivisection on humans. If they let us do that, we'd be ruling over America's second empire by now with the world at our feet. It would be 1945 all over again."

"Yes, but with that kind of progress they must suffer a failure rate of two in three."

"Either you have Darwinian capitalism or you don't," Dr. Pink says, probing around inside the carcass. "I bet ol' Polonium doesn't lose any sleep over his casualties. He would probably use Chechens anyway."

"Is it true that Polonium himself has been enhanced?"

"I heard that. I don't know if it's an urban myth or not. All that superman junk he's into, though . . . maybe."

"And if Polonium is in deep now, you can bet the rest of the world apart from the U.S. and Western Europe will be doing it in ten years' time."

"So we find ourselves at the end of the food chain and have to play catch-up. So we have to break the rules in the end anyway and everyone gets to call us hypocrites."

"Our people do some cheating too," White says as he examines the abdominal cavity. "On the quiet. You know that. What the Corporation won't allow is vivisection on human children, because the scandal if it broke would close them down. Comparisons would be made with Hitler and Mengele. That's where these guys beat us every time. They don't worry about a free media."

"I know that," Dr. Pink says. "We have this taboo, but we'll have to break it sooner or later. Kids don't necessarily suffer as a result of the research. Anyway, who in hell would ever find out? This program is SECRET, in capitals. I had to go through five hoops, they tapped my phone, talked to my friends and colleagues and everyone who's known me since high school, followed me around for six months—and that was just to get on the consultancy list. I've had five different identities in as many days, and tonight I am Dr. Pink. No, no, nobody is ever going to bust us. Not only does the President not know about what we do, ninety-nine percent of the CIA have never heard of it."

"Well, they put us all through the same rigor. The military isn't subtle, but the money's good."

"You got that right. Why do you think I'm here? I earn more in three days than I get in a year on civil research projects."

"Anyway, going back to what you were saying, you're right, the kids don't suffer at all for the most part. You start to put synthetic cable in a kid's spine at age about seven, by age seventeen you have a superman with an unbreakable back. Where's the suffering?"

"Like this one," Black says. "Shot through the spine with a hollow-nose and he was still walking. We're gonna have fun with the reverse engineering here. I'd sure like to know how they did it."

"Running," the gunman says, as if he has an inner need to keep repeating the story. "Running at full speed. I guess he was about a yard from me when I hit him with an exploder full in the chest and he finally went down. I was sweating it, I can tell you."

"Well, let's turn him over, let's see how well they've done here."

The body it seems is quite heavy. It takes the three of them to turn it over so the face is staring at the ceiling. We all groan, myself more loudly than anyone. I cannot believe it.

"Wow!" Pink says.

"They're winning," White says. "As good as won, I would say."

"Will you look at that?"

Everyone in the room is constantly switching their attention between the creature on the floor and Captain Asset.

"Damn it!"

"Can you believe it?"

Dr. White is so shocked he wants to check with me, as if I am a fellow scientist. "Have you ever seen anything like that?" he asks, stabbing his finger toward the Asset then back again at the creature on the floor.

"No," I say. "Never."

The Asset also is transfixed. The face of the perp is a perfect replica of his own, as is the near-white hair and the crew cut. "Does it come off?"

"It must," Dr. Pink says. "He sure wasn't born like that."

"It probably fits by suction or glue," Black says.

The Asset kneels beside it. "I'm going to touch it," he says.

"No gloves?"

"No. I did a program. I can tell what material it is, skin to skin. Yes, a graphene trellis," he says, caressing the dead one's cheek. "I think they've grown skin and hair follicles on top of it."

Dr. Black examines further, wearing surgical gloves. "I think you're right, Captain."

Pink shakes her head. "If they've gotten that far, they've as good as won the contract," she says. "We can only do masks using the living original. We can't copy or imitate like this in graphene—they must have done it from photographs. Probably thousands of pictures fed into a software program to get this kind of accuracy. We can't model this material at all except on a living face, that's way beyond our capabilities at this point in time."

"So they've won already," Black says.

"Except for the control thing," White says.

"We don't even know that," Pink says. "This HZ is not here on a private debauch. This baby came here tonight for commercial sabotage—right, Captain?"

"Correct," the Asset says, "to discredit me. The Russian lobby in Beijing have already started a campaign. I'm an uncontrollable child murderer, a tearer-apart of innocent kids, an undisciplined mutant."

A certain frisson passes through the group. I guess only the Asset is allowed to use the *M* word.

"The control thing was our best selling point—now they're using it against us?"

"Sure," the Asset says. "We would do the same. Three years ago they nearly clinched a deal with the ministry, until we pointed out how bloodthirsty these guys are. And how ugly. Now they're turning it around."

"That mask, though. It worries me a lot more than the unbreakable spine. I haven't studied it yet, but from what I've seen, there can be no doubt they are way ahead in the manipulation and shaping of graphene. You all see the implications, right?"

"If that mask can pass a standard isometric test, which it probably can, and they already know how to fake fingerprints and DNA, which they do, then say goodbye to identity. Sure, they're ahead of us. We can't impersonate like that—we wouldn't even know where to start."

"Face is everything. If someone can steal that, you're done. As a person and as a society. You produce a spy identical in every way to a spy on the other side, who behaves in every way like that spy, whose wife and kids are even fooled, who in the end actually *becomes* that other spy—so who in the world is who? You don't just get social chaos, you get a full-blown psychic winter. People walking around in circles like broken toys."

"You spent time in L.A. lately? What else is new?"

"Take it off," the Asset says.

"Take off the mask here? Now?"

"Yes," the Asset says. "Take it off now."

The instruction has a strange effect. No one wants to be the one to take off the mask. "It is probably a full hood, including ears and eyes."

"Including? Oh, man! I was thinking—"

"We saw it on the other example," the Asset says. "They preserve the ear/eye nerves and cords, extend them and cut off the original organ, use a synthetic replaceable. Looks like they would have no trouble making ears and eyes out of graphene." He jerks a chin at the team. "I need that information now," he says. "Pull off the mask. Do it."

Whatever is under the mask, even a seasoned team like this doesn't want to see it. The Asset nods. "Amazing, isn't it? Nobody can bring themselves to look. Only a freak can face a freak, right?"

He bends over the body again then plunges a hand down under the T-shirt at the back of the neck. "I was right, it *is* a full hood, stops just above the shoulders, I can feel the graphene trellis. Okay, I'm going to pull."

He manipulates the material between a thumb and forefinger, as you would open a very thin plastic bag, then pinches something and starts to lift. The material is so fine as to be invisible at first, then as the light catches the dust and the Asset lifts farther, I cannot *see* but have to deduce a transparent sheet so thin it is two-dimensional, rising from the face. It is also very strong. He is holding the amazing material in a fist and pulling until some of the perp's face has gone, but it is not possible to tell what lies underneath. The mask is stuck. Now I have some idea what to expect, and so do the others. We all move back as the Asset pulls harder. It will not come away, though, because the material is trapped under ears and eye sockets.

"Those will be artificial organs," one of the team says. "You could probably pull them up with the mask. That graphene isn't going to break, that's for sure."

The Asset pulls still harder, things pop. Now the mask is a tiny crumpled piece of material mixed up with two ears and two eyes embedded in it.

What lies underneath? R, you don't want to know, really you don't.

Okay, you do, but it's hard to describe. If it were simply animal, it would be easier. If I could report to you that the new artificial humans are some godforsaken splicing of ape and man, with an ape head and long hairy arms and a British accent, etcetera, it would be easier for you to deal with. What we have, though, is definitely not animal. And it's not human either. Neither is it a space alien. With a huge domed fishlike forehead, two high-tech cables for eyes and another two for ears, a thin face, cruel mouth, and a set of teeth like a baboon's . . . No, R, I simply cannot do justice to it, because to describe the surface is to miss the point. When you look at it, you experience a feeling deep in your gut that the Neanderthals must have felt when they first set eyes on *Homo sapiens: This hideous thing is smarter and more ruthless than us. This thing is taking over. There goes the neighborhood.*

I must have started to talk to myself or mumble out of shock, because the rest of the team has stopped to look at me.

"It's okay," Dr. Pink says. "I was like that the first time."

"Our whole species suffers from hubris because we have no experience of creatures mentally superior to ourselves. This is the beginning of payback," Dr. White says.

"Imagine how a dog feels, having to live in a world full of humans with superior cunning and intellect who keep tricking and fooling and exploiting and tormenting it. Well, that's how humans are going to feel when this thing takes off. When the artificial intelligence becomes self-evolving and independent of us."

"Accelerated learning enhancement? ALE has taken off already," the Asset says, and everyone falls silent. "And by the way, you wouldn't want me to remove *my* mask, would you?" He checks his watch. "Three minutes to go."

Three minutes later the team has rolled the cadaver up and four men are lifting the tarp exactly at the moment a battered black Toyota Carryboy screeches to a halt outside. The six-foot roll is placed carefully in the back, the rear door closed and locked, the car squeals away—and I'm alone at the crime scene, which has been cleaned and tidied. Even the Asset has silently disappeared. I step out onto the marketplace and understand without a shadow of doubt that sometime over the past decade the world changed radically forever—but the event was top secret and may be classified for the next fifty years.

When I take out my phone I see it is three zero-five a.m. There is only one person I know who might just be awake at this time. But I don't much care if she's awake or not, I need to call her anyway. I press the autodial button and let it ring. She answers after about three minutes. I tell her what has happened.

"There in ten," she says and hangs up.

The streets are pretty much empty except for a predawn garbage truck and some drunks in an alley with a flashlight. It takes Krom no more than ten minutes, as she promised, and now here she is in her own battered little white two-door. She has pulled on a pair of shorts and T-shirt. Close up in the front passenger seat I become aware of how muscular her legs are. They are elegant enough, but firm, like an athlete's. She lets a couple of beats pass until we are half a mile away from the market area.

"So, you saw an HZ—a humanzee? I'm jealous." I stare out of the window, watching the silent city go by, working my jaw. "Is it true that they're too ugly to look at?"

"Yes," I say.

"But is that because, you know, we're just not used to seeing that kind of being?"

"The opposite. We've all seen them before, in our worst nightmares — something tells you: this is the future you've been running from all your life."

"Tell me more, tell me everything."

"*You* tell *me* everything," I say. "It's time. You know a lot more than me. What is that creature? Who is that creature? How is that creature? Why is that creature? And why did you refer to the Asset as *Messiah* when you spoke to the FBI?"

"I've been promoted. Thanks to you. In the top circle we refer to the Asset that way. It's the protocol. You'll see."

She flashes me a glance while she changes gear at an intersection. The glance resembles the way a woman might take a quick look at a cake baking in an oven, to see if it's done yet. "Okay," she says. "Okay. But you must have guessed most of it."

We have come to a set of red lights. Stopping is optional at this time of night, especially for cops, but she brakes anyway, her hands resting on the steering wheel. "The new technology is not expected to change the way wars are fought. In the future, *security* will mean controlling and suppressing the have-nots of a global economic system that has collapsed. For that you need transhumans: THs. According to all the experts, that is the most economic and probably the only way of doing the job. A TH can wait like a sleeper until needed, collecting information on neighbors, friends, and employers, then use his or her special skills in conjunction with conventional security services when revolutions start. A TH has no loyalty to any normal human because a TH is a superior order of life. In a riot one trans could hold off as many as ten rioters indefinitely, but it's exponential. Ten THs could hold off not a hundred but a thousand, by acting in perfect coordination. The problem all along was how to inject enough ferocity in the product without having a rogue mutant on your hands. It became a problem of personality." She flashes me a look. "Which is kind of funny, if you think about it."

"Why?"

"Because from the military point of view, the personality is one of those little vanities that only nonmilitary wimps worry about. That's what threw them fifty years ago in Vietnam. It's what drove Goldman crazy and the reason why he teamed up with Dr. Christmas Bride. You've guessed that, right?"

"Through a glass darkly."

"So Goldman took the children of those spaced-out vets who were born at the camp. But he screwed up. That's one of the things most freaked Richard Helms, who was running the CIA at the time: records of disastrous interventions with children. No wonder he blatantly destroyed the files right in the middle of the inquiry. Dr. Bride's point was that the human personality is the product of a hundred thousand years of evolution based on archetypes: what our forefathers called gods. Although we like to be cynical about it, those dead deities are actually very important to our functioning, like enzymes in digestion. We simply don't want to be a part of the world if we can't dream about transcending it. What he gave to those kids was the transcendent. And it worked. You've met the Asset. For many in the transhuman community he is the most accomplished, advanced being on the planet."

"You really believe he's Jesus Christ?" I mutter in disbelief. I had not realized how much I had come to rely on her cynicism.

"He is," Krom says, that incongruous tone of reverence in her voice, the same she used when talking to the FBI. "You just have to see it right, as a historical mandate."

"He also kills people, scares the shit out of them, plays with their emotions."

"You can't make omelets without breaking eggs. Save your judgmentalism. How was he tonight?"

"Functioning perfectly."

"See? That's what I'm getting at. In a dangerous fix with an HZ killer who could easily take out a dozen trained men, he functioned perfectly."

"Maybe you should fill me in on the HZs," I said.

"Look at it like this: transhumans are the only way to go. Americans and Russians both experimented in the last century, failed, and in the American case caused a huge scandal. Naturally, the experiments continued in the USSR based on Professor Ilya Ivanov's work with apes, and the Americans continued with vets and volunteers in secret in various locations, mostly in Southeast Asia. Both had breakthroughs at the same time. Both found the funding to be difficult since it was extremely expensive and officially was not happening. The country that most needs to bolster its internal security is China, with a population that soon will reach nearly two billion. China has a minor TH program of its own based on chemicals, but is way behind the other two. The PRC is very interested in *breeding* transhumans rather than producing them through specially designed drug regimes they already have, most of which were sold to them by Dr. Christmas Bride. They let it be known they would be interested in buying into someone else's research, which means Russia's or America's, but they need reassurance that the assets produced by such a program are stable and reliable. So Russia and America are in competition. The one who succeeds in selling to China will inevitably grow close to the PRC, with all the commercial and economic benefits that implies. They will also receive a massive injection of nonstate funding from sale of the system. Naturally, the U.S. doesn't want Russia to be close to China, and Russia doesn't want the U.S. to be close to China, and neither party wants the other to race ahead thanks to an injection of billions of tax-free nonaccountable dollars. There's more than just commerce at stake."

"So the competition is fierce and deadly."

"You saw it tonight. The way the Russians tried to discredit the Asset by making it look as if he is a child molester and killer—just what the Chinese are afraid of with this program. Polonium's people even knew you are the Asset's half brother and that you long to find your father—hence the writing on the mirror in a murder in the center of District 8." She pauses. "But the point is the technology you witnessed. That will get everyone excited, including the Chinese when they are briefed. Nobody knew the Russians had gotten that far. You said one of the scientists thinks they're further ahead with graphene technology than America? That's going to get a lot of people's attention. You see, masks turned out to be key. The human being in its evolution sacrificed almost everything to vanity. Soft beautiful skin instead of protective hair, large seductive and vulnerable eyes, muscles and tendons allowed almost to degenerate for the sake of producing shapely limbs, etcetera. You want to put primate intensity back into the mix, you have to sacrifice aesthetics—big time. This results in a product that is too ugly for anyone to look at; even hardened military men can't stand to look at a full HZ without its mask on." She scratches her ear. "Amazing, isn't it, the one thing nobody thought of: beauty. It tripped them up big time. But graphene masks are the way to go. That's why you had three world-class specialists there tonight. Some ass is going to get kicked in Virginia soon as they realize they're so far behind Polonium. It'll be the space race all over again."

I grunt.

"What's the matter, is all this too much for you?"

"I'm just a simple cop."

She laughs cynically.

"But I *am* a cop and so are you, and I'm wondering why we're conveniently ignoring the main point."

"Which is what?"

"Which is how you know so damn much."

She lets quite a few beats pass. "Didn't I tell you I was recruited?" she says simply. Then adds, "Look, why don't you come back, see how I live, we'll talk some more?"

35

You work with someone, inevitably you build up a picture of the way they live. So: Krom is a single young dyke who lives in a bedsit somewhere between Ekkamai and On Nut, probably in a modern four-story walk-up on a side street, she is polite but strange with neighbors, she rarely entertains save for one-night stands that take place discreetly so as not to cause outrage; if she has a second bedroom, it is full of cardboard boxes of old clothes and outdated gadgets, on her wall hang posters originating in the lesbian blogosphere, there is a ruthless kind of masculinity in the minimalism, right? Wrong.

To judge from the direction we have taken in her old Toyota, it seems as if she resides in the most expensive part of town, between Ploenchit and Lumpini Park; but not all the land around here has been developed for tall apartment buildings. Throughout the city you still find die-hards, people who like to live in a wooden house on stilts in a generous orchard with plenty of plants, pools, cats and dogs, even monkeys and parrots, while the wall of high-rises rises higher and higher all around.

It is still dark when we arrived at the iron gates. Krom uses a remote handset to open and close them behind us. Safety lights make it possible to discern perhaps a half acre of land with a couple of fish pools, some banyan and frangipani trees, grass that is cut irregularly; a dozen cats' eyes stare from improbable elevations when we get out of the car. Krom leads me up a wooden stairway and uses an old-style latchkey to enter the house, which is already inhabited and filled with light. Someone is not merely awake, someone is working at this hour.

"It's late afternoon on the East Coast of America," Krom explains. "You'll see."

We are standing in a corridor. By my calculation the room at the far end must run the width of the house and offer a fine view of the garden with the pools, trees, and cats. It must be like old Siam in that room. Krom leads me to the door, knocks gently: "Can we come in?"

"Come."

The woman in the far room is tall for a Chinese; perhaps she owns Manchurian genes, for she is around five eleven and slim, about fifty years old in a comfortable silk housecoat, her black hair tied back in a bun. She leans lightly on a shelf next to her hand, holds her head at an angle, waits expectantly; but it is the shelf that now grabs my attention—actually, all the shelves do. The room is a library of perfume bottles, tens of thousands of them, which cram the shelves in colorful sets six deep, like a paperback library. Meanwhile, discreet and intriguing aromas play games with my head. It's difficult not to feel a happy kind of high in this room, as if the aromas were proxies for love and money.

"I have brought a visitor," Krom tells the Chinese woman.

"Yes," she says, "I can smell him well enough from here." She smiles. "Krom has told me all about you," she says. Then, when the Chinese woman decides to move and continues to hold her head in a certain way with eyes apparently focused on the ceiling, I realize she is blind. "I'm afraid I have a call from New York in about two minutes," she says and dips a hand in the pocket of her housecoat to pull out a smart phone to show us.

"I'm sorry," Krom says. "Shall we leave you alone?"

"No, it's only business," she says. "What is your friend's name again?"

"Detective Sonchai Jitpleecheep. Detective, this is Madame Gloria Ching—but I call her *Yai*, because she is almost my mother."

"There's no *almost* about motherhood," Madame Ching says with a smile, still holding her head at an angle, her unfocused eyes pointing at the ceiling. "And Krom is way ahead of me in most things."

"Except perfume," Krom says.

"Yes. Perhaps." Now her phone rings and she fishes it out of her pocket. "Hello, Gloria Ching speaking." Her English is perfect, of the kind only taught in expensive Asian private schools.

"She's the daughter of a PRC cadre," Krom whispers. "Nothing but the best for her, especially since she was born sightless. Her father was on the Central Committee, he was a kind of minister of defense, but they purged him and he's been under house arrest for two decades. He still has connections, though, and tons of dough offshore."

"I'm afraid I'm not so keen, to be honest with you," Madame Ching is saying to her caller in New York. "He needs to bite the bullet and put in some more skatole for the base notes . . . No, *skatole* is civet shit, more precisely, the *smell* of civet shit . . . But what it really needs, and I'm generously giving free advice here, is a touch of hyraceum . . . It's made from the petrified excrement of the Cape hyrax. It has the power to make perfume intriguing instead of merely pleasant . . . You see, aroma is like any art, you don't get anywhere without contrast and depth . . . I don't mind the bergamot at all, I think he's done a fine job with the bright floral theme, and the citrus is very well anchored, it's just that it lacks intrigue, which is what you need for evening wear . . . Yes, I'll talk to him or put it in writing if you like . . . Well, you want to sell to Asia, you have to do a lot of floral highlights, we're not so dark and animal as the West, he's got that right . . . I'll have someone send a bill for the consultation before the end of the month . . . Goodbye."

Madame Ching closes her phone and clicks in our direction. At first I was not sure I had heard right, or if the middle-aged woman had some eccentricity that caused her to make clicking sounds. It is clear she intends to join us in the sitting area at the other end of the room, and I assumed that Krom would guide her, or she would use a stick. Instead, she keeps up with the hollow-sounding clicks, then walks toward us with perfect assurance. She sits on a chair next to a sofa we are sitting on, smiles in my direction. Krom is staring at me, waiting for a reaction.

"You've been enhanced," I say, because it seemed to be expected. I turn to Krom. I do not say, *Gimme the whole story this time or I'll kill you,* I just feel like saying it.

"I was nineteen years old," Krom says, "and getting ready to die. Look at that picture again." She goes to a credenza and finds an iPad. "Look at it on the big screen, you'll see more." She locates something on the iPad and shows it to me. It is the same portrait as the one she showed me of herself on her phone, but on the iPad it's huge and easier to study. There is that obvious intelligence in her eyes, but drug abuse of some kind is a given. Another unhappy outsider: lost, utterly lost, and about to fall further into something tragic. There is no direction in that soul, none at all. I look from her to Madame Ching and back.

Krom takes the iPad to examine the photo. "Look at me. Just another third-world girl feeling like a piece of consumer trash waiting to be gobbled up."

"But you're not . . ."

"Not in the same league as the Messiah? No, of course not. Nothing is permanent with us, we need injections every six months."

"What happened?"

"The PRC learned about Dr. Christmas Bride quite early on, they made contact. In return for a mountain of dough Bride was able to advise them on certain superficial kinds of enhancement that can be acquired in adulthood, without the high risk of implanting circuits in the brain. His research with LSD and its variants enabled him to develop extra sensitivities in certain areas. We call them Apps, like for smart phones. Yai had the olfactory App, didn't you, Yai?"

"And echolocation. Both changed my life."

"And it was Yai who they appointed to take care of my initiation, wasn't it, Yai?"

The Chinese woman sniffs and smiles. "Now you have the Detective's attention," she says. "He is emanating aromas of awe. I think he is finally getting it. Don't stop, whatever you do."

"It's just another revolution," Krom says. "Technology developed in war shocks everyone when it is revealed. Who would have predicted forty years ago that people of the future would spend most of their lives staring at computer screens?"

"But this is different," I say.

"Yes. This is the big one. We are all supposed to be discreet for the moment, waiting for the tsunami to hit." She shrugs. "Because that's what it's going to be. Quietly, secretly, a few research groups have been working on something that will sweep the world like cell phones, and for the same reason: it's what we want."

"Enhanced bodies?"

"For the masses who love to play with themselves. For the elite, something more radical. Enhanced brains, enhanced horizons. New personalities. The most important thing you will ever witness in your life is the transformation of the Asset. He is ready to spread his wings and fly. Bride and Goldman successfully married his human intelligence and his artificial intelligence so that he has reached the moment where his capacity to learn is accelerated way beyond the human. When he told you he was Jesus Christ he was simply stating a truth within the terms of present-day mythology. What was the original Jesus if not an enhanced human? The Bible is full of stories of humans enhanced by God. Change your definition of God . . ."

The Chinese woman starts to laugh. "Krom is in total awe of Christmas Bride, whom she's never met. I met him only once, I could smell the devil in him."

Krom grins. "Yai thinks Bride took revenge on his Catholic mother by turning himself into God. After all, he is the one who produced the Asset, aka the Messiah."

"Who also happens to be the most efficient killing machine in human form ever produced."

"No, the HZs are ahead in that."

"So," Madame Ching says, "this is a conversation that will take up the whole of this century and the next as well. Are we good or bad, we transhumans?"

"We are inevitable," Krom says. "End of conversation." She turns to Madame Ching.

"Transhumans are a highly evolved, creative, and exciting new species with a weakness for sadism," Gloria Ching says with a smile.

The two women filled me in on a few more details. It was dawn before I left them. Madame Ching clicked her way to the door to see me out, and Krom busied herself feeding the cats. All around the garden the gleaming pink walls of giant skyscrapers rose above the quaint old house, but I couldn't help feeling that this small center of personal enhancement had the edge on the high-rises. The future, surely, was right here. True, nobody knew that yet, but it would not be long. It was hard to take in, as if the world I inhabited was already so out of date as to be irrelevant. Nothing we do today that will not be swept away in a heartbeat, once the story breaks. How do you feel about that yourself, R? Did we miss the yacht, you and I? We are the Old Humans: OHs, already. If we're lucky, the NHs will find us quaint; otherwise it's a choice between the reservation and the zoo. Personally, though, I'm kind of drained this merry morning. They are heavy people, those transhumans, very heavy.

36

Apologies to you, R, what with all the action and stress I've only just realized I left you hanging after the FBI TH gave me that thumb drive with the hyper-secret recordings that self-destruct after six hours. You remember? I'll shove it in here, if that's okay. BTW, is there something wrong with the high-tech brain that causes it to miss the obvious? I played the recording aloud into an old-fashioned tape recorder. The files on the thumb drive self-destructed, but I still have the conversation. It is quite interesting and goes like this:

Goldman [out of breath, slightly hysterical]: *I'm scared, Control, I have to admit it. I'm damn scared.*

Control [in a neutral tone]: *What about, G8? The thing we talked about three days ago?*

Goldman: *Yeah. The same. Only three days is a long time with the ALE.*

Control: *He's threatened you?*

Goldman [sighing heavily]: *I told you, he doesn't need to threaten.*

Control: *Oh, yeah. You know him so well, you can read his mind. And what you read there is an intention to harm you?*

Goldman: *Are you being sarcastic?*

Controller: *No, just summing up so we can understand each other.* [Pause] *So, tell me about it.*

Goldman: *I've been with him so long I can smell when he's about to kill. Do you understand me? The air around him starts to die, it's like when there's too much ozone.*

Control: *Ozone?*

Goldman: *I'm trying to give you the feel of it. Fuck you.*

Control [sighing again]: *Well, you trained him to kill, didn't you?*

Goldman: *Yeah, I trained him to kill. With approval and assistance from—*

Control: *Don't say it.*

Goldman: *I didn't say it. But it's true.*

Control: *I wasn't on the case at the time, G8. I was about seven years old when you started this phase of the project.*

Goldman: *So, what are you saying, you're not qualified?*

Control: *I'm saying this has been going on one hell of a long while and from what I've seen of the file you've had full operational control all that time. Forty years, G8. Forty fucking years on Ultra II. Actually, more.*

Goldman: *That's right, forty years I've been serving my country, mostly in the jungle. Now I want some help.*

Control: *You want help. I want to know what's suddenly gone so wrong. You're holding out here. Let me put the possibilities as I see them: you're having a nervous breakdown because you're way too old, too clumsy, and too out of date for your own program, which you are losing control of just like any old guy.* [Silence. The Control continues] *The other is that this Asset is no better than all the others, all of whom died at your hands. That's what I think, by the way. And you can't admit it because this Asset is all you've got right now. The deal with China goes wrong, you are out, discredited. I hope you put some money away for what's left of your life. Now, there's just one thing you can tell me that might, just might, get me on your side. What I want is an explanation as to why the Asset is, in your opinion, going wrong now instead of later or earlier?*

Goldman [in an okay, I'll come clean tone of total despair, as if he is coughing up his own guts]: *Bride double-crossed us.*

[Silence]

Control [in a tone expressing disgust and disbelief]: *Bride? The wizard himself? Do you have any idea how many wonderful, laudatory, praise-my-man memoranda and minutes you—*

you personally, G8—have placed on record throughout four decades precisely in order to keep that jungle shaman on the case when others were in favor of eliminating him, in the old-fashioned sense of the word?

Goldman: *I know. I know that. I also told you he is a genius. And a Brit. The combination produces eccentricity like you wouldn't believe. He made his Asset an expert on Italian cuisine, classical arts, and the French Revolution—and just about every goddamn religion under the sun. An Asset designed for essentially military operations, yet. And who can tell in advance what direction a man will take thirty, forty, fifty years down the track? Nobody, nobody on this earth thought the thing would take this long.*

Control: *I'm with you there. Looked at objectively, you could say this program is even older than you. About eighty years since those maniacs Dulles and Gottlieb started on this Frankensteinian extravaganza.* [Wearily] *So, tell me about your problem with the Brit nut job.*

Goldman: *I don't think he has any intention of selling to China. He's letting the Asset kill the deal.*

[Long pause]

Control: *How's that?*

Goldman: *A truckload of small things, hints.*

Control: *For Christ's sake, man.*

Goldman: *Okay, I can't prove it and I don't have the evidence, but I think the Old Man programmed his Asset, as in deep, deep psychic penetration, long before he handed him over to us.*

Control: *Well, now at least I understand why you've been quiet about your doubts up to now. You mean you've connived knowingly or unknowingly with a total con, a half-century long, during which time the Company spends untold millions on a project which is preprogrammed to revert to the use of a private person who is not even a U.S. citizen? Is this call a request to take out the Brit?*

Goldman: *Not specifically. What I need you to think about is this. Like you say, this thing has been going on too long. The Brit is already a billionaire and he's damned old. He discovered a lot of stuff in the jungle, not just hallucinogenics. I think he can keep himself alive for at least another decade, maybe more. He's like a Celtic magus—weird but successful.*

Control: *So?*

Goldman: *So, why would he content himself with being the midwife to a revolution that will change the way governments govern and control population worldwide?*

Control: *Why not? Doesn't sound like a humble role to me.*

Goldman: *Because his intention is to rule that world himself. I tell you he's deep and European—he doesn't think utilitarian or democratic. And he doesn't need money. Like you said, he's a billionaire already thanks to the private chemical programs he sold to China.*

Control: *You're going vague on me again, G8.*

Goldman: *He thinks the greatest motivating factor today, and certainly for tomorrow, for the whole of humanity, is a search for meaning.*

Control: *Search for meaning? What, he's reverting to his hippie days?*

Goldman: *You could say he never stopped thinking that way. He was brought up religious. His main point is that what people want is a new god. Culturally and psychologically the global situation is almost identical to that of Palestine and the eastern Mediterranean two thousand years ago under the Romans.*

Control [bemused]: *Yeah?*

Goldman: *Apparently it was total chaos, with new cults sprouting up all over the place. The search for meaning was universal and a powerful political force in itself. Apparently even a lot of Roman soldiers became Christians, even while he was alive.*

Control: *Who was alive?*

Goldman: *Jesus fucking Christ.*

Control [sounding interested]: *So what if that is true today as it was two thousand years ago, which it might be. What does it have to do with the price of false tits? What does the Brit magus intend to do?*

Goldman: *Send his only begotten son to take over. The only one left, anyway. Same as last time.*

Control [disgusted]: *You need a vacation, G8. You need a long vacation.*

Goldman: *You're cutting me loose? That's a death sentence, you know that?*

The line is cut.

37

So I'm in the canteen at the station grabbing my evening meal, holding the phone to one ear listening to the Colonel while I'm loading up a plastic plate with pad Thai, and at the same time there's a *bleep* that tells me that I've just received a message, but I don't know my phone well enough to risk checking the message while the Chief is talking for fear of cutting him off.

"But that's Satorn," I'm saying, "that's not District 8. I have no authority to investigate."

"I know. But it's a special address. I'm not saying more over the phone. Inspector Krom is already there. Let's say you're both to give specialist counseling without taking over the case."

So now I'm forgetting the pad Thai and leaving my plastic plate on the counter, rushing through the swing doors and down the steps to the street trying to decide which would be quicker, a cab or a bike, and thinking Satorn is a long way on a bike but there's so much traffic on Sukhumvit I could be sitting in the cab for an hour so I decide on the bike and stride to the end of the bike line and tell the jockey where to go and he doesn't want to go that far because it encroaches on other bikers who are known to protect their patch with ferocity and knives so I have to promise to pay him double as danger money and we're on our way before I remember the message on the phone:

How can one as talented as I ever consent to be a mere soldier or policeman? I felt degraded in front of you the other night. What in heaven's name were they thinking when they tried to bend me that way? Don't they know by now how negatively I react to such indignities? I put up with it, then when I can't stand it anymore . . .

If you don't know, Sakagorn's principal residence is off Soi Langsuan, and Bully Boy Goldman's is on Soi 24, Sukhumvit, which I think you once visited. I have tried to amuse you with a reference or two to Caravaggio: a brute but a genius for whom I have a soft spot. You will see immediately how well I have channeled his Goliath. For the lawyer, though, how could I not reference that propagandist David? (I do so adore teasing you with clues, it's such fun.) Good night, good night! Parting is such sweet sorrow, that I shall say good night till it be morrow.

A lot of the houses on Sakagorn's *soi* are of the old-style wedding-cake type, built by millionaires before the local rich learned to imitate the international rich and built super-modern homes designed by hip international architects. Most, though, are large mansions pretty much in the European high-bourgeois style: complex and elegant roofs, gables, five-car garages, plenty of bedrooms, attached guest cottages de rigueur, CCTV everywhere, guards and electronic gates. No prizes for guessing which is Sakagorn's; the road outside is already blocked with police vehicles and media rats with video and sound equipment. Black cables thick as anacondas lead to humming vans. A female reporter for one of the local channels is talking into one of the cameras, holding a microphone. When she sees me she tells the viewers the "famous detective Sonchai Jitpleecheep has just arrived," then she calls out. I smile automatically, shake my head and mime, *Not my patch.* The cop at the gate presses a button. I squeeze past as soon as the gap is wide enough. The cop presses the button again and the gate closes behind me. *What is that weird music?*

Inside the house, where the music is even louder, there are a half-dozen police from the local station standing around on the marble floor. They see me and jerk their chins at the double staircase. Then they point to their ears and shake their heads and look at me for answers. I shrug, but now I think I know what that music is. I climb up to the master bedroom. Krom is there in her black boiler suit, hands in her pockets. It looks as though she has finished issuing orders and is stumped for the moment. She nods when she sees me.

"I can't figure out how to turn off that damned music. There must be hidden cables with an independent power source. We can't just smash the speakers. Do you know what it is?"

"Yes," I say, for I've remembered. I am no kind of classical music buff, but the memory goes back to Fritz, who was the first of my mother's customers to become a full-fledged person to me, rather than mere food source. He loved the work of some crazy Renaissance prince called Gesualdo, told a story of a genius who murdered his wife and her lover then shut himself up in his castle where he had his servants whip him for the rest of his life. The off-key music he produced was a direct expression of his spiritual death, his private hell. Is the Asset finally saying something real here?

"It's composed by an Italian murderer."

"It's so creepy."

I raise my eyes. She jerks her chin toward the bathroom where the forensic team has finished with the video sweep and is now kneeling to take still photos of minute details that might or might not be useful. They've left Sakagorn where they found him, naked in the bath. I stare and stare.

The tableau is very famous, so famous I have come across it often in my endless travels through time and space on the Net. Now I realize who *David* is in this context. I open my smart phone, key in *French Revolution, David, Marat, death of,* and there they are: the picture on the phone and the still life, so to speak, in the bathroom. I show it to Krom. Her eyes flick from the miniature image of David's masterpiece to the dead lawyer in the bath over and over again, perhaps as many as a dozen times.

"Amazing," she murmurs. There is something quite strange in her tone, as if she is admiring a triumph of classified technology. "How he set him up like that . . . I don't know. It's not like anything I've ever seen." She glances at me. "Murder as art? The final *farang* decadence?"

She is referring to the way the cadaver has been arranged to perfectly imitate the painting of the revolutionary Marat, with a few differences. For example, instead of a letter, Sakagorn is holding a barrister's brief in his left hand. Instead of a cloth around his head the perp has wrapped his long hair up into a bun. Instead of an ink pot on a side stool, my half brother has wittily replaced it with an Apple laptop. But, as in the painting, one arm hangs out over the side of the bath, there is a light-colored towel with bloodstains under the armpit and a green towel also draped over the bath, and he is lurched to one side with his head almost resting on his right shoulder, his mouth slightly open and the fatal wound in his upper chest. As in the painting, the body has been dead just long enough to acquire a greenish tinge.

"Let's go," I say, and tell her about the Asset's e-mail and the reference to Bully Boy Goldman.

There is a rear entrance to Sakagorn's mansion, which we slip out of and hail a cab. I snatch glances of Krom from time to time as we race to Goldman's apartment. I myself am still sufficiently human to be shocked by the lawyer's death. I cannot say I liked him much or respected him, but it was not difficult to relate to his all-too-human weaknesses. Krom, though, I can tell, sees only a technical and cultural marvel in his murder and can hardly stop smirking. She has been enhanced, after all, she is no longer one of us. Now I watch carefully as she does that special thing with her mind. Krom closes her eyes and seems to retreat deeply into herself until the world is entirely blocked out. It takes only a few seconds, then, when she opens her eyes again she is a different person. There is a new, steely strength in the atmosphere around her and even a slightly metallic timbre to her voice.

"How many . . . I mean, how long before the revolution?" I ask.

She shrugs. "Good question. A lot depends on your half brother, actually." She smiles. "Like any applied science, once it's seen to work it can't be stopped. That's why I gave in—you can't fight the future."

"Which is what?"

"Exactly. That's the question, isn't it? Maybe a replay of the fifties when the world and Superman were young and no one in the USA had heard of Vietnam."

The cab turns into the driveway of Goldman's apartment building and our conversation ends.

Are you familiar with the work of the baroque artist Michelangelo Merisi da Caravaggio, R? I myself was not and had to fish out my iPhone again to consult the Wiki. It seems he was another Italian murderer, on the run from Rome with a price on his head, literally: anyone who brought his head in a basket to the Pope could expect to receive the reward immediately in gold. In an attempt to express penance by painting his way out of the fix, he did a *David with the Head of Goliath* in which he features not as the triumphant David but as the head in the basket. For this reason our Asset has given Goldman a false black beard and a long black wig. He must have shaved the head and used strong glue for the wig, because it is hanging by some strands from a bronze statue of—well, you guessed. Where he found a man-size copy of Michelangelo's *David* in Bangkok I cannot say. In any event, he was unable to imitate the painting exactly and had to hang the head around David's neck and so arranged the piece to face us immediately on our opening the front door to Goldman's apartment. Beheadings are, of course, notorious for the mess they make. The floor is slick with blood pooling in hollows. It is still liquid, though. He must have done Goldman quite recently. Now my iPhone bleeps.

> *Let us go see our father together, Dear Brother, I would like that and I'm sure he would too. BTW as a professional I do hope you don't find my work too fussy? I'm feeling just a touch of stage fright.*

I show the message to Krom, whose eyes glitter. It must be the drugs she takes that give her a weakness for heroic madness. She shrugs. "Go, you can't arrest him, he has diplomatic immunity, and anyway the Americans would never allow it, he knows that, he won't hurt you."

"But why murder the two people in the world who were closest to him?"

"Ask him when you see him."

38

I sulked. I hate it that I cannot arrest the Asset; it disgusts me that some kind of elitism is already at work regarding transhumans. It enrages me that he can walk around free; this is Bangkok, not Baghdad. I tell you, R, you only have to come from a semifeudal society to develop an extreme aversion to a future where the whole planet will be under the heel of an aristocracy of Enhanced Ones. Take it from the third world: you really don't want to go down that road, you've forgotten what it's like, cast your mind back, why did your ancestors get on the *Mayflower* in the first place? Oh, never mind, I know it's too late. Anyway, I have to see him, don't I? I replied to his message with a taciturn OK.

In the meantime the results from the swab tests didn't come. Instead I received a letter from the Trustee for the Bankruptcy Court of the Eastern District of Kentucky who regretted that the Know the Father Corporation, now in receivership, was being investigated by the FBI, who suspected the KTF of fraud, money laundering, blackmail, conspiracy and intimidation within the meaning of the RICO provisions, and employment of unqualified personnel who posed as technicians: in brief, my swabs would not be processed, and it was unlikely I would get my money back.

I could try again, of course, with another DNA tester, but I don't think I will. What difference would it make? The search for self is a continuum, what closure can an old man in a coma offer? Of course, I've known that forever and chose to ignore it up to now: continuums, you never see them until it's too late.

———

So Jesus Christ arrives to pick me up at the station in the late Sakagorn's sky-blue Rolls-Royce, with the deceased lawyer's driver in livery, of course. It seems that the Asset was already living at Sakagorn's mansion while the lawyer spent most of his time at a luxury apartment a few miles away. Now the Asset, aka Messiah, treats the mansion, the car, and the driver as his own. I am tight-lipped and cool when I get in the back with him; but he's the Asset, he's enhanced, a master of moods. He also speaks Thai perfectly. I want to believe he has been studying it for years; the possibility that he might have become fluent in a month or less is too awful to contemplate. But I remember what Sergeant Lotus Bud said: only a couple of weeks ago the Asset had only basic Thai and they had to communicate in Khmer.

At first I refuse to react to his small talk, but when he makes a pun in Thai that turns the driver to Jell-O (puns are a chronic national weakness: hard men collapse in giggles; we're not as bad as the Cantonese, but we're close) I find myself seduced. Why not sit back and enjoy the company of a multiple killer who carves up his long-term workmates to intrigue and charm his elder sibling? After all, he's Superman. Clearly, he approves of my change of mood.

"You see, my dear, you cannot be angry with me for long. That's what I always wanted, a blood relation who would forgive my foibles. Even Doc Bride could not foresee that. Do you feel the same way, now we have bonded?"

I decide to check his commitment to our blood brotherhood with a forensic question. "Why did you do them in, Jesus? Exactly, why?"

"Ah! You mean—"

"Goldman and Sakagorn. Surely you haven't forgotten already?"

"Doctor's orders. They were about to double-cross the Old Man with a secret deal with China—they were scared the Doc was double-crossing *them*, so they planned to double-cross *him*: basic intelligence community stuff. They even tried to buy my compliance—a truckload of dough they offered. How dumb can you get? Couldn't they figure out that the first programming the Old Man inserted in my brain was loyalty to him? I told him what they were up to and he gave the word. You don't betray your own creator. I'm not sure he was expecting anything so ornate, though, that was all for you. I have the younger sibling's need to impress the elder."

I stare at him. "Killing humans means nothing at all to you, does it? Is that because you do not see us as part of your species?"

He thinks about it. "I do believe you are looking at it the wrong way, dear one. Who on earth gives a damn that Goldman and Sakagorn are dead? My vengeance is just. Their families are much better off now, and Sakagorn's new young mistress is financially independent—he left her millions in his will. Broaden your view somewhat to include, let's say, all life on earth, except man. Then broaden it further to include all the life in whatever spiritual spheres you believe in, if any. Then broaden it to include ghosts of the dead, if they exist. Then broaden it to include all the extraterrestrials on all the viable planets in all the cosmos—"

"Yes?"

"So, in none of those areas of research will you find anyone or thing who gives a fuck or a fart for human life. That's it, you see, the last enhancement is the broadest: humans have no use or importance except insofar as they may one day produce transhumans. There's no other excuse for their confused and pathetic existence. Fecundity in the production of lab rats aside, there's nothing humans have that the universe wants. The best they can hope for is a global system presided over by THs who will make the earth run smoothly." He casts me a glance. "If you don't agree, name one moral advancement by humanity in the past ten thousand years. The social order and moral code of Stone Age man was far more rigorous and demanding than anything today. Neanderthals would consider a modern human as a psychopathic monkey with gadgets."

The Asset tells the driver to let us out at the hospital entrance, where everyone stares at the sky-blue limo and the irresistible hunk who gets out. I lead him to the lift that takes us to the head department, which is quiet with dimmed lighting. Jack's two buddies have already been discharged and it seems they left him there in permanent bliss in accordance with their jungle customs. We stand by the bed of our primogenitor. I have no words for the occasion and neither does the Asset, who stares at the old vet in a state of confusion. I think this could be the first time he's seen him since childhood and is not prepared for the devastation that time has wrought on that body and face. I think, also, he finds it difficult to imagine that he originates from such stock, for it is as Krom foretold: this Asset has entered a phase of rapid change, his responses are faster, more commanding, more godlike by the day.

"This is the Doc's gift to me, brother. I asked him to arrange it. Our father will be in a state of bliss now until he dies. Are you pleased with me?"

"Ah, yes."

"Let's go," he says, bored after a few minutes.

Back in the limo he tells the driver to take us to the mansion of the late Lord Sakagorn. Now I realize the meeting with our father has tripped some fuse in him; anything from the soft, mediocre, human zone puzzles and disturbs him. Me, for example, I puzzle and disturb him considerably.

"How was I the other night?" he asks. "Not too military, I hope?"

"At the shooting of the HZ? You were perfect, efficient, brilliant, commanding, responsible with terrific leadership."

"I was sweating it, I can tell you. It would only have needed one more HZ to beat us. No way we could have coped with two or more, they would have torn us apart. I was seriously intimidated. Did you see the teeth on that thing?" He casts me a regretful look. "I'm being frank here, they're better than me. Stronger, faster, more ruthless. They could beat me to a pulp with one hand tied behind their backs—naturally that was always the sales line the Russians used with the Chinese."

"You've met HZs socially—the enemy?"

"Sure. It's not like you think. The transhuman community is . . . eccentric. Sometimes there are mutant conventions in remote places that I attend along with HZs. It's quite jolly, the HZs play chess all the time."

"HZs play chess?"

"They're fanatics, you can't keep them away from the board. They allow less than one second per move, the games play at lightning speed, and they can hold an intelligent conversation at the same time, except when they get drunk on vodka and start singing. That can really drive you to suicide, when they try to sing—those barbarians didn't even try to produce vocal cords capable of basic harmony. Their bodies are unbelievably strong, though—they would have won the contract years ago except that the Chinese learned of a serious flaw. They start to go into decline after about five years—and there's no way of telling exactly when or how. They tried to convince the Chinese that we had the same problem, that's why they had one impersonate me like that."

"What do they do with them after five years?"

"Unclear. Probably Polonium has them shot and they salvage the high-tech parts for recycling."

I take a couple of beats to process the implications. I guess it won't be long before artificial organs leave the dead bodies automatically and make their way to the nearest depot. "You were really scared that night?"

"Shitless, frankly. How can anyone look on that and still find meaning in life?"

"But you took control perfectly."

He nods. "That's the programming, they drummed it into us, the military mind. But I always feel bad after a performance like that. It's such a violation of higher intelligence, all those straight lines and sharp corners it plants in your skull. Doc Bride warned me about it. We discussed it a lot."

"You discussed with Dr. Bride the future structure of your mind, your personality?"

"Certainly. I was the building site and the junior architect both. Almost from the start. He warned me, you see, that a clash would come between the stuff he'd crammed into my head and the stuff the military would cram in. But he was sure the chemicals and the inserts would cause an acceleration of development that would lead me to drop the military side eventually and become a world spiritual leader. *Play your Gandhi against their Stalin,* he advised me." He smiles. "He said I would have to be Christ to survive." He shrugs. "He would have preferred Apollo or Zeus or Zoroastrer or Krishna, and frankly so would I, but he felt compelled to take revenge on his mother by manufacturing his own Jesus . . . Complicated fellow, the Doc. He trained as a Freudian, you know, before he switched to Jung."

He gives me a smile oozing with kindness, fondness, spiritual goodwill, preparedness to die for me, a fraternal adoration that will last an eternity, an utterly convincing beam of divine love; then he turns it off. "Christ is as good as any, I guess, and there's very good product recognition. We can build on that. It's a lot easier than starting from scratch, and I'll only have to flash a few miracles, just like two thousand years ago, and most of the seven billion suckers on the planet will fall for it."

"I see. What will you use for corporate identity? Will you stick with the Cross?"

"Oh, no. Just like two thousand years ago, we'll take a universal symbol, something with total worldwide recognition as had the Cross in its day—and tweak it a bit."

"What symbol would that be?"

"An S with two vertical strokes, of course." I gasp. "Shall I tell you why you gasped just then, dear brother? Because at that very moment you saw that our little project is not only possible but inevitable. Indeed, it has already started. Is it not so?"

I shake my head in wonder. "You're really going to start a new world religion, take over the earth?"

"Depends." He grins. "I might hate the paperwork. But I'm not going to hang around in the CIA's program any longer, that's for sure. I'm bored with it even if there are oodles of dough to be made. They'll have to find some other mutant to sell to the Chinese. Anyway, like I said, it's still basically Doctor's orders. He's not greedy, all he wants is world dominance before he dies."

We get out at Sakagorn's mansion and the Asset leads me to the large garden at the back. There is a long covered swing that kids and adults alike might use to relax in the shade. We sit in it together and he plays a game of using one arm to pull and push the double swing to its limits, holding us out almost horizontally for a full five minutes before slowly letting the seat come down again with total control. He gives me a sheepish look.

"Sorry, I shouldn't show off, should I?"

"Do you need to?"

He gives me the divine smile. "It's all your fault, for being such a perfect elder sibling, it makes me a little giggly. But we are still not fully bonded, are we? I'm not sure. From time to time you look bewildered, my brother. Sometimes you have an expression on your face that tells me I'm violating some cultural rule of intimacy they never told me about. I wouldn't know, we didn't do a lot of love training at the camp.

There were tons of torchlight processions down into the depths of the cave, with cannibalism as a kind of ultimate consummation. That was the big event: eating someone else."

He pauses and rebuilds the adoring smile. "Shall I tell you a secret? I first saw you from a distance some time ago—more than a month. Goldman pointed you out. We were in Soi Cowboy and you were about to enter your mother's bar. The minute I saw you I knew that you were my brother. I was stunned. I *knew* you immediately. It was my baptism in the Jordan, that's when I became the Messiah of this age. After that I couldn't stop myself, every few days I would slip back to the *soi* to take pictures of you. I must have taken over a hundred on that iPhone. It was such fun spying on you like that. And then making sure you received the phone—and the Doc's number in Contacts. I was in agony for days wondering when you'd finally get through to him. The old fool turns his phone off when he wants to think about something. Or when he's on one of his opium binges. Or when he's on acid—especially when he's on acid and . . . Well, he's a different man. I expect he struck you as a wonderful, eccentric, brilliant, charming, highly polished old English gent, did he not? Those are merely relics of a personality he used to own, before Angkor. He needs opium to keep up the pretense. Acid reveals the truth."

The Asset gives a grandfatherly smile and folds his arms over his stomach. "Then, when you did call him, *he* had to call *me* right away because I hadn't told him about you and he didn't know where you were coming from at all. What a laugh—he was mad as hell, but he forgave me. Poor old Doc. And I was the one who insisted he take you to the camp, because I wanted you to know *everything*, you are my only living blood relation on this earth, aside from that old guy in the hospital."

"Tell me about the opium. It's terribly injurious, especially for a man his age. Why doesn't he use LSD all the time?"

The Asset gives me a shrewd look, as if I've stumbled on an inconvenient truth. "He takes the Spirit only rarely these days. Very rarely. You could even say he uses opium to avoid acid."

"Why?"

"Because when he's on LSD his demon takes over completely. That's really what all this is about, you know." The Asset lets this bomb drop with a yawn. "He sold his soul to the great demon of Angkor forty years ago on a ten-day acid binge, but he'll never admit it." He checks my face. "That doesn't mean the project won't succeed. The opposite. With a demon like that backing us, how can we lose? The Khmer spirits are taking over the world again, using the weapon they know best: magic." He smiles conspiratorially: "It's quite fun, isn't it?"

I realize that, outlandish though it seems, this is as sincere as the Asset is able to be. He really means that he is the Messiah. Frankly, R, I am experiencing the original policeman's hell here: stuck with a perp who won't stop confessing and no power of arrest.

"But Jesus, you are not Jesus," I say. "You murder, you intimidate, you mutilate, you hypnotize men into killing their nearest and dearest, you scared my wife half to death, you are a war machine—" I stop, ashamed of my own exasperation.

"Hmm, the military lobby does keep cropping up, doesn't it? It's a concession we had to make. The Doc says I'll grow out of the boy-soldier stuff pretty soon now. I'm sorry I scared your wife, it's a kind of reflex they taught us."

"What is?"

"Scaring the shit out of people: psychic dominance, to give it its military title. It's quite clever, it involves all sorts of subtle factors like standing at a certain distance, control over facial features, total physical superiority, posture, and something you do with your eyes that isn't mystical but looks it, then you call attention to the very sensitive area around the mark's navel, which is a terrific fear center—and basically you convince the mark that you have killed many times before and might be about to do so again, which isn't difficult when it's true. It's part of riot-control training. You pick a pack leader and reduce him to a whimpering wreck without even touching him. Very effective."

"But the killings?"

"*Dy yang sia yang*," he says in a perfect Thai accent. Roughly translated: *You can't make omelets without breaking eggs.* "If I killed them, it must have been the will of God, mustn't it? The Doc and I talked about that a lot. 'Transcend killing by turning it into an art form,' he advised. 'Everyone has to die, but not everyone dies in the form of a handcrafted masterpiece—think of your victims as privileged to be killed by you. Above all, the Messiah is an artist.'"

"Dr. Christmas Bride said that?"

"Mm, when he was on acid, the old devil." He gives me a grand smile. "Anyway, I don't do violence anymore, I'm bored with it."

"Since when?"

"Since I killed Sakagorn and Goldman. Just one little murder of the right person in the right place at the right time did the trick. What a liberation! My evolution has speeded up, just as the Doc predicted. You must have noticed. In a couple of months I'll be the type who bursts into tears at the sight of a dead sparrow. But there is one thing I owe you, isn't there? One more gesture before I slouch over to Bethlehem to be reborn."

"What's that?"

"This," the Asset says, and reaches behind his head to remove his graphene mask. It is a striptease: slowly a wide brow emerges, then eyebrows, then the eyes . . . He completes the unveiling with a quick pull, and now, finally, I am looking into the face of the devil, who could also be Christ. I cover my mouth. "Oh, no!"

It is simply too much. The poor mind eternally misled by everything thanks to the myth of the normal, the ordinary, is now confronted by the impossible, the extraordinary—and does its best to turn off. I'm holding on to the swing, white-knuckled with stress, wonder, and horror, for it is *the face of Dr. Christmas Bride!* Not, to be sure, aged eighty-plus, but that Bride of the ancient photo taken with a Kodachrome more than fifty years ago: young, godlike, brilliant, and mad.

"God made me in his own image," the Asset says, a tad forlorn. "I've never shown anyone before, only you and the Doc know. What do you think?"

"How did he do it? Plastic surgery isn't *that* advanced. Are you sure that's not another mask under the mask?"

"Genius always finds a way," he says, still in that slightly doubtful tone. He shrugs, smiles, and replaces the graphene mask. Just then the doorbell rings.

"Ah!" he says.

We return to the house and he uses a remote to open the front door. Footsteps in the hall.

———

I am able to guess who it is, for the occasion, which is religious, calls for a specific kind of devotee, one whose dedication is blind and therefore absolute.

"Matthew," the Asset says with a smile. "On time as usual."

The FBI is not Thai and yet he offers that most perfect expression of local devotion known as the high *wai*. He raises palms pressed together as high as his forehead and smiles at the Asset with uncritical adoration that seems to say, *Kill me if it be your pleasure, I will never know a greater god than you.*

Or something like that. It's a little embarrassing, but also impressive. He gives me the high *wai*, too, I guess to acknowledge me as God's half brother. This is heady stuff. I find my imagination channeling what one knows about the origin of churches: a small group of dedicated followers with a message so powerful it redirects humanity. The sort of community, in other words, that pariahs like me never join. The Asset flashes me a look as if he knows what I'm thinking.

"Matthew," he says and puts an arm around the FBI, "there's one special little thing I'd like you to do for me, right now. I want you to tell my dearly beloved brother your story—in that succinct lawyer's way of yours. Just the essential parts. He is a very quick study, essentials only will do."

I do not think the moment has been rehearsed; it didn't need to be. Fanatics have only one song to sing, and they don't need much prompting.

"I was lost," the FBI confesses. "A man, my father, escapes the corrupt, criminal, despotic, repressive police state of China and lands in the corrupt, criminal, despotic, repressive police state of the USA. What formula for survival does he pass on to his son? It is this: *Above all, be impeccable in your hypocrisy, let not a drop of the human seep out of the polythene with which you have packaged yourself. Replace affection with Teflon, love with ambition, fairness with ruthlessness, the milk of human kindness with the acid needed to burn your way to the top. And never let your agony show.*"

He pauses and gives a quick glance to the Asset, who nods, smiling.

In a trembling voice the FBI continues: "This was excellent advice. Without it I never would have lasted. But what is the use of lasting? As the spirit was slowly crushed in me, it responded by burning all the hotter. I was sure I would explode. I became fascinated by stories of young men who stockpile firearms before their terrible coming out. I recognized a godseed in me that was violated with every conforming thought or act, that was drowning in the superficial. No matter how much the world rewarded me, *I* condemned me for the coward and slave I had become. But where was the real message? Who was speaking words of truth? Who had the strength and the vision to show the way out?"

He stops shyly. There is great courage and sensitivity in the way he forces himself to look at me with tears in his eyes. "I once was lost but now I'm found," he says and turns away.

I see in him what, I suppose, most people would see: a man, no longer exactly young, who has chronically failed to find love. My mind flashes to my darling, if wayward, Chanya. Compared to him, I am lucky.

"See what I mean?" the Asset whispers to me out of the corner of his mouth. "See the hunger that drives him? There are billions burning in silence just like that. Humanity festers in its clingwrap."

Now the Asset says something to the FBI. The FBI nods, shakes his head to clear it, and smiles at me with evangelical warmth.

"Matthew will take you to see some friends who will help with your initiation," the Asset says. He turns on his heels and abruptly returns to the garden.

I have become used to sudden changes in my half brother; this is the first time he has been quite so open in his arrogance, like one who perceives that the need for patience and civility is almost over. Like a man whose time has come.

I do not recall consenting to any initiation; nevertheless, I follow the FBI out of the house and sit next to him in the back of the sky-blue Rolls-Royce. The driver knows where to go, and within about ten minutes we arrive at the old Siamese house on stilts in the middle of the jungle of high-rises. During the ride I send SMSs to Chanya and try to call her several times, but as before there is no reply. The first, sly suspicion that the Asset has sent me away from him so that he can abduct her enters my vulnerable heart.

Matthew waits in the limo while I climb the stairs to the front door. I have no doubt all has been arranged and choreographed and that Krom will answer.

The door does open on the first press of the bell, but it is Madame Gloria Ching who opens it. Her eyes stare sightless at the sky while she sniffs me. We *wai* each other politely and she invites me in.

"You've just missed Krom, who popped out on an errand," she says in those hyper-English tones and adds a smile as she leads me clicking down the corridor.

"I don't believe you," I say, mimicking her smile.

The contradiction startles her for a moment, then she relaxes. "Of course, I should remind myself, a detective is not an ordinary human being." She turns her blind eyes to me and breathes deeply. "You're right, it was decided that I would have a few words with you first."

We are in the panoramic back room with all the perfume bottles. As before, I am overwhelmed by the range of aromas that hit me in half a dozen vulnerable and exotic places. It is impossible not to feel high and intrigued in this room, as if a thousand mysteries could be solved through the subtle computations of smell.

Gloria Ching settles herself on the sofa. "I am supposed to simply tell you about myself. I grew up suddenly during the Cultural Revolution, before I was smuggled out of the PRC. I experienced collective barbarism close up. Basically, there has always been and will always be two kinds of humanity. Up to now the civilized have kept the hordes at bay with technology. Now that technology has risen to a different level. We no longer need the masses, they can be replaced by machines. Their riots and revolutions can be put down, we have no need to be intimidated anymore. Let them have their pornography and their football and their TV series while we-the-saved take over. The New Humans are simply those with the civilization and the learning skills to acquire talents that would only destroy the inferior half of our species." She turns her head to the ceiling. "If I were in your place, I would be thrilled at the chance to get on the program at all. To have the kind of future they are offering you, as brother to the Messiah—you have it made, my friend. You are literally the luckiest man on earth. That's what they wanted me to tell you. And now I think I hear Krom in the hall."

Gloria Ching takes me, clicking, to the door and opens it on Krom, who cannot look me in the eye. I follow to her room, which is not at all what I expected: none of the ruthless minimalism of a willful dyke, more like the boudoir of a practiced seducer. All over the room, including the ceiling, the female form is celebrated in oils, watercolors, photographs, and, naturally, lady lamps. The counterpane on the bed is midnight-blue silk; a replica of a primeval mother goddess, with huge breasts, belly, and vagina, hangs on the wall above.

"Chanya was here with you, wasn't she?" I say. "I can feel it. Where is she? What have you done with her?"

"She's safe, Sonchai. You'll see her very soon. You're nearly there, man. Just one more hurdle to go."

"What are you talking about?"

She seems about to reply, then changes her mind. "The way we're doing it, we're showing you the life stories of different initiates, but you already know mine."

The room sports a bentwood rocker in a bay window that looks over the garden. I cannot bear to look at her, so I sit in it, staring out at the frangipani trees and the bougainvillea, the pond and the cats all prone around it. She speaks while I stare.

"You know what I was, because you've seen so many examples. A trashy dykey piece of female garbage that nobody wanted, a total non-entity like someone dying at the bottom of a well. I think you know what I'm talking about. I think you've been there. There's only one thing that remains when you're in that state. Just two primeval words that won't go away: *I am*. It's not a lesson you ever forget. *I am* plus body. My beautiful, young, female body that so loves to be with other female bodies. Basically life is either money or sex, and for me it was a no-brainer. Naturally, I had them give me the sex App soon as I was ready."

"There's a sex App?"

She draws a chair up and sits obliquely behind me so that I can feel her breath on the back of my neck.

"Sonchai, it's not just because you're a man that you have no idea. Most women don't realize either."

"What?"

"What a world of sensuality lies just under a woman's skin. Thousands of years of male jealousy and dominance have left us stupefied and totally cut off from our own sexual identity, which ought to be so vivid, so life-filled. There are ways of releasing that, my friend, ways for a woman to come out, to wake up to her deep, hungry, life-affirming *power*."

"You used some kind of drug on her?"

"Don't kid yourself, it's not just a matter of chemicals. It's *something inside so deeply denied* . . . As the song says. You know that much about her. I can help you. That of which I speak is not exclusively homosexual. Even a man can learn how to enhance a woman's sensuality. I have to give her back to you, anyway. There, I've said it. I'm not allowed to keep her. You are the brother of the Messiah, you win. You only have to join us, which you almost have anyway."

"But why is everyone so keen on me, Krom? I'm flattered. Why is it so damn important that I become one of you?"

"Your genes, Sonchai. I don't know the details. It seems all your father's kids at the camp were unusually gifted. After he met you, Dr. Bride confirmed that you seemed to have those characteristics, that same kind of genius."

We let quite a few beats pass, then Krom coughs and starts to talk again.

"Face it, Sonchai," Krom says. "Chanya is all you've got, man, the only real relationship in the world, your only anchor. Would you even be able to sleep tonight if you went home without her? Or tomorrow? Or the next night?"

I let that hang, refusing to respond.

"It's all over for the nonenhanced, Sonchai. You're an elitist yourself at some level. You're certainly a lot smarter than average, and you detest most of modern culture. Even without enhancement you're all too alert to the pathetic state of the world—the imminent squalor of war and economic disruption that the sad seven billion homunculi are going to live through during the next few centuries: you've seen that. You *want* a superbrain, a superbody, membership of the new race of humans who really will reach the stars—admit it, you do, don't you?"

"I don't give a damn about any of that, I want to see Chanya," I say. "I want to hear her tell me how she feels, what she wants to do."

"Okay," Krom says. "Okay."

She stands and I stand with her. At the front door she seems deflated, as if some superior power, which happens to be male, is about to take her favorite doll away. I check the limo, which has not moved in the drive.

In the back of the Rolls, Matthew speaks so softly to the driver I cannot hear the name of our destination. I'm not entirely surprised when we wind up back at Sakagorn's mansion. Matthew has his own key. There is no one around when he lets us in and takes me up to a room at the top of the house. He nods at the closed door, turns and leaves. I knock. A familiar voice says *Come in.* I enter.

"You're okay?" I blurt.

Chanya is standing by a window from which she must have turned when I entered. She holds up both wrists. "Look, no handcuffs. I'm free to come and go. No kidnapping. No coercion. Nobody has molested me. I can walk out of this house anytime I like." She steps forward and we embrace. I hold her tight, she puts up with it.

"Then let's do that," I cry in a sudden flash of hope. As if life is ever that simple. "Let's get the hell out of here."

She sighs. "What would that solve? Wouldn't we be back in some state of constant denial? We need to sort this out, Sonchai."

"Sort what out?"

She holds both my hands and stares into my eyes. "Darling, you are our ticket out of this. I can't believe how fortunate I am to be married to you. The opportunity being offered is just totally mind-blowing."

"What opportunity?"

She wrings her hands. "I can't believe it. They're offering you the world and you pretend not to understand. How perverse can you be?"

"Let me get it straight, you want me to have their implants?"

"Why not? It's the way the world is going. There will be the enhanced and the slaves. They're offering you the ultimate enhancement, the God implant. I don't fully understand, but the difference it would make to us, Sonchai! From a life of squalid pettiness to governors of the universe."

"They've drugged you, they must have done. This isn't you talking."

"But this *is* me. I just dumped my liberal left-wing conscience with all its bullshit. It's time, Sonchai, it's high time. We did our best. As it happens we are smarter than the rest and don't deserve to rot with the masses. We are just not second-class people. Let's be real here."

"What you're actually saying is you can't love me if I don't become a mutant?"

Our voices have been rising and my last remark was almost a shriek. It caught us both off balance. The *M* word in particular carries quite a kick.

She glares at me, her lower lip trembling. "Then I'll have the implants myself. They've offered. I don't have your talent, your genes, the operation could kill me or send me to a mental hospital, but I'm willing to give it a try, anything to get off this dirty, stunted, petty, squalid, empty level we live on."

We are a bloody, glaring couple now, fresh out of words to yell. In the silence I see that she has expressed her base values as a human being—and for me the disappointment is distilled bitterness. Without a hint of drama I turn, leave the room, and close the door behind me. Depression hits.

At the top of the double staircase I look down on the polished marble of the ground floor and the two figures who have appeared there. They are waiting near the bottom of the staircase, too polite to look up. I descend slowly. Very slowly. This is the dead point, after all, the evisceration. I am quite sure I have nothing left with which to resist. No soul's night gets any darker than this. I hardly have the strength to walk.

They wait until I've reached the last step before locking eyes with me. I surmise from the way they examine me that they are deeply interested in my mental state. Have they gone too far in presenting me with grim truths about life on earth and the future of man? Or not far enough? The transfusion of one form of consciousness with another is a delicate task, apparently. They step back to assess me for a moment, then point to three armchairs set together in the middle of the hall. Dr. Christmas Bride, with that extraordinarily mobile face that endlessly processes every human thought and emotion from Adam to Mickey Mouse, is wearing a cream tropical two-piece suit with white flannel shirt and a lemon silk cravat.

He says in that charming Brahmin accent, "Sonchai, my dear fellow, how wonderful to see you again. Have you been well?" His handshake is warm while mine is limp. "Shall we make ourselves comfortable?"

We sit in a circle of three. I have no idea why I am playing their game now, except that I'm too empty to think.

Up close to the Doc, I become aware that this is not quite the same charming old Brit I spent time with in the jungle. I suspect him of ascending to level seven.

"The Spirit rules," Dr. Christmas Bride says in a solemn voice, as if saying grace.

"Amen," the Asset says. I don't know if Bride is on LSD or not; I am certain, though, that the demon of Angkor has taken him over.

The Doctor smiles faintly while he takes out a packet of Camel cigarettes, fits one to his ivory holder, and lights up. "We are all truly sorry that your final initiation should involve heartache, but that's the way it is for everyone in the end. To be entirely free we must all break—and break utterly—from the endless torments of biology." He stares into space. "You think you love your wife, but you are advanced enough to be aware of the illusion. What does woman mean to you? A false promise that with enough groveling and emotional dependence you will, somehow, acquire intermittent rights of readmission to amniotic bliss. Do I need to tell you that the price is your freedom and your manhood? You are very smart, but even you have a problem relinquishing that fallacy." He stops, nods at something invisible, then starts again. "Our path is merciful, however. You can have her back—is that not so?"

The question is addressed to the Asset.

"You can have everything you want, dear one—practically everything at all. Money, enhancements, fame, longevity, that woman or some other woman. For the enhanced shall inherit the earth—is that not so, Father?"

Bride nods.

"So why me?"

"Your genes," Bride says.

"Because Jesus Christ is my half brother?"

"Sort of," Christmas Bride says with a smile. "You see, he alone survived of all the original . . . ah . . ."

"Lab rats?"

He coughs. "If you will. But the point is the genes. He and all your half siblings were uniquely gifted with regard to the program."

"But you killed all the others by pushing them too far?"

"Brother, they were incredibly smart," the Asset says. "Way ahead of all the others. Our father's genes must have something special they haven't been able to locate yet."

"So, why—"

"Adolescence," Bride says, taking a toke on the Camel. "You may think me a brute, but I assure you I did all I could. Mid- to late teens is inherently unstable—I took every possible precaution. Don't you think

I wanted them to live more than anything in the world? Your brothers and sisters were all brilliant, like you, and in much the same way, a speed of apprehension that one can enhance with the most modest of surgical inserts. They possessed a latent talent that the others could not come close to. Of course, it is deeply regrettable they could not carry those gifts through to adulthood—the transition from prodigy to mastery is notoriously difficult, only five percent make it in any profession."

"So why would I—"

"Because you have the stability of a grown man. You could pass the program with flying colors, you're so clever and amazing," the Asset says.

All the time I feel the intensity of their combined psychic focus, like a steel band tightening around my skull. When I cease to respond, we sit in silence for a minute, then the Asset leaves his throne to stand behind my chair and embrace me. I twist around and he gives me a big dopey smile that would be pathetic on anyone less sinister.

"I understand your reluctance, brother," he says. "Do you know I have my doubts, too? And I'm changing, changing, changing. You wouldn't believe the worlds upon worlds that open up, once the ALE kicks into high gear. I do believe I'm entering the realm of the divine. I'm receiving visions of flawless four-dimensional symmetry, it's like living inside perfect crystals, gateways to a higher heaven. I really don't think I want the job anymore—I mean the Messiah thing. Too much admin." He sighs. "But karma is karma, is it not?" He caresses my head and chucks my cheek. "We could ramp you up into Buddhahood in a year, isn't that so, Doc?"

Bride smiles and nods. "It's just a case of tweaking the inserts."

It is difficult to convey the effect the Asset is having on my head while he stands behind me. He is very charming in this mood, and quite comical with his crack about *too much admin*, but it's the dynamic disconnect that somehow penetrates to the medulla oblongata. I am being seduced by a killer clown, a sociopathic god on the Greek model who must win not because he is good but because he is of a higher order of being: quite irresistible. All the while he is smiling and teasing there is a relentless will bending my mind. I cannot help remembering that moment in the tennis ball video when he turned demonic with an ugly expression on his face before he mastered the game. And he is invisibly supported by the others, including Chanya, who form a kind of chorus in my head, adding their silent wills to his. I remember the young man in the boat at the beginning of all this: a Thai boy who killed his mother under just such relentless pressure. Now the Asset stands in front of me and fixes his gaze on the area of my navel and I'm racking my brains for a way out of here.

Too late I become aware of a force even greater than the Asset's. Bride is also staring at me. As I succumb I am aware of what you might call the backdrop against which all this is playing out. I remember the words of the late Lord Sakagorn on the subject of Angkor: *That huge dark rotting Wat the size of a city block, those hideous stone pyramids like Aztec architecture, that sinister little shrine right in the middle, the whole atmosphere of the thing.*

I see that sinister shrine at the top of the steep stairs, and there, filling the corbeled vault—how shall I put it? The *Beast* himself, there is no other word for it.

"You want me to be . . . Who? Saint Paul? John the Baptist?"

I stare at the Asset, who smiles. "Anyone you like. The electrical circuits in the left and right lobes are tiny, you can hardly see them, they're about the size of a fingernail. Admit it, dear one, you do want to be enhanced, don't you?"

Now, between you and me, R, he has a point. I'm wondering what I'm going to do with the rest of my life without Chanya, and I have to confess I wouldn't mind some of those Apps. Would you? To stroll around confident that you could beat the hell out of any ten thugs who crossed your path: that would be basic and I wouldn't say no, but it's the others that are so intriguing. Suppose you could understand all the calculations that prove $e = mc^2$ in five minutes just by following the logic? Suppose you could learn an Asian language to fluency level in a month? Then there's the enhanced sex App: create eager sex slaves with every erection, that would be worth the inserts, don't you think? And there's the total makeover of the personality: from timid urban paranoid to strutting world conqueror in no time at all. I bet there's a synaesthetic App, too, that would let you experience music in terms of color and even as direct sensual experience. (Would it be fun to automatically ejaculate at the end of Beethoven's Ninth? I'm not sure but I'm willing to give it a try.)

"Sure," I say. "But I don't want to be a sociopath."

The word takes them by surprise.

"I'm afraid you don't really have a choice, my friend," Bride says. "Not because we will coerce you—frankly, that is not possible, only a willing recruit could succeed in the program. But because you alone are qualified to save the world. Or, at least, that part of it that remains when the dust has settled on the catastrophes to come."

My jaw drops. Silence. They wait, confident of my final capitulation.

I wish I could claim credit for some brilliant scam by which I escaped their psychic bullying, but as you know, R, I'm always honest with you, and I hope you're not too disappointed when I confess I invoked an imperative no culture can afford to ignore.

"Excuse me, I have to use the bathroom," I say, and slip out the back way that Krom showed me when Sakagorn was still in the bath.

Now, R, I cannot claim that I am unaffected by the extreme bullying to which I have been subjected. I am, frankly, terrified that I will succumb in due course, as Chanya has. Their argument is backed up by the evidence, that is the problem. The Asset really does exist, such beings really will be all too common in the future, the ordinary man and woman can look forward to a life of politically correct slavery, a feudalism as rigid as the Hindu caste system, while the THs lord it over us like barons on horseback from the Dark Ages. And I really could be one of them. Come to think of it, I do believe I'd be pretty good. I mean, I'd try to be fair, humane, make sure nobody whips the slaves too hard (under my stewardship everyone would have a roof over their heads, hot and cold running water, plenty of food and fuel to keep warm, TV so long as they're obedient and work work work) . . . I would only have to sacrifice my humanity at a time when no one values it anyway. Somewhere, however, there is a deeper truth, I know there is, I simply don't seem able to reach it right now.

———

However, by some quirk of dharma I have the medicine to hand—and the cure. I'm racing to the hovel on the back of a motorbike. I promised the jockey triple the usual fare if he can beat the traffic. As a result we spend a lot of the ride on the sidewalk, trying not to knock over pedestrians. When we arrive I tell him to wait while I dash inside to pick up a packet of Marlboro Lights and the rest of that oil Krom gave me. Once back on the bike I tell the jockey to take me to the police station. The plan is to find me a nice subterranean cell where no malevolent vibes can reach me. There I shall avail myself of the power of Buddhist meditation boosted by cannabis. It won't take more than a couple of joints and some intense breathing exercises. It happened once before on the Green Sash case where we found the head but never located the torso: I totally freaked out, but with the healing herb and the wisdom of the Buddha and the seclusion of the cell I was able to reach the underlying reality of Universal Mind. As for Chanya, don't worry, she'll be fine once I've got some herb into her; we must not judge her too harshly: empty days weaken all of us, and she does have an adventurous streak.

Now, I don't want to lead you astray, R, and probably such radical therapy is not for you, but as I explained once before in an evangelical moment, compassion is the cosmological constant of the psyche, just like the speed of light in physics: at the end of the day everything is measured against it. So that's where I'm headed right now. I'm not being sentimental or religious, it's simply the only enhancement worth having. There is the slight problem of desolation, though. It's where the treasure's buried, and you do have to cross that desert, as the holy man said. Did you ever reach this moment yourself, R, where you take a deep breath and gulp before you bite the last bullet?

I am yours in dharma, Sonchai Jitpleecheep.

A NOTE ABOUT THE AUTHOR

John Burdett was brought up in North London and worked as a lawyer in Hong Kong. To date he has published seven previous novels, including the Bangkok series: *Bangkok 8, Bangkok Tattoo, Bangkok Haunts, The Godfather of Kathmandu,* and *Vulture Peak.*

A NOTE ON THE TYPE

This book was set in Electra, a typeface designed by W. A. Dwiggins (1880–1956). It is not based on any historical model, nor does it echo any particular period or style but has a feeling of fluidity, power, and speed.

Typeset by Scribe, Philadelphia, Pennsylvania

Printed and bound by Berryville Graphics,
Berryville, Virginia